FROM THE FIELDS OF
PORTHLENN

FROM THE
FIELDS OF
PORTHLENN

A CORNISH ROMANCE, BOOK FIVE

DEBORAH M. HATHAWAY

DRAFT HORSE
PUBLISHING

BOOKS BY DEBORAH M. HATHAWAY

A Cornish Romance Series

On the Shores of Tregalwen, a Prequel Novella

Behind the Light of Golowduyn, Book One

For the Lady of Lowena, Book Two

Near the Ruins of Penharrow, Book Three

In the Waves of Tristwick, Book Four

From the Fields of Porthlenn, Book Five

Belles of Christmas Multi-Author Series

Nine Ladies Dancing, Book Four

On the Second Day of Christmas, Book Four

Seasons of Change Multi-Author Series

The Cottage by Coniston, Book Five

Sons of Somerset Multi-Author Series

Carving for Miss Coventry, Book One

Timeless Regency Collection

The Inns of Devonshire—The Coachman's Choice

Christmas Escape Multi-Author Series (Contemporary)

Christmas Baggage

For Cornwall

PRONUNCIATION GUIDE

Porthlenn – porth-LENN
Tregalwen – treh-GAWL-when
Golowduyn – goal-oh-DEW-in
Lowena – low-WHEN-uh
Penharrow – Pehn-HAIR-oh
Tristwick – TRIST-wik
Dulatha – dew-LAH-thah
Glastaish – glass-STAISH
Fynwary – fin-WARE-ee
Morvoren – more-VOR-in
Trevik – TREH-vik
Cadan – CAD-in
Isolde – iz-OLE-duh
Elowen – EL-oh-win
Hedrek – HEH-drik
Edern - ED-ern
Trevethan – treh-VEH-thin
Gwitha – GWIH-thuh
Tegen – TEE-gin (hard 'g')
pasties – PAHS-teez
ye – ee

CHAPTER ONE

Cornwall, May 1820

White sails marked the division between land and sea, the ship's red ensign billowing in the wind, signaling to the world that the *Defense* had now embarked on another journey. Her course was set, her destination decided, though what she would find along her way was anything but certain.

The men aboard the ship were sure to be buzzing with anticipation for their new adventure. All men did who joined the ranks of His Majesty's Navy. They would now be breathing in the salty air that surrounded them, the air that spoke of freedom like nothing else on earth. Because it wasn't *of* the earth.

It was of the sea.

How Lieutenant Edmund Harris envied them. Standing at the edge of the Cornish cliffside, the long grass brushing against his leg like the swish of a horse's tail, he trained his green eyes on the ship forging farther and farther away from him.

An emptiness gaped in his chest, his heart torn away from his body as it joined the crew on the *Defense*, leaving him broken, fragmented. He wouldn't be whole again until the ship returned and he rejoined his brothers-in-arms.

Unfortunately, he wasn't a stranger to this feeling. He never had been whole until he'd joined the navy at the tender age of eleven anyway. What was a few weeks of feeling empty when he'd spent his entire childhood in such a way?

With a heavy sigh, he readjusted the dark blue sling around his neck, shifted his aching left arm in the fabric, then picked up his portmanteau that rested in the grass beside him.

Life was not fair. He'd known that for nearly thirty years now. But the fact that he was landbound for the next few weeks, commanded to nurse a wound he'd accrued six years ago, seemed more cruel than normal—especially being stationed in Cornwall. Why couldn't it have been Wales or Brighton? Even France would be better than this.

"You are a detriment to the safety of the Defense, *Lieutenant,"* Captain Jones had said. *"Because of your arm and your mind. Take care of yourself, and I will keep a position for you aboard my ship upon our return from Channel patrol."*

Edmund had tried to protest, but Captain Jones would not yield. Edmund still wasn't even certain what his captain had been speaking of, accusing him of not being in the right frame of mind to sail.

Perhaps Edmund *had* been a touch distracted recently, arriving at his officer's watch a few minutes late and forgetting his responsibility to weigh anchor. But he was certain that was only due to the fact that he'd taken back-to-back assignments over the last three years without a single break.

Most men could easily bear such work. Edmund could, too —though not according to Captain Jones. Still, he would respect his superior's commands, no matter how silly he thought them.

"I will be ready to resume my position soon, then, Captain," Edmund had promised. *"I shall not let you down."*

And he would not. His forearm had given him grief before

—the bones lightly protesting ever since he'd broken them six years before. But after a lighthearted tussle with a handful of sailors at one of the port towns they'd stopped in a few weeks ago, his wound had flared up far more than it ever had before.

Still, he was sure he'd feel far better in three weeks' time, and his mind would return to its usual sharpness. Until then, he would simply bide his time in Cornwall.

For the hundredth time, Edmund swept his gaze across the rugged, rolling cliffsides, softened with tufts of green grass and pockets of pink sea thrift clumped together in trembling crowds. The turquoise water just below sparkled with the brightness of a thousand precious gemstones, rivaling the waters of the Caribbean he'd seen on his journeys aboard a number of His Majesty's vessels.

Very well. Cornwall wasn't so horrible a location to be marooned.

As if the wind could hear his thoughts, it rushed against him, whistling in his ear in retribution.

Fine. Cornwall was an utter dream. In truth, he'd never seen its equal. He merely harbored ill will to the county due to his heart having nearly been broken by the girl he'd offered it to three years before. A girl who had been…

Well, never mind what she had been to him. He held nothing against her. Otherwise he would not be heading to the very place they'd met.

Golowduyn Lighthouse. Where it had all begun.

He ran his fingers through his thick, brown hair, raking any negativity from his mind. Three years and a half had passed since he'd stepped foot on those cliffs and he'd been rejected by the woman.

She was no doubt married by now, perhaps even with a child or two.

Well, good for her.

And good for Edmund for moving on as well. Not with just any one woman, but many women.

The *Defense*.

The *Florentina*.

The *Duchess*.

In his years he'd spent away from Cornwall, he'd come to realize that the only place he would ever belong was on the deck of a ship, where he was accepted as a wanderer, a free spirit moving from vessel to vessel and port to port.

No ship would ever think to tie him down. Even the *Defense* would welcome him back as first lieutenant in three weeks, and all would be right with the world again.

Until then, he would keep his chin up. He would return to the lighthouse, visit with his old friend, Captain Kendricks, then leave for Penzance where he'd take company in a bottle and a deck of cards until his lady once more returned for him. He'd convalesced in Cornwall before. He could do it again.

Only this time, he wouldn't be distracted by any fisherman's daughter who boasted warm brown eyes and a charming, dimpled smile.

He'd allowed Poppy Honeysett to receive a glimpse of his heart before. He wasn't about to let her do the same thing again.

"Cloaks and shoes off first, girls," Poppy Honeysett whispered as she entered Golowduyn Lighthouse, two toddlers filing in after her. "Remember, we must keep quiet."

She closed the front door as the girls nodded in silence, their endless energy having apparently found its end after they'd played on the beach for the better part of two hours that afternoon.

The early-May sun had lingered longer than usual today, but the winds had picked up, bringing a sharp chill across the beach and whipping sand into their faces. As such, they'd been required to end their fun prematurely.

It was just as well. Poppy needed to accomplish a few more chores before she left the lighthouse. She'd soak in her time with the sea later that night, as per usual. Watching the waves always did wonders for her mood.

The Kendrickses' oversized Newfoundland dog, Gwitha, pattered down the corridor of the lighthouse, greeting Poppy and the girls with a few sniffs and drool across their skirts. Once he'd left his mark, he tapped down the corridor once again, no doubt on his way back to Mrs. Kendricks's room. He could always be found looking over his mistress.

"Can I see Mama?" Elowen asked, as if considering Gwitha's departure as well. She handed her blue cloak up to Poppy, the girl's dark red hair standing out in a tangled mess caused by the sea's winds.

"I do think she still be sleepin', love," Poppy said gently, accepting the cloak.

The three-and-a-half-year-old's face fell, though she nodded all the same, sitting down on the rug in the front corridor.

Poppy's heart reached out to her. The poor girl was suffering nearly as much as her mother, Mrs. Abigail Kendricks, who had been instructed by Dr. Kent to remain abed after nearly losing her second child a month ago.

Poppy knew the woman quite well, having labored alongside her incomparable work ethic for six years now. Even though the woman was willing to do whatever it took to save her life and the life of her unborn child, being confined to the house and resting all day was clearly wearing on Mrs. Kendricks's spirits—and her family's.

"Ye know what might cheer ye up?" Poppy asked. "Why don't we look at the shells we collected and find one to give to your mother? Would ye like that?"

Elowen's head popped up, the light returning to her blue eyes instantaneously. "Yes!"

Poppy held a hushing finger to her lip, then stared down

the corridor to the side rooms where Mrs. Kendricks—hopefully—still slept. "Ye must keep quiet, though," she gently reminded.

Elowen raised her shoulders with a sheepish grin.

"I find shells, too, Auntie Poppy?"

Poppy looked down at her two-and-a-half-year-old niece, Isolde. The girl sat down on the rug, her legs sticking straight out from her as she tapped her shoes together at the tips, waiting patiently for Poppy to untie them.

"'Course ye can, ye little mimsey," Poppy said.

She knelt down beside the toddler, pulling the ends of the ribbons to untie her shoes.

Isolde clapped her hands with a broad grin, looking to Elowen with excitement. "I love shells!" she exclaimed in a whisper, her white-blonde hair as windblown as Elowen's.

Poppy smiled at their enthusiasm. She loved watching these girls, their vivacity for life, their quick smiles produced from the simplest of things—finding swift crabs on the beach or picking fresh flowers for their mothers.

It wasn't always sunshine and sea pinks, especially when trying to clean with the girls one step ahead of her with their messes, but Poppy would choose caring for them at Golowduyn over spending hours in the fishing cellars at Tristwick any day.

Her chest tightened. Of course, she hadn't always felt this way. She used to love processing fish in the above-ground, cobblestoned courtyard. The women would often sing and visit as they pressed the oil from the pilchards that their husbands, brothers, and fathers had caught the night before. It was a ritual she'd always loved.

But ever since the accident, things had...changed. The music had ceased, and the chatter was nonexistent. Any chance Poppy had to ignore those changes, she would take it. That was why she always volunteered to bring her niece with her to Golowduyn, so Mother and Morvoren—Poppy's sister-in-law—could work at the cellars instead of her.

"Oh. Sorry, Poppy."

Poppy pulled out of her reverie as Elowen and Isolde stared down at the rug that had amassed large pillars of sand from the girls' shoes.

"Goodness," Poppy breathed. How that much sand could be carried in such little shoes was beyond her.

She should have had them remove their footwear before coming inside, but with that chill in the air, Poppy had rushed the girls into the shelter of Golowduyn without another thought.

She'd certainly pay for it now, but then, when had a little rug-shaking and floor-sweeping hurt anyone?

"That be all right," Poppy said, quelling the girls' worried brows. "I'll clean it up while ye sort out the shells."

After the rest of the sand had been dumped onto the rug —heavens above, how was there more?—Poppy situated the girls in the kitchen with the shells they'd collected in her reticule, spreading them on an old rag splayed out across the table.

As the girls looked through them, Poppy grazed her eyes over the selection. Most of them were broken, but there were a few she could use for her shellwork that evening before bed. She was nearly finished with the little dress she was making for Isolde's rag doll. A few of these shells would be the perfect addition to the hem she'd been sewing.

With the girls occupied at the table, Poppy left the kitchen to clean up the sand waiting for her by the front door, her mind still focused on the shells. After the doll's dress, she'd get started on those boxes Trevik had found for her. Perhaps she'd design a few waves or even a whale or two on top. She'd grown quite talented at fashioning shapes out of the shells. While they didn't fetch more than a few pence in St. Just, any extra money she could provide her family with was more than worth her efforts.

Still deep in thought, she reached down to pick up the rug, flicking the sand toward the middle when a memory she'd kept locked away for years slipped to the forefront of her mind.

"I can't imagine being so creative with seashells. You are quite talented, Poppy."

The words pierced her heart like a lightning bolt far in the distance above the sea—silent but powerful—just as it always was when *his* voice echoed in her memories.

Without hesitation, she carefully opened the lid to her heart and returned the memory securely within.

She wasn't ready to reminisce about the past. She had learned to live, to be happy again. She had learned to not wait for him any longer. Allowing his voice within her mind would only threaten the peace she'd worked so hard to bring back into her life.

Focusing on her task at hand, Poppy pulled the rug carefully up from the floor, holding the sides together with one hand as she reached for the door handle.

"Poppy?" Elowen called from the kitchen.

Poppy paused, staring down at the rug. She needed to get rid of this sand.

"Just a moment," she called over her shoulder in a softened tone, keenly aware of Mrs. Kendricks's need to sleep.

She fixed her eyes down the corridor as she opened the front door, praying the girls wouldn't come running up behind her with thunderous footsteps.

With one last moment of hesitation, she made quick work of her task. Angling her head away, she took a step outside onto the lighthouse landing. With her breath held and eyes closed, she released half of the rug and flung the sand into the wind.

A sputtering and coughing sounded in front of her not a moment later, and she gasped, opening her eyes to discover a sand-coated man standing in front of her. He ducked his head and waved his right hand in front of him, clearly attempting to lessen the sand she'd pelted him with.

"Oh, sir! I be that sorry!"

She dropped the rug to her feet. The fierce wind tugged at her skirts and blew a few strands of loosened hair across her face, so she brought her hand up to brush them aside.

The man straightened, though his bicorn still covered his face as he hacked. A portmanteau rested at his feet, his white waistcoat was coated in sand, and a blue naval officer's jacket stretched across his broad shoulders.

Poppy gasped, bringing a hand to her mouth as her chest tightened. There was only one man whom she'd ever seen in a lieutenant's uniform at Golowduyn Lighthouse.

Surely this was not true. Surely it *could not* be true.

But when the man looked up, settling his green eyes on her, she could no longer deny it.

"Poppy." There was no question in his tone, nor did surprise register in his expression.

But shock struck through Poppy's body, weakening her limbs as she teetered back.

Those eyes. That voice. She'd know them from anywhere. They belonged to the man she'd fallen in love with. The same man whose heart she'd broken three years before.

So it *was* true. Lieutenant Edmund Harris had returned to Cornwall.

CHAPTER TWO

*P*oppy could not draw a full breath, soaking in the lieutenant's firm brow, angled jawline, and defined cheekbones.

He'd returned. When? Why?

He looked away from her as he released another cough, continuing to brush the sand from his blue jacket.

Her cheeks pinked as she once again realized what she'd done. "I-I be so sorry," she stammered as Edmund—or should she call him Lieutenant Harris again?—delivered yet one more dry cough. "I didn't see ye there."

He hacked again, blinking hard as he brushed his fingers through his hair, sand flying out from the brown strands and disappearing into the wind and the grass below.

"That's all right," he finally responded, clearing his throat. "A little sand never hurt anyone. Though, my eyes might not agree with me at the moment."

He rubbed them again before looking at her, the whites of his eyes watery and red with irritation.

"I be that sorry," she repeated, her voice falling quieter that time as the situation became absurdly clear to her.

Lieutenant Harris had returned. He was standing right in

front of her. And she'd just covered him in sand.

Her stomach tightened, her thoughts spinning. Why had he returned? Was it…because of her?

"What…I…Ye…" She shook her head, unsure of what to say, how to respond to his presence. He hadn't changed much, though his face had matured, and more lines stretched out from his eyes and around his lips. She had never thought the man could grow more attractive, yet somehow, he had.

"I be surprised to see ye," she finally settled with, her thoughts still spinning.

"I'm surprised to see you, as well. I wasn't aware you'd still be working at the lighthouse after all these years."

Was this truly Lieutenant Harris—the man she'd dreamt of nearly every night since his departure—standing before her, speaking with her in his smooth, deep voice?

She swallowed with a nod. "Yes."

No other words came as she cast her gaze about him once again. Her eyes caught at once on the blue sling holding up his arm, though the jacket draping across his shoulders hid most of fabric. She frowned, worry twisting her stomach. "Are ye injured?"

His eyes dropped to his sling, and he raised it easily away from his person. "This? No, it's merely my old injury giving me grief once again."

"From the shipwreck?"

He nodded. "I've been put on leave for a few weeks due to a small amount of discomfort, so I came here to visit with the captain. I'll be off to Penzance tomorrow."

Poppy hadn't realized how high her spirits had soared upon seeing Lieutenant Harris until they plummeted to rest at her feet. That answered her foolish question from before—he was not there to see her. He was there to see Mr. Kendricks.

He and the previous captain of the shipwrecked HMS *Valour* had been close friends at sea. Following the incident, Lieutenant Harris had then helped out at the lighthouse with his injured arm, all while Poppy and her mother first started to work there as well.

At the thought, the bottle of memories Poppy had secured before in her heart flew wide open, assaulting her mind as past mingled with present.

The first time she'd met the lieutenant had been at that very lighthouse six years before, when she was nearly sixteen and he, four and twenty. He'd made a joke, she'd laughed, he'd winked…and she'd fallen in love.

Then her world fell apart.

She pushed aside memories of the last time they'd spoken together three years ago, when he'd shared his plans for his future and they hadn't aligned with hers. Time had passed, and the bridge between them had been shattered into a million pieces, never to be reforged again.

"Do you know if Captain Kendricks is home?"

His voice broke through her thoughts, and she was once again struck with the knowledge that he stood before her. "No," she replied, "'e be in St. Just. 'E ought to be 'ome soon, though."

He looked down the road that led to Golowduyn. "And Mrs. Kendricks is away, as well, I take it?"

Poppy glanced over her shoulder, the door ajar only a fraction. The girls must not have heard their visitor yet, or they would have already accosted him with questions and stares.

Better that than sand.

"Yes, Mrs. Kendricks be 'ome." Poppy hesitated. "But I don't know if she be up for visitors."

Concern furrowed his brow. "Has she taken ill?"

"She be poorly with child. Required to stay abed 'til the little one comes."

"Oh, I'm sorry to hear that."

Lieutenant Harris looked away again, and Poppy watched him in silence. This had to be some sort of dream. How else could she explain seeing him after so many years and speaking to him as if nothing had occurred between them—when *every-thing* had occurred between them?

He was just behaving so naturally, so comfortably, all while she was bumbling around like a pilchard pulled from the sea. There wasn't a chance he could have forgotten all that had been said between them, was there? Or had the three years apart truly been enough for him to forget her?

His eyes pulled up to meet hers, and she chewed the inside of her lip with hesitance. Poppy had always enjoyed the fact that she could read Lieutenant Harris's expressions very clearly. Before, he'd always met her gaze with a wink or a mischievous grin. Or he'd make a joke to get her to laugh.

Now, though his lips turned up in a smile, his green eyes were devoid of that same mischief, and she knew, somehow she knew, it was because of her.

"Well," he said when she made no further move to speak, shifting his body away from her, "I don't suppose you'd be willing to let Captain Kendricks know that I've…"

He turned toward the road at the sound of hoofbeats, his jaw more angled than she'd remembered.

"If it isn't the man himself," Lieutenant Harris murmured.

Poppy pulled her eyes to where Mr. Kendricks rode forward on his black horse. His narrowed eyes focused on Lieutenant Harris and Poppy before a smile broke out on his lips.

"Edmund Harris?" he called out, pulling in his horse and leaping off the saddle.

Lieutenant Harris had already left Poppy's side, his long stride taking him directly to his old comrade.

"Captain," he greeted with a touch to his bicorn before he removed it completely.

Mr. Kendricks laughed, pulling Lieutenant Harris in for an embrace. "What the devil are you doing here? Come to torment us in Cornwall again, have you?"

Lieutenant Harris laughed, clapping the man's back with

his free arm. "How did you know?"

Poppy watched the interaction with thinly veiled interest. She'd seen the men together before, their friendship heartwarming to even those on the outside of it. But in that moment, she wanted to slink back inside without another word. This was the lieutenant she remembered—warm and cordial. A friendly tease, never serious. Not the one she'd been speaking with before.

Mr. Kendricks shook his head, taking a step back to better see his friend. His smile faltered when he caught sight of Lieutenant Harris's sling. "What on earth did you manage to do to yourself now, Harris? Fall off another ship, have you?"

Lieutenant Harris cradled his left arm in the sling with his right hand. "If only I had so noble a tale to tell. But this is merely my injury from the *Valour* being a minor inconvenience. Nothing to worry over. I'll be back aboard the *Defense* in a matter of weeks if I have any say in the matter."

"I don't think any captain could keep you from his ship if he wanted to," Mr. Kendricks said with a chuckle.

He glanced beyond Lieutenant Harris's shoulder for the first time since his arrival, casting hesitant eyes between Poppy and Lieutenant Harris.

"My apologies, Poppy," Mr. Kendricks said. "I hope I was not interrupting the two of you."

Poppy's cheeks burned, and she shook her head, ready to defend herself. All of Cornwall knew of her love...of her past love of the lieutenant. She could only imagine what Mr. Kendricks was thinking about the two of them together again.

"No, you were interrupting nothing," Lieutenant Harris said at once. "I was only asking after you when you rode up at the most opportune moment."

Poppy stared at the lieutenant. Was he just as anxious to clear the air, or had the words been said for Poppy's benefit alone?

Mr. Kendricks hardly looked convinced, but he seemed to accept his friend's words, nonetheless. He faced Poppy again with a sobered expression, his handsome features pulling down in a frown. "How is Abigail?"

Her tone lowered as she recalled Mrs. Kendricks's inability to smile that day. "She be a bit low in spirits, sir."

Mr. Kendricks swallowed, the lines in his brow creasing. "Thank you for watching over her."

Poppy nodded. Lieutenant Harris pulled his gaze away from her and adjusted the sling round his neck.

"Dinner be made as well, sir," she continued. "It might be a touch cold, but ye can warm it up fine enough."

"That will be perfect. Thank you, Poppy."

She glanced again to Lieutenant Harris. "There be enough for your guest, too, sir, if 'e be wishin' to stay for dinner."

Mr. Kendricks looked to the lieutenant in question. "Would you, Harris?"

"Only if I'm not imposing."

"Not at all. You heard Poppy. There's more than enough. Besides, you can't leave without seeing Abigail. If you left without a word, she'd skin you alive, lying abed or not."

Lieutenant Harris chuckled. "Now that is the truth if I've ever heard it."

Poppy took a step toward the house. She couldn't bear this any longer. She needed to escape. Fortunately, with Mr. Kendricks's arrival, she didn't need to linger a moment more.

As if the girls sensed Poppy's and Isolde's impending departure, Elowen shot forth from the front door and bolted straight for her father, barreling into his leg and curling her arms around his thigh.

Isolde, however, moved quietly behind Poppy, taking her hand in silence as Poppy gave her fingers a light squeeze.

Lieutenant Harris's curious gaze lingered a moment on

Isolde and Poppy before he shifted his body toward Mr. Kendricks.

Poppy paused. What had that look been, that slight flickering frown that had crossed his features before he shifted away?

"Ah, there's my girl," Mr. Kendricks said, peeling Elowen from his leg and pulling her up to embrace her. "Were you well-behaved for Poppy today?"

Elowen nodded. "Yes, Papa."

He narrowed his eyes playfully. "Are you certain?"

"Honest! Wasn't I, Poppy?"

Poppy smiled. "Ye were perfect, as usual, Elowen."

"See, Papa? Perfect."

"I should expect no less," he responded with a tap of his finger to the tip of her nose.

She rubbed her nose, then wiggled free to the ground. "I'm choosing a shell for Mama. You must see, Papa."

She tugged on his fingers, pulling him toward the house, and he chuckled. "Just one moment, El. Would you care to greet our guest?"

Elowen paused, looking to Lieutenant Harris then with a curious gaze. "Good morning," she greeted.

"Afternoon," Mr. Kendricks corrected, but Elowen didn't bother speaking again, watching Lieutenant Harris give a bow.

"How do you do, Miss Kendricks?" he said with a warm grin.

"She is a replica of her mother, is she not?" Mr. Kendricks said proudly.

"Indeed, she is."

"Come, Papa, I want to show you the shells," Elowen said, tugging at his hand again.

"Very well." Mr. Kendricks moved forward, motioning for Lieutenant Harris to follow. "We must see these shells. Apparently, it is of utmost importance."

Lieutenant Harris smiled once again, then followed Mr. Kendricks toward the house.

Poppy stepped aside, finally finding her moment to break free. Never mind the shells still splayed across the table. She would not stay there a moment longer. "If ye ain't be needin' anythin' else, sir, I'll be headed back 'ome."

"Excellent. Thank you again, Poppy. We shall see you in two days' time?"

"Yes, sir."

He moved toward the house, and Poppy hesitated a moment before glancing to Lieutenant Harris. Her nerves were unhinged, her thoughts jumbled.

Was this the last time she would see him again for another three years? Or would it be forever this time?

Pushing the thoughts aside, she dropped into a quick curtsy. "Pleasure to see ye again, Lieutenant. I do 'ope your wound be fitty soon."

Lieutenant Harris gave a single nod, his joy absent from the smile he'd expressed upon seeing Mr. Kendricks. "Thank you, Poppy. Good day."

Poppy. He'd called her that earlier, too. She shouldn't be surprised. She was never 'Miss Honeysett' to him—or anyone, really. She liked her first name far too much to be called by anything else.

Still, the level of friendship that first names spoke of was now, she was certain, nonexistent between them.

Giving one last fleeting look across the man's features, she turned on her heel with Isolde's hand in hers and walked away from Golowduyn Lighthouse and Lieutenant Harris, all the while wondering if the past quarter of an hour had been reality, or if her recurring dreams had twisted into some sort of nightmare where Lieutenant Harris had returned to Cornwall but still had yet to forgive her.

She was more inclined to believe the latter.

CHAPTER THREE

$\mathcal{P}$oppy held Isolde's hand the rest of the way home, singing songs about mermaids and ships and sharing tales of The Hurlers of Bodmin, mischievous piskies, and giants who made islands their homes.

Such stories and songs were typical for their walks back to Tristwick to keep Isolde from dwelling on the long journey, but this time, Poppy was vigilant in ensuring both of them had their minds occupied so Poppy wouldn't dwell on Ed—on Lieutenant Harris any longer.

The last time he'd left, she'd found even the simplest of tasks impossible to do, from rising out of bed every morning to greeting her neighbors. She wouldn't allow herself to be the same way again.

After her stories had dried up for Isolde, Poppy took to pointing out distant dolphins popping in and out of the sparkling sea and herring gulls coasting across the calm waves in search of their next meal.

"Auntie Poppy?" Isolde asked as they paused to smell the Alexanders. The small, yellow flowers gave off a pungent, near-spicy scent, the blue ocean visible through their tall, spacious stems.

"Yes, Isolde?"

"We havin' fish?"

Poppy smiled. Elowen had a perfectly proper accent, being raised by a lady and a gent. But Poppy couldn't help but prefer Isolde's broken, Cornish accent. "For supper? I believe so. Ye be fine with that?"

Isolde sighed, tapping the stem of one of the Alexanders as it bounced in the wind. "I not like fish."

"Ye don't? Why not?"

"I not like the eyes."

Poppy smiled. "What if we eat everythin' but the eyes?"

Isolde seemed to think for a moment, then settled with a simple, "No."

Poppy gave a short laugh. This darling girl always made Poppy's life exponentially better. How she would have regretted missing out on seeing Isolde's childhood, leaving Cornwall when the lieutenant had asked her to.

She shook the thought from her mind. "We ought to be grateful for the fish we 'ave, love. Without 'em, I think we'd be very 'ungry."

Isolde sighed, staring out at the sea instead of responding.

Poppy felt for the girl. She, herself, had grown weary of eating fish at times, but then, she was old enough to realize that there might be a time in the not-so-distant future when fish might become even more of a precious commodity than it already was. Especially for the people of Tristwick.

Soon enough, she and Isolde rounded the ridge of the cliffside, the small hamlet coming into view with a dozen or so quaint, stone houses nestled deeply within the cove.

Even after her twenty-one years of living there, Poppy had yet to grow used to the sight each time she witnessed it anew. Not only did Tristwick evoke feelings of a fairytale with greenish blue waters and light-green cliffsides marked with gray stones, but the hamlet had always brought an instant warmth to her heart, letting her know that all was well in her little world.

Because each time she looked at Tristwick, she witnessed her father throughout it all—the cellars he'd built himself, the cottages he'd pushed to develop, the pathway he'd created after years of walking the same trail. He had poured his heart and soul into their home, into ensuring everyone had a place in their community, and everyone, Poppy especially, admired him because of it. Each time she saw that hamlet, she saw her father's love engrained in it all.

But in the last few months, things had changed. The hamlet still held that otherworldly beauty, but Tristwick had lost half of what made her home feel like *home*.

Before, people would sit outside their cottages, peeling potatoes and shelling peas, greeting one another after a hard day of work. Now, the path was nearly empty, and most of the houses they passed by were vacant, their owners having left after the tragedy that had struck in February.

She and Isolde walked hand-in-hand down the quiet pathway toward the center of the cove where the cellars rested. As they neared the tall stone walls, Poppy looked up the pathway to her home, which was situated at the far south bend of the cove, wondering if her family was already there.

Recently, the number of fish hauled into Tristwick had been abysmal. So much so that the women would finish their work in half the time as usual. While the idea of having half a day off from their daily toils of stacking fish and pressing oil *seemed* fine, the fact remained that the residents of Tristwick might not have enough food for winter, which was more than troubling.

With no smoke coming from their home's chimney, and no windows propped open to allow in the sound of the sea, Poppy redirected her focus to the cellars.

Blinking away from the vision of Lieutenant Harris's green eyes that continued to appear before her like two incessant specters, Poppy peered down at Isolde. "Let's see if your mother and grandmother be in 'ere, eh?"

Isolde responded with a wide-open yawn.

Poppy reached for the large cellar doors, but they swung open before she had the chance. Mrs. Bosanko appeared on the inside with her twelve-year-old daughter, Tegen.

"Mrs. Bosanko, Tegen," Poppy greeted lightly. "I be surprised to see ye still 'ere."

The middle-aged woman wiped a hand across her weary brow, her smile weak. "So were we. There be a fine catch. Me 'usband be pleased with 'ow much they were able to 'aul up."

Poppy pressed a hand to her chest. "Oh, I be that glad." A whole day of pressed fish would last the village weeks if they were conservative. What a godsend that was.

"'Ow be Mr. Bosanko?" Poppy asked next. Gryffyn Bosanko worked as a roller aboard Poppy's brother's ship, the *Pilferer*. He was the gentle giant of Tristwick, ready to defend his home to the death, but sweet and kind to everyone he met.

"'E be little better," Mrs. Bosanko responded, her features falling even more as the past few months weighed upon her spirits. Tegen's frown matched her mother's. "The catch today 'elped."

Poppy nodded understandingly. Gryffyn, along with Poppy's brother, Trevik, had been hit the hardest with the deaths that had occurred aboard their eight-man fishing lugger. They took it upon themselves when the rest of the crew had broken apart.

But just as Poppy was aware of the tragedy, so was Mrs. Bosanko. There was no need to drag the woman farther down. "Let us pray they 'ave better catches in future, too. I be certain they will." She turned to Tegen next. Poppy had her own concerns to deal with—namely a certain lieutenant's return that had yet to vacate her thoughts—but she would far rather help Tegen than dwell on herself any longer.

"Are ye lookin' forward to the hurlin', Tegen?"

Tegen looked away, and an uncomfortable silence filled the air. Poppy glanced to Mrs. Bosanko with uncertainty.

"Tegen ain't sure if she be wantin' to attend," Mrs. Bosanko explained softly, an arm around her daughter's shoulders. "She 'asn't the heart after the Pennas left."

Poppy's own heart twisted with grief. The Pennas were one of the families who'd suffered so much with the accident that they'd left Tristwick for good. Tegen, who was overtly shy, had been the best of friends with the Pennas' youngest daughter. She must be suffering a great deal without her nearby. How daft of Poppy to have brought up such a sensitive subject.

Poppy leaned forward slightly, anxious to right the mistake she'd made. "I understand if ye don't wish to come, Tegen. But I do know that the countrymen be needin' your support." She paused, narrowing her eyes playfully. "Unless ye be thinkin' o' rootin' for the townsmen?"

To her pleasure, Tegen shook her head with a smile. "No, I ain't supportin' the townsmen."

"In that case, I think ye ought to come." Poppy smiled. "We be needin' your loud cheerin' to push these men to victory. And..." She leaned forward. "I did hear of a minin' family with a few young girls 'round your age who will be there. They be new and lookin' for a friend." She shrugged, attempting indifference. "I could introduce ye to 'em if ye'd like."

Tegen hesitated before nodding, her eyes taking on a lighter note. "Thank ye, Poppy," she said softly.

Poppy smiled warmly before glancing up to Mrs. Bosanko, who placed a grateful hand on Poppy's arm. "Thank ye, dear. Ye always be a bright spot in our day."

Poppy's chest swirled with warmth. She couldn't go on the lugger and cast nets out to catch fish, nor could she sell enough shellwork to support all of Tristwick. She could not even help herself by keeping the lieutenant from her weakened mind.

But she *could* help those who remained in the hamlet by spreading joy, if only just a small amount.

Mrs. Bosanko drew a step away. "We'll let ye go now to deliver this little one to 'er mother," she said, motioning to Isolde, who'd been swinging on Poppy's arm for the duration of the conversation.

Poppy nodded, and after saying goodbye to the Bosankos, she and Isolde entered through the doors.

Silent cellars greeted their arrival. Where singing and chatter had once filled the open courtyard, their footsteps now clicked and echoed about the towering four walls and across the otherwise quiet cobblestones.

"Do ye see 'em, Isolde?" Poppy asked, looking past the piles of olive-brown pollocks—the most frequent catch of the month—stacked between layers of salt.

The room was seemingly vacant of any other souls but theirs.

"No," Isolde responded, her brow low.

Finally, beneath the lofts that were built above the court-yard's back end, Mother and Morvoren—Isolde's mother—stood from their seats near the barrels of fish.

"Be that me darlin' Isolde?" Morvoren said, her tongue sounding more Cornish by the day. Beaming, she held her arms out to her daughter.

Isolde's lips split into a grin, and she released her hold of Poppy's hand immediately, sprinting toward her mother.

"Oh, 'ow I've missed ye today!" Morvoren wrapped her arms around Isolde, picking her up and spinning her in circles.

Her blonde hair was a shade darker than Isolde's, but thick and shining, despite Morvoren having worked all day. Her locks were pulled mostly back, though a few tendrils hung down at the side of her face, detailing her already stunning features.

Poppy had always thought her the most beautiful woman

she'd ever seen—as stunning as a mermaid and as generous as a saint. Morvoren had richly blessed their lives ever since joining them, being the sister Poppy had never had.

Mother smiled at Poppy as she approached, greeting her with a hug from the side.

"Are ye not to spin I 'round like that, Mother?" Poppy teased, motioning to Morvoren and Isolde.

Mother laughed. "'Fraid not, daugh'er."

Poppy looked at the pollocks in front of them. "I did hear the men 'ad a good catch last night."

"Oh, a fine one. Trevik and the others be right pleased."

"And the women?"

Mother hesitated. "Not much change, I be afeared. It be a somber mood again in 'ere."

Poppy's heart lowered. She didn't know why she'd expected anything to change. After all, they were all suffering.

The storm that had come last February had rocked Tristwick's community, roofs being torn apart, cellar doors ripped open, windows blown in. But nothing could have prepared them for the waves that overpowered the *Pilferer*, two men losing their lives as they were thrown into the merciless sea—Enyon Penna, the skipper, and Kenver Roskelley.

After their deaths, the community had been torn to pieces. Hedrek Roskelley, Kenver's brother, moved his family away to St. Ives, the Pennas leaving shortly after to Devonshire. Only four remained who could man the lugger, Trevik, Mr. Bosanko and his son, Charlie, and Jowan Cardy, whose grandfather Edern was no longer of an age to help aboard either.

Having such a small number of men was all well and fine during the mackerel and pollack seasons, but once the pilchard watches began in August, they would need a full crew.

Those who remained in Tristwick now suffered with not only the inability to man the boat in a timely manner and retrieve a hearty number of fish, but they were also left behind to pick up the pieces of the broken hearts scattered around Tristwick. It was beginning to wear on them all.

But Poppy wouldn't dwell on such matters. She had a duty to Tristwick, to her family, to her friends. She would not see her home fall to sorrow.

"At least we 'ad some fish today," she said. "And we could very well 'ave more tomorrow."

"Right ye are, Popp," Mother said with a smile. She turned to face her more directly. "'Ow be the Kendrickses?"

Poppy hesitated. Lieutenant Harris had been in the back of her mind since leaving Golowduyn, lingering in a heavy silence, like a storm on the horizon waiting, hovering as it gained more strength before it would douse those on land with its downpour. She didn't want to speak about him, especially to her family, but she could not withhold the storm forever.

"They be fine," she said. "Mrs. Kendricks finally slept… But somethin' else 'appened."

"What?" Mother pressed, clearly concerned.

Morvoren came over to them, holding Isolde in her arms as her sea-green eyes fixed on Poppy.

Poppy searched for the right words before simply spitting them out. "Lieutenant 'Arris be there."

Mother let out a soft gasp, and Morvoren's brow wrinkled.

"'E never," Mother breathed.

"Oh, Popp," Morvoren said, her brow wrinkled. "Are ye well?"

Poppy appreciated the sentiment, but she didn't need her family to worry about her or pity her. What she needed more than anything was a way to forget about Lieutenant Harris once and for all.

After all, he'd clearly been able to overcome any feelings he might have had for her.

"I be more 'an well," she reassured them. "I was shocked at first, but we 'ad a cordial conversation"—if she could call throwing sand in his face and speaking a few sentences a conversation at all—"then Mr. Kendricks came 'ome. The lieutenant ain't 'ere for long. Just today."

Morvoren set down a wriggling Isolde, who wandered toward the fish, prodding at them as she wrinkled her nose.

"What did ye say to 'im?" Morvoren asked.

Poppy shrugged. "Nothin'. 'E asked after Mrs. Kendricks. I asked 'im 'bout 'is stay. That be all."

"'Ow was 'e?" Mother asked next.

Poppy sighed with barely restrained frustration. How could she respond? That Edmund was still as remarkably handsome as ever? That now he appeared perfectly happy with Mr. Kendricks but unbearably guarded with Poppy?

"'E seemed…content," she responded.

Morvoren looked more worried than ever. "Are ye sure ye be well, Popp?" she asked, pain in her expression.

Morvoren had been the first one to encourage Poppy to share her feelings with the lieutenant years before. The woman had taken it as her own fault when things hadn't worked out between Poppy and Lieutenant Harris, but of course, Poppy did not blame her in the slightest.

With as convincing a smile as she could manage, Poppy reached out to rest a hand on Morvoren's. "I be more 'an well, I promise ye. I know ye both be worried, but when I saw 'im, it be so sudden and over so quickly, I 'ardly 'ad time to think at all." She thought for a moment. "In truth, I'd like to forget I e'er saw 'im."

Footsteps sounded behind her. "Forget ye e'er saw who?"

Poppy closed her eyes, cursing her fortune before turning around to face her brother. Trevik's face was unshaven, his eyes bloodshot with grey circles hanging beneath them.

"Who?" he asked again, standing beside Morvoren and placing a kiss to her cheek in greeting.

Poppy hesitated. This was the last thing her brother needed on his already overflowing plate.

"'E'll find out eventually, Poppy," Mother said.

Trevik's frown grew. "Find out what?"

Poppy sighed. "Lieutenant 'Arris be back in St. Just."

Instantly, Trevik's eyes hardened, his lips white as they pressed together. "What does 'e want?"

His firm tone did nothing for Poppy's hesitancy. "Nothin'. 'E only be visitin' the Kendrickses tonight, then 'e'll be off to Penzance tomorrow."

Trevik nodded, apparently satisfied with this information. "Good."

Poppy glanced to Morvoren, who shared her look of relief.

Trevik and Lieutenant Harris had started out as friends, but the moment the lieutenant had shown even the slightest interest in Poppy, Trevik had reverted into her protective elder brother, mistrusting Lieutenant Harris in every way. Matters only worsened when Poppy and the lieutenant's relationship fell to pieces. Poppy had tried to explain that Lieutenant Harris was not at fault, but Trevik would always take her side —a fact for which she was grateful.

"Did ye speak with 'im?" Trevik asked next.

"Only for a moment," she replied. "'E only be 'ere for Mr. Kendricks."

Trevik scowled, shaking his head. "I don't believe that for a second. 'E be back 'ere to rile ye up again."

Poppy's spirits picked up for the briefest of moments, but she reined them in. "'E don't want nothin' to do with I, Trev. I can promise ye that." Her shoulders sunk from the weight of the truth of those words.

Trevik's defenses lowered, and the frustration in his eyes weakened to reveal his weariness once again. "I be sorry, Popp. That 'e came back 'ere, I mean. 'E 'as no thought for ye, otherwise 'e wouldn't do such a thing."

She looked away. Wasn't that what she'd said before? That Lieutenant Harris had no thought for her, that he no longer loved her? So why did hearing her brother say the same thing cut so deeply?

"We just don't need 'im comin' back 'ere and ruinin' things for we again, askin' ye to give up all manner o' things," Trevik continued, rubbing his fingers against his neck.

Morvoren placed a comforting hand to his back.

"I know, Trev," Poppy repeated. "That be why I wasn't plannin' to tell ye in the first place. There ain't nothin' 'tween Lieutenant 'Arris and me. Not any longer."

He gave her a wary look. "So we ain't be at risk o' losin' ye to 'im?"

The words she'd written to Lieutenant Harris flickered in her mind.

I don't see meself e'er leavin' Cornwall for anythin', Lieutenant.

Poppy blinked, dragging her mind to the present. "No, ye ain't goin' to lose I. Not now, not e'er. I be stickin' with all of ye whether ye like it or not."

He gave a half-smile, then drew a deep breath. "I be glad to hear that. 'Specially now."

All eyes fell on him. Morvoren's smooth brow puckered in a frown. "What do ye mean, love?"

He couldn't meet any of their gazes. "I received word back from Hedrek Roskelley. 'E don't want to come back to 'elp we fish. There ain't nothin' to convince 'im otherwise."

Poppy watched her family react to the news. Mother's eyes dropped to the floor. Morvoren released a disappointed sigh. The circles beneath Trevik's eyes seemed even darker than before.

Having Trevik reach out to Hedrek had been a poor bet. They all knew the man would not return to Tristwick after his younger brother's death. It was too painful a reminder— something the Honeysetts understood all too well.

Nearly eleven years had passed by since Father's death, and still, Poppy was numb with grief at times. She'd barely managed to come out of the stupor of darkness his death had put her into, as she had definitely not escaped unscathed.

"So what now?" Morvoren asked. "Ye can't find any

others to man the lugger. Must ye go down to three nights a week? Two?"

Poppy listened with growing discomfort. Trevik had only managed to find a temporary fix to their shortage of sailors, hiring three men from Sennen who could only sail a few nights a week for a handful of hours at a time—as opposed to the six nights a week and nearly eight hours at a time they were typically used to.

The lack of fish hauled was concerning, but it was better than nothing.

Trevik shrugged. "I ain't certain yet what we can do. The men we be payin' are satisfied for now, but they won't last forever." He looked to his family, regret pulling across his features. "I only be sorry to be puttin' ye all through this."

Before Poppy could encourage her brother, Mother shook her head and spoke first. "Ye don't think a second longer on it, son. We be a family, and we stay together as a family. Ye don't 'ave to go through this alone."

Her words seemed to buoy him as he nodded. "Ye be right, 'course, and I be grateful for it." He let out a sigh. "Whate'er we do, we must produce a solution quickly. I fear none o' we will be able to last much longer at the rate we be goin'."

Morvoren nodded, following her husband out of the cellars as Trevik picked up a halfway-sleeping Isolde. He cradled her in his arms and smiled for the first time since Poppy had seen him that afternoon.

Poppy followed behind Mother as Morvoren and Trevik continued their conversation of Tristwick's troubles, but Poppy closed off her ears. She didn't wish to hear it any longer—nor what was needed to fix her home. Every idea they produced would surely change the face of the hamlet altogether.

She knew change was inevitable in this life, but why did it always have to be bad change? Father dying. Tristwick falling apart. Lieutenant Harris leaving.

She followed her family home, keeping her eyes fixed on the sparkling sea. Trevik was right. None of them needed the extra worries that came with Lieutenant Harris's arrival in Cornwall. The last time he'd left her, she'd been cast back into the throes of darkness for months. She would never risk going back there again, especially not when her family needed her.

Thank heavens the lieutenant wasn't staying longer than a day. Neither she, nor her family, nor her home, could bear it.

CHAPTER FOUR

*E*dmund had almost forgotten how incredible food could be. After living off of hard tack and water-thinned stew as a ship's boy for years, he had been thrilled to graduate to the fresh bread and spiced meats he paid extra for as a lieutenant.

Still, that food desperately paled in comparison to the fresh herb and citrus roasted chicken with potatoes Poppy had left behind for the Kendrickses. Each bite filled his stomach with sunshine that was thick and bright and beautiful.

He'd always remembered Poppy's mother being a spectacular cook when he'd spent months convalescing at Golowduyn. Apparently, Poppy had taken the talent and run with it.

At the thought of Poppy for the hundredth time that evening, the image of her standing before him flashed in his mind's eye. He'd attempted not to look at her for too long when he'd first seen her, not wishing to encourage any sort of relationship beyond acquaintances between them, but he'd been unable to help himself.

She had matured, grown even more beautiful over the years. The girlish roundness of her face had given way to a more slender, smooth shape, and her body boasted a new feminine figure with her curves.

Her voice had changed from what he remembered, too. It had softened—along with her arched lips that had only smiled when the young girl had wrapped her arms timidly around Poppy's leg.

The girl. She was obviously Poppy's daughter. They both had the same freckles and wide-eyed expressions. Did she take after her father, too? Poppy's…Poppy's husband? She must have settled down with someone from Tristwick, a neighboring farmer or miner. Was she Mrs. Roskelley now? Or Mrs. Treen?

Edmund rubbed the sudden pressure against his chest and pushed the thought away. It didn't matter to him whom she married—nor how strange it was to think that he should no longer call her 'Poppy.' He was happy for her—just as he was happy with his own life.

After situating Mrs. Kendricks with her meal in her room, Kendricks and Edmund had eaten their meal with Elowen in the dining room, gobbling up the food with second helpings for each of them.

Soon after, Kendricks put Elowen to bed, then finally helped Mrs. Kendricks from her room, carrying her and her swelling belly into the sitting room and laying her out on the settee. Her large dog stretched out across the floor in front of her, keeping a watchful eye on his mistress.

Once the initial greetings had been made, Kendricks excused himself to see to the lamps in the lighthouse above.

"Have you been unable to find anyone to replace me?" Edmund joked, recalling the few months he'd helped watch over the light of Golowduyn.

Kendricks paused in the doorway, his hand on the frame as he turned around. "On the contrary, we've found someone better. Cadan Sholl has *two* working arms."

Kendricks walked away, and Edmund chuckled before

facing Mrs. Kendricks.

"It is wonderful to see you again, Edmund," she said, her smile vibrant though marked with weariness.

She had always been a reserved woman, quite anxious when it came to social matters and trusting others due to past experiences, but Edmund had always enjoyed her tenacious spirit. After all, how could he not, when that very spirit had once saved his and Kendricks's lives?

"It's wonderful to be back," he returned. "I trust the captain has been taking care of you."

Kendricks had been retired from the navy for five years now, but still Edmund had been unable to fully rid himself of calling his friend 'Captain' now and again—out of habit and out of respect.

Mrs. Kendricks rested a hand to her swelling belly. "Better than anyone ever has. Though that will come as no surprise to you."

"His days as captain must be showing," Edmund joked.

"Indeed." Her blue eyes clouded over, worry pursing her brow as she looked to the closed window, only the periwinkle sky visible from their viewpoint. "I will admit, I do not like being unable to help him. He puts so much on himself. I worry for his sake."

Edmund hesitated, not knowing what to say to ease the woman's burden. Her love for her husband was obvious, as was Kendricks's love for his wife. What would life be like to share such feelings, to experience a person's willingness to sacrifice everything for another?

Poppy's wide, brown eyes flickered before him, though he blinked the vision away. He'd tried with Poppy before, but some people were just unwilling to give.

"So, Gavin tells me you will be recovering for quite some time," Mrs. Kendricks said, smiling once again, though the worry in her eyes remained. "Will you be staying at Golowduyn?"

"Oh, no. I couldn't burden the two of you with my recovery again." Nor was he willing to remain near a certain woman he was trying desperately not to think about. "I'll spend some time in Penzance, I believe. Then perhaps return early to St. Ives."

"I'm sorry you will not stay here. Gavin will not say so, but he has missed you a great deal. I believe you help him feel closer to his days at sea."

Edmund could only imagine the feeling. To live off of the sea, away from the ships forever? That was the last thing he wished for.

"How long have you been commanded to rest?" she asked next.

"A little less than three weeks is what I'm hoping for. I am anxious to set sail again."

She nodded, a knowing look in her eyes. "So we are both forced to rest from the one thing our spirits yearn for. Me with the lights, you with the sea."

"It would appear so. Although, I am resting purely for the sake of my arm. Your ordered rest is for much more altruistic reasoning." He paused. "But then, that is just like you, isn't it? Giving up your life for another."

Their eyes met, understanding passing between them about their pasts that had converged years ago. A moment later, Kendricks joined them, his boots thumping across the wooden flooring.

"All finished," he said. "Cadan is on duty for the evening, so I am free to visit." He settled down in his seat, looking between his wife and friend. "What have you been speaking of since I was away?"

Edmund leaned back in his seat. "My plans for convalescing. Our days at sea. How much of a rigid, unforgiving captain you were."

Mrs. Kendricks's eyes smiled with amusement.

"Of course I was," Kendricks said. "There was no chance

we would've even set sail with you unruly lot, had I not been rigid."

Over the next half hour, the three of them chatted together, catching up on the last few years of each other's lives and reminiscing about the past until Mrs. Kendricks shifted in the settee.

"I do hate to cut my part of the evening short, but I fear I am rather tired," she said.

Kendricks was quick to jump to his feet. "I'll help you back to bed."

Edmund stood, as well, taking Mrs. Kendricks's hand and placing a quick kiss to the back of it. "Rest well, ma'am," he said with a bow. "You deserve it."

She smiled warmly, and Kendricks carried her back to her bed, the dog padding right behind them. Edmund took the moment alone to walk to the window, peering out at the gilded sunshine spreading its wings across the cliffside and tinting the green grass with a golden orange.

He'd always appreciated the view from Golowduyn, especially in the tower where the twenty-one lamps were lit to ward off any ships sailing through storms and darkness.

Though he'd spent many a night at the raggedy St. Just inn prior to being invited to stay at Golowduyn for his final months, his time convalescing in Cornwall had always been a wistful memory, filled with happiness, laughter, and excitement.

How different things were now.

After a few moments, Kendricks returned, and he and Edmund left the lighthouse behind to descend the steep hill toward Golowduyn Beach, the small section of land situated just south of the lighthouse.

They walked across the sand, their conversation pausing as they took in the sunset before them. Puffy clouds lingered just above the sun, their shadows dark grey against the soft blue sky, edges lined in copper. Farther out, the sea was still, but nearer to the shoreline, white froth kicked up from the rushing waves, racing up the sand in fluid motions.

Edmund shook his head. "Sometimes, I forget the beauty that can be seen from land."

Kendricks kept his eyes trained on the view. "Just like I forget the beauty that can be seen from the sea."

Mrs. Kendricks's words slipped through Edmund's thoughts. "Do you miss it, being at sea?"

"At times the ache is potent. I allow myself a moment to feel sorry, then I compare what my life *was* to what it is *now*, and I instantly see how I am immeasurably happy. Life at sea, though grand, is…lonely. I never really knew how much it was until I met Abigail."

Edmund's brow twitched. Lonely. He wasn't lonely. He was a lieutenant with hundreds of other men aboard the ships upon which he was stationed. How could he be lonely?

Then he recalled moments at night on the sea, swinging back and forth in his hanging cot, hearing the snores around him, seeing nothing but blackness. In those moments, it was true, he did feel lonely. But what was the issue with feeling lonely a time or two?

"It seems like only yesterday, doesn't it? The shipwreck?" Kendricks said, motioning to the jagged cliffs Golowduyn rested above. Waves slammed against the rocks that protruded into the sea, fanning water out in every direction with white bursts of power. "It is remarkable to see how our lives have changed since then."

Edmund made a noise in response, unable to think of anything else to say. The shipwreck on Dulatha cliffs *had* changed both of their lives. Mrs. Kendricks, previously Abigail Moore, had been the one to pull Captain Kendricks and Lieutenant Harris from the sea when the other men had been secured on land, rowing out in the storm to rescue them both as they were tossed about in the water.

Kendricks had ended up marrying the girl and inheriting

the work of a lighthouse, thereby changing the course of his life forever.

And Edmund? Edmund had fallen for a girl too young, waited at sea for her to grow older, returned once she had, then had his heart broken.

Yes, indeed, their lives certainly had changed.

"We surely would have perished had Abigail not risked her life for us," Kendricks said, interrupting Edmund's thoughts. "We were fortunate to have her help then. And I'm fortunate to have her now."

Edmund narrowed his eyes. Kendricks was behaving strangely, though Edmund couldn't put his finger on why. Was Mrs. Kendricks worse than everyone was letting on? Or was something else the matter?

"How are the both of you?" Edmund asked, facing his old captain directly. "You can tell me, sir."

Kendricks hesitated, his shoulders lowering in a way Edmund hadn't seen since the captain had been forced to come to terms with the *Valour* colliding with Dulatha Cliffs.

"In truth, Harris?" Kendricks shook his head in a helpless gesture. "I'm struggling. And so is Abigail. You know how she is only herself when she works and watches over the lights." He ran his fingers through his hair. "It is taking everything within her to remain abed. And it's taking everything within me to get her to do so. If something happens to the baby, if something happens to *her*, I don't know what I'll do."

The vulnerability in his friend's voice twisted Edmund's heart. Of all the people in Cornwall, Gavin and Abigail Kendricks deserved happiness more than anyone. "How long until she could deliver the baby safely?" he asked.

"Preferably a month. But each day feels stretched into eternity."

Edmund winced. "I'm sorry, sir. I wish I could help you both."

Kendricks nodded his gratitude, taking a deep breath

before clearing his throat and facing Edmund once again. "So, you mentioned going to Penzance to receive your rest."

Edmund hesitated, not wishing to change the subject yet. Was there truly nothing Edmund could do for them? "Yes, I'll be headed there for a time."

"And I suppose you'll spend your time in the comfort of a few drinks, a game of cards, perhaps even a woman or two?"

Edmund flashed a smile. "You know me well, Captain."

Well, he *had* known Edmund, the old Edmund. The Edmund who hadn't cared a shade about having a connection with a woman before kissing her.

But he'd changed since Poppy. No, not since Poppy. He'd changed since he'd grown older. He'd matured.

"I thought I might also return to Derbyshire," Edmund continued. "Visit Sunningway House, perhaps. I would like to ensure my tenants of the estate and those leasing the house are well taken care of."

"And will you be visiting your family whilst in the north?"

Edmund had to laugh. "No, indeed."

Kendricks knew better than anyone that Edmund's relations with his family were strained at best. Edmund's mother and two older brothers resided in Lincoln, more than seventy miles from the house Edmund had inherited from his father in Derbyshire.

Edmund had written to his eldest brother a time or two, but he'd not seen any of his family since he'd left for the navy at eleven. Truthfully, he had no desire to change that any time soon.

"You still haven't forgiven your mother, then," Kendricks continued, "for her pushing you toward the sea? I would have thought you'd be grateful for her introducing you to such a life you cherish."

Edmund looked away, guilt shaking his conscience. He had always held fast to the story that his mother had pushed him out of the door to join the navy, when in truth, Edmund had joined the navy to escape her treatment of him. Saying as much had never endeared him to others, however, so he'd had to change his narrative.

Still, the fact that he hadn't even been honest with Kendricks put him on edge. "While I do appreciate my life now, I don't believe I will be visiting her this time."

Kendricks nodded, rubbing his hand against his chin as he faced the waning sunshine. "And at the risk of insufferably prying, may I ask after you and Poppy?"

Edmund's nerves pinched. He'd figured this conversation would occur at some point during their visit. "What about the two of us?" he asked with false naivety.

Kendricks raised a knowing brow. "You may claim ignorance, Ed, but the last time you were in Cornwall, Abigail and I were under the impression that we were soon to hear an announcement that you and Poppy had become engaged."

The forthright words shook Edmund's standing. He shifted his feet in the sand, fiddling with a thread that poked out from the hem of his shirtsleeves. "Does she still wish to be called by her given name?"

Kendricks gave him an odd look. "Why would she not? We have always called her Poppy."

Edmund was fully aware of such. He knew no one who called the girl 'Miss Honeysett.' Even *he* had attempted to call her the formal name in his thoughts to create distance between them, but it simply did not fit.

"But now that she is married, does she not wish to be called by her husband's name?" he asked, averting his gaze.

He did not want Kendricks deciphering the reason Edmund was asking his question—to simply learn to whom exactly the woman had attached herself.

"Married?" Kendricks pulled back. "Poppy is not married."

A jolt shot through Edmund's stomach, his heart skipping a beat before racing to keep up. Poppy, not married. How could that be so? "But the girl from before…at the lighthouse…"

Understanding lit Kendricks's eyes. "You are referring to Isolde? She is not Poppy's daughter. She is her niece. Trevik and Morvoren's daughter."

Edmund's lips parted in shock, though he had no reason to be surprised. Of course that blonde-haired child would belong to Poppy's golden-haired sister-in-law.

Still, his mind reeled. So Poppy *wasn't* married. Nor did she have a child with another man. Did that mean, perhaps, that she had yet to move on from their relationship?

Truly, he had no notion as to why such news buoyed his spirits. No doubt he was simply happy for her brother and sister-in-law for their new addition to their family. Either way, his lightened heart was not due to the fact that Poppy did not have a husband. In truth, he would have liked to see her happily settled.

"So what happened between the two of you?" Kendricks pressed as Edmund remained silent. "And before you respond in some jesting manner, know that Abigail has put me up to this. She will know when I tell her your response if it is the truth or not."

With his head still spinning, Edmund sorted through his thoughts. He truly did not mind that the Kendrickses wished to know what had occurred. All of Cornwall seemed to have some notion of Poppy's infatuation with him, courtesy of her trailing after him as a sixteen-year-old girl. But he would sooner share the truth with the Kendrickses than anyone else in St. Just.

He drew a steadying breath, reminding himself of the years that had passed, the time he'd spent healing, and the fact that he was far, far better off at sea than anywhere he would have been with Poppy.

"It simply…did not work out between us," he said, raising his voice to be heard above the whistling wind and tumbling waves. "I could not leave the sea, she could not leave Cornwall. Without a solution, we chose to go our separate ways, and I have never looked back."

Kendricks narrowed his eyes, clearly attempting to see if what Edmund spoke was the truth. It was, in essence. After all, there was no need to go into detail about how things had fallen apart.

Once his arm had healed and Edmund had first returned to sea, he'd written Poppy when she'd turned seventeen, asking her to wait for him—at the risk of Trevik having Edmund's neck. When a full year had passed, and Poppy had finally reached the age of eighteen, Edmund had returned, and the two of them had fallen swiftly for each other. Or so Edmund had believed.

On the beach in Tristwick, he'd told her of the home he had planned for his future wife at Sunningdale House, naively hoping for Poppy to be the one.

"When I return from this final assignment, I shall retire," he'd said with all the naïve hope in the world. *"I'll be able to leave the sea and we can be together in Derbyshire."*

He could almost now feel how the warmth in her gaze had slowly shifted, her expression falling and eyes skirting anxiously about when he'd tried to draw closer to her. The humiliation of that memory was poignant and painful, one he would not relive, one he would keep locked away forever.

He did not obtain an explanation for her rejection until he'd been at sea for more than a month. She had explained to him in her first letter that she would not leave Cornwall for anything. Her second and final letter had asked when Edmund would return to Cornwall, offering him a place in Tristwick aboard the *Pilferer*.

But he'd already made his decision. The pain and embarrassment, the confusion he'd been met with from her rejection, had been excruciating. After all, he'd offered her a home, a future with him, a place to grow old, wealth she'd never known. But everything he offered, everything he was, was simply not enough for her.

As such, he told her in a single response that he did not know if he ever would return to Cornwall. And there, their communication had ended.

"So there is nothing between the two of you any longer?" Kendricks asked, drawing Edmund back to the present.

"No. There is not."

Kendricks nodded, seeming to think for a moment. "Well…then what would you say if I made you a better offer than your current plans on how to spend your convalescence?"

"A better offer than cards and drinks and women? I'm intrigued."

Kendricks paused. "Very well, perhaps not entirely better, but I can promise a bit of port and fine conversation."

Unease crept up on Edmund. "What do you have in mind?"

"Stay here at Golowduyn. Earn your keep by helping around the house as you once did."

Edmund stared. "You are serious?" He'd been expecting an offer as a guest, not an aide.

Kendricks sobered. "Unfortunately, I am perfectly serious. You must know how hesitant I am to ask this of you, Edmund, but I am desperate."

The request left Edmund scrambling for logic. He couldn't remain here. That would lead to all sorts of trouble. "I'm certain I wouldn't be of much help with only one arm."

"It would be just as before," Kendricks reassured him. "You could exercise the horses, feed the chickens, watch over the light at times. There's plenty you can do while ensuring your arm receives the rest it requires."

Well, Kendricks had taken care of that issue swiftly. Still, Edmund wasn't convinced. "Surely I would be imposing. You already have a full house as is—and an assistant. Would not

Abigail be even more anxious?" He'd already imposed enough by arriving at Golowduyn unannounced.

But Kendricks was quick to give another rebuttal. "In truth, Abigail was the one to suggest the idea first. You see, her biggest concern is being a burden on me and others. Your presence here, with the help you give and the assistance you offer, will give her the permission she needs to allow herself to rest."

"Is your new assistant not help enough?"

Kendricks gave him a dubious look. "Do you really believe that Abigail would ever trust a man of three and twenty with lighting the lamps after a mere two months of knowing him?"

Edmund could not help but laugh. "No, you are correct." It had taken ages for her to learn to trust Edmund with watching over the light, and even then, she'd never allowed him to light the lamps.

Still, he sighed. He could understand Kendricks's plight. Truly, he could. And frankly, remaining at the lighthouse sounded far more appealing than being with strangers in Penzance—or even worse, being near his family in Lincoln.

But there was one glaring issue he could not solve. How could he work at Golowduyn for three weeks while Poppy Honeysett did the same? He was not concerned for his own sake, of course. But Poppy had been infatuated with him for years. If she *had* been married, her husband would have at least created a barrier between them. But now, what if she attempted to rekindle the past?

"Abigail trusts you, Edmund," Kendricks said softly. "And you know that trust is difficult to come by."

The words settled on Edmund with a force he hadn't felt in years. It wasn't a powerful force, but it struck him with a humility he was in sore need of. Abigail Kendricks had literally risked her life to save his, and the captain had kept him safe for years at sea. They were the closest people he had to a real family, a family who not only cared about him, but *showed* how they cared about him. Could Edmund truly not spend a few weeks at Golowduyn to ease the burden this couple was sharing?

Poppy or not, he knew what he had to do.

"Very well. I will remain here for as long as you need me, sir."

Kendricks watched him for a moment, the relief in his eyes apparent. "You are certain?"

"Absolutely. I am happy to help in any way I can."

Kendricks released a breath. "I cannot thank you enough. Abigail will be delighted. And I…" He shook his head, clasping Edmund on the shoulder in silence.

Edmund could feel his friend's gratitude without hearing a word. To avoid showing too much emotion, however, he shrugged it aside. "I never would have thought to see you, Captain Kendricks, so lovesick."

Kendricks grinned. "I'll be making you climb the steps to the lamps tonight if you are not careful with your words, Lieutenant."

"Ah, I can't climb those steps. Me broken arm, see," he joked, raising his slinged arm and putting on a common accent from up north.

"Already trying to get out of work. This is like being aboard the *Valour* all over again." Kendricks chuckled with a shake of his head. "How I've missed you, Harris."

Edmund smiled in response. "There is a great deal to miss."

After another chuckle, the men watched the sun's final descent into the sea.

Edmund drew deep, calming breaths, allowing the breeze from the sea and the salty air to calm his nerves. He'd made the right decision. He knew that. But even so, that would not make the next three weeks easy. Of course he could handle it. After all, he'd left any thought of Poppy in the past.

But had Poppy done the same with him?

CHAPTER FIVE

*E*dmund posted a letter early the following morning in St. Just, alerting his eldest brother, Algernon, that he would be convalescing in Cornwall and would therefore be unable to make it to Sunningdale.

Sending the letter was a bit of a relief to Edmund. In the first letter he'd received from Algernon in over a year, his brother had inquired after Edmund's intentions for Sunningdale House. Why he cared about its future was beyond Edmund, as Algernon, the eldest son, had inherited Father's largest estate in Lincoln, Norest Park.

Still, Edmund was certain his brother would disapprove of his decision to stay away. Algernon had always been the most responsible of the three Harris sons, attending Oxford, taking over his father's estates at the ripe age of seventeen, and always putting his mother first. There was nothing the man could do wrong as the pride of Mother's eye.

Edmund, however, was the opposite. It was no wonder Algernon barely tolerated him, and Cecil, who was just older than Edmund, had not contacted Edmund once since he'd left for the navy. Mother had clearly poisoned his brothers against him.

"Your brother is a selfish boy," she'd say. *"He is an embarrassment to our family in every way."*

It was just as well. Edmund did not want any connection to the woman. Why would he, with a mother who'd never loved him? Thank heavens there was such distance between them both. They were a mother and son who were never meant to coexist.

Leaving his disappointing thoughts behind, Edmund departed from a teeming St. Just, heading in the direction of the cliffsides. He didn't recall the town ever being so busy before, the streets filled with rolling carriages, the shops doubling in size and number.

He was relieved he didn't have to stay at the Golden Arms at all this time around. Housing at Golowduyn was far more pleasant. He much preferred being surrounded by a rugged Cornish coast to being pushed and prodded down busy streets and sharing a room with strangers.

With renewed determination to leave any thought of his family behind, he focused on the imagery around him. The tall green grass curved over the dirt road he walked along, casting spindly shadows beneath them, and the yellow flowers dotting the countryside demanded attention with their happy colors.

Though he'd tried to deny it, he had missed the scenery here, the rolling fields, the dramatic coastline, the tors stacked high in the distance. The landscape was incomparable.

As he drew nearer and nearer to the sea, Edmund thought he could hear the faint sound of the waves calling to him, but farther ahead, he'd realized the noise was coming from a carriage rolling around the bend.

Standing aside, he allowed the carriage free passage, but he watched in surprise as it slowed, stopping to settle right beside him.

He waited, intrigued to see who was within the carriage walls. But as the footman opened the door, only a vaguely familiar face appeared within as a young woman poked her head forward.

"Why, Lieutenant Harris," the woman said. "It *is* you."

Edmund narrowed his eyes. Was he supposed to know this woman? "Yes, it…it is I."

She shook her head, her dark eyes twinkling. "I don't suppose you remember me. Mrs. Rennalls? My husband saw to your wound after the shipwreck."

Recognition dawned, and Edmund's lips parted. "Of course, Mrs. Rennalls. I thought I recognized you."

She beamed, clearly pleased with his words. "I had no idea you were in Cornwall again."

"Yes, it was an unplanned visit. I am on leave for a few weeks, so I thought I would visit with the Kendrickses while I can."

Her eyes dropped to his arm in the sling. "Oh, heavens. Another injury?"

"The same one, unfortunately."

"Oh, well you must see Dr. Rennalls. He will surely know what to do to help you be on your way soon."

Edmund nodded, though he would never again agree to visit with the physician. He was fine enough, but his wife—now that Edmund's memory was returning—had been the type to sit in the adjacent room in order to hear all of her husband's patients. She'd always entered the room just as soon as the examinations had been completed, asking all manner of personal questions in a roundabout way.

He supposed that was why she was such an informed gossip.

"So you are to stay with the Kendrickses, then?" she asked.

He nodded, and her brow puckered.

"Then you will have heard of poor Mrs. Kendricks," she questioned next.

The woman was fishing already. Heavens above. "Yes, I have."

"Unfortunate business, that. Even more unfortunate that she has taken to seeing another physician instead of my husband."

Her eyebrows were drawn high with sadness, but her tone was pinched, revealing she was more annoyed than sorrowful.

She waited in silence, but frankly, Edmund had no notion as to how to respond to her words. Mrs. Rennalls must have realized this after a moment as she continued.

"Speaking of such, I do have quite tragic news," she said, lowering her voice, as if they were going to be overheard on the vacant road. "My husband and I are to quit Cornwall. Permanently."

Edmund's brows raised. "Are you? I am sorry to hear that."

"Yes, as am I. My poor Rennalls has been unable to cope since that new physician came to St. Just. Dr. Kent." Her tone flattened as she said the name. "He charges next to nothing for his patients, sometimes accepting fish as payment." She shook her head. "I cannot imagine his choices to be very sustainable at all."

Edmund recalled hearing about Dr. Kent from Kendricks and Abigail. He didn't have much of an opinion of the physician, but anyone who the Kendrickses trusted, he knew he could trust, too.

Still, he was sorry to hear about the Rennallses' move. "Where will you go from here?" he asked, hoping to divert attention away from her disparaging another physician.

She did her best to hide her smile, but the edges around her eyes crinkled, and she raised her chin. "We are to go to London."

"Are you? That will certainly be a change of pace." And not at all a pleasant one. He far preferred quieter settlements to the bustle of Town.

"Yes, indeed. But we are most ready for the challenge. Rennalls says I belong in the high society of Town."

Edmund pressed his lips together with a nod. "I'm certain you do, Mrs. Rennalls."

She smiled, flattered. "Yes, we are quite ready to quit Cornwall, find somewhere we can be appreciated. Though, we are not the only ones to have fallen on hard times, mind. St. Just has grown, but Wheal Jenny has veritably run out of copper, and even some of the fishermen are now suffering for food. I'm certain you've heard what occurred in Tristwick. Terrible tragedy."

Edmund's chest pressed in, making it difficult for him to breathe. A tragedy in Tristwick? He hadn't heard of a single mention of it. Still, he needed to tread carefully with Mrs. Rennalls. "I have not heard of this tragedy, unfortunately," he admitted.

"You mean, you have not been to Tristwick yet?"

"No, I haven't."

Her eyes widened with intrigue. "There was a terrible storm a few months ago, you see. It caused the loss of two fishermen's lives. Since then, more men have left, leaving the Honeysetts, and those few others who remained, scrambling."

The air Edmund tried to breathe in stuck in his throat. Two men. He'd known each of the men who worked aboard the *Pilferer*. Which ones had perished?

"Do you happen to know which men died?" he asked, his voice rigid.

Mrs. Rennalls strained to recall the names. "A Roskelley and...a Penna, I believe."

Edmund nodded in response. Both men had been wonderful people. They'd spoken with him, invited him to celebrations on Tristwick's beach. Mr. Penna had even attempted to arrange Edmund a marriage with his daughter, Mary.

Working on the sea always provided a risk to every man

who chose to do so, though it was never easy when anyone lost their lives to the waves. How were their families and those who survived? Tristwick had as tight a community as he had ever seen, but how could they remain valiant if they had no fish for the coming months and no one to man the boats?

Of course, none of this was his responsibility or his concern. Still, his heart ached for them.

"I am quite shocked Poppy Honeysett didn't tell you of the tragedy when she saw you," Mrs. Rennalls said. "Unless…you have not seen her yet?"

This was the question he knew she'd been dying to ask. Though why a woman of the upper class was interested in the affairs of a fisherman's daughter and a visiting lieutenant was beyond him. But then, perhaps gossip was difficult to come by in St. Just.

The woman was certainly going to have the time of her life when she moved to London.

"No, I have seen her," he responded simply.

Her lips pressed tightly together, as if she were attempting to stop herself from asking further questions. Her prevention lasted a total of two seconds. "And…how was your reunion? Shall we hear wedding bells at last?"

Edmund pulled on a look of confusion. "For whom?"

Mrs. Rennalls blinked. "Why, between you and Poppy, of course. The last time you were here, all of us were under the impression that you and Poppy had become engaged, and then all of a sudden, you vanished."

"Heavens, are folks still speaking of this? It occurred nearly three years ago."

Mrs. Rennalls looked slightly affronted at being accused of old news, but still, she leaned forward even further in her seat in the carriage. "You cannot blame a woman for wondering, can you?"

Yes, actually, he could. First Kendricks, now Mrs. Rennalls. Who had first circulated this false engagement throughout St. Just? Or was it merely what people naturally assumed after seeing Poppy and himself together?

Either way, he would set the record straight, if only to keep him sane for the next few weeks at Golowduyn.

"I do not know where you received your information, but I'm afraid to say that you *were* misinformed, Mrs. Rennalls. You see, Poppy and I were never engaged."

Her brow twitched. "Oh. I see. That is surprising. Especially considering the state Poppy was in after you left."

His stomach jolted, though he readily quelled his nerves. What did she mean, Poppy's 'state'? Blast it, if Mrs. Rennalls hadn't intrigued him. Still, he wouldn't satisfy her with a question of clarification.

To no surprise of his, she continued on her own. "She was forlorn, you see. Quite so. Didn't leave her house for weeks."

Edmund's mind swirled with the information the woman had delivered to him in such a short amount of time. Moving to London, deaths due to storms, Poppy disturbed by his departure.

Honestly, he didn't know what was being exaggerated and what was the truth. If Poppy did have a difficult time when he'd departed Cornwall, that certainly made him feel better about the nights he used to spend wide awake, trying to stop his thoughts from dwelling on her.

But then, why would she have been upset at all? She was the one who had ended any chance of a relationship burgeoning between them.

"I do hope you weren't terribly distraught with the whole affair," Mrs. Rennalls fished again.

Edmund pulled on a smile. He would not allow this woman to spread an ounce of false information about him. "All I can say, Mrs. Rennalls, is that I am perfectly happy with how things turned out. I couldn't be more pleased to spend the rest of my days at peace on the sea."

She narrowed her eyes, as if trying to deduce if he was

speaking the truth. "Well, I'm very glad to hear that, sir. I only wish I could say the same for Poppy. I'm sure the poor girl still longs for you. One does not forget a first love."

Edmund shifted his body away from her. He was finished with this conversation. He needn't have any more ideas shoveled into his mind or reminders as to how Poppy used to be. How she used to beam with pride whenever she'd made Edmund laugh. How she'd been an adorable young woman and had now grown into a stunning individual.

An individual who had carved his heart straight from his chest and dropped it into the depths of the sea.

Frankly, he would feel quite satisfied if the woman had yet to overcome her love of him—if she'd ever even called it love.

"So tell me," Mrs. Rennalls continued, "do you…"

Her words faded as her lady's maid, who'd remained silently tucked away in the confines of the carriage, whispered something to Mrs. Rennalls. Mrs. Rennalls gasped, then looked over her shoulder in the carriage through the back window.

Swiftly, she faced Edmund through the door again, her eyes wide with excitement. "If it isn't the very woman herself, come to trail after you again."

Edmund tightened his eyes. What was the woman on about?

But as he caught sight of the movement behind the carriage, he turned to see Poppy Honeysett walking toward them, her gaze on Edmund's until she pulled it swiftly away.

To add insult to injury, his heart jumped at the sudden sight of her. Honestly, he should have been expecting this. How often had she crossed paths with him when she was younger? Finding him on cliffsides, catching him on the spiral steps of Golowduyn, running into him on beaches. If he didn't know any better, he would think that she'd just *happened* to find him this morning, too. Except the fact that she'd no doubt expected him gone by now.

Did this mean he was accurate in his assumption the night before when he'd discovered that Poppy was not married after all? And did this mean Mrs. Rennalls was correct—that Poppy had yet to overcome her infatuation with him?

"Poppy? Poppy Honeysett, is that you?" Mrs. Rennalls called out with excitement, waving a hand from her carriage.

Poppy came to stand beside them. "Mornin', Mrs. Rennalls," she greeted, skirting a glance at Edmund. "Lieutenant."

Mrs. Rennalls looked between them like she'd just been given two gifts and now had to choose which she'd like to accept. "How providential that you are both here," she said, eyes gleaming. "We were just speaking of you, Poppy."

"Were ye?" Poppy's eyes landed on Edmund, a flicker of intrigue in their depths.

His jaw flinched. Of all the things for Mrs. Rennalls to say, *that* was the worst. If the very idea of Edmund speaking of herself perked Poppy up, that was evidence to him that Mrs. Rennalls had been rightly informed in one regard.

Poppy still had feelings for him.

But he would not allow this to carry on a single moment further. Poppy could do what she wished, feel as she wished, but *he* could not live through this again.

He would make it inexplicably clear that he'd moved on— and he'd do it that very moment.

Finding herself at liberty for the first time in days, Poppy had thought it a fine notion to head to St. Just to inquire of Mr. Pedrek if he would be interested in purchasing her shellwork to sell in his jewelry shop again.

Never had she thought she'd find Lieutenant Harris on the same road. After all, he was supposed to have left St. Just already, had he not?

She forced her eyes off of Lieutenant Harris again, wondering what he could have been speaking of with Mrs. Rennalls. Or had the woman been telling a falsehood? It certainly wouldn't be the first time.

"What were ye speakin' of 'bout I?" she asked.

"Oh, nothing of great importance," Mrs. Rennalls said enigmatically. "We were also speaking of how long it has been since the lieutenant has graced us with his presence."

Poppy nodded carefully, knowing whatever she said could very well be used in gossip later on. The only reason the woman was even remotely interested in Poppy was because a lieutenant was involved—or at least *had* been involved.

"It 'as been long," Poppy responded.

Mrs. Rennalls opened her mouth to continue, but she paused when she spoke with her lady's maid inside the carriage.

After a moment, Mrs. Rennalls's nodded, then she turned back to Poppy and Lieutenant Harris. "I fear I must leave the both of you now, as I've an appointment with Mrs. Follett that cannot be missed." She leaned forward. "I am to order a very fine gown for my arrival in London. Of course, I will have to have an entirely new line of dresses created while there, as London fashion is far different than that of our quaint Cornish country-side." She gave a little laugh then pulled back inside the carriage. "At any rate, I am certain the two of you have much to discuss after all these years." Her eyes sparkled. "Good day to you both."

The footman closed the door, then hopped onto the back of the carriage before it rattled down the road toward St. Just.

The moment Poppy and Lieutenant Harris were left alone, an awkward silence settled heavily between them, and Lieutenant Harris's smiling features settled once more into a tight expression, as if his lips didn't know what else to do but frown.

For a moment, Poppy wished for Mrs. Rennalls to return,

if only to see his smile again. But then, she wasn't so naïve as to think she deserved his smiles any longer.

Shaking her head, she faced him with what she hoped was calm nonchalance. There was no reason the two of them could not speak like civilized adults. So much time had passed, after all.

"I thought ye would've left for Penzance by now," she said lightly, praying her words didn't come off as accusatory.

He shifted his boots on the road, peering down at them. "No, I was asked to stay on at Golowduyn for a few weeks to help Mr. Kendricks while Mrs. Kendricks is abed."

Poppy tensed. A few weeks? Heavens above.

She didn't blame Mr. Kendricks for asking Lieutenant Harris to stay. After all, they were close friends, and Mr. Kendricks was experiencing a great deal of anxiety. But then, what was she to do, simply work alongside the lieutenant as she'd done before as if nothing had changed? Such a thing was sure to be impossible.

Then another thought occurred. What was she going to tell Trevik?

"I trust my staying there will not be a problem," Lieutenant Harris said, no doubt wondering at her continued silence.

"A problem?" she questioned. "Not at all. Why would it be?"

He raised a brow. "I haven't the faintest. But your silence tells me you do take issue with my staying here, despite your words stating otherwise."

Poppy stared. He'd always been infuriatingly accurate when reading her. Once, when she was sixteen, she'd been caught by the nettles around Golowduyn after straying too far from the pathway. Despite being in a great deal of pain, she'd managed to hide her injuries until the very end of the day. Before she left, Edmund had taken one look at her, dropped his gaze to her arm, then found a bit of salve to ease her wound.

How she'd admired him for coming to her rescue that day.

How times had changed.

Pushing the memory aside, she made to defend herself. She truly did not take issue with his staying there, especially if it was to help the Kendrickses—regardless of how she felt. She could handle being around him. She would be fine. More than fine, she would be marvelous.

But before she could respond, he blew out a heavy sigh.

"Poppy," he began, "I feel I ought to be frank with you. Whatever happened between you and me before…I no longer feel what I once did." He looked away. "In truth, I'm not even sure I felt anything at all. But what matters is that I've changed. I've moved past what occurred." He glanced up at her with a compassionate wince. "I believe it is time you do the same."

Heat rushed through her limbs, burning her cheeks with humiliation. How she regretted her behavior as a young woman, following after him, silently begging for his attention, for his affections.

She knew already Lieutenant Harris didn't have feelings for her now, even if he had when they were both younger. He'd made that clear when he'd chosen to remain at sea instead of taking her up on her offer to share a home with her in Tristwick.

"You've asked me if I will ever return to Cornwall," he had written to her. *"I cannot give an answer, other than, I do not know."*

Her heart had fully broken that day she'd finally received his correspondence, for it had solidified what she'd always feared, that he did not love her.

So now, to hear him state that he had *never* loved her—and to hear his accusations that she still loved him—she could not bear the humiliation.

As swiftly as her embarrassment had taken over her person, pride and indignation soon followed.

She raised her chin and faced him directly. Lieutenant Harris didn't wish for a relationship of any sort with her— friendship or otherwise. So she would make it as clear as the Cornish waters that she felt the same.

"I don't know what ye be thinkin' 'bout I, sir," she stated, "but rest assured, I 'ave moved on."

"Are you certain?"

His look of disbelief rattled her patience. "Ye find that difficult to believe?"

He shrugged, readjusting the sling around his neck. "The evidence would suggest otherwise."

"And what evidence might that be, Lieutenant?"

"Well, you are not married, nor do you have children of your own." He tipped his head to the side. "And you are still working at Golowduyn. All signs would point to you living the same way as before, so why would I not assume you are *feeling* the same way as before?"

Her mouth dropped open. The sheer audacity of the man. This was not the Edmund Harris she remembered, the Edmund Harris she'd fallen in love with. Thank heavens she'd truly lost any feelings for him.

"Well, what about ye, sir? Ye ain't married. Ye 'ave no kids. Ye still be pinin' away at sea. Per'aps ye chose to work at Golowduyn to be closer to I." She took a step closer, her voice lowering. "Why else would ye be talkin' to Mrs. Rennalls 'bout I?"

His soft scoff informed her how preposterous he thought the idea. She knew her words were ridiculous, but honestly, the man deserved to be taken down a few notches.

"You haven't changed from that sixteen-year-old girl, have you, Poppy? You still possess that wild imagination." He gave her a solicitous half-smile. "I assure you, I am happier now than I ever have been before in my life. I believe that is proof enough for the both of us that I have moved on."

Poppy hardly recognized this pompous, self-assured gentleman standing before her. Had the humble, playful Lieutenant Harris of her past been swallowed up so completely? That lieutenant would have never thrown her age in her face. That lieutenant had always been respectful, kind, and considerate. Had the sea changed him? Or was this new, unflattering behavior merely a façade to mask how he truly felt about what happened between them?

Either way, she would not throw a fit, proving his words right. Never mind that she had always possessed a wild imagination—thinking that piskies had taken over her room when she was a girl and believing that she saw a large, cat-like beast crawling across the moors.

She was far more sensible now, and she would prove it.

"Well, I be glad that ye be so 'appy, sir," she stated, sobering. "I only 'ope ye can feel the same for I. 'Cause I *'ave* moved on. Ye won't be findin' I pinin' after ye any longer, if that be what ye be wantin' I to do still."

Slowly, his eyes hardened, his lips drawing into a thin line. "No, I would hardly expect you to do that again."

"Fine," she stated. "I be glad we've come to an understandin', then."

"Indeed." He took a step back, bowed, then straightened with an impassable gaze. "Good day, Poppy."

Poppy watched him walk away, fighting the regret she felt for engaging in such an argument. She had no notion as to why they were even bickering. Did it stem from their pride? Or their still-open wounds?

Either way, she knew one thing for certain. She was going to do her best to ensure Lieutenant Harris never made the mistake again of thinking that she was still in love with him.

Because Heaven knew she was not.

CHAPTER SIX

*P*oppy had straightaway told Morvoren and Mother that Lieutenant Harris would be remaining in St. Just. Her sister-in-law had offered to find a time to tell Trevik herself, and Mother had shared her encouragement throughout the day and well into the following morning when Poppy had to report back to Golowduyn.

"Don't let 'is presence bring ye down, love," Mother said as they stood near Tristwick's dock at dawn, awaiting the *Pilferer* to sail in after a night of fishing. "Ye 'ave a gift to understand what folks be feelin', like your father 'ad. If ye use that gift, I think ye will see there be more to the lieutenant's story than meets the eye."

Poppy agreed to go along with her mother's suggestion, but as Poppy and Isolde left the handful of women in Trist-wick to process the fish, she couldn't help but long to join in the work instead of toiling at the lighthouse.

Life was cruelly ironic in that regard, when only just a few days before, she had been glad to have a break from the cellars.

Even though she'd tried to be honest with her family before, Poppy had been far too embarrassed about Lieutenant

Harris's accusations to tell them all of what he'd said about her pining after him—mostly because she'd feared they'd agree with him.

After all, they'd seen more than anyone how she'd followed him around like an infatuated kitten, desperate for his love. She did not feel the same way now, of course. Especially because she was exceedingly grateful that she'd remained in Cornwall. Her family needed her. Tristwick needed her. And there was no way she could've helped from afar.

Still, knowing such did very little to improve her mood until she and Isolde reached Golowduyn, greeting Elowen who had been reading a book in Mrs. Kendricks's bed, Gwitha sitting nearby with his chin resting in his paws.

"'Ow ye be feelin' this mornin', Mrs. Kendricks?" Poppy asked as the little girls greeted one another with multiple embraces.

Mrs. Kendricks gave a tired smile. "I slept more last night than I have in weeks, so I'm doing much better."

"I be that glad to 'ear it," Poppy said as she went about her routine, sliding the curtains open and adjusting the window so it allowed more of the sea's sounds within the room.

"I'm sure I can attribute my rest to having the lieutenant here. I can already feel Gavin relaxing."

Poppy stiffened at the mention of Lieutenant Harris, though she folded the blankets at the foot of Mrs. Kendricks's bed with a smile. "That must be nice for ye both."

Mrs. Kendricks was silent for a moment, her calculating gaze on Poppy. "I know it is a little late to ask you this, but are you all right with the lieutenant staying here for a time?"

There was no chance Poppy was going to tell the woman the truth and risk her and her unborn child any discomfort. She pulled on her best smile and nodded. "'Course. What 'appened 'tween the two o' we be long since past. Seein' 'im now, more 'an ever, confirmed it."

Mrs. Kendricks did her best to hide her disappointment, but Poppy could see it in her eyes. Apparently all of Cornwall wished for her to wed Lieutenant Harris. Well, perhaps she ought to tell all of Cornwall just how pompous the man had grown, then she'd see if they took his side any longer.

Her mother's words echoed in her ears again, and she drew a calming breath. She needed to give the lieutenant a chance, like Father would have.

That had always been one of his strengths, believing there was good in everyone and allowing them the opportunity to show it. Surely she could try a little harder to be like him.

An hour later, she had the perfect opportunity to do so when she and the girls plucked a few weeds from the gardens and Lieutenant Harris and Mr. Kendricks arrived from an early-morning ride.

Mr. Kendricks appeared more refreshed than Poppy had seen him in months, and Lieutenant Harris himself fairly beamed as he sat astride Mrs. Kendricks's dappled grey mare. But when his eyes met Poppy's, Lieutenant Harris's smile faded away.

"Morning, Poppy," Mr. Kendricks greeted as warm as ever.

Lieutenant Harris, however, barely acknowledged her presence. He delivered a simple, straight-faced bow, then took up his conversation about the navy with Mr. Kendricks again.

Clearly, the man was bound and determined to prove his words from the day before, that he was happier now than he ever had been—and it was because he was not with her.

Unfortunately, as the day progressed, she saw exactly that as she went about her chores and as he took up his old tasks at Golowduyn.

While she fed the chickens alone, Lieutenant Harris and Mr. Kendricks fixed the hinge on the stable door, their deep laughter rising above the constant sound of the waves below.

Later in the day, when she'd swept the kitchen floor from

Isolde's and Elowen's spilt flour—"It's snowing, Poppy!"—
she'd overheard him speaking with Mrs. Kendricks in the
sitting room. He'd even managed to get her to laugh thrice,
which Poppy hadn't heard in weeks.

Of course, Lieutenant Harris had this effect on everyone.
He was charming, energetic, and filled with an abundance of
charisma—like a male siren infused with the power of Eros's
arrow.

But when he was around Poppy, he was silent, encom-
passing the mood of a Sunday sermon gone on for far too
long in a stuffy, boiling church.

How she despised him for it. She'd have to apologize to
her mother when she returned home. Poppy was in no mood
to give the man even a sliver of her empathy when he was
clearly not suffering in the slightest.

Fortunately, Isolde and Elowen kept her busy enough to
not dwell too greatly on her misfortune of having to work in
the same house as a man she'd been daft enough to fall in love
with all those years ago.

However, when she settled the girls down at the kitchen
table with a pile of excess dough from the steak and kidney pie
Poppy had made for the Kendrick's dinner, Poppy was frustrated to hear the lieutenant's words drifting in from where he
cleaned the fire chute in the sitting room.

She couldn't make out what he said, but as Mr. and Mrs.
Kendricks both laughed, she cringed.

Poppy was grateful the Kendrickses were so happy. Really,
she was. But for some reason, her annoyance with the lieutenant—and his ability to bring more joy to the Kendrickses
than Poppy ever had—could not be squelched. How could he,
after all these years, simply return from the sea and have
everyone still love him?

She huffed out a sigh, then turned away from the sitting
room. In a huff, she uncovered the plate of mint lemon curd
shortbread she'd baked before the pie. She always had a habit

of finishing the dessert before dinner. Now, she'd never been more grateful for the practice—or for the Kendricks's generosity.

Her family could rarely afford such luxuries as lemons, so baking with such expensive ingredients was a dream come true. Consuming them, on the other hand—with the Kendricks's permission, of course—was unrealized heaven.

"Eat whatever you wish, Poppy," Mrs. Kendricks had told her for years. "We have too much food as it is."

Typically, Poppy only allowed herself to indulge in dessert or a small taste of dinner to ensure the food was well-cooked.

Today, however, would have to be the exception.

Ensuring the girls were too occupied with their dough to witness the indelicacy of their caretaker, Poppy turned her back to them, sliced a thin sliver from out of the cast-iron skillet, then stuffed the lemon-filled shortbread into her mouth.

Instantly, the tangy, sweet taste infused her tongue like sun-soaked sand. Now this…this was bliss. This made everything better. This made all her worries simply—

"Poppy?"

She sucked in a breath, inhaling a few crumbs of short-bread crust which resulted in a hacking cough.

Did the lieutenant have to ruin *everything*? Even her dessert?

She covered her mouth to ensure the pieces of the short-bread didn't end up all over the rest of the skillet, then she cleared her throat and turned to face him, still chewing on the remainder of her mouthful.

Heavens, she didn't realize she'd stuffed so much in there.

His green eyes focused on her, impossible to read.

With his continued silence, she knew she'd have to be the one to speak up first. She lowered her hand. "Yes?"

To her horror, a piece of her masticated shortbread shot forward, landing at his feet.

He stared at it, his lip twitching. "If I was your target, I'm sorry to say you missed."

A lightness twinkled in his eyes, but it vanished before she could fully register his teasing.

He cleared his throat. "Mr. Kendricks has asked me to inquire if you have a spare bucket you are not currently using. We need an extra one for water to clean the hearth in the sitting room."

She took in the sight of his angled features, smudged soot along his jawline and just above his right brow. How was he even more handsome while in sore need of a washing?

She chastised her thoughts, pulling to the forefront of her mind all that had occurred the day before—all that he'd accused her of.

Swallowing hard the rest of the shortbread, she turned. "Yes, sir."

But before she could retrieve the bucket, she caught sight of Isolde and Elowen flinging pieces of their dough onto the floor beside them. She course-corrected to end the mess before it became any worse.

"We must keep it off the floor, girls," she reminded, tossing the pieces back onto the table.

Isolde frowned, looking at the dough that had stretched across her fingers like spiderwebs. "It sticky, Auntie Poppy," she complained in her broken words.

"Let me fetch the bucket for the lieutenant, then I'll wash ye off," Poppy responded.

But Isolde's blonde brows pulled together, her eyes widening with a panicky look. "But it sticky!"

Poppy couldn't help but smile. Isolde loved playing in dirt and sand and mud, more often than not coated from head to toe in all three. But the moment anything sticky touched her—be it jam, honey, or, apparently, dough—she was done for.

Elowen, however, already had the dough sticking to dozens

of strands of her red hair. Perhaps this was not one of Poppy's best ideas.

"I am more than happy to wait so you may help the lady in distress," Lieutenant Harris said with a smile in Isolde's direction.

The two-and-a-half-year-old hardly noticed, her eyes focused so intently on her hands, one would have thought she'd lost the use of them.

Poppy did as the lieutenant suggested, grateful for the distraction the girls provided, though the awkwardness in the air still held strong between her and Lieutenant Harris.

After retrieving a rag, she wiped the girl's fingers clean and inspected them with a close eye. "Be that better, love?"

"There be more." Isolde said, pointing at a small speck of dough on the back of her hand.

Poppy wiped the girl's soft skin carefully, acutely aware of the lieutenant's eyes on them both. She definitely should have retrieved the bucket for him first. She hated to imagine what he was thinking.

Poor Poppy, still as stuck in the past as the dough is to Isolde's hands.

She tightened her jaw. "That be fine now?"

Isolde nodded, her smile returning. "Thank ye, Auntie Poppy."

She kissed the girl atop the head, then moved to retrieve the bucket. She was ready to see the last of this pompous sailor.

But as she crossed the kitchen, footsteps sounded near the doorway, and Golowduyn's most recent assistant, Cadan Sholl, appeared in kitchen.

Poppy's mood instantly brightened, and she shifted away from where the bucket rested near the fireplace. "Cadan! I be wonderin' when ye were goin' to arrive."

Cadan, who had just turned three and twenty, had relocated to St. Just last year, living in the north of England previously. He started work at the lighthouse only a few months ago but had instantly found a place at Golowduyn due to his ever-present smile and dedicated hard work.

Isolde and Elowen hopped down from their chairs at the table, running to greet Cadan with an embrace around each of his legs.

"Ah, me girls," he said, patting their backs with a grin. "Are you havin' fun today?"

The girls nodded in unison before Cadan turned to Poppy with a grin that caused his blue eyes to veritably disappear. He reached out and placed a firm kiss to the back of her hand. "And how is me favorite flower in all of Cornwall?"

She laughed. Poppy always found herself in a better mood when talking to Cadan, and unsurprisingly, the two had become quick friends because of the fact.

"Ye charmer." She gave his arm a half-hearted tap in admonishment. "Ye only say as much 'cause ye be smellin' me lemon-curd shortbread."

He pressed a hand to his heart. "Will you ever forgive a weak boy such as meself?"

She pretended to think for a moment. "I s'pose. But only if ye taste a bit o' the shortbread and tell me if it be fine enough to serve."

He delivered an exaggerated sigh. "If I must." Then he grinned with another wink.

The wood of the kitchen floor shifted near the door, and she glanced to where Lieutenant Harris still stood waiting for his bucket. She'd nearly forgotten he was there.

Or so she liked to tell herself. In truth, she was keenly aware of every breath he breathed and every blink he blinked.

She made for the bucket once again, then paused, slowly turning to look back at Lieutenant Harris. That scowl of his. It certainly hadn't been that fierce before. And why was he directing it at Cadan?

Poppy narrowed her eyes, but when he caught her gaze, he blinked and looked away.

Her heart tripped. If she didn't know any better, she would say the lieutenant was…but, no. That was ridiculous. Lieutenant Harris couldn't be jealous of Cadan and Poppy's camaraderie.

But Mother's words popped into her mind. *"Ye 'ave a gift to understand what folks be feelin'."*

Could it be true? Did Lieutenant Harris truly feel envious of her relationship with Cadan, even if it was a purely platonic friendship?

She supposed there was only one way to find out—and it certainly wasn't by giving him the bucket and having him leave the kitchen.

Edmund thought Poppy was finally going to give him the bucket as she moved to stand right next to where it was situated near the stove.

Instead of retrieving it, however, she merely stood beside it and removed the rag from the shortbread where it rested on a small table near the stove.

So that was what she'd spat toward him when he'd entered the room—shortbread. She'd certainly offered a different greeting to Cadan. No spit involved and with a smile as brilliant as the sunrise.

"Heavens, but they smell divine," Cadan said, drawing in a deep breath.

Edmund did his best to avert his eyes from the man, not wishing to be caught scowling at him again. He'd only met Cadan on one occasion before, Kendricks introducing him as the "best assistant Golowduyn has ever seen."

Of course, Kendricks had only said so to tease Edmund for when *he* had worked as an assistant.

Still, all of Golowduyn seemed to have fallen for the man nearly seven years Edmund's junior. Even the toddlers fawned over him when he entered the room—though Elowen and Isolde had since returned to their dough at the table.

More than anyone, Poppy appeared to like Cadan, as well. Edmund hadn't seen her light up with that broad of a smile since before he'd left Cornwall.

"'Ere ye go, sir," Poppy said, her skirts brushing against the bucket as she cut a small slice out of the dessert and offered it to Cadan.

Had she entirely forgotten about Edmund's presence? Honestly, what did a man have to do to receive a simple bucket?

Cadan reached for the shortbread, but Poppy pulled it back swiftly. "Be your 'ands clean?"

He stared down at his palms with a shrug.

Poppy clicked her tongue, though her eyes remained bright. "Ye must allow I to feed it to ye, then."

Cadan's brow rose as Edmund's lowered.

"If you must, my lady," Cadan responded.

She held it close enough for him to take a bite, and she laughed. "Ye nearly bit me 'and off, sir."

"My apologies," Cadan said, his mouth full as he chewed.

Honestly, had he no manners?

Edmund blew out a breath, tired of the ridiculous scene unfolding before his eyes. He would have retrieved the wretched bucket himself ages ago, were it not placed so closely to Poppy's leg.

Cadan's exaggerated moan stole Edmund's attention again.

"This is…" Cadan exhaled again. "This is the best short-bread I've ever eaten."

Poppy's cheeks blushed a lovely red, like a rose blooming for the first time. "Ye just be sayin' that."

"No, I speak only the truth."

Her smile grew, and Edmund's chest tightened.

Their conversation from the day before returned to his

mind—as it had done many times since they'd ended it. He'd regretted his pompous behavior instantly, but it was the only way he could think to put distance between them.

He hadn't believed her for a moment when she'd said she'd moved on from him. But seeing her now with Cadan, he couldn't help but wonder...*had* she moved on with the lighthouse assistant?

"I'd like the rest now please, me flower," Cadan said, and Poppy happily fed him the remainder of his shortbread.

Flower. How unimaginative. If this man was courting Poppy, he surely could do better than that. What did Poppy see in this Cadan Sholl anyway? He obviously had no wealth, no inheritance.

Or did she merely like him because he would keep her in Cornwall?

Edmund pushed aside his bitterness, reminding himself to be happy for the woman. After all, he was supposed to have moved on.

Unfortunately, his worsening mood remained like a permanent shadow.

Cadan glanced to Edmund, as if aware his thoughts had turned to him. "Have you had a piece, lieutenant? I swear, I could perish right this moment and leave this life a fortunate man, indeed."

Poppy didn't laugh this time, her searching gaze on Edmund.

"I haven't the desire to taste anything Poppy creates," Edmund said gruffly. "I'm afraid I'm only here for a bucket."

Poppy's smile faltered, and guilt twisted in his chest. Why had he been so harsh in his response? She most assuredly would have offered him a taste of the shortbread otherwise.

But then, some part of him had feared that she *wouldn't* have allowed him a taste, that she would have rejected him. After all, it wouldn't be the first time.

"Ah, yes," Poppy said softly. "The bucket."

She turned around, finally pulling out the large, wooden bucket he'd been coveting for far too long.

"Don't feel too badly, sir," Cadan said, swallowing the last of his food. "It took months of knowin' Poppy before she allowed me the pleasure of tastin' her food before she serves it."

Memories he'd forgotten about until that moment accosted Edmund's mind, hurtling him back years ago to when Poppy had helped her mother in this very kitchen. Mrs. Honeysett would often offer him the chance to taste meals, as well, which he'd always accepted.

He'd make some comment about how delicious the food was, then tease Poppy about becoming a fine cook herself one day, to which she'd respond with a blush—but never with any words.

Obviously, Cadan had no notion that Edmund had already known Poppy beyond six years now, nor that he'd once been the taste-tester for the Honeysetts.

Edmund had been replaced. Of course, that was all well and good. Expected, even. So why did this hollow feeling continue to expand in his chest?

Instead of exploring the answer, Edmund trained his eyes on the bucket. Why did she simply hold it there? Could she not give it to Edmund so he could be on his way?

"Well, I fear I've spent far too long prolongin' my duties," Cadan said, clapping his hands together. His eyes fell on the skillet of shortbread again. "I don't suppose..."

Poppy laughed again, handing Cadan another piece. Obviously, seeing to Cadan's needs was more important to her than seeing to Edmund's.

Cadan snatched the shortbread from her fingers again with his lips.

"That be all now," she warned.

"Yes, ma'am," he mumbled, eating the lemon-curd shortbread like a bird, cocking his head back as he lipped the food into his mouth piece-by-piece.

Poppy laughed all the harder. "Ye be ridiculous, Cadan."

"But you love it," he responded.

Poppy didn't deny it.

Finally, Cadan nodded his head to Edmund, waved at the girls, then winked at Poppy before he left.

Instantly, the room fell silent.

Poppy extended the bucket to Edmund with a lingering smile, but he knew the grin was not meant for him. "Here be your bucket, sir."

Then she turned away, covered the skillet with the cloth, and faced the girls with a smile.

Edmund held the bucket in his hands, staring down at it. So that was it. That was all he would receive from the woman —a simple bucket with only a few words.

He really didn't have the right to feel so annoyed, so... neglected. And yet, he did. He'd always felt at home, at peace during his time at Golowduyn. Now, he was beginning to feel as if he was no longer welcome, which was utterly ridiculous. After all, the Kendrickses wanted him there, that much was clear.

But Poppy's indifference...

"Be there somethin' wrong, sir?" Poppy asked, motioning to the bucket in his hands.

He blinked. "Pardon? Oh, no." For some reason, his eyes flittered toward the covered shortbread.

Poppy gave him a questioning look. "Ye be wantin' some?"

"No, thank you," he responded at once, though his words had sounded less than sure.

What the devil was wrong with him? He had his bucket now. Why didn't he just leave?

"Are ye certain?" she asked. "Ye be more 'an welcome to. So long as I don't 'ave to feed ye meself."

She'd meant her words as a joke, as was evident by the sparkle in her eyes. But he couldn't bring himself to smile. Poppy had never behaved in such a way with him as she had with Cadan. She had flashed a smile or two at Edmund or goaded him into more footraces than he could count. But she'd always been too shy around him to do anything further than that.

And now, the fact that Poppy had been able to flirt with Cadan when she'd never done so with Edmund placed a burr beneath his saddle—one he couldn't remove.

"No," he repeated. He needed to get out of there. "At any rate, you ought to save your food for your admirers. They will appreciate it more."

Then he walked away with the bucket in his hands and a pinch to his chest that he couldn't begin to remove.

CHAPTER SEVEN

"*Y*ou seem anxious this evening, Harris. A bit unstable atop the horse still?"

Edmund smiled, albeit tightly, as he and Kendricks rode across the cliffside away from Golowduyn the next day. Despite his friend's teasing, Edmund had actually taken to riding Mrs. Kendricks's mare quite easily—despite many sailors never finding their bearings on a horse.

He always felt such clarity while sitting atop the animals. It was the same as standing at the bulwark of a ship, feeling the wind in his hair and being a part of something bigger.

He had to admit, though. That night, he *was* feeling anxious. But it wasn't because of the horse.

"I'm not anxious," he lied. "Just a touch…distracted." Edmund blew out a breath. Perhaps Captain Jones had been correct about Edmund's state of mind being a touch agitated. But wasn't being on land supposed to quell his nerves? After all, going back to Tristwick shouldn't be causing him any sort of discomfort.

Entering the Honeysett's home, however…

He adjusted his seat in the saddle as best as he could with only his right arm to help, keeping his left arm steady in the sling that chafed against his neck, despite resting beneath his collar. The blasted thing always proved to get in his way, even while riding, but he wasn't about to allow it to stop him from enjoying it now.

One thing *would* prevent him, however.

"Are you certain I was invited to come tonight?" he asked.

Apparently, Trevik had called for those in Tristwick and any neighboring areas to attend a meeting to decide what could be done with the failing fishing cove.

Edmund had heard more from Kendricks about all that had hit the small community. He didn't think he could be of any service to them, but Kendricks thought otherwise.

"Absolutely," Kendricks reassured him. "I told Trevik myself that you might have insight into the issues they're facing, and he agreed to have me bring you along." He paused, giving Edmund an odd look. "Why do you keep asking that?"

Edmund hesitated. "It is only that, well, Trevik Honeysett and I haven't been on the best of terms since…"

"Since he discovered his sister enjoyed your company?" Kendricks finished for him, and Edmund nodded.

"As far as I'm aware, he seemed perfectly fine with the idea of you coming," Kendricks reassured him. "I wouldn't give it any more thought."

He was right. Edmund was overthinking this. Although, Trevik *had* threatened him on more than one occasion in the past.

"Ye keep away from me sister or ye'll 'ave both arms in splints."

"If ye 'urt 'er, I'll ne'er let ye get away with it."

Surely the man had overcome his issues now that Poppy had severed her ties to Edmund. Perhaps he and her brother could even become friends again.

At the thought, the tightness in his shoulders eased. Honestly, Trevik was probably too busy being angry with Cadan now to spend any more time being upset with

Edmund. Unless, of course, Poppy's brother liked Cadan better than he had ever liked Edmund.

Rubbing the back of his neck, he tried to dispel the tension that had returned and bunched together there like snagged fabric. He needed to relax. He was going that evening for one reason, and one reason alone.

He was concerned for Tristwick. And though he knew he really had no reason to be—he hadn't had any connection to anyone there for three years—he would do his best to help in any way he could.

The men rode mostly in silence, both of them clearly deep in thought as they finally rounded the ridge to Tristwick, and the hamlet came into view. Edmund had always loved visiting the quaint cove, the stone cottages nestled comfortably within the embrace of the hillside.

And yet, he could see the difference three years had made. Only half the houses had smoke drifting from their chimneys, and most of the windows of the vacated cottages had been boarded up. The *Pilferer* still bobbed up and down in the small harbor, her sails lowered, but the thin strip of beach that stretched down the opposite side of the cove was uncharacteristically empty.

He had gathered on that beach with the people of Tristwick often for food and games. He could imagine the gathered group now, Poppy included, as they'd take part in footraces on the sand. Her cinnamon eyes would flash with excitement, her smile happy and carefree.

Back then, her smiles and bright eyes had only been meant for him. Now they seemed to extend to everyone *but* him.

A twinge of sadness plucked at his heart. Poppy had chosen what she loved more than anything in the world—Cornwall. And he could never compete with it. Deep down, he wanted her to be happy. So why did this terrible jealousy continue to rear its insufferable head inside of him?

Drawing a deep breath, he pulled up his horse alongside

Kendricks, the two of them tying up the mare and gelding near the processing cellars before continuing the rest of the way up Tristwick on foot.

As they approached the last house on the south side of the bend, Edmund greeted the other men and women straggling into the Honeysetts' home. Most of them were pleased to see him, greeting him with smiles and claps upon his back.

But when he stepped over the threshold, ducking his head through the low-hanging door, he came face-to-face with a stoic Trevik.

How ridiculous that Edmund had faced down enemy vessels, had been tossed overboard from a wrecked ship, had dealt with numerous injuries—and *now* he was nervous.

Trevik greeted Kendricks first with a shake of his hand. "Thank ye for comin', sir."

Kendricks nodded. "More than happy to." He turned then to Edmund. "You remember the lieutenant."

Edmund longed to clasp his hands behind his back, though his sling prevented it. He needed something to calm his nerves from the fisherman's firm look that could have shriveled up a wave-soaked seaweed. "Good to see you again," Edmund said stiffly.

When Edmund had first arrived in Cornwall, he and Trevik had become fast friends, meeting often at the Golden Arms for a drink or a quick meal. They'd bonded over their mutual love of sailing and overeating, but things had changed once Poppy had begun to be vocal about her interest in Edmund. Trevik had assumed a protective stance over his sister and never went back.

"Lieutenant," Trevik said with a clipped nod, "thank ye for comin'."

Edmund could feel the struggle behind Trevik's words. The man didn't offer a handshake. Instead, he walked away and moved to greet the others now entering his home.

Edmund breathed a sigh of relief, shuffling to the back of

the house where a few more men stood mingling. Thank heavens he'd gotten that over with. Fortunately, his meeting with Trevik had gone over better than he'd expected. Of course, he'd envisioned Trevik taking him by the collar and throwing him down the cliffside into the sea.

As Kendricks spoke to the men beside him, Edmund took the opportunity to look around the home that had remained nearly unchanged in the three years since he'd been there. The same brown curtains were drawn near the windows. The same rickety furniture faced the hearth. And the same warm atmosphere greeted everyone like a welcome embrace.

Light poured forth from the open windows, the sun taking its time to set that evening, and a modest fire burned within the confines of the small hearth. Beside the hearth was the family portrait Poppy had painted of her family years ago, the frame decorated with seashells.

That would be Poppy's shellwork. She'd always had a particular affinity for shells, whether it was finding them, admiring them, or working with them. Did she still feel the same way, or had she changed in that regard, as well?

Despite the extra bodies of men and women—and a few children—filling the room from wall to wall, the faint scent of hevva cake wafted through the air. Naturally, his eyes drifted toward the kitchen, and only then did he notice the movement within the back room.

Mrs. Honeysett stood facing the stove, and Morvoren Honeysett—who had always been kind to Edmund—stood nearby, delivering Isolde the hevva cake he'd smelt before. The girl's eyes widened with delight.

His own mouth watered as the delectable scent became even more potent. The cake almost smelled as good as the shortbread Poppy had fed Cadan the day before. Would they be serving the cake that evening? He could only pray his stomach wouldn't sour as it had before with the shortbread.

Of course, he was fairly certain Cadan had been the reason for that.

Edmund's eyes fixed on the kitchen again, and Poppy stepped into view. Her hands were propped on her hips as she spoke animatedly about something he couldn't make out. She paused, listened to something her sister-in-law said, then broke out in the most stunning smile he'd seen on her yet.

Edmund still hadn't been able to come to terms with how the woman had changed in the last few years. She still had the same features and qualities, but the way she held her chin level with the floor exuded a quiet confidence he hadn't seen on her before. She'd grown into herself and her desires, seeming perfectly content in her own skin.

In the next instant, her eyes found his, and his stomach jolted. Fortunately, a body moved between them not a moment later, breaking their contact.

Edmund drew in a breath and snapped his attention away from her. Now that he knew she was in the kitchen, he could avoid her at all costs.

And yet, when her laughter chimed out above the noise of the growing crowd, he couldn't help himself. He looked back to the kitchen, pure joy radiating from her as she laughed. Had her dimples always been so deep? They were like small pockets of joy, spreading warmth with a single appearance—despite the somberness of those gathered in her home.

She turned around, her back facing the doorway as she piled squares of the hevva cake onto a plate on the table. Her skirts swished back and forth as she moved, her profile appearing every so often as she spoke with Morvoren, her smile remaining.

"I believe everyone be 'ere now. Shall we begin?"

At the sound of Trevik's voice near the front of the room, Edmund tore his eyes away from Poppy. How had he ended up staring at her again?

"First, I'd like to thank ye all for takin' the time out o' your evenin' to come an 'elp." The room was silent as Trevik shifted his feet near the hearth, his eyes on the floor ahead of him, brow knit as he continued. "As ye all know, Tristwick be fallin' under 'ard times now. The fact that we all can fit in one room be a testament to exactly 'ow we've suffered."

A few heads bobbed up and down around the room. Edmund looked around him, the impact of Trevik's statement finally sinking in. Before, Tristwick's community had filled the sands of the beach. Had they truly lost half of their men and women, half of their families?

"I do wish we were meetin' under different circumstances," Trevik continued, "but the fact remains, that ain't possible for men in our line o' work."

More nods moved about the room. Another movement shifted in the corner of Edmund's eye, and before he realized what he was doing, he looked to the kitchen again. The Honeysett women were still bustling about, albeit far more quietly. Well, Morvoren and Mrs. Honeysett were.

Poppy was spinning around in circles, holding a giggling Isolde. After a look from her mother, Poppy stopped, shushing Isolde with a finger over her own grinning lips. Poppy watched until her mother turned around, then she picked up spinning again in quick circles with her niece.

Edmund's lip twitched at the sight. That. That right there. That was the Poppy he remembered, the Poppy he had not seen until that moment. Had she changed so much as to not reveal that side of her so very often—or was it merely Edmund's presence that prevented it from coming out?

"Now," Trevik continued, "I do 'ope together we can formulate some sort o' plan to benefit we all. That be why I brought in others who don't live 'ere."

He motioned to the men who'd chosen to stand at the back of the room, each of them nodding as his name was called.

"Dr. Kent," Trevik began. "'E be one o' the smartest men

I know, not to mention the most generous. Ye all know 'e be helpin' we all for 'alf the price as what we used to pay."

Edmund looked to the physician with mild interest, Dr. Kent humbly lowering his head. So he was the one disturbing Dr. Rennalls's work in St. Just. Well, if he provided better, less expensive medicinal services for those who could not afford it, good for him.

"Ye all know Mr. Kendricks, 'course," Trevik said, continuing his introductions. "'E's been 'elping we all since the beginnin' with his funds to help Tristwick and his connections and capital to repair the *Pilferer.*"

"And I'll continue to do so," Kendricks responded.

Trevik gave a nod of thanks before his eyes settled on Edmund's. His lips parted, then snapped back closed before he shifted to introduce the next man, Mr. Causey.

"I suppose he hasn't forgiven you after all," Kendricks whispered for only Edmund to hear.

Edmund gave a knowing half-smile. "I believe I've offended the entire Honeysett family now."

Before Kendricks could respond, Trevik continued. "Mr. Causey knows just about every man in Cornwall. We do 'ope ye can provide us with insight as to who to go to for more 'elp."

Edmund recognized Mr. Causey at once. He had been at the heart of nearly every gathering Edmund had ever been to in St. Just. If there was a man to help spread the word for aid, he'd be the one to do it.

"And finally," Trevik said, "we be grateful to Mr. Jack Trevethan for carvin' time out of 'is busy schedule to be 'ere with us, too." Trevik cast his eyes around the group. "As ye all know, last year, Mr. Trevethan purchased the land Tristwick rests upon. If anyone 'as a vested interest in 'ow we families survive, it be 'im."

Mr. Trevethan nodded in response before Trevik carried on.

"Now, I know this goes without sayin', but the fact be obvious. We need 'elp. We need more men and women and children. Good men brave enough to fish. Devoted women strong enough to process. Robust children who ain't afeared o' hard work."

Edmund glanced toward the kitchen. Morvoren and Mrs. Honeysett had taken to standing in the doorway, both of them listening to their husband and son give his speech. Poppy, however, stood farther back in the kitchen, quietly eating slices of hevva cake with Isolde, the two smiling at each other like mischievous thieves.

He looked away before he could crack a smile. Was she able to hear Trevik from within the kitchen? Did she not feel the dread that had seeped its way throughout the room? Or was she simply distracting herself and Isolde from it all?

"So," Trevik said, "we be needin' some fine ideas to draw folks to Tristwick permanently. Surely together, we can find a way out o' the mess that's been made for we." He waved his hand across the room. "I'll open it up to all of ye now. Don't hesitate. We need all the ideas."

He faced them expectantly, but no one said a word. Shuffling sounded near the kitchen, and most of the eyes turned to watch as Poppy and Mrs. Honeysett appeared in the doorway with trays of brandy wine and cake. Morvoren remained inside the room, taking Poppy's place with Isolde.

"No one gets any o' me mother's or sister's food 'til ye give us ideas on 'ow to save Tristwick," Trevik joked.

"Ye only say that to keep the food yourself," Poppy said, progressing throughout the space.

The room rumbled with laughter.

Edmund did his best to keep his eyes off of Poppy, his stomach reaching out to the spiced scent trailing out behind the cake.

An older resident of Tristwick seated on the bench in the

front room raised his hand first as the food was brought around.

"Yes, Edern, please," Trevik said with an encouraging nod.

As Edern offered up a few suggestions as to how to first solve Tristwick's basic needs, Mrs. Honeysett came up in that moment with the cups of brandy wine. There was no chance there would be enough for everyone, so Edmund graciously declined her offer.

The woman paused beside him with a warm smile. "It be good to see ye again, Lieutenant," she whispered genuinely, then she carried on to the next person who accepted a cup.

"At least there is one Honeysett who appears to like you," Kendricks whispered.

Edmund could only sniff in response.

The conversation shifted as it continued, moving on from solving the issues of lack of food for winter, to how to bring in more men to Tristwick more quickly.

"Gryff?" Trevik called on the burly man at the side of the sitting room next.

"We discussed the possibility of per'aps buildin' new 'ouses to draw people in from other towns," Gryffyn Bosanko responded, his arms crossed over his broad chest. He'd been one of the men who'd greeted Edmund outside.

"They be too much money, they be," another man piped up.

"I can certainly approve the funds to build more houses here," Mr. Trevethan said at the back, "once the ones that have been vacated are filled."

"What would we need to do to see to that?" Trevik asked.

Mr. Trevethan pulled in his lips. "Simply show me there's enough interest, and I'd be happy to look into it."

Edmund glanced to Poppy as she drew closer and closer to where he stood, smiling at each person with whom she shared the cake.

"Thank ye, Mr. Trevethan," Trevik continued from the front of the room. "Howe'er, we still need to decipher 'ow to bring people to Tristwick." He paused, looking across the room. "I know there be some concerns 'bout bringin' in more families and growin' our 'ome, thereby changin' the overall feel o' the place we all love. But sometimes, we 'ave to embrace change for the benefit o' we all."

Poppy glanced to her brother, her smile faltering, her eyes clouding over before she shook the look from her face and handed the hevva cake to the next individual.

Edmund narrowed his eyes. What had Trevik said to have produced her concern, changing Tristwick? Surely that was the only logical solution the community had to solve their issues. Building new houses would only fix the problem of an influx of new residents—something with which they were not struggling. But changing the hamlet in other ways was the only way to bring more people in to fish.

As Dr. Kent spoke up with the suggestion to appeal to the miners who worked below ground with the promise of healthy, fresh sea air instead of being underground all day, Edmund continued to watch Poppy until she finally approached him and Kendricks.

"Thank you, Poppy," Kendricks whispered, taking a piece of the dessert in hand.

"Mrs. Causey watchin' o'er your wife tonight?" she asked in a low tone.

"She was gracious enough to do so, yes."

Poppy nodded, then shifted to Edmund, slightly raising the tray of cake toward him. "Would ye like one, sir?"

Edmund was keenly aware of Kendricks's attention on them both, so he quickly took a square piece of the cake dotted with raisins and nodded his gratitude.

"So ye be fine with me hevva cake but not me short-bread?" she whispered.

He paused in bringing the cake to his mouth, his words

refusing to come until he saw the twinkle in her eyes. "No, I...
I would have loved one. I only..."

He what? What exactly was he trying to say? That he'd
been too prideful to accept it from her before? That he was
even too prideful to eat one with the Kendrickses after dinner?

Instead of waiting for him to continue, Poppy simply gave
a knowing smile, then walked to Dr. Kent with her tray.

"How did she know you didn't eat her shortbread?"
Kendricks whispered.

Edmund flushed. "She offered me a piece before dinner,
but I...I refused."

Kendricks smiled with a shake of his head. "No wonder
you've offended her."

He faced forward again as heat fed up Edmund's neck.
Edmund wasn't used to this, Poppy speaking with him in such
a way. He'd always been the one to make *her* blush.

More than that, he wondered at her sudden change in
mood. She'd been silent and shy their first meeting, harsh and
biting after he'd spoken with Mrs. Rennalls, and entirely indif-
ferent to Edmund around Cadan. He could hardly keep up
with her.

The conversation around them continued, but once again,
Edmund was pulled into his louder thoughts. Admittedly, he
hadn't been on his best behavior when Poppy and Cadan had
flirted, when really, he had no reason not to be. Had Poppy
perhaps taken his actions the day before as jealousy on his
part?

He released a silent sigh, shifting his feet on the wooden
flooring. He would need to clear the air between them again,
it would seem. Not only that, but he was fairly certain he owed
her an apology. Two, even. One for not accepting her dessert,
and two for how presumptuous he'd been after speaking with
Mrs. Rennalls. Clearly, Poppy *had* moved beyond their past. It
was his duty as a gentleman to let her know how happy he was
for her.

Besides, he had to prove his words. He'd declared his progress over the years. It was time he showed her proof of the very same.

"Another question continues to surface, though," Trevik said, his words finally pulling Edmund from his thoughts. "Many folks 'ave 'eard 'bout the accident. Now they be afeared o' the same thing happenin' to 'em."

"Well, tain't like the navy be sunshine and roses," piped up another. "'Ow do they keep the men to stay there?"

All eyes shifted to Kendricks and Edmund, who stood near the back.

"The threat of flogging kept me there when I was a boy," Edmund joked. "The threat of death for deserting keeps me there now."

The room chuckled, even Poppy smiling in response. But Trevik looked less than entertained. Perhaps this wasn't the best time for Edmund to share his teasing.

"Lieutenant Harris is only partially accurate, of course," Kendricks said with amusement. "Wages play a pivotal role in keeping the men at sea, as does the promise of prize money. They receive no income until after their assignment is completed, so if the men desert their posts, they collect nothing." He glanced to Edmund. "Anything else, Harris?"

Edmund, anxious to redeem himself in Trevik's eyes, hesitated. "It is difficult to say. In my experience, being involved in the navy at a young age solidified my desire to continue with it. With young boys, officers can mold them, shape them to love the sea and the work so they continue to come back for more, no matter the risks."

"Like me son," Gryffyn said, a hand on the young man beside him. "Charlie's grown to love fishin' as I did at 'is age."

Charlie nodded, his thin, lanky features the opposite of his father's.

A mumble of approval rippled through the group, and Trevik's jaw twitched. Clearly, he hadn't expected Edmund to bring his brain to the meeting after his less than helpful comment from before.

Without even responding to Edmund, however, Trevik looked around to the others. "Anyone else?"

Edmund bit back a scoff, looking to the floor. He couldn't blame Trevik for being protective of his younger sister. But after all that had occurred, he couldn't deny the fact that Trevik was behaving rather pettily.

Edmund's eyes traveled toward the kitchen again. Mrs. Honeysett was now taking a turn with Isolde, and Morvoren cleaned up a few things on the table. Poppy, however, stared out the window, her eyes distant, no hint of a smile on her lips. If Edmund didn't know any better, he'd say the woman appeared…sorrowful.

But Poppy was never sorrowful. Was she?

CHAPTER EIGHT

*P*oppy had been doing her best not to listen to the discussion in the next room all evening, but as slivers of the conversation reached her ears, her mood had taken a sharp decline.

Not even Lieutenant Harris's gaze in her direction could help her now. Well, it helped to a small degree.

Her flirting with Cadan the day before had been just the thing to solidify her questions about the lieutenant. He'd been unsettled with her friendliness with Cadan—had shared an unyielding frown from the moment the lighthouse assistant had stepped into the room—and there was only one explanation for it. Edmund did not like the attention she'd shown Cadan.

Whether that was from simple irritation or a more pointed jealousy, she couldn't be sure. Either way, her confidence had returned at the knowledge—and at the very fact that the man still watched her now.

She glanced toward him, but he pulled his gaze swiftly away, which produced another half-smile on her lips.

She had wondered if he would be attending that evening,

so when she'd seen him standing in her home, she was able to overcome her initial surprise within a matter of moments.

No doubt Mr. Kendricks had invited him along, as Trevik surely wouldn't have done so.

She sighed, shaking her head and staring back out the kitchen window, the sky swirling with pink clouds as it met with the green countryside.

She was grateful for Trevik's continued protectiveness of her, but sometimes his behavior was a little *too* protective. Just like his defensive nature with Tristwick.

Her chest pressed against her heart once again. Trevik would do anything to save the hamlet, as was evident by the meeting that evening. She appreciated his efforts, of course. But when the suggestions started coming through—how to populate the area, how to change Tristwick to an unrecognizable town—she couldn't bear it. She knew Trevik was listening to all the suggestions of the hamlet to allow them to feel heard, even if they weren't the most exceptional of ideas.

But still, her frustration mounted. Why did Tristwick have to change at all? She knew they needed a few more families to help with the *Pilferer* and the cellars, but why bring in more than was necessary? Why change Tristwick to be as large as St. Just? To lose the quaint, magical quality of their hamlet, inevitably losing the view of the sea? Father had built it the way it was, and it had been good enough for him. So why was it not good enough for the others? Certainly he would be on her side, were he still alive.

She moved away from the kitchen window, pulling her eyes to the view in the sitting room instead. Beyond the bodies, she could just make out the blue seas sparkling in the golden sunshine, calling her to their peaceful waves.

But she couldn't answer that call. Not until the meeting came to an end.

Fortunately for her sake, only another half hour passed by before Trevik ended the conversation. "Well, I've kept ye all for far too long, though I'm certain we could speak 'bout this for hours." He paused, holding his hands together in front of him. His lips parted, and Poppy could see his hesitation.

She braced for the coming words.

"I know we all would like to go back to the way that things were," he said softly. "But the truth o' the matter be that we can't. We all must be ready for the change that be comin' to Tristwick. 'Cause there *will* be a change, whether we want there to be or not."

Poppy knew it. All of Tristwick knew it. But it didn't make it any easier to hear it. Tristwick—*Cornwall*—was her one constant in this life. Even her family wasn't immune to change. If Tristwick was taken from her, changed to the point beyond recognition, to the point where she could no longer see her father's memory in the hamlet, what would happen to her? What would happen to her family, her mindset…her joy?

A dark chasm hollowed out in her chest, expanding until it reached the expanse of her heart. She held her breath, focusing all of her energy on the light, but nothing could brighten the darkness that threatened to engulf her.

She'd felt this way before, whisperings of darkness and shadow. There was only one thing now that could stamp out the night before it flourished within her like poisonous vines.

As the group filtered from the house, Poppy slipped out the back door, taking the smaller pathway behind the houses to avoid happening on anyone. Fortunately, most of those in attendance would be headed to their homes, readying their children for bed and remaining in for the evening, so Poppy could enjoy the beach alone.

It was not that she did not want to speak to her friends and neighbors. She was simply not in the right frame of mind to allow herself to speak with anyone. At least, not until the waves soothed her worries.

Once she reached the beach, Poppy sat straight down in the sand, removing her stockings and boots before standing once again to wiggle her toes into the millions of minuscule particles that massaged every section of her feet.

She closed her eyes and drew deep, methodical breaths. Instead of ignoring her anxious thoughts from before, she allowed her mind to process them before ultimately giving them to the sea. The waves took them out one by one, burying them deep within the ocean where she could no longer feel the effects of her concerns.

As her heart rate slowed and her mind cleared, she opened her eyes and took in the sight before her. This was her favorite time of day. When the light still glowed from the sun, but in a far gentler way as it sunk toward the horizon, promising of a glorious sunset.

The world was preparing to rest, the waves lazy as they half-heartedly drifted up the sand before giving up to join the sea once more. The sun was already putting on the show it had promised her, pink and yellow and purple decorating the sky in soft strokes of paint.

In the far distance, waves with more strength slapped against the rocks, creating a golden mist that lingered in the air, causing the protruding cliffs to appear as if they floated just above the water.

She could have sworn she'd seen a mermaid once out there by those rocks. No one had believed the word of a twelve-year-old, but she couldn't deny the large tail that had dipped down into the water before she'd been able to catch a better look. A few years later, however, the town of Tristwick —Poppy included—had nearly believed Morvoren to be a sea maiden. She was only slightly disappointed to discover that her sister-in-law was, in fact, a human.

Some folks said mermaids weren't real. Other folks said that about God, too. But Poppy had always been of the mindset that she'd rather believe in something than not. Why wouldn't she when believing was far more adventurous? Far more *hopeful?*

She looked past the creamy turquoise water to where the golden sun cast its pillar of light across the waves, approaching the horizon closer and closer.

This view simply could not be beaten. Nor could the brisk wind in her hair, playing with the tendrils at the back of her neck, or the muted briny smell that permeated the air around her like a blanket of comfort.

She tightened her shawl around her shoulders and took a few steps forward, leaving her belongings behind as she approached the water. It took a few tries, but finally, a wave stretched toward her, its long arm sliding up the sand and brushing the tips of her toes.

"Good evenin'," she whispered to the water. "Did ye miss I?"

The waves slunk back before reaching out even further, covering the tops of her feet and causing the sand to sink beneath her.

She grinned. "I thought so."

Yes, out here, all was well with the world. Out here, she didn't have to worry about the meeting or about who suggested what. Out here, she didn't need to be so concerned over the future of Tristwick. She didn't need to fear forgetting her father's memory. And she didn't need to worry about how she would be when Lieutenant Harris left again.

She winced. Not even the sea could keep that gentleman from her mind forever.

Without another thought, she pulled her focus over her shoulder to where her house stood high on the cliffside. From her vantage point, she could just make out Gryffyn still conversing with Trevik by the door, though most of the pathway had emptied.

When her eyes traveled down the rest of the pathway, however, she was surprised to discover Dr. Kent, Mr. Kendricks, and Lieutenant Harris speaking near the cellars.

Well, the physician and Mr. Kendricks were speaking. The

lieutenant had his eyes focused on Poppy, this time not bothering to look away when he was caught staring.

Poppy looked toward the water, however, and refused to glance back. For years, she'd been far too concerned about where the lieutenant was or when he'd come back. She couldn't bear to be that way again.

The soft water crept toward her, turning sand over in its wake as it splashed down against the beach. How she loved watching the tide draw in. She could remain there for hours and still would not be able to receive her fill of staring at those mesmerizing waves.

"Good evening."

Her heart vacated her chest as it stuttered to a halt. She turned to find Edmund had left Dr. Kent and Mr. Kendricks and came to stand beside her.

"Evenin'," she responded, her mind racing with possibilities as to why he'd approached her. Was he coming to tell her to overcome her love for him again? She was no longer angry for his presumptuous words—especially after how he'd reacted with Cadan. But she wouldn't be able to curb her tongue if he did start throwing accusations again. "Can I 'elp ye with somethin', Lieutenant?"

"No, only forgive my intrusion." He stood a hearty distance from her, rolling his shoulder back, no doubt in an attempt to ease the discomfort his sling caused him round his neck. "Dr. Kent was speaking with Mr. Kendricks about his wife, so I thought to give them a moment's privacy."

She nodded, peering out at the sea in silence. She knew she ought to say something further, but was it so very wrong of her to expect the lieutenant to put forth some effort? He had been the one to join her, after all.

"Are you well?" he eventually asked.

She glanced up at him. "Why, do I look sickly?"

"No. That is to say, I saw you slip out of your house

without a word and thought, perhaps..." He trailed off again, shaking his head. "I was merely inquiring, that is all."

He'd seen her leave the house, too? Heavens, how long had he been watching her? "I be more 'an fine, thank ye." It wasn't a lie. Not really. She was feeling far, far better than before. "I just needed to be on the sand 'fore the sun set fully."

"I see."

Did he really? Poppy didn't bother asking him if that was true.

"It is stunning this evening," he said.

"It be stunnin' every evenin'," she corrected.

"Just so."

More silence filled the air between them, and Poppy's peace slipped through her fingertips. There had been a time when she would have loved to stand and watch the sunset with this man. Now, it was too painful of a reminder of what could have been.

She would be better off retiring early. "Thank ye for comin' tonight," she said, thinking it a fine notion to end their conversation on a word of gratitude. "To me brother's meetin', I mean."

"Oh, it was no trouble. Mr. Kendricks requested that I join him."

Just as she'd suspected.

He looked away, his brow furrowed. "I was sorry to hear of the losses you have all experienced in Tristwick."

So he wished to speak with her further? "Thank ye," she said halfheartedly.

She knew people mentioned other's difficulties to express their condolences or show how deeply they understood their pain. Typically, she appreciated these words. But there were times when she wished she could bury her head in the sand and pretend that all the world was filled with sunshine, seas, and shells.

She eyed another approaching wave, allowing it to cover

the tips of her toes again, but Lieutenant Harris drew back to avoid his boots getting wet. He had never been one to mind the water, but rather to remove his boots and walk in the sand barefooted. Had that changed?

Peering down where the water had left behind a sheen across the sand, a few shells had been unveiled, tucked halfway beneath the shifting sands.

She reached down and retrieved a pink and white scallop shell, pleased to find it unbroken. She wiped the excess sand and moisture off the shell against the side of her skirts, then brought it forward to brush off as much as the sticking sand would allow.

"You still collect shells?"

Did he think it childish of her to do so? "I do."

"You haven't changed in *that* regard, I see."

The subtle accentuating of the word 'that' in his sentence gave her pause. He was obviously pointing out that she'd changed in other ways. Had he not changed, as well? Such a thing was impossible after so many years.

So then why had his words felt like such a criticism?

CHAPTER NINE

*E*dmund didn't know why he'd gone over to Poppy. It was true that Dr. Kent and Kendricks had been speaking of Mrs. Kendricks, and Edmund hadn't wanted to impose. But the forlorn look Poppy had exhibited toward the end of the meeting at the Honeysetts' had contrasted so greatly with what he was seeing now, he'd just allowed his curiosity to get the better of him.

More than anything, however, he'd seen the chance to apologize without any prying ears, so he'd seized the opportunity like a true, stalwart naval officer unafraid to back down from his duty.

Even though at that very moment his palms were as soaked as the sea from the memories this beach brought to his mind.

He held an arm bent behind his back and secured his footing in the sand, hoping his firm stance would give him the courage to face his own past.

"Poppy, I fear I owe you an apology."

Her eyes darted to his, and she had the decency to appear surprised, as if she truly didn't know what he was about.

"After seeing you and Cadan interact, I can see how wrong

I was about the need for you to move beyond…" He paused, waving a hand between the two of them. He wanted to look up at her to see if she understood his gesture, but he forged on. "At any rate, I hope you can forgive me for my pompous assumption otherwise."

He ended, focusing hard on the sea as she remained silent.

Eventually, he saw from the corner of his eye as she shrugged her shoulders. "It be no trouble, sir. While I don't think ye owe me an apology, 'course I forgive ye."

She would forgive him, just like that? She'd been so angry that day after Mrs. Rennalls had left. Could she really not be upset about it still? But as he observed her staring at the waves again, not a hint of unpleasantness in her expression, he found no reason to disbelieve her.

Well, then. He'd done his duty, now he could be off.

Before he could take a step, however, her words stopped him.

"In what ways 'ave ye found that I've changed?" she asked, her eyes fixed on the sinking sun, her face aglow with warm light.

How had she changed? He eyed the smooth curves of her face, her brown hair that had somehow gained a glossier appearance, and her lips that had grown more supple.

She turned to look at him, no doubt wondering why he was taking so long to formulate his response, but he snapped his attention away. "I am unsure," he lied.

She eyed him with an unreadable look. "Ye've changed, as well. Ye be more serious now."

More serious? No, he was not. Never mind that Captain Jones had said the very same thing about him. He knew himself better than anyone.

"I s'pose a life at sea will do that to a person," she continued. "Do ye still love it as ye did 'fore?"

"Even more so now, if that is possible." The sea was the one thing upon which he could rely. The water was no respecter of persons. It simply accepted a man as he was. Unlike people.

"And you," he continued, "do you still love Cornwall as you did before?"

He tried to keep his voice level, though his feelings from the last six years fought to break through.

"I do," she responded. "I be 'appy 'ere, with me family."

Edmund's jaw twitched. He could read between her words.

"I'm happy with my choice to not be with you, Edmund."

Well, that was fine, wasn't it? Because he'd essentially said the same thing about her.

A heavy silence nudged its way between them, as muddled and unending as the sands they stood upon. Both of them were clearly thinking of the same thing, neither of them willing to breach the subject.

Until...

"Lieutenant," Poppy began softly, her words so quiet, he had to read her lips to hear her completely, "I be needin' to apologize to ye, too, sir. For 'ow things ended 'tween we. For not explainin' more fully me feelin's."

He struggled to keep the door to his past shut, narrowing his eyes to focus harder on the sun halfway hidden by the horizon. "It is no trouble, I assure you. All is well with me and my life." He could be proud of how unaffected his words sounded.

"Truly?"

He turned to look at her, disbelief etched in her eyes.

"Of course. It was in the past. Why would matters not be well after so long?"

She hesitated. "I'd like to believe ye, sir. But ye just seem to be *actin'* like everythin' be well, when in reality, 'tain't."

Her straightforward words startled him, though they shouldn't have. He'd said himself that Poppy had changed.

But he still wasn't used to *how* she'd changed—her courage, her pointedness, her ability to flirt with Cadan.

As his strength faltered, so did his resolve to ignore the memories still trying to squeeze their way into his mind.

The first time they'd stood on this beach alone together, Poppy had told him she loved him. Edmund hadn't been able to tell her the same, though he'd berated himself for the feelings he had to continually fight off for the sixteen-year-old. The second time they'd stood there, he'd expressed his desire to be with her, he'd attempted to show that desire by sharing his affection, but she'd...

He shook the thought from his mind. He would not allow himself to continue down this path. "Thank you, Poppy, for your apology and for your concern. However, both are unwarranted. We have already established that we have different desires, different hopes for our futures. Dredging up the past will do neither of us any good."

Hurt sliced through the warm brown of her eyes, but he refused to feel an ounce of regret.

"I only wished to explain, sir, as I didn't really 'ave the opportunity to do so 'fore ye left."

Edmund's brow furrowed. Didn't have the opportunity? She'd had *ample* opportunity.

Those same memories from before flooded his mind, permeating every inch of his soul, unable to be dammed.

He'd been crushed beyond words at Poppy's rejection. Even now, it was as if the weight of the *Defense* pressed harder and harder upon his chest. He needed to leave before he was pressed to death.

Glancing over his shoulder, he found Dr. Kent and Kendricks still speaking. Edmund would simply retrieve Mrs. Kendrick's horse and ride home himself. He couldn't bear the humiliation of the fact that he had yet to overcome his past— that he still felt for...

"Excuse me," he blurted out, taking a step back. He'd be

hanged if he revealed that much to this woman. "I must return to Golowduyn."

Poppy stared after him, confusion swimming across her features. "Will ye not allow I to speak?"

He was unable to stop the hurt from rushing over him—the hurt that so cleverly disguised itself as anger. He stopped, turning to face her again. He shouldn't engage. He knew he shouldn't. And yet...

"Forgive me, Poppy. I seem to recall plenty of opportunities for you to share with me your concerns, but you remained silent until your letters."

Her brow twitched. "I was young. Ye asked I to leave behind so much. I didn't know what to do. And when ye didn't return..."

His ears started ringing, a soft, subtle noise like the distant sound of a fog bell warning of danger. "I didn't return?" He needed to stop, but the ship had already left the dockyard. His tongue was unhinged, his feelings as raw as how they were three and a half years before.

"Surely you know why I did *not* return," he continued. "Why I *could* not. I did not ask you to leave everything behind for nothing. I was offering you a home, a future beyond what you knew. I was willing to sacrifice everything for you—the sea, my career in the navy." He shook his head. "I was willing to do all of that, but you were not. You must speak the truth, Poppy. You did not want a life with me. It is as simple as that."

How could this even be reality, the two of them speaking of what had occurred in the past? He'd had nightmares aboard the *Defense* of this very thing happening, having to relive his humiliation all over again of a county being chosen over him.

Tears brimmed in her eyes, just as they had when she was sixteen. But he would not allow the sight of them to penetrate his defenses. Not again.

"I was young," she repeated. "Surely ye can know what it would feel like to leave me family, me 'ome."

The words slashed through his heart, reminding him exactly why he'd closed it off to begin with. With a set jaw, he faced her one last time.

"That is just it, though, Poppy. I do *not* know what such a thing would feel like. I never had a family. Not a real one, anyway. But I did have a home at sea—a home I was willing to leave behind for you, so we could build a family *together*." He shrugged, taking a step back as he adjusted his lower arm in the sling. "I was only stupid enough to believe that would be enough for you."

"Edmund, I—"

His name on her lips sealed his heart shut. She did not have the right to speak of him in such an intimate way any longer. "Goodnight, Poppy."

Then he walked away to his awaiting horse without a look back.

Edmund had always thought that he'd progressed, that he'd forgiven and forgotten the pain he'd felt from his time with Poppy.

How very wrong he'd been.

CHAPTER TEN

*P*oppy never enjoyed being in a terrible mood, but she couldn't help it as she worked at Golowduyn the following day. Her conversation with Lieutenant Harris had not gone well at all.

His words had rattled her. He'd said he'd wanted to create a family with her, that he'd never had one of his own. But then, had he not mentioned a father and two brothers? A mother he hadn't seen for years?

Questions about his past aside, one thing she couldn't understand was why she needed to join a new family by completely abandoning her own. She knew women left their homes more often than not, some traveling far away and never seeing their parents or siblings again.

But that wasn't for Poppy. She couldn't fathom a life without her mother's guidance. Without her brother's protectiveness and teasing. Without the sister she'd only just gained in Morvoren. And without the sweet spirit Isolde had brought into their family.

That was why Poppy had said no. That was why she'd written to him the second time, asking if he'd ever consider starting a family in Cornwall, but he'd never responded to her offer—merely told her that he did not know if he would ever return.

Her world had revolved around waiting for that man to return from the time that she was sixteen to after she'd turned eighteen, and then beyond. But he stopped coming back.

Until now. Now when it was too late. Now that they'd both traveled down their chosen paths, paths that could never align, merely crossed over one another occasionally.

Instead of returning to the darkness that had once cloaked her mind in sorrow, she allowed herself to be angry. Angry that he still did not understand. Angry that he had made her wait. Angry that he had returned to Cornwall when he never told her that he would.

She did her best to put on a smile with Isolde, Elowen, and Mrs. Kendricks that day, but whenever she could, she snuck away to allow herself the opportunity to stomp about. Throwing the feed to the chickens in the henhouse. Tearing apart the weeds in the garden. Beating the rugs with far more vigor than was called for. Cleaning up after Gwitha's slobber he smeared across the front door.

After releasing some of her pent-up aggression on an unsuspecting spot on the corridor floor with her mop, Poppy settled the girls in the sitting room with their dolls, then went to see what Abigail had written down for the dinner plan that evening.

Cornish pasties or stargazy pie, one for this evening, the other for tomorrow.

She enjoyed making both meals, just as the Kendrickses enjoyed eating them. Not having the energy to decide, Poppy closed her eyes. Moving her finger around in circles above the meal plan, she plopped her finger down after a few seconds, landing closer to pasties.

Pasties it was, then.

With the girls occupied—if only for a moment—Poppy pulled out the ingredients, pausing for a moment when she caught the sound of Mr. Kendricks and Lieutenant Harris coming down the spiral stairs of the tower.

"I'm starved," Lieutenant Harris was saying. "I've forgotten how much Golowduyn can work up one's appetite."

Mr. Kendricks chuckled. "I trust you are pleased you don't have to eat what food they offered aboard the ship."

"Anything is better than hard tack."

Mr. Kendricks huffed in agreement. "Although, I would wager that Mrs. Honeysett or Poppy could make even that taste as fine as anything."

Poppy's ears perked at the sound of her name, but the lieutenant didn't respond, irking her further. Did he not enjoy her cooking? Or was he too prideful to admit it?

"Do you still have an affinity for pasties?" Mr. Kendricks asked, their voices drifting down the corridor.

Poppy pulled farther back in the kitchen to avoid being seen.

Lieutenant Harris made a groaning sound of delight. "I'd be content to live off of them for the rest of my days. I'd be double my weight, but contentedly double my weight."

Poppy stared down at the flour, sweet cream, potatoes, onions, and salt spread before her. Suddenly, she did not have the desire to make these pasties at all.

"You are in luck, then," Mr. Kendricks said. "I believe Abigail has requested pasties for this evening. Poppy certainly makes a remarkable one."

Edmund didn't respond, which piqued her further.

"Although *all* of her food is remarkable," Mr. Kendricks kindly continued. "Her roasted chicken, her stargazy pie."

Their boots sounded near the front door, and Poppy had to strain to listen to hear their final words.

"You know, I am quite a supporter of Cornish cookery," Lieutenant Harris said. "But I fear stargazy pie is the one dish I cannot begin to stomach."

"Truly? I've always enjoyed it," Mr. Kendricks said.

Their voices faded as they made their way outside. Poppy glanced to the window, seeing their broad shoulders shift back and forth as they walked to the oil hutch, empty pails in hand.

Thank heavens the lady of the house had given Poppy the option as to what to choose to cook that evening. Because she knew what she would be making for dinner, and it most certainly would not be pasties.

By the time she'd finished with the pie, Poppy regretted her petty behavior, but it was too late to turn back now. Why did she have to behave so childishly, making a dish she knew Lieutenant Harris hated? Why couldn't she have simply swallowed her pride and continued with the pasties?

Desperate to leave Golowduyn before the men could see what was on the docket for dinner that evening and suspect her of choosing the pie on purpose, she sprinted around the kitchen, setting the dining room table and cleaning up the pots and dishes she'd used as swiftly as she'd ever done.

She set the pie in the center of the table, then placed a clean cloth over the top of it just as the front door opened.

With Elowen already in her mother's room, Poppy motioned for Isolde to join her, managing to leave the kitchen and enter the dining room just as the men joined her.

Her plan was coming together perfectly. She may not be able to take back her foolish decision to make stargazy pie in the first place, but she sure as heaven didn't need to be there when they discovered her mischief-doing.

"Poppy," Mr. Kendricks greeted, eying the set table, "it smells divine in here."

She nodded her thanks. Fortunately, he could not tell the difference between pasty and pie.

Lieutenant Harris entered soon after, his eyes landing on Poppy before promptly looking to the cloth-covered dish. She had every intention of leaving before they could discover what was beneath the cloth, but now, she couldn't help herself. She *wanted* to see Lieutenant Harris's reaction.

She waited with far too much interest as Mr. Kendricks raised the cloth, the man clearly expecting the pasties he'd promised the lieutenant earlier.

But when he revealed the pie, he paused.

The crust was a perfect golden brown apart from the six, silver pilchard heads sticking out from the top of it, peering up at the ceiling with lifeless, translucent eyes.

The pie was one of her favorites, but she could see why the lieutenant might be put off by its appearance.

"Stargazy pie," Mr. Kendricks murmured, then he glanced to Lieutenant Harris with an amused grin.

She knew a fraction of guilt for having Mr. Kendricks expect one food and delivering another. But when Lieutenant Harris's smile faltered as he stared at the pie, a shot of satisfaction pulsed through her.

His eyes dropped to Poppy's, and she swiftly wiped the smile from her face and turned to leave.

"Mrs. Kendricks ordered the pie or pasties for this evenin'," she explained simply as she headed for the doorway. "I do 'ope ye ain't be too displeased with the pie, Mr. Kendricks."

"Oh, no. *I* am not," Mr. Kendricks responded.

"I be that glad." She looked down to Isolde. "Let's be off, love."

With the men's eyes still fixed on her, she scampered from the dining room toward the front door, opening it just as Isolde tugged on her arm.

"Auntie Poppy, me shoes," she gently protested.

Poppy's eyes dropped to her niece's stockinged feet. "When did ye take those off, eh?" She stifled a sigh, unwilling to become upset with her niece for Poppy's own need to escape swiftly. "Never ye mind. Where did ye leave 'em?"

Isolde led the way back to the kitchen—of course they would be in the kitchen—just as Mr. Kendricks moved down the corridor with a helping of the pie on a plate, clearly on his way to deliver the meal to his wife.

He paused. "Did you forget something?"

"Shoes," Poppy said, and Mr. Kendricks smiled.

"You can't get very far without those, now can you?" he said, making a silly face to Isolde, who smiled shyly in response. "Thank you again for your help today, Poppy. See you on Monday."

She nodded in response, then followed Isolde's tugging. With the kitchen attached to the dining area by only one access, Poppy had to enter the dining area—where Lieutenant Harris was now seated alone—to retrieve the shoes.

His eyes fell on her as she walked by him, but she kept her gaze trained ahead. She did not need to pretend false politeness now. Not when they were alone. She knew very well how he despised her, and that evening, she was not keen on him, either.

Once safely in the kitchen, she knelt down to help Isolde with her shoes, finishing with a swiftness she'd never exhibited, before helping her niece off the chair and leading her back to the door.

Her footing stopped, however, as she came face-to-face with Lieutenant Harris standing in the doorway, his eyes fixed on Poppy.

"Ye be needin' somethin', sir?" she asked innocently.

He narrowed his eyes. "You seemed quite pleased with that pie you made this evening."

She skirted her glance away. "Aye, sir. I always be pleased with me cookin', see."

"Or you could be pleased for another reason."

She lowered her brow with as much confusion as she could muster. "And what other reason would that be?"

He was silent for a moment. "Did you do it on purpose?"

She paused, pulling her lips in before responding. "Do what, sir?"

A slight smile inched across his lips. "You heard Mr. Kendricks's and my conversation about the pie earlier, didn't you? I can see that mischievous look in your eye clear as day."

Blast her transparency. "I don't know what ye be goin' on about, sir. Mrs. Kendricks did order one of two options this evenin'. I just so 'appened to pick stargazy pie o'er pasties. That be the luck o' the draw, see."

His eyes narrowed, then to her utter shock, a smile tugged at his lips. "I should have known."

Desperate to leave before she could smile in response, she took a few steps toward him, unable to hide the mischief in her tone as she spoke. "Well, if ye'll excuse the both of we, sir. We best be gettin' 'ome. Makin' pasties for me family tonight. Don't wish to be late."

His smile grew, but he stepped aside all the same, and Poppy scurried past him with Isolde trailing after her.

He spoke just as she reached the other side of the dining area. "I'll find some way to pay you back for making me eat this, Poppy Honeysett."

She glanced back over her shoulder, a spark in his eye she hadn't witnessed since his return—the spark of a challenge, the promise of a contest. And she couldn't help but respond in the same way.

"I'd like to see ye try, sir," she said.

Their eyes connected, and for a brief moment, that care-free feeling within her heart and the look of humor in the lieutenant's eyes pulled Poppy back to the past. They'd always had such fun when competing with one another. The past could not simply be wiped away, nor could the hurt and mistrust. But dared she hope that this might be a start to return to how things were?

Before anything could be said to erase the hope kindling

within her, Poppy delivered a quick curtsy in departure. "Good evenin', Lieutenant 'Arris."

Even as she sang with Isolde on the way home, Poppy was continually distracted by the vision of those green eyes sparkling happily down at her.

"Look, Auntie Poppy," Isolde said, drawing Poppy's attention to the fields they walked alongside, two cliffsides up from Tristwick. "It be Powflenn."

Poppy smiled at her mispronunciation of the word. "Ah, so it be! I didn't realize we'd made it 'ere already."

Powflenn, or Porthlenn, were the fields Poppy always pointed out to Isolde on their way home. She'd been so caught up in her thoughts, she'd nearly missed it.

"Do ye love these fields, too, Isolde?" she asked.

Isolde nodded her little head up and down with vigor. "Yes, Auntie Poppy."

Poppy narrowed her eyes in a playful manner. "And do ye know what flowers bloom in those fields?"

"Poppeeth!"

Poppy laughed. "Yes, indeed. Poppeeth."

They stopped near the fields to take in the sight of the poppies that had yet to bloom, their long, hairy stems and bulbous flower pods bobbing up and down in the wind as if they were caught up in the country jigs the ladies danced to at the public assemblies.

She'd attended a few of those dances when they could afford it a few years before. While they were enjoyable, she far preferred watching poppies dance to men and women—especially once the flowers were in bloom. She realized it was a bit silly to have poppies be her favorite flower as well as her name, but she couldn't help it. They were simply the most delightful flower in existence.

The red carpeting the cliffside was always a spectacular, unforgettable sight. Easily one of Poppy's favorite places to be. She had lost count of the number of times she'd sat in the midst of the flowers—careful not to tread on a single one, of course—and watched the seas shift from turquoise to navy blue as the sun set.

From her viewpoint, she could see Tregalwen Beach and the very edge of Tristwick's dock to the south. To the north, beyond the broken chimney of the Penharrow ruins and the small house of Lowena, she could just make out Golowduyn's tower.

And it was here, from the fields of Porthlenn, where she'd watched for Lieutenant Harris's return. She couldn't read any ship's name from that far, of course, but she always fancied the vessels to be carrying him safely back to Cornwall. He wouldn't even be able to wait to get to St. Just before he would return to her, sweep her up into his arms and express his undying love for her.

But none of that had ever happened. And instead, she'd sat in those fields alone, waiting until she knew how fruitless such an action was.

That was when the darkness had returned, the darkness that had only relented with the presence of her family, memories of her father, and time in Tristwick and the sea. What would ever happen if she lost them? What would ever happen if she *left* them?

Poppy wanted to be positive. She wanted to move forward with hope, but then, she needed to remember the past to protect her future.

"Auntie Poppy, we go 'ome now?"

She looked down to Isolde who'd been patiently waiting. With a calm breath and a forced smile, Poppy nodded. "Yes, Isolde. Let's go 'ome."

CHAPTER ELEVEN

*E*dmund used the backs of his fingers to flick off the thick mud, sand, and water the Kendricks's dog had left behind on his shirt, but he only succeeded in making matters worse.

He'd taken Gwitha with him for a walk on the beach that afternoon to ensure the rowboat had remained secure during the storm that had raged against the lighthouse's tower last night. The boat had remained safe. Edmund's white shirt had not.

Once he'd climbed back up from the beach, reaching the muddy pathway toward the lighthouse, the dog had barreled toward Edmund, coming up on his hind legs to pounce against him. Edmund had barely remained upright, but mud and drool had spilled down his open shirt and now trickled down his chest in the most unpleasant of manners.

Served him right for walking without his cravat on and waistcoat fastened. This was especially infuriating this morning due to the fact that he had no clean shirts available to him—only ones drying on the line.

Ah, well. At least his waistcoat had escaped without a

mark. One shirt would be easier to scrub mud from than a waistcoat, cravat, *and* a shirt.

Besides, walking with the winds blasting off from the waves had been just the thing to invigorate him enough to awaken him, as he'd spent half the night keeping watch below the lamps so Kendricks could remain with his wife and Cadan could take the night off.

Before his annoyance with Cadan could return, Edmund distracted himself by pulling again at the mottled fabric sticking to his chest. He needed to change before he was driven to madness.

As he approached the lighthouse, he caught sight of the clothing line stretching from the side of the tower, where a few shirts had been fluttering since that morning.

Would they be dry by now? He could only pray that they were. The mud and slimy drool was beginning to irk as it dripped down past his stomach.

Wriggling with discomfort, he walked toward the line, knowing a moment longer with this watery mud licking down his chest would do him in.

He progressed across the grass, the sun warming the back of his head and shoulders like a thick blanket as the light shone directly above him. The cool, salty wind played with his hair, reminding him of the countless times he'd stood upon the deck of the *Defense*, the wind against his face, the rigging and blocks tapping above him, the waves slapping upon the bulwark.

A mere six days had passed by since his time at Golowduyn had begun. Less than two weeks remained before he'd be back at sea where he belonged. He would be able to manage that much longer, would he not?

Then again, after only a week, he'd insulted Poppy, apologized, bickered again, then teased her as if they were still friends.

Well done, Edmund. Well done, indeed.

Why could he not remain apathetic around the woman? Cordial, unaffected, calm. He'd take any of it over the frequent, volatile irritability he'd been exhibiting over the last week.

Reaching the shirts, he looked at a hem, finding the initials that marked the first one that was hung up.

G.K.

Kendricks's shirt.

He moved to the next and the next, finally discovering the third shirt to be his. Removing it from the line, relief filled him to discover its dryness.

Kendricks had plans for the two of them to polish the refractors behind the lamps that afternoon while the lights were doused. Edmund would have to hurry if he wanted to be of any help at all. He'd just bring this inside to swiftly change in his room.

He made to retreat, but his boots made a slurping sound as he stepped away from the mud he'd been too distracted to notice until then. He raised his boots one at a time, noting the sheer amount of mud now beneath each sole.

He sighed. This would take ages to clean up. The dog's saliva-mud mixture now twisted against his chest hair, pinching and pulling unbearably.

Tapping his fingers against his thigh, he looked up, casting his eyes across the grounds of Golowduyn from his vantage point beside the tower. Not a soul was in sight. Kendricks was still in the tower, Mrs. Kendricks was in bed, and Poppy was clearly occupied with the girls.

Yes, he'd have to clean off his boots in order to go inside, but at least if he changed his shirt out here, he'd no longer have to suffer with this oppressive mud.

With determined movements, he got to work, removing his sling, then wriggling out of his waistcoat and pulling his shirt off over his head.

His left arm protested with a twinge of pain, so he rested it against his side as he took the clean section of his soiled shirt in his right hand and used it to wipe the mud free from his chest.

Edmund could handle many uncomfortable things, sea-soaked clothing, sand in his hair or even teeth, but for some reason, that mud was simply—

A soft gasp sounded behind him, and he whirled, coming face to face with Poppy. Her eyes rounded as she stared at him, standing still with an empty basket in her arms. Her eyes scanned the length of him half-dressed, and a blush instantly glowed on her cheeks.

Edmund's lips parted, and he hurried to explain himself, heat rushing to his brow. "My apologies. I'm afraid I was in a little mishap with the dog and caked in mud. I thought I'd…"

His words trailed off of his own accord. He thought he'd what, simply undress outside? This had to be his worst idea yet.

Poppy hardly seemed to notice that he'd even spoken, standing to the side, her eyes focused on the grass. "That be fine, sir. I just came to gather the clothin'."

Her eyes glanced across his chest again, her cheeks a lovely shade of apple red, and his embarrassment faded away. Did she enjoy what she saw, then? For reasons he refused to explore, he could not deny the pleasure that filled him at the thought.

Once she looked away again, he took a quick glance at his bare chest himself, scrubbing at the dirt before he paused. Looking up to Poppy, he took stock of the empty basket in her arms.

She had been washing his clothing? Such a thing should have been obvious, as she was essentially working as the Kendricks's maid. How could he have not thought of this before?

He grimaced. Never in a million years would he have ever wished for Poppy Honeysett to be washing his clothing. Even if matters would have been different for them and they would have married, he would have hired out a maid to do the task. He simply couldn't bear the idea of her doing such a service for him when he was literally doing nothing in return.

"You have been doing my washing?" he asked, sliding the shirt down his front to finish up the cleaning process he'd nearly forgotten about.

Her gaze skittered down his chest. "Yes, sir." She narrowed her eyes at the shirt in his hands, as if she was trying very hard not to look anywhere else. "Be that another shirt ye need washin'?"

"Oh, no. Not at all." There was no chance he'd have her wash another. From this point forward, he would be doing his own washing.

Her eyes remained on the mud-smeared fabric. "Ye call that clean?" Her brow furrowed, then she extended her hand toward him. "Allow me, sir."

"No, that's all right. I can do the washing myself."

He pulled the shirt back, holding it to his side and revealing his chest more fully in the process. Her eyes lingered on his torso, and a flame sparked within him.

Many years ago, he'd found it humorous when sixteen-year-old Poppy used to watch him. Now, with this matured woman clearly admiring his physique, her stares felt different. It caused his heart to beat unnaturally. He wasn't certain if he liked it or not.

Before another moment passed, he flung the soiled shirt over the line, then pulled on his clean one, wincing as his arm twinged in protest again from his swift movements. As his sight reappeared, he found her once again staring until he pulled the fabric down to cover his torso.

He felt far less exposed now, though her eyes still glazed over the top of his chest where the shirt split open.

Yet again, his heart sputtered, as if coming up for air after being submerged in sea water.

"Did I do somethin' wrong with it, Lieutenant?"

He paused, pulling his sling back on and readjusting it around his neck. He could not wait to be rid of the contraption. "Pardon?" he asked. She motioned to the shirt he wore. "No, I do not believe so."

"Then why won't ye allow I to wash your other one?"

"Oh, I just…" He paused, scrambling for words. "I just do not believe it fair of me to take advantage of your services to the Kendrickses when you are receiving no extra payment in doing so."

She gave him an odd look. "They increased me pay the moment ye arrived, sir."

"Oh. I see." That took care of that. But then, how could he explain his other reasoning—that it seemed far too intimate for her to be washing his clothing? "Should I not at the very least be paying you out of my own pocket?"

"Nay, sir. Mr. Kendricks be more 'an 'appy to do so for 'is guests and those who work 'ere. I wash all the clothin', the Kendricks's, Cadan's."

Edmund forced his expression to remain unchanged. Well, if she was cleaning the assistant's clothing, she must not have a problem with anyone's clothing, then.

He shifted his footing to rid himself of the discomfort rising in his chest, the thought of Poppy's fingers on Cadan's clothing nudging its way to the forefront of his mind.

She held her hand out toward the sullied shirt once again. "If ye don't mind, I'd like to earn me wages fairly by cleaning your clothing…and cookin' ye delicious dinners, as I did on Saturday."

He caught sight of the sparkle in her eye. It was the same one she'd held when she'd revealed exactly why she'd made the stargazy pie—because she knew he didn't like it.

She'd shared that look with him when she was younger and usually up to no good. During his first convalescence in St. Just, she'd spotted him in town, speaking with him for a moment before Trevik had come looking for her. Begging Edmund to keep her presence a secret, she darted behind a wagon. Little had Edmund known that she'd jump out a moment later, scaring the devil out of her brother. She'd laughed an inordinate amount, which eventually led to Edmund and Trevik joining in, as well.

Edmund had always enjoyed a good joke, but it had been a long time since he'd been properly teased. There simply was no time for that in the navy, as he'd learned in his youth. But seeing that spark in her eye, feeling the laughter bubbling up in his chest, he couldn't deny how greatly he missed it.

"I did not have the opportunity to properly thank you for that pie," he said, trying to forget about his clothing being cleaned by the woman. "It was quite delicious."

Her eyebrows flicked up in disbelief. "Was it now? I be that glad. Did ye eat an entire slice yourself?"

He could see her amusement from her own comments dancing in her eyes. "As a matter of fact, I did." He looked away. "Well, nearly. It was more of an entire forkful than an entire slice, rather."

She laughed. He hadn't felt this delighted by a laugh in years.

She walked past him, sidestepping the mud and taking the soiled shirt from off the line herself, tossing it in the nearby wooden tub filled with soapy water.

"So 'ave ye found a way to get back at me yet for cookin' ye such a fine meal?" she asked, removing Kendricks's clean shirt from the line next.

He shook his head. "I'm afraid I haven't had a moment to consider anything." In truth, he'd been attempting to forget he'd ever said such a thing.

It had been a moment of weakness, her smile dumbing his logic and tricking him into playing along with her teasing. Such a thing was never wise with Poppy. The last time he'd done so, she'd swept him up in her playfulness to the point where he'd been convinced to give up the sea for her.

Thank heavens he'd seen reason before it was too late.

"Well, I might 'ave an idea for ye meself."

"Do you now?"

"'Ave ye heard o' hurlin', Lieutenant?"

"Mr. Kendricks may have mentioned a thing or two about it."

In truth, Kendricks had asked him to join in. From what Edmund understood, two opposing sides—townsmen and countrymen—fought to bring a ball to their respective end goal with no other rules beyond that. The men were allowed to hit, push, trample—all of it was fair. Honestly, hurling sounded as mad as folks who believed in piskies and merfolk.

She moved to the line, removing the pins holding up the other clothing stretched across it. "Well, ye ought to go. We'll not be playin' on a Sunday, so there ain't be no risk of ye turnin' to stone. And they could use someone with your…" She glanced over her shoulder, her eyes settling on the top of his chest again before she faced forward. "Your experience in the navy."

What the navy had to do with hurling was beyond him, but Edmund let her words go. He had immediately protested Kendricks's idea to join the game due to his arm. There was no chance he'd risk prolonging his return to the navy. Or worse, prolonging his stay in St. Just. But his friend had assured him there were other ways to play that didn't involve physical contact with others.

Edmund had to admit, he was intrigued by the idea of attending, even more so with Poppy mentioning it. "So how would that satisfy my revenge for you feeding me stargazy pie?"

"It wouldn't exactly." She removed another shirt from the line, again sidestepping the mud he hadn't managed to avoid. "But it would drive me brother mad to see ye there. Which'd serve 'im right after 'e disregarded your comment at the meetin' the other day."

He stared. He hadn't known she'd been aware of Trevik's snub. Not wishing to bring up *that* night again, he gave a half-smile. "You still enjoy tormenting him, then?"

"Ain't that what little sisters be for?"

The smile she gave him caused a longing within him to see the full vibrancy of one of Poppy Honeysett's grins—the ones she now only bestowed on her family and a certain lighthouse assistant who would remain nameless.

"So where does my revenge for you come in to play?" he asked, if only to keep his mind focused.

He and Poppy were speaking. Civilly. They were not arguing. They were not fighting. It felt as if nothing had changed between them. As if they hadn't just argued days before about how hurt they were by the other's actions.

"There be a party afterwards at the Hawkins's home, Fynwary Hall." Poppy removed a pair of Mr. Kendricks's breeches from the line. Or were they Cadan's? "They've invited everyone who be playin' for country's side with the promise o' games."

She folded the breeches and secured them in her growing basket of clothing. "I do recall ye bein' near to beatin' I whene'er we played on the beach." She shrugged one of her shoulders. "Per'aps we could see who be the victor 'tween us now. After all, ye know 'ow I 'ate losin'."

The invitation hung in the air between them. He couldn't very well answer now. He needed time to think on the possible outcomes of attending an event where Poppy would be present.

Already, he knew the idea was dangerous—playing games with her, finding joy in being around her. He couldn't do such a thing, not when he'd been so damaged the last time. But as the moments ticked by, and hope flashed across her features, he found himself nodding without his own accord.

"Perhaps I will attend," he said. "You and your brother could both use a dose of humility, I believe."

Her barely restrained smile almost made his words worth it.

"We look forward to givin' ye the same, Lieutenant," she returned.

Then she raised the laundry basket to her hip, moved around the mud, and walked past him with a slight curtsy.

Edmund kept his eyes on the sea, refusing to turn back and look at her swishing skirts as she departed.

He'd said 'perhaps.' That certainly wasn't a very strong commitment. He could still back out, he could still make the wise decision and remain far, far away from the girl who'd broken him years ago.

And yet, even now, he knew he would attend the blasted hurling competition and the games afterward. Because he was a glutton for punishment—just as he always had been.

CHAPTER TWELVE

*P*oppy craned her neck left and right, standing on her tiptoes as she scoured the faces in the crowds around her. St. Just teemed with even more people than usual, the roads overflowing with men, women, and children alike as nearly everyone in both the town and the countryside had seemed to join together that morning for the hurling competition.

Shop owners had boarded up their windows to prevent broken glass from rowdy participants or rogue balls, though a few carriages and men on horseback still attempted to travel down the streets, braving the risk of being overpowered by the crowds. Anticipation buzzed in the air for the game to finally begin as women pulled their younger children back from the center where the men gathered, hushing their cries of wishing to participate in the dangerous sport.

Poppy loved the excitement hurling always brought to the town. The sport was not as popular as it once had been, many towns losing the tradition altogether. But she was glad Tristwick had not, as it was a welcome distraction to the hardships they faced.

She glanced around the crowds again, looking for no one

in particular. But when one specific individual's face didn't appear in her search, she sighed with disappointment.

"Lookin' for someone, Popp?"

Poppy glanced to Morvoren, standing right beside her in the middle of the square in St. Just.

"Yes," she answered swiftly, having prepared for just such an occasion. "I just be ensurin' Tegen Bosanko be havin' fun with the girls."

Morvoren nodded, though she hardly looked convinced. Poppy looked to Tegen, if only to make her words more credible. She wasn't telling a full falsehood. The girl was so painfully shy, Poppy wasn't sure she'd enjoy meeting the girls she'd promised to introduce her to a week before.

But as she found them in the crowds, Tegen laughing and smiling with the two young bal maidens from Wheal Favour, Poppy's heart was full. It was good to see her happy. Perhaps Tegen would now begin to heal after the Pennas's departure.

Hopefully Poppy would be able to do the same when Tristwick changed.

Her heart twisted. Trevik had spoken to the family again last night. He'd gathered a list of names for Mr. Trevethan of those who were interested in living in Tristwick, spending hours scouring the countryside, taking referrals from others, going far beyond St. Just. But the number of individuals he'd written down was far more than Poppy thought he'd find, and the knowledge sent a small thread of panic through her heart.

Of course, the people on the list were only interested in the *idea* of living in Tristwick and the thought of working aboard the *Pilferer*. Only time would tell if they would follow through with their wishes.

"They ought to be startin' soon," Morvoren said, her voice raised to be heard above the overwhelming crowds, though the two of them stood on the outskirts of the others. "Everyone be 'ere from the countryside."

Well, not everyone.

Poppy still didn't know what had possessed her to invite Lieutenant Harris to the sport. Perhaps she was simply attempting to bring back the past, before she'd ever shared her feelings with the lieutenant, when they were simply and irrevocably friends.

"I do think we be waitin' on a couple more men," she said carefully. "Mr. Kendricks and...and I do think I 'eard that Lieutenant 'Arris might be comin', too."

Instantly, Morvoren's eyes were on her. "Is 'e?"

Poppy nodded, feigning nonchalance, but of course Morvoren could see straight through it.

"Poppy, ye've 'ardly spoken of 'im since 'e came 'ere. Are ye sure ye be fine?"

Poppy sighed. She'd never kept things from her sister-in-law before. Why start now? In truth, she'd been desperate to speak with someone about all that had occurred, but every time she'd tried, Trevik was present, and there was no chance she'd risk speaking of the lieutenant with her brother around. He was far too protective of Poppy—and far too mistrustful of Lieutenant Harris to not break her heart again.

Perhaps now, in the midst of the crowds, she could express to Morvoren how difficult matters had been, how she and Lieutenant Harris had argued, fought, accused, and teased each other, all in the matter of a week.

"I'll admit," she began, "I 'aven't—"

"Trevik be comin'," Morvoren interrupted, looking over Poppy's shoulder before smiling at her approaching husband. "We can continue this tonight, yes?"

Poppy nodded, turning to greet Trevik, as well. Blasted brother that he was. How did he know just exactly when to interrupt matters?

Still, she couldn't be upset with him for long. Not when he was, in reality, a very *good* brother.

He greeted them with a smile, kissing his wife on the cheek

before taking a look around them. "Crowds be 'eavier than they were last year."

He looked exceptionally more disturbed that morning than he usually did, always having the weight of the world on his shoulders. Poppy and Morvoren exchanged looks, knowing very well what was upsetting him today.

"We'll be all right, Trev," Morvoren said. "Poppy and I 'ave already discussed remainin' away from the crowds."

He hardly looked relieved with their attempts to assuage his concerns about them being in attendance. It wasn't anything unusual to have women and children there to watch the sport, but Trevik was, again, worrying about nothing.

"Per'aps the crowd becomes too raucous and ye get 'urt?" he asked. "I'd just as soon as 'ave ye both join Mother and Isolde at Golowduyn."

"So we miss all the fun that ye get to 'ave?" Poppy asked, her brow furrowed. "Not a chance."

Morvoren rested a hand against his back, calming him in a way no one else could. "We'll be fine, Trev. I promise. And I promise to keep 'er out o' harm's way, as well."

"That be a lofty goal," Trevik said with a smirk at his sister.

Poppy swatted her brother on the arm, and he smiled before his expression grew serious once again. "Popp, ye ought to know, that lieutenant be 'ere."

Poppy perked up despite her best efforts not to. "Oh?" She glanced around, wondering how she'd managed to miss him. But when Trevik's wary gaze increased, she paused. "What?"

"I know what ye be thinkin', Popp. Just…be careful. 'E be a charmer."

Heavens above. Was he going to deliver his typical speech again where he told her she was far too impressionable? Where he instructed her not to be so silly, to grow up and put her family first?

"I ain't a child anymore, Trev," she said with a heavy sigh, taking a step to the side to allow a family to file past them.

"'E doesn't think ye are," Morvoren said with a glance of instruction to Trevik. "'E just be worried 'bout ye."

Poppy nodded. "I know. Ye all be worried. All the time. But ye don't 'ave to be. I be more 'an capable of withstandin' the man's *charms*." She said the word with a pointed look. "I know 'e don't want to remain in Cornwall, and I do, so I ain't in danger o' fallin' for 'im again."

As she spoke the words, they were once more solidified in her heart. She *wouldn't* fall for him again. But surely a carefully guarded friendship with an old acquaintance would be just the thing to boost her spirits.

Trevik would simply have to accept the fact that she could make her own decisions.

She faced Morvoren and Trevik again, a silent conversation occurring between their mere glances at one another.

"Would either of ye care to allow meself into the conversation?" she stated.

Morvoren gave an apologetic smile before Trevik spoke. "Sorry, Popp. We just want ye 'appy. 'Appy and safe. Our family knows better than anyone what comes o' trustin' untrustworthy folks."

Poppy solemnly nodded, his words humbling her pride. They *did* know what came of trusting folks like that. Father had believed the word of a snake and suffered because of it, to the point of his very death. But Lieutenant Harris was no snake. Still, Trevik would never see him as anything other than the man who'd rejected his sister.

With that in mind, Poppy responded far more softly. "Thank ye for your care. But I be smarter than I was before. I won't do nothin' to risk hurtin' me or me family."

Trevik eyed her warily, but as the crowd quieted around them, visibly shifting toward the center of the square, they turned their attention elsewhere.

"Settle down! Settle down!" came Thomas Causey's voice as he stood atop a crate to be seen above the rest of those in attendance.

Trevik's jaw set. "I best be off." He turned to face Poppy and Morvoren with a pleading look in his eye. "Please, keep safe."

"We will, love," Morvoren said. "Ye be safe, too."

She placed a sound kiss to his lips, then sent him off.

"'E be such a worrier," Poppy said, shaking her head.

"'E simply be makin' up for your lack o' worries," Morvoren said with a pointed but playful look.

Poppy smiled as best as she could. She'd known Morvoren was teasing, but the words hit Poppy hard. In truth, she did have worries—an exceptional number of worries. But the difference between her and Trevik was that she very rarely let them show.

"I believe we are ready to begin," Mr. Causey's voice chimed out again. Being the winner for the countrymen the year before, he was the man chosen to introduce the game this year. "If all the men participating could please join me in the center here."

Movements shifted around the crowd as the men weaved their way in and out of the masses, but Poppy could hardly see a thing beyond the backs of bobbing heads. She glanced behind her, settling on a few chairs situated near the front of the bake shop.

Nudging Morvoren, she motioned to the chairs. "We'll be able to better see from there."

Though Morvoren hesitated, Poppy led the way toward the shop, pulling up her skirts and stepping up before helping Morvoren to do the same. Finally, atop the chairs, Poppy could fully see above the crowds below.

Mr. Causey continued his speech, welcoming those in attendance and encouraging fair play as Poppy half-heartedly listened, her eyes still roving over the crowds.

Finally, she spotted Mr. Kendricks astride his black horse near the back of the crowd. Sure enough, Lieutenant Harris stood beside him, his left arm still propped up in a sling.

At the sight of him, her eyes dropped instinctively to his chest and torso now covered with clothing. Seeing him near the clothing line the day before had been…eye-opening.

She blew out a breath to steady her heart.

Of course it was nothing she hadn't seen before. She blushed to think of the countless times she'd spied on him swimming in the sea when she was a girl. But three years was a long time, and she'd somehow forgotten how straight and rigid his collar bone stretched below his neck and across his shoulders. Or how formed and defined his features were, not only on his face, but across his whole front.

She stood a little straighter atop the chair, hoping to catch his attention, but his eyes focused on Mr. Causey, as hers should have been.

"The goals are marked with a red flag," he continued. "Countrymen, you must cross the barrier to the west. Townsmen, the east. Whichever side reaches their goal first—or whomever manages to break through the parish boundaries—will win for their team."

A few more cheers sounded.

"Now, be aware of the families watching and the shops who have chosen to close their doors—and quite literally their windows—for this event." He paused, then raised the apple-sized silver ball in the air. "Are we ready, men?"

The crowd erupted into cheers, and Poppy grinned. She couldn't see the writing on the ball from as far away as she and Morvoren stood, but she knew "Town and Country" was etched into the band welded around it. How she longed to be a part of the fun. Then again, she'd seen the tackling that typically went on during the sport, and she didn't really have the desire to be trampled by a group of overeager men.

"Town and country, do your best!" Mr. Causey shouted, raising the ball ever higher. "For in this parish, I must rest!"

He called for three cheers, the crowds roaring louder and louder as excitement overflowed from each person in attendance. Finally, Mr. Causey pulled his arm back then released the ball into the air.

A mad dash occurred as the men from both sides ran toward the ball, though it had already been buried in a sea of men piling on top of each other, clambering across bodies to reach the ball rumored to bring good fortune.

Poppy watched the chaos with delight. The whole thing was madness. Chaotic, delightful madness. After all, she'd heard of deaths occurring with the sport. Did she really wish to die due to her competitiveness? No. She would simply wait to expel her pent-up feelings at the house party that evening at the Hawkins's home.

"Ought we move farther back, Popp?" Morvoren asked, worry pursing her brow, despite their distance from the crowd.

"Nay, we be fine, Morvoren." There was no chance Poppy would lose the only spot she even had the possibility to see the ball from. "We be safer than those two cakey folks."

She pointed to two middle-aged women dressed in fine silks, standing far too close to the crowd, their necks twisting and turning as they searched for the ball, though they were pushed aside as the crowd migrated a mere foot to the west.

The women gasped in horror, scowling at those who dared to mistreat them so, though they moved back a hearty distance.

Poppy could only grin. This crowd was clearly no respecter of persons. One risked injury by standing too closely.

At the thought, she searched for Lieutenant Harris again. Mr. Kendricks still sat atop his horse behind the crowd, though the lieutenant had shifted to the opposite side of the throngs of people, fortunately still standing a good distance away from the center.

The men gave each other a nod, then faced the group of men crowding around the ball.

Poppy narrowed her eyes, wondering what they were about before a loud cheer sounded. She swiveled her eyes to the pile of men just as the ball surfaced, hurled toward the direction of the town's goal line.

A moment later, the men piled atop each other once again, flooding the area like a swarm of bees to honey. This huddle lasted longer, pushing a quarter of an hour. Morvoren's attention soon strayed, but Poppy kept her eyes trained on the pile—when she wasn't looking at Lieutenant Harris, of course.

After far too long, she finally caught his attention, his eyes landing on hers as she watched him. He nodded his head in greeting, then turned back toward the game.

Poppy struggled to keep her smile at bay. Now that he'd seen her, would he look back at her again?

She shook her head, stamping out her pride. The man had more important things to pay attention to—like the group of men who could very well trample him to death.

When the ball finally resurfaced, the man holding onto it flung it into the air toward the town's side. Arms reached up as others jumped toward it, but the ball flew past them all to land squarely in Lieutenant Harris's right hand.

Without waiting a moment, he whirled around and released the ball toward Mr. Kendricks, who caught it with ease atop his horse, taking off in the direction of the countrymen's goal.

Poppy couldn't stop her cheers at the exciting turn of events. As the group neared his horse, Mr. Kendricks tossed the ball down to Mr. Trevethan, then took off in another direction to distract half the townsmen.

The other half of them, however, tackled Mr. Trevethan to the ground, halting the gameplay once again.

"Be that legal?" Morvoren asked, motioning to Mr. Kendricks tearing away on his horse.

"Ain't no one be protestin' 'bout it," Poppy said with a laugh. "That be incredible, whate'er it was. See the ground that be gained?"

And none of it would have been possible without Lieutenant Harris. She glanced to him, and her breath halted when she found his eyes on her. She gave him an impressed look, holding up her hands and clapping as if just for him. He bowed in response and straightened with an amused look before setting his sights on the ball once again.

Poppy was breathless.

Before long, Morvoren nudged her with her elbow, motioning to two women headed in their direction.

"Poppy!" Merryn and Nessa Argus, the apothecary's daughters, came skittering toward her with broad smiles as they dodged in and out of the constantly shifting crowds.

"Mornin', girls," Poppy greeted. The Arguses were a kind family, their daughters just the same, if not a little silly. But then, who was Poppy to judge in that regard?

"Isn't this excitin'?" Merryn, the elder sister asked, her accent somewhere between upper and lower class. Her black hair glinted in the sunshine. "Don't ye just wish we'd be allowed to take part in it?"

Poppy nodded. "Maybe we ought to start up a women's hurlin' sport."

Morvoren looked at her with an amused grin. "Good luck with that. Trevik'd ne'er allow it."

Didn't Poppy know it. She turned back to the girls, noticing Merryn nudge Nessa subtly with her elbow.

"We didn't expect to see ye here today," Nessa said, a strange look to her eye. She was far shorter than her elder sister.

Poppy paused. "Why wouldn't I be 'ere?"

The sisters exchanged glances again. "Because of the lieutenant's return, of course. Isn't it uncomfortable for ye to be around him?"

Poppy shifted her standing on the chair, looking out to the crowd. Her eyes unwittingly settled on Lieutenant Harris. He was no longer on the outskirts, having somehow moved toward the center where the pile of men still only shifted about a foot at a time.

She frowned, eying his sling. He had best take care.

The girls watched her expectantly.

"Why would it be uncomfortable for I?" Poppy asked in return. "There ain't nothin' 'tween us."

Again, the girls looked at each other. When Merryn turned back to Poppy, her eyes were alight with excitement. "So ye aren't pursuin' him any longer?"

Poppy shook her head. "No, 'course not."

After Lieutenant Harris had accused her of still pining after him, there was no chance she would allow word to get back to him that she was still interested in him. Because she wasn't. But if he changed his mind and wanted to remain in Cornwall...

She shook her head. That would never happen, so there was no point in even entertaining the thought.

Nessa bit her lip, her own eyes bright as she raised on the tips of her toes to appear taller. "So ye wouldn't be mad if we decided to pursue him?"

Poppy's stomach turned, her mouth turning as dry as sand. "What, both of ye?"

They grinned.

"Why not?" Nessa said with a simple shrug.

Poppy glanced over the heads of the girls, seeing Lieutenant Harris draw closer and closer to the center crowd and farther and farther away from her. What she'd said was true. Poppy wasn't pursuing him any longer, and he wasn't pursuing her. With that being the case, why did she regret her words so greatly?

"So ye don't have a problem with it?" Merryn asked, her black curls bouncing at her temples.

Poppy shook her head in a sort of daze. "No, not at all. Good luck to both of ye."

The girls giggled, then linked arms. "Will ye be at the Hawkins's tonight? Ye can see for yourself who wins between us."

Poppy had never regretted agreeing to go to a party more than in that moment. "I believe I will be, yes."

The girls nodded, then left Poppy with their heads close together, no doubt discussing the plans they each had to entrap the lieutenant.

Poppy had to have known this was coming, that Lieutenant Harris would move on with someone else. In truth, she wished him to be happy. But was it terrible of her to wish to not *see* him be happy if it was with another girl?

"Be that true?"

Poppy looked to Morvoren. "What?"

"Do ye not take issue with 'em pursuin' the lieutenant?"

Biting her lip, Poppy struggled for a response, finally settling with a depleted shrug. "I don't know. But I know I don't 'ave the right to be upset if I was."

Morvoren's brow pulled together. "Do ye regret not goin' with 'im to Derbyshire?"

Poppy had asked herself that question countless times, but only to keep her desires in check. "I be sad at times," she answered truthfully, "when I think o' what could've been. But every day I be reminded o' what I would've missed 'ad I agreed to leave ye and the others and Tristwick. And I can't regret that."

Morvoren gave a soft smile, then wrapped an arm around Poppy's shoulders. "I be sorry, Popp. 'Bout all o' this. But I do be 'appy to 'ave ye with us."

They stood there for a moment, Poppy drawing on the strength she received from her friend and sister's companionship.

Because even if Poppy was glad to be at home with her family in Tristwick, it only lessened the ache in her heart to a degree, for she could not help but contemplate the future family she had given up with Lieutenant Harris.

And how he might have a family one day with someone else.

CHAPTER THIRTEEN

*E*dmund had been tossed around at sea during storms and enemy engagement. He'd found himself in countless tussles with the other ship's boys when he'd first joined a crew. And he'd been roughed about at home when he was even younger.

But being shoved from person to person in the streets of St. Just? This was something else. Gavin had warned him to stick to the outskirts of the crowds, but Edmund had been unable to help himself, drawing closer and closer toward the ball, itching to feel the surge of energy that rushed through his limbs the last time he'd thrown it.

Usually, the altercations he had been involved in resulted from anger, involving a great deal of tension and fear. But with this sport—though there was a fair amount of aggression included—the overarching feeling was simple pleasure.

Still, he needed to take care. His arm was already beginning to protest, the sling a good reminder to not become too involved.

As the crowd moved and shifted, Edmund took a moment to breathe, eying the outskirts where the women, children, and older men watched the sport from the sidelines. He caught sight of the apothecary's daughters again, who waved at him with delight any time he even glanced past them.

He nodded his head, then looked swiftly away. They were pretty girls, albeit a touch overeager. The last thing Edmund wanted to do was encourage any connection to them. He'd learned his lesson with Poppy.

Unable to help himself, he glanced back to the brown-haired beauty standing above the others near the bake shop. She had beamed as brightly as the sun that day, despite watching from the sides. He could only imagine how she itched to play, to take the ball and sprint all the way to the goal marker.

And yet, now, her smile dimmed as she stared into the crowds. But, why? What could have happened to have stolen her joy?

"Harris!"

Edmund swiveled. Kendricks had dismounted from his horse and now stood in the middle of the crowd, throwing the ball toward Edmund.

Snapping to attention, Edmund backed up, jumping to catch the ball, but Trevik came up to his side before he could, bumping against Edmund's left arm and catching the ball instead. Edmund grimaced, gritting his teeth to keep from grunting as pain shot through his arm.

Trevik hurled the ball toward Dr. Kent, but a townsman leapt from the ground and intercepted it before being tackled by the others.

Edmund scowled at Trevik, who was already heading back for the ball. Honestly, the man was impossible. "We're on the same team, Honeysett," Edmund shouted.

Trevik looked back at him with a fierce scowl. "Then pay attention to the game 'stead o' lookin' at me sister," he growled back, then he shoved his way into the crowd.

Despite his anger, heat rushed over Edmund like a wave of the sea at being found out. He glanced again to Poppy, who watched him with concern, but he looked away in an instant. There was no chance she'd heard their words, though she had obviously seen their interaction.

Frustration overwhelmed him as he forced his way to the center of the scuffle. He was not responsible for what had occurred between himself and Poppy. *She* had been the one to choose not to go with him. *She* had been the one to break his heart. So why was he receiving Trevik's wrath?

Using his right elbow and guarding his injured arm as best as he could, he nudged his way through the group, using his anger to propel him forward before he finally had access to the silver sphere.

As he caught it, however, Trevik swiped it from his hands and tossed it elsewhere, a townsman interceding yet again.

A huddle progressed with Trevik and Edmund on the outside, pushing to get to the ball first. The joy Edmund had felt before had vanished, competition and anger now fueling his actions.

The other men must have sensed the mood shifting between them, their aggression picking up, as well, their shoulders pinning together due to the pressing crowds.

Trevik shoved Edmund to the side, causing his arm to cry out in pain once again.

Edmund typically prided himself on remaining patient, on finding humor even in the worst situations. But as Trevik shoved into his side again, he couldn't hold back any longer.

Entirely buried in the crowd, he shoved Trevik right back. "Keep your distance, Honeysett," he growled. "I'm just attempting to play like everyone else."

Trevik wouldn't meet his gaze. "No one wants ye to play, 'Arris." He tried to leave, but the men were pressed too tightly against one another to move more than an inch.

"No one, or just you?" Edmund returned.

Trevik didn't respond, so Edmund—already knowing he shouldn't—nudged him with his shoulder.

Trevik turned wild eyes on Edmund, pushing him to the side with two hands. Edmund did his best to remain steady, but with his blasted sling, he could hardly do a thing.

The two continued their scuffle, pushing into each other until Trevik pulled Edmund away from the crowd and pushed him down an empty alleyway, the two of them continuing their tussle like foolish schoolboys. Had Poppy seen their actions? Edmund glanced over his shoulder, but she was no longer in sight.

Without his vigilance, Edmund was too late in discovering Trevik barreling toward him, the fisherman knocking Edmund against the side wall of the shop. His arm blasted against the brick next, and white-hot pain flashed through his limbs.

"Stop!" Edmund demanded. "I *will not* do this with you any longer, Trevik!"

Edmund cringed at the weakness he revealed in stopping the fight, but he couldn't go on. Who knew how many days his convalescence would be set back now if his arm didn't stop throbbing. He never should have engaged Trevik in the first place.

Trevik stood before him, his fists clenched, his chest rising and falling with heavy breaths—same as Edmund's. The crowd still roared, but the alleyway seemed to mute the noise as people filtered past, unaware of the both of them.

"Then leave," Trevik said, tossing his head behind him. "That be what ye do best, ain't it?"

Edmund ignored the slight. "Fine. I'll leave the competition. Will that solve everything for you, then?"

Trevik's scowl increased. "I ain't speakin' o' the competition. I be tellin' ye to leave Cornwall."

Shaking his head in disbelief, Edmund slid his hand behind the sling around his neck, the fabric rubbing his skin raw. "That's what I'm trying to do. You attempting to injure me further, however, will only prevent my departure from occurring sooner."

Trevik didn't seem to hear him. "We don't need ye 'ere any longer, disruptin' all our lives."

Edmund could see the man was unhinged. Truthfully, he could almost understand his plight. Trevik had always been protective of his family—and for good reason. The stress he was under must be monumental. But he clearly wasn't seeing matters straight.

"I am not here to disrupt anything," Edmund responded, attempting to remain calm. "I came here to see an old friend, and I am remaining here to help that old friend. That is all."

"Ye be a coward, 'Arris."

This man was truly testing him. "Is that really what you think of me, Honeysett?"

Trevik drew a step toward him, his brown eyes dark. "What else would ye call a man who promised the world to a young woman, only to leave 'er and ne'er return?"

Edmund's blood boiled. "Poppy didn't want me, Trevik. I offered her everything, but she did not want me."

He'd expected Trevik to reel back in shock, or at the very least, blink in surprise. But his scowl remained intact. "Ye 'ave no idea what she wanted," he bit back.

"I do, she—"

"She waited for ye," Trevik interrupted, a slight tremor in his tone as he continued. "Every day, she watched for your ship to return. For weeks, she sat out there, always waitin'. But ye ne'er did come back. 'Til now."

Edmund stiffened. So it was true, then? Mrs. Rennalls had been speaking honestly? Anger filtered out of him as guilt spurted within his heart, like water into a ship ridden with cannon fire.

"I told her," he began, "I wrote to her and told her I didn't know if I'd ever return. I did not know she would wait."

His words sounded pathetic even to his own ears.

"Exactly," Trevik said, his lips white with anger. "Ye were too focused on yourself and what ye wanted. Ye didn't give a care for a young girl who ye promised everythin' to, only if she left everythin' she did ever know. And now ye come back, flauntin' your presence in 'er face." He pointed a finger at Edmund, speaking through his clenched teeth. "Ye be the worst o' men, 'Arris. The worst o' men."

Edmund blinked, attempting to hide the wince that followed such a true statement. Still, he scrambled to his defense, unsure of what else to do. "She and I wanted different things. I can hardly be blamed for that."

But Trevik was clearly finished with the conversation. He backed away with a look of disgust. "Ye stay away from Poppy. That be me final warnin'."

Edmund knew Trevik was a man of his word. But Edmund needed to clear the air.

"I have no designs on your sister," he said, his pride fully damaged. "You have my word. I will not injure her again."

"Your word means nothin' to I," Trevik stated. "After all, it be the word of a coward."

Edmund's heart contorted, pain packing into every inch of his chest as Trevik walked away. Edmund didn't try to call the man back. There was no purpose in doing so, even if he explained how *he* felt throughout the ordeal. It was quite common—indeed, it was *most* common—for a man to uproot a young woman from her hometown and provide a living for her elsewhere.

Yet, no matter how Edmund attempted to assuage his aching heart, he could not be rid of the image continuously flashing through his mind of Poppy sitting on the cliffside, watching ships as they sailed to and from Cornwall, hoping Edmund would be aboard one of them.

Had she truly done such a thing? Did that not prove that she *did* have feelings for him, then? And yet, what did it matter if Poppy had already moved on with Cadan?

With a throbbing arm, Edmund leaned back against the shop wall, hiding in the shadows of the alleyway until the crowd shifted forward. He would feel horrible for leaving Kendricks behind without a word, but he had no choice but to slip out of the alleyway and head back to Golowduyn.

He couldn't participate any longer. His arm—nor Trevik —would no longer permit it.

As he walked away from the town, still hearing the shouts and jeers rising up in the air behind him, he recalled Poppy's words from yesterday, when Edmund had teased about giving a dose of humility to Poppy and Trevik both.

"We look forward to givin' ye the same, Lieutenant."

How unfortunate that Poppy had been right.

CHAPTER FOURTEEN

*T*he countrymen took the victory four and a half hours later. The crowds cheered louder than ever before as Mr. Trevethan held the silver ball high in the air for all to see. Soon, he was carried toward the pub to dip the ball into a pint of brandy—which would be shared with all who wished to take a sip and receive extra luck.

Everyone seemed anxious to participate in the celebrations. Everyone, that is, but Poppy. She couldn't celebrate. Not after she'd seen the tussle that had occurred between Trevik and Lieutenant Harris. She'd watched them nudge each other before she'd lost sight of them in the crowds, and her stomach had dropped with worry until Trevik had resurfaced near the ball.

The lieutenant, however, was still nowhere in sight.

Poppy couldn't help but feel for them both. Trevik was only doing his best to defend his family. The lieutenant was only doing his best to defend his honor. And she was caught in the middle of it all.

With the hurling lasting well into the late afternoon, most of the women left St. Just directly after the celebrations to make ready for the party at the grand house, Fynwary Hall.

Poppy did her best to keep her mind busy as she and Morvoren helped each other with their hair and dress before they left for the Hawkinses'.

Mother was to stay home with Isolde that evening—"I'll leave the party-goin' to ye young folk"—and Trevik was set to fish, so Morvoren would serve as Poppy's companion.

The two of them chatted comfortably together as they walked to Fynwary Hall, Morvoren steering clear of any mention of Lieutenant Harris, which Poppy was grateful for. She didn't need any other reasons to think of the man more than she already was.

Would he be there that evening? Or had Trevik somehow managed to scare him away? Whatever had occurred, she was fairly certain she owed the lieutenant an apology for her brother's actions.

After plucking a few yellow wildflowers, Morvoren tucked them securely into Poppy's curled and twisted hair, then they neared Fynwary Hall.

"It be so grand," Morvoren breathed.

Poppy had to agree. The house, with its three stories and beige stone, was as fine as any she'd ever seen, and now, more than ever, she was grateful she'd taken Morvoren's advice to wear her nicest dress, a golden yellow, patterned gown with long sleeves. It wasn't fit for the usual games she'd take part in on the beach, but Morvoren, having grown up in the upper echelons of society, assured Poppy the games they would play that evening would be a far cry different than placing a stick far out into the ocean-covered sand or having foot races on the beach.

Poppy glanced to the carriages that rolled up the long drive to Fynwary Hall, fine silk gowns and dark jackets exiting as miners, fishermen, and farmers arrived on foot.

Most of those attending that evening from the lower class had never stepped foot on the grounds of such a fine estate, nor had many of them interacted with the upper class frequently—or at all.

However, Poppy didn't give those fine carriages a second glance. Certainly their lives were easier—their tables were nearly always filled and their clothing always fine—but they were no better than she was, and she was no better than they. So why should she be concerned with interacting with them? She had enough friends and acquaintances in both classes to count herself fortunately at ease with them both.

Poppy followed Morvoren—who wore a dark blue gown that accentuated her glowing, blonde hair—as they migrated with the rest of the crowd to the back of the estate, being greeted by Mr. and Mrs. Hawkins, their hosts for the evening.

If ever there was a more striking couple than those two, Poppy was sure to have never seen them. Mr. Hawkins was tall, lean, and had a face fit for a deity, and Mrs. Hawkins was a rare beauty, what with her black hair, vibrant blue eyes, and porcelain skin.

If they weren't so kind and possessed such wonderful hearts, Poppy was certain the couple would have many an envious enemy.

After greeting heaven's chosen couple, Poppy joined the others where large, fabric canopies had been set up on the vast grounds of Fynwary Hall. Beneath one of the coverings, long tables were set up with countless foods and desserts covering every inch of the pristinely white table coverings.

Clean chairs were placed beneath the other tents to provide coverage for those who desired shelter from the evening sun, though the large trees near the front of the house already cast long shadows across the grass.

Poppy and Morvoren took a seat near the Causeys, waiting until the last of the guests arrived before Mrs. Sophia Hawkins welcomed those in attendance, inviting them to eat to their heart's content and simply enjoy their time together.

"You men deserve the chance to celebrate after such a

victory," she said. "And we women deserve a chance to rest after hearing the continuous boasting from our men, do we not?"

Laughter resounded before Mrs. Hawkins ended her speech, and the group migrated toward the tables filled with food.

A few of the upper-class individuals—the Stedmans and the Madderns—were clearly uncomfortable with the presence of the lower class, raising their chins and positioning themselves at the far end of the gathering with frowns of disapproval, but as for the majority of those in attendance, they intended to enjoy themselves and the victory they'd received earlier that day.

So why was Lieutenant Harris not there to celebrate that victory, as well? Discontented with his absence, she tried to focus on the excitement buzzing in the air, but her sinking spirits and disappointment at not seeing him that evening could not be removed from her heart.

After gathering a modest plate of the finest fruits, pastries, cheese, and rolls she'd ever seen, Poppy mingled with friends and did her best to enjoy herself, attempting to forget about the lieutenant's absence.

A quarter of an hour after the party had begun, he finally made his appearance. Her heart skipped a beat as a rush of excitement overcame her, finding him speaking with the Hawkinses, a charming smile on his lips before he turned his eyes to Poppy.

Had he known she was there already? Or had he felt her gaze on him first? He gave a measured smile, to which she responded with a tip of her head, then she calmly looked away.

Biting her lip and looking in the opposite direction, Poppy willed herself to quiet down.

He had come. And her thrill at the knowledge could not be checked.

That is, until she caught the Argus sisters grinning across the way. Poppy knew that look in their eyes. It was the very same look Poppy had exhibited when she was young and filled with girlish fantasies about falling in love with a naval officer and living out the rest of her days in blissful peace.

Sure enough, the two of them headed straight for the lieutenant, cornering him near a set of chairs. Lieutenant Harris smiled, seeming pleased with the attention he received from them both.

Poppy's excitement disappeared, a sinking filling her chest, as if her heart couldn't stay up a moment longer.

This was for the best, having the Arguses pursue the lieutenant. She had become far too excited at his mere presence —just as she'd done before.

But he would be leaving in less than two weeks now, and she couldn't bear another departure like last time. The girls would provide just the barrier she needed between her and Lieutenant Harris.

And yet, as an hour passed by, and the girls remained at the lieutenant's side, her stomach tightened. He seemed perfectly at ease with the women. Did that mean he enjoyed their attention?

After another plate of cherry tarts simply to improve her mood, Poppy leaned back in her seat, half-heartedly listening to Morvoren, Mrs. Causey, and the Summerfields—Mrs. Causey's maternal grandparents—as they discussed the current situation of Tristwick.

Unwilling to be dragged down into the depths of despair on *two* accounts, Poppy excused herself to refill her glass of lemonade.

Pouring the yellow-tinted liquid herself, she leaned her hip against the table and fully faced away from the party to observe the estate's expansive grounds.

"Good evenin', Poppy."

Poppy turned to see Mrs. Gwynna Trevethan coming up

toward her with a warm smile. "Mrs. Trevethan, it be a fair while since I've seen ye. 'Ow are ye, ma'am?"

Mrs. Trevethan—once a bal maiden working for a copper mine—had married the mine owner's gentleman son in a match that had shocked all of St. Just.

"Oh, more than fine, thank ye," she responded. "And yourself? Enjoyin' the lovely spread?"

Her accent had changed a great deal, sounding far more refined, but she still maintained that warmth and generosity in her smile.

"A little too much," Poppy joked. "I don't know if I'd e'er get used to eatin' such fine foods."

Mrs. Trevethan raised a brow. "I still haven't. Sometimes, I wake up in a cold sweat, thinking I must be forced to eat pillas with water every morning again."

They shared a laugh. The mining families were typically poorer than most fishermen around the area, so while Poppy had never seen food the likes of that evening's, she also knew how fortunate she was to have the food she did possess.

She faced Mrs. Trevethan with a curious gaze. "'Ave ye adjusted well to the life of a lady?"

Mrs. Trevethan gave a half-smile, her copper eyes looking out across the fields. "Well enough," she responded, her tone low. "Fortunately, I've had many friends to help me along the way, and an endlessly patient husband. But the rules of Society are...difficult to maneuver. I do sometimes miss the simplicity of spallin' at the mine." Her eyes took on a faraway look. "Breakin' down ore is far easier than plannin' parties, sometimes."

They shared a smile before she motioned toward the outskirts of the gathering, where her husband chased around two boys, whose laughter filled the air with joy. "My Jack and the twins make it all worth it, though. He won't tolerate unkindness toward me of any kind, so I swear he's stopped talkin' to half of St. Just." She shook her head, her eyes still watching Mr. Trevethan. "But oh, I love him all the more for it."

Poppy could see the love she held for him and could understand why. In the year that Mr. Trevethan had purchased the land Tristwick rested upon, he'd been kind, respectful, and more than determined to help keep the residents happy.

"'E seemed right pleased to 'ave made that goal for the countrymen today," Poppy said, recalling the man's beaming smile as he raised the ball in the air.

"Well, ye know why, don't ye?" Mrs. Trevethan asked with a sidelong glance. "The twins teased that he couldn't possibly win, so he had to show 'em up." She gave a playful shake of her head. "Like father, like sons."

Poppy smiled in amusement. Then, because her mind seemed incapable of dwelling on anything other than Lieutenant Harris for longer than a minute at a time, she glanced toward him.

He still stood with the Argus sisters, laughing at something one of them said.

Poppy's stomach turned again. She needed to stop punishing herself by watching them together.

"How have ye been since his return?"

Blast. She hadn't realized Mrs. Trevethan had seen her staring at the lieutenant. It was just as well. There was no hiding the fact that she'd been transparent as a child, revealing her love of the man for all of Cornwall to see.

"I've been fine," Poppy responded, the word starting to sound odd to her ear after having said it for far too long now. "It just be strange."

Mrs. Trevethan nodded. "I was sorry to hear when he left. But ye be a good person, Poppy," she said, her accent reverting for a moment. "Happiness in marriage be well on its way for ye."

Poppy could only muster a half-smile. She used to believe

that to be true. But now…perhaps she ought to resign herself to find joy without the man she'd loved.

Mr. Trevethan trotted over in that moment, his dark hair falling over his brow, causing that rakish look to appear again that had caused nearly every single—and not single—woman to stare with admiration at the man.

"Mrs. Hawkins is looking for you, my love," he said. "I believe she wishes for the games to commence." He turned to Poppy with a smile. "Good evening, Poppy."

"Evenin', sir."

"Is your brother not in attendance this evening? I haven't been able to locate him."

"'Fraid not, sir. 'E be preparin' to fish this evenin'."

"Ah, well. Perhaps next time. How go his attempts to save Tristwick?"

She shrugged, attempting flippancy. "Little better. Folks still be frightened o' the sea swallowin' 'em up if they sail aboard the *Pilferer*."

Mr. Trevethan's brow furrowed. "I wish him better luck in the future, then. When you see him, though, would you mind very much telling him that I received his correspondence with the list of individuals who wish to take residence in Tristwick? I am working on a plan to see what is plausible to improve the houses already purchased before we build anything further. Perhaps that will encourage others to come to Tristwick, too."

Poppy swallowed the sand that seemed to coat her throat. "Yes, sir. And well done on your victory today."

He nodded his gratitude, then the Trevethans excused themselves from Poppy, Mrs. Trevethan linking her arm through her husband's.

"Speaking of victory," he said, speaking quietly to his wife. "I deserve a little prize for it, do you not think?"

Mrs. Trevethan swatted his chest and looked around, though not behind her where Poppy could still hear. "Hush, Jack. Someone'll hear."

"Only if you promise to speak to me in your accent this evening," he said, raising a quirked brow as he stared down at her.

She grinned. "For ye, sir, I be willin' to do anythin'."

They shared a kiss, and Poppy darted her eyes away from them, though a smile marked her lips. If the Hawkinses were heaven's couple, the Trevethans were the impish equivalent.

Poppy glanced back to the crowd, looking to see where Morvoren had gotten to when she found Lieutenant Harris, this time with his eyes on her.

His lips held no smile, as they had for the Argus girls, so Poppy looked away without hesitation. Mrs. Trevethan was right. Happiness was in her future.

But she would not find it with Lieutenant Harris.

CHAPTER FIFTEEN

*P*ain pinched Edmund's heart as Poppy walked back to her sister-in-law without a smile in his direction. Had Trevik told her of their scuffle? Did she blame Edmund for the cause of it, and was she now unhappy with his presence there that evening?

In truth, he had been resolved not to go. Were it not for Kendricks asking him to specifically give his regrets to the Hawkinses for not being able to attend, Edmund would be back at Golowduyn, sulking in his room.

He'd even offered to watch over the lights that evening, but Kendricks had already told him Cadan would be there before sunset to light the lamps.

"You must go, Harris," Kendricks had said. *"Enjoy yourself like you used to."*

Not wishing to give the impression that he was avoiding the Honeysetts on purpose now, Edmund had finally relented, intent on speaking with the Hawkinses, then leaving for the Golden Arms.

Of course, then the Argus sisters had made it impossible for him to depart. The only fortunate matter in all of this was the fact that Trevik was absent.

At least Edmund wouldn't be provoked into another brawl.

He found Poppy again, sitting beside the others, her head lowered as she stared at the drink in her hands. As if he could see into the past, his mind flashed once again to her waiting for him, and his chest ached.

How he regretted his actions. He should have made his intent to remain away clearer. He'd been so tormented, feeling as if he wasn't enough, just like he wasn't enough for his own wretched mother.

He pushed the thought of the woman aside, listening half-heartedly to Miss Argus ramble on about the ribbons she'd purchased with her sister specifically for that evening.

Obviously, such a topic didn't hold his interest for long, and though he responded with as much fascination as possible —"I can see why such a shade was chosen, as it does bring out the color of your eyes quite superbly"—his own eyes found their way once again to Poppy.

He wanted to speak with her, to ask her if her brother's words were true. In his worst moments at sea, after all that had occurred, he'd despicably wished for her to suffer as much as he was suffering. In truth, he never thought such a thing was possible. After all, she was the one who'd chosen to remain in Cornwall.

But now, at the very notion of her suffering, Edmund could hardly bear it. He needed to speak with her, just to know.

A few moments later, however, before he could break away from the Arguses, Mrs. Hawkins gathered the group together for games.

With the children in attendance playing with the Causeys in another part of the garden, and married couples, older and younger, choosing to sit and watch the festivities instead of joining in the fun, the unmarried, younger folk gathered together in the green, where chairs had been situated in a large circle fit for nearly twenty players.

Poppy joined the group of unmarried people—upper and lower classes included—so Edmund remained back. He had no desire to participate that evening, especially when Mrs. Hawkins explained that forfeits would be in effect.

He'd only played them at Christmas once or twice during the rare occasion he'd been stationed near a navy friend's family and invited to join them. More often than not, the forfeits included kissing games, which he was not willing to participate in. Should he be paired up with Poppy and have a repeat of what had occurred the last time he'd tried to kiss—

He cut the thought off, unwilling to dwell on it a moment longer.

Unfortunately, in his moment of distraction, the Argus sisters had managed to pull him a degree toward the gathered group. Still, he protested, claiming his arm needed rest as he held a hand to the sling.

But when Mrs. Hawkins counted those who had gathered, her brow puckered. "All right, now I know I counted an even number of both men and women who will be participating in the games. Which of you men has somehow escaped my notice?"

Edmund took a step back in the crowd, but it was to no avail, the Argus sisters pointing him out at once.

"Ah, there you are." Mrs. Hawkins waved him toward her. "Come along, sir. You mustn't be shy."

Shy? Edmund wasn't shy. In fact, it was the last thing he was. He simply didn't wish to put himself into a situation that he knew he'd later regret.

Averting his gaze from Poppy, who had been watching him with the rest of the crowds, he shook his head. "I'm certain there's another gentleman who'd like to take my stead."

Mrs. Hawkins looked around her, but no man stood forth.

"There, you see? You are our only option. Come along, sir. I promise I shan't make the games too difficult." She winked at the crowd. "At least not all of them."

The gathered group laughed, and Edmund took heavy steps to join the others, those who watched standing outside of the circle as Mrs. Hawkins introduced those in the group to one another.

Edmund moved to stand beside a few of the men—one of whom included Cadan, which he was none too thrilled to discover—but Miss Nessa Argus pulled him to her side instead, Miss Merryn Argus quick to follow up on his other.

Years ago, Edmund would have loved the attention these women were giving him. But now all he could think of was a wounded Poppy, crying over her loss on the cliffside.

He glanced toward her, but she was hidden behind the other players.

Did these Argus women actually wish to see which of them could win him over? Had they no notion that he would just as soon choose neither of them to avoid either of them becoming hurt as Poppy was?

"Now," Mrs. Hawkins said, "my dearest friend Mrs. Trevethan and I will be keeping track of forfeits, which, as you all know, shall be acquired each time a loss is accrued in every one of the games we play." Her bright blue eyes shone with delight. "We shall not require raucous forfeits to be paid, however, we can promise lively fun when all of the games are completed."

Cheers erupted, and Edmund stifled a groan.

Miss Argus leaned forward to speak around Edmund, though her voice could hardly be constituted as a whisper. "I do hope she'll call for kissin' forfeits."

"As do I," Miss Nessa agreed.

The girls giggled, glancing up at Edmund, but he couldn't bring himself to look down at either one of them.

Before, when he'd actually wanted to attend, he'd had the

desire to compete against Poppy. Now, he had a different reason to win—so he wouldn't have to pay a single forfeit to anyone in attendance that evening. But then, he knew Poppy, and her competitiveness knew no bounds. If she won, which she was more than likely to, how could he *not* pay a forfeit?

With nerves as rattled as the rigging of a ship during a storm, Edmund listened to the rules of their first game, a variation of Blind Man's Bluff.

Miss Argus was the first to be blindfolded over her dark hair in the center of the circle of chairs and guests. The players moved about the circle, shifting their seating around before allowing Miss Argus to begin her task. Edmund took a seat three spaces down from Poppy, just enough to see her from the corner of his eye.

Had he done that intentionally? Perhaps.

Was it wise for him to do such a thing intentionally? Not at all.

Without using her arms, Miss Argus moved forward about the circle until she bumped her knee against a man with blonde hair, wearing a blue cravat.

"Who goes there?" Miss Argus said with a smile, reciting the words of the game.

The man in question was allowed to respond three times in any way that would disguise his voice, so as to make it more difficult for Miss Argus to discover with whom she spoke.

"Is it Mr. Kevern?" Miss Argus guessed.

The man shook his head, and Mrs. Hawkins alerted Miss Argus that she had earned a forfeit, to which the young woman giggled behind her fingertips in response.

Edmund cringed. He might have to escape before the forfeits were called, after all.

As Miss Argus touched the next knee, which just so happened to belong to Poppy, she repeated the phrase, "Who goes there?"

To the shock and utter delight of those watching and those in the circle, Poppy responded with a perfect horse whinny.

Edmund bit back a laugh, though the rest of the group couldn't help but chuckle at the sound.

Miss Argus smiled, then awaited her second hint.

Poppy snorted like a pig, which the crowd laughed at again, before she delivered her third sound, which was the bleat of a sheep.

Miss Argus guessed wrong again, adding to her list of growing forfeits, but Edmund hardly noticed, unable to pull his eyes off of Poppy.

This was the woman he'd grown so accustomed to seeing —the carefree, silly, joyful Poppy. She had no inhibitions, no concern over embarrassing herself. Merely the simple desire to enjoy herself and, of course, to win.

How could her spirits have been brought so low when he'd left when she was always chipper, always filled with hope? Did that mean that she'd truly felt something for him? Something deep and immovable?

Miss Argus eventually guessed a person correctly when she bumped against her sister, though she'd earned herself a hefty six forfeits before being allowed to remove her blindfold.

"Ye ought to 'ave made animal noises," Poppy said to Miss Nessa as she stood to retrieve the blindfold herself, and the crowd laughed again. This time, Edmund joined in.

After a few more rounds, none of which included Poppy or Edmund gaining a forfeit, the next game was brought about.

Edmund thought his dread would have increased significantly with a new game, but as the Ribbon Pull was announced, he found his desire to leave had lessened to a degree, if only to catch a glimpse of the Poppy from the past —the Poppy he had yet to bring out himself.

The group was formed into a tight circle, a gentleman between each lady, with Edmund standing directly across from

Poppy. He tried to catch her gaze, but she hadn't looked at him since she'd spoken with Mrs. Trevethan near the tables.

Instead, she leaned closer to Cadan—who had unfortunately been positioned right next to her. He said something for only her to hear, and she responded with a nod and a beaming smile.

Edmund pulled his gaze away, refusing to dwell on what the man could have possibly said to have made Poppy brighten like the awakening sun.

Mrs. Trevethan explained the rules, then she handed each player a ribbon before tying the opposite ends together in the center of the circle, the ribbons appearing like the spokes of a wheel.

One by one, Mrs. Trevethan would call out one of two commands. "Let go" was for the players to keep hold of their ribbons, and "pull" required them to release them, causing the ribbons to drift toward the ground.

To Edmund's relief, Cadan was one of the first players to be eliminated as he pulled the ribbon instead of dropped it. He made another comment to Poppy, and she laughed once again.

Edmund grimaced, unfortunately at the exact moment Poppy's eyes finally met his. Swiftly, he looked away, not wishing to give away his feelings on the matter.

As more commands were called, more players were removed, and Edmund once again stole glances at Poppy. He couldn't help but smile at the spark in her eye, or the pleasure she revealed each time she succeeded in passing another round.

The crowd laughed and cheered and bemoaned every person who was removed until finally—and not to any surprise to Edmund—only he and Poppy remained.

She clearly attempted to avert her gaze from his, but as they each took up a ribbon that they'd dropped to the grass in the last round, their eyes met across from each other.

Edmund had never known Poppy to be insecure—shy, perhaps, when she was younger—but never insecure. And yet, as she looked at him, he could feel her hesitancy. He was certain most of the guests in attendance that evening were aware of what had occurred between him and Poppy. Was that why she was so discomfited? Or did she fear his rejection for some reason, that he would perhaps ignore her before all of these onlookers?

Anxious to set her nerves at ease—and to prove to everyone watching that he and Poppy held no animosity toward each other—he gave a half-smile.

"This reminds me of those games on the beach," he said quietly, the murmur of the crowd ensuring his words were just for her. "Down to the two of us."

Her lips curved ever so slightly. "Ye be still just as competitive."

"And you are not?"

Her grin grew.

"Ready?" Mrs. Trevethan asked.

They gripped their ribbons, their eyes remaining on each other's.

"Let go!"

They both kept hold of their ribbons, their smiles growing as the crowd cheered for them both.

He raised his eyebrow in a challenge, and she narrowed her eyes, their dark depths shining like stars in the night's sky.

"Let go!" Mrs. Trevethan cried again.

Still, they kept hold of their ribbons, though this time, Poppy flinched.

The crowd continued with their responses, and Edmund smiled. "Nearly lost it that time," he teased.

"Pull!"

Immediately, the both of them released hold of their ribbons, and the crowd cheered once again.

This continued four, five, six rounds, neither of them

willing to lose—both of them reluctant to gain a forfeit. Each time another round passed, Poppy's confidence returned brighter and bolder, her reticence vanishing.

"Ye must give up, sir," she said. "Ye know I'll win in the end."

CHAPTER SIXTEEN

*E*dmund knew Poppy was right. There would be no victory over the woman. She was far too stubborn, far too determined, far too...wonderful.

As they awaited their next instruction, their eyes met over her white ribbon and his green one. Something happened within him as he watched her. Time stood still. The warmth in her eyes, the smile on her pink lips, slid around his heart, cupping it in warmth and security, coaxing it to open.

He knew he shouldn't allow it. He needed to keep his heart secure, under lock and key, safe in his keeping so he couldn't be injured again.

But as her eyes softened, he could almost feel *her* feelings. He could almost know of what she was thinking. Finally, he allowed his heart to open, if only but a sliver.

A thousand emotions rushed over him, recollections of the wonderful times they'd shared together overpowering his senses. But one memory in particular stood out above the rest.

Poppy had been but sixteen. Edmund had thought her adorable, with her freckles and slightly turned up nose, but he hadn't allowed himself to think anything more of the girl due to the nearly ten-year gap in their ages.

But one summer day, her family and a few others gathered to play games on the sand. She'd invited him to come along when she'd seen him at Golowduyn earlier that day, and he'd accepted, if only for something to pass the time.

It was his first time playing with them. He hadn't expected anything more than a pleasant evening spent in their company. But when he'd joined the families, their laughter and smiles had been contagious like nothing he'd ever experienced.

There was love engrained in each of them, and he'd been welcomed into their families with open arms. Poppy had gone out of her way to ensure he felt at ease, though she'd blushed to high heaven whenever he even so much as looked at her.

And yet, when the games were played, she'd blossomed like a bright yellow hellebore, just like now. As he stood across from her—a mere two ribbons and a history between them—he was looking at that same woman from before. How deeply he'd missed her vivacity for life, the way she exuded peace when she looked at the sea, or love when she looked at her family.

In that moment, he could almost just believe that they were still the same people they'd been before. That nothing had happened between them, that they were still friends who simply wanted to enjoy one another's company—just like it used to be.

But nothing was like it used to be. Never mind the stirring now taking place in his heart. Never mind the warmth Poppy's smile embraced him with. Too much had occurred between them to pretend as if it had not.

Hadn't it?

Visions of Poppy waiting on the cliffside for him flickered in his mind like a flame being threatened by opposing wind. Had she really felt something for him? Did she really feel something for him now?

"Pull!"

Edmund pulled the ribbon without a thought, realizing too late that Poppy had released hers with both hands high in the air. The grin on her face told him everything he needed to know. He'd made a mistake, and she'd just won.

But just like before, he couldn't be upset over his loss. Not when Poppy spread warmth and light wherever she shone.

The crowd cheered her on with claps and grins as she faced Edmund.

"Well done," he said with a feigned look of disappointment, then he bowed at the waist with a hand to his chest.

Poppy's returning grin was enough to cripple him. There it was. He'd finally earned one for himself.

The next games were introduced and played, but Edmund's mind lingered on Poppy throughout the evening, so much so that he earned himself one more forfeit.

He could only pray that Mrs. Hawkins and Mrs. Trevethan wouldn't require him to do anything too humiliating. Because as much as he was taken by these reminders of the past and how he'd once felt about Poppy, he still needed to remember that she'd chosen Cornwall over a life with him.

When the games were completed, Mrs. Trevethan and Mrs. Hawkins took themselves away for a moment to count up the forfeits accumulated by each player—even Poppy having obtained one after Cat and Mouse.

The group mingled with the others, a few of them merging toward the drink table as the Argus sisters latched themselves to Edmund's sides once again. He listened as best he could as they spoke of their duties at the shop, but when he spotted Poppy sitting beside Cadan, his heart tripped. Because her eyes weren't on the lighthouse assistant.

They were on Edmund.

A softness warmed their brown depths, snatching his breath away as she kept her attention on him. He knew he needed to look away, but then, why should *he* have to do so when she was the one staring?

He drew a calming breath, though his heart raced round his chest as the beauty continued her pensive gaze until Mrs. Hawkins walked between them and finally broke their gaze.

When the forfeits were finally called, the men were once again situated between each woman, Mrs. Hawkins directing them where to sit and looking entirely too gleeful as she did so.

"You sit here, Miss Nessa. No, no. Mr. Carne, you must sit here. And Miss Lanyon, over there by Mr. Pethick." Next, she reached for Edmund's arm just before Miss Argus could. "Now, Lieutenant Harris, you sit right here. And Miss Honeysett, there you are. Just left of the lieutenant, please."

Edmund stiffened. Poppy did so, as well, but only for a moment before she sat down beside him.

A heavy silence rose between them. They didn't need to speak as they awaited their instructions for their forfeits, but then, the fact that he couldn't think of what to say made things worse.

He pulled his hands together on his lap, glanced around the group still being situated, then finally thought of a question.

"How many forfeits must you pay?" he asked, though he already knew the answer.

She didn't look at him as she responded. "Just the one."

He shook his head, attempting to put her, and himself, at ease with more teasing. "You are filled with far too much luck."

"Luck." She scoffed. "It be skill, as simple as that."

He smiled in response, and the tension in his shoulders eased. That is, until Mrs. Hawkins finished positioning the players and gleamed in front of the group.

"For the first forfeit," she began, "each man must turn to the lady on his left and deliver four compliments."

Edmund's chest tightened.

"The twist is," Mrs. Hawkins continued, pausing for

dramatic effect, "each of the compliments must be delivered without the use of the letter '*L*'."

The group laughed in response, but Edmund's mind was already racing as to how he could possibly escape the forfeit. But then, doing so would only hurt Poppy. How could he do that again?

"Now ladies, no matter how fine or how ridiculous these compliments may be, you must accept them with a simple, 'Thank you, sir,' before he may continue. You may begin when ready."

Mrs. Hawkins stood back, and the compliments began.

That is, everyone's compliments but Edmund's. He had no idea what to say to Poppy without possibly encouraging any feelings between them—something he definitely did not wish to do.

"Ye don't 'ave to do this, Lieutenant." Poppy's voice was soft as she spoke, her wide eyes looking up at him. "I know it be uncomfortable for ye to…"

Her words faded away as he shook his head. He would do this, if only to not injure her further. "Are you tempting me to shirk my duty and earn another forfeit?" he teased.

She smiled, her dimples deep.

"Now, allow me to begin." He pretended to think for a moment. "I would—"

"That be an '*L*', sir."

He paused, her lips twitching to reveal her smile. "So you will hold me to that, then?"

She nodded. "Ye must play fairly, sir."

"Just so." He stopped to think for a moment, ignoring the warmth her smile infused into every ounce of him. "My first compliment…that also has an 'L', I suppose."

She laughed, and his heart soared.

"Number one," he started again carefully. He knew just the thing to compliment her on that would be perfectly harmless. "You, Poppy, have more determination to win than anyone I've ever witnessed."

"Thank ye, sir," she said with a slight smile.

That had been relatively painless. Only three more to accomplish. Now what else could he mention that would not be misconstrued by either of them or the crowd as true admiration? Not that he didn't admire her, of course. Just as an acquaintance, of course.

"You have a marv—no, delightf—no, that won't work either."

She laughed, and he feigned a frown. "You imagine this to be easy, do you?"

"Far easier than ye be makin' it out to be," she said with a humorous shake of her head. "At this rate, the party'll 'ave dispersed by the time ye be done."

"All right. I—"

"That be an L."

He frowned. "'All right' wasn't part of my compliment now, was it?"

Her eyes shone with delight.

"Now, if you will allow me to continue?" He waited, and she pulled her soft lips in so he could no longer see them.

Shame.

"I do like...No, I do *enjoy* the shape of your...ears."

She laughed. "Me ears?" She held her fingers to them. "I do think that be the first time me ears 'ave been complimented."

He smiled. "Then that should be all the more flattering."

"Very well. Thank ye, sir...I s'pose."

Their eyes met, but Edmund looked away before he could get lost in their depths. His common sense nudged at the back of his mind, warning him to be aware. But he hardly needed to be cautious when he was merely playing a little game.

Now for the third compliment. She clearly hadn't been very fond of him pointing out her ears. Perhaps he ought to do something else to counteract his words. Her cinnamon eyes? Her full, pink lips? The smooth curve of her jaw?

He blinked away the thoughts, settling on something far more platonic.

"Your…" He paused. 'Dimples' wouldn't work. He'd have to find another way to describe them. With a smile, he continued, speaking each word slowly to ensure they were void of any L's. "The marks in your cheeks are quite…charming."

Now that was a compliment any gentleman ought to be proud of. He looked to Poppy for her response, but she looked away, a blush spreading across her cheeks, though her smile—and her dimples—remained.

Such a sight really shouldn't have brought as much pleasure to him, but he found himself wishing to cause that blush to deepen. It accentuated the amber in her eyes and brought an even more feminine quality to her features.

He'd done the very same when she was younger—always saying how impressed he was with her abilities. What else could he say now to do the same? Compliment her on the swish of her skirts as she walked? Point out how her nose wrinkled delightfully when she laughed? Or how the hair blowing across her brow right now made his fingers itch to brush it aside for her?

"Are ye havin' that difficult a time thinkin' o' something else, sir? Would ye like me to 'elp?"

He cleared his throat. Everything he thought of had been far too personal to compliment her on—not to mention that they'd hosted a plethora of L's.

Glancing back up at her, he was intent on mentioning something about her dress, but when their eyes met, he paused. She may have been teasing earlier, offering him help, but in the depths of her eyes, he could see as clear as day the vulnerability that shone within them again.

She had watched him day in and day out as a sixteen-year-old, had expressed her love to him as a seventeen-year-old, and had expressed her desire to marry him as an eighteen-year-old—nearly all of which he'd not been able to share in return due to her age.

So now, to see that vulnerability enter her eyes again as he struggled to give her a compliment, he knew that insecurity had been produced from his leaving. Somehow, he knew it. And his heart ached because of it.

Anxious to set aside even a small degree of his shame, Edmund drew a deep breath. "I have quite often admired how your eyes shine as amber when you watch the sea."

Just as he'd hoped, her blush continued, and a shy smile spread across her lips. "Thank ye, sir," she said softly.

How grateful Edmund was for the laughter that filled the air around them as the group listened to the superfluous compliments of the other gentlemen, for if they'd heard his own sincere words, they would have had no other choice but to assume that he felt something for Poppy once again.

What was concerning, however, was that Edmund *did* feel something. Whether it was a simple memory of his past feelings or a rekindling of something new, he couldn't be sure. But he was certain that this woman still did not wish to leave Cornwall, and he was certain he wanted to return to the sea.

Or at least, he *had* been certain once.

Mrs. Hawkins moved to the center of the circle, clapping her hands to draw the attention toward her. Edmund tore his gaze away from Poppy and faced forward, conflicting feelings battling in his heart.

"Shall we all cheer our gentlemen on for such lovely compliments for these delightful ladies?" Mrs. Hawkins asked first. The crowd obliged with cheers and clapping before she continued. "Now, I'm sure you will all know who I shall call to the center to pay for the one forfeit she gained this evening."

At once, everyone turned to look at Poppy, who looked dazed for a moment, as if deep in thought. Then she blinked, smiled, and joined Mrs. Hawkins in the middle.

She faced the crowd with a tense smile, her eyes flicking away from Edmund's.

"All right, my dear," Mrs. Hawkins began, taking Poppy's hand, "as victorious as you have been this evening, Mrs. Trevethan and I believe it will be quite advantageous for you to share three pieces of advice to each player from this evening."

The crowd clapped, and Poppy's shoulders lowered a fraction, no doubt out of relief.

Edmund breathed a sigh of relief, too. Perhaps Mrs. Hawkins and Mrs. Trevethan wouldn't be requiring kissing this evening.

Poppy began her task as soon as Mrs. Hawkins left the circle, approaching each individual with three offers of advice before moving on to the next.

At first, her voice was soft, her advice stinted, but with each new person she spoke with, her spirits returned as she made the crowd laugh time and time again.

With the sun lowering in the sky—though sunset was still two hours out of reach—a golden light had slipped through the trees nearby, casting dancing patterns across her yellow dress as she moved from person to person.

Seeing her dressed without her working clothing was rare, and though Edmund could—and had—admired the woman in anything she wore, there was something about her that evening that pulled at him. Poppy, dressed in the color of the sunshine, was fitting. Stunning. Spellbinding.

And he didn't know what to do with that fact.

CHAPTER SEVENTEEN

*E*dmund watched with anticipation as Poppy moved around the circle, drawing closer and closer to him. Her advice for the women was fairly simple—suggestions of trying different colors of ribbons or to branch out from their daily routines to catch fish with a spear—but when she progressed to Cadan, Edmund's chest tightened.

"Now, Cadan," she said, shaking her head with an amused smile that Cadan instantly returned. "I don't know what I can say to ye, as ye be nearly perfect already."

The crowd laughed, but Edmund was fairly certain his own smile looked as forced as it felt.

"But I will say this," Poppy continued, "ne'er lose your ability to compliment a woman's food, as ye do it so well."

Edmund winced. Had that been a slight upon his own compliments? He supposed he could have mentioned her food over her ears.

She really did have fine ones, though. Especially when the tips of them poked out from her elegant hair that evening.

Cadan smiled like a schoolboy, looking up at Poppy with veritable stars in his eyes.

Edmund shifted uncomfortably in his seat.

"Next," she continued, "I think ye ought to wear a blue waistcoat more often, as it brings out the color o' your fine eyes."

Fine eyes? What were they, blue? Those were fairly close to green, were they not? Did she consider green eyes fine, too?

"And finally, ye must find it in yourself to be more competitive, as I do believe ye 'ave more forfeits than all o' we combined."

The crowd broke out into laughter again, even Edmund finding it impossible not to smile at her wit.

Cadan chuckled, as well. "You be right about that, Popp."

Popp? Edmund pulled a face. He, himself had never called Poppy the nickname only her family used. Did that mean Cadan was close to being family?

Finally, after four more turns, Poppy reached Edmund, and he looked up at her with as much confidence as he could muster, though his stomach was a flutter of butterflies.

Poppy, however, looked perfectly at ease. "Now for ye, Lieutenant Harris," she began, "I'd beg ye to learn to love stargazy pie." She turned to the crowd. "It be a Cornish staple, ain't it?"

Most of the lower class cheered loudly, and Edmund smiled with amusement.

"Me second piece of advice for ye is to avoid dogs who be out after a storm. I do 'ave it on good authority that they muddy shirts somethin' terrible."

The advice had been casual enough that no one would have thought she'd spoken of personal experience, but the look she shared with Edmund told him all he needed to know.

"Finally," she continued, her smile softening, "might I suggest that ye take time to walk barefooted in the sand again? It'll do your heart and your mind a world o' good."

The crowd delivered an audible, "Aw," then cheered with agreement to her advice.

She smiled at him, her eyes lingering a moment longer

than they had on anyone else before she moved to the next individual.

Edmund hardly heard her next piece of advice, his attention remaining on what she'd said to him. She may have been teasing at first, but that final suggestion...she had meant it sincerely, and he knew it.

He hadn't really thought about it until that moment, but he had yet to walk barefooted in the sand, when he typically had done so at least once a day when he'd convalesced the last time in Cornwall.

Granted, he was busier now than he had been before. But that was no excuse. He'd simply not made time for it, and somehow, Poppy had known.

The rest of the forfeits were paid over the course of the next half hour, Poppy swiftly finishing hers before the others were tasked with paying out their own.

Edmund had been required with a few other men to pay another forfeit in the center of the crowd as they pretended to be statues of Greek gods, pulling poses as suggested by the audience. That hadn't been as painful as he thought it would be, what with Poppy's cheers and laughter in his direction.

After that, he'd been able to sit back in his seat, enjoying all the others as they made quick fools out of themselves. He and Poppy shared comments every now and again, laughing together as Miss Lanyon was required to sit on Mr. Pethick's back as she rode around the circle.

Finally, with one forfeit to be paid by an unannounced gentleman, Mrs. Hawkins stood in the center of the crowd with an untamable smile.

"All right, my lovely friends and neighbors," she began, clasping her hands in front of her. "I regret to announce that this shall be our last forfeit. However, as I have received a number of requests from more than half of you, we shall end the evening with one that must be paid by playing Fishing for a Kiss."

Those beyond the circle cheered, while those *within* the circle were divided between looks of excitement and looks of dread. Edmund, however, settled farther back into his chair with a satisfied sigh.

He knew he was not the gentleman who had to pay another forfeit that evening, and since he knew he wouldn't have to watch Poppy doing so either, he could fully relax.

"Are we ready to see which of your men shall be called upon to proceed with the greatest of honors?" Mrs. Hawkins asked.

The crowd cheered, and she waited a moment longer before finally continuing. "Cadan Sholl," she announced.

Edmund clapped at first with the rest of the crowd. The man deserved this, after all, what with his failure to win a single game. But when Edmund noted Poppy's cheers and observed Cadan's willingness to fairly canter to the center of the circle without so much as a beat of hesitation, a knot settled in the pit of Edmund's stomach.

Mrs. Hawkins explained the rules of the game, and an odd ringing sensation in Edmund's ears occurred as she finally walked out of the circle, allowing Cadan to begin the game.

"Now," he started, repeating the lines Mrs. Hawkins had instructed him to recite, "who shall be my little fishy?"

Edmund's fingers tightened where he held them on his lap. He could see Poppy's amusement from the corner of his eye, her smile bright and posture relaxed as Cadan stood in the center, circling around slowly as he met each woman's gaze with a charming smile.

Edmund stifled a sigh. The man was certainly enjoying this attention, what with his blue eyes and his ability to like stargazy pie.

Of course, Edmund didn't really know if he liked the pie. But if Poppy made it, Cadan surely did.

Edmund forced his shoulders to relax. He didn't know

whom Cadan would choose. There was no use in worrying about it until—

"Ah," Cadan said. His eyes focused to Edmund's left, and Edmund's jaw tensed. "My favorite flower shall now be my favorite fishy."

The group laughed, whooping as Poppy was chosen, but Edmund could hardly draw a breath. He needed to get out of there. He couldn't sit through this.

And yet, all eyes were on Poppy and Cadan. If Edmund left, they would all know he took issue with her kissing another man—when he *shouldn't* take issue with it.

His only consolation was the fact that this was not Poppy's choice, it was Cadan's. It didn't speak anything as to what *she* wanted to do.

Cadan's slow approach to Poppy stole Edmund's attention once again, and Edmund folded his arms and leaned back in the chair, forcing a pleasant smile on his lips, though his insides were in turmoil.

Producing the makeshift fishing pole Mrs. Hawkins had fashioned for Cadan—a thread with one end tied to a twig and the other to a piece of barley sugar—he drew closer and closer.

Edmund couldn't help himself any longer. Stealing a quick glance at Poppy, he surmised her reaction to Cadan's intentions, instantly wishing he had not. Her eyes had been on Edmund, and he thought he witnessed a degree of hesitation within her. But in the next moment, she faced Cadan with an easy smile.

With his own happy grin, Cadan reached her, lowering the baited sugar into her mouth, which she accepted with a laugh. "That do be the finest bait I e'er tasted," she teased.

Edmund couldn't even bring himself to crack a smile.

Cadan raised a victorious arm in the air. "I have hooked her!" he exclaimed, still reciting the lines from the game. "A famous fish. What if it should prove a mermaid? Oh, how gloriously she nibbles. I..." He paused, his brow furrowing as he clearly forgot which lines to say next. More laughter ensued before Mrs. Hawkins fed him his words. "Ah, yes. I must take care not to lose her, as I am an old sportsman."

"Ye be losin' I soon as this bait be gone," Poppy joked again, her words puckered as she continued to suck on the sugar.

Cadan beamed. "Well, then there is nothing to be done with such a lovely fish, except by playing her oh, so...well." He finished his last words slowly, straying from the script and raising his eyebrows in a daring motion.

"Get on with it, then, ye old sportsman," she said, and the crowd laughed again.

Cadan removed the string from the stick, placing the other end of the thread into his mouth as he fed it through his lips and drew closer to Poppy, who remained seated.

Edmund's chest ached so greatly, he was no longer able to breathe. He tried to look away, tried to pull on a look of amusement like all the rest of the crowd, but his eyes once again darted to Poppy's.

She still held the sugar in her mouth, the wrinkles around her eyes revealing the smile she could not fully express. She'd sat straighter in her seat, as if leaning toward Cadan, and Edmund winced.

He had hoped she wouldn't accept the kiss. That she would have rejected Cadan as she had rejected...

But it was futile. She was clearly anticipating this kiss as much as Cadan was.

At the full realization of that fact, Edmund's heart cracked, splitting off from the small section he'd allowed to open before. The memories spilled forth without his permission, draining him from feelings until he was as dry as the sand untouched by the sea.

In his last moment with Poppy, after he'd offered her a home, a chance to start a new life with him. He'd foolishly, stupidly, leaned toward her to kiss her. But she had pulled back, turning her head to the sea and pretending she hadn't known what he'd been about to do.

Humiliated and overcome with regret, Edmund had instantly pulled away, unwilling to kiss her if she didn't wish to as well. But he'd been so confused. He'd as good as proposed to her, had already made plans to return a few months later when he could retire from the navy and spend weeks with his new wife. But she hadn't even wanted to kiss him.

So now, to see her willingly accepting—anticipating—Cadan's kiss…his heart couldn't bear it.

His stomach roiled, his chest burning hot as Cadan finally closed the distance between himself and Poppy.

The connection lasted only a moment, their lips pulling apart as the crowd expressed their delight over the sight with laughter and delightful hollering.

Poppy's cheeks were tinted with a bright pink as she grinned at Cadan, shaking her head in amusement. But Edmund hardly saw. White sparkles appeared in his eyes as his vision blurred. He drew a deep breath to calm his pounding heart.

"Did you like that, Popp?" Cadan asked with a wink.

She shrugged. "What, the barley sugar? Oh, yes. That be more 'an fine."

The crowd roared with laughter. Cadan took her hand in his, kissed the back of it, then took a bow to the applauding crowd.

Mrs. Hawkins stood, thanking her guests for participating and coming to Fynwary, but Edmund hardly heard her.

Had Poppy and Cadan kissed before? Was that why they'd both appeared so at ease?

He didn't realize he was still staring at her until her brown eyes met his. She still smiled from her moment with Caden, as if to say, *"I did tell ye that I'd moved on."*

How Edmund wished to respond with an unaffected smile,

but his lips refused to move. He'd said for so long he felt nothing for Poppy Honeysett any longer. But with his insides burning with jealousy and embarrassment, he knew he could no longer deny it.

He just didn't realize how badly it would hurt to see the proof right before his eyes. Poppy loved Cadan more than she'd ever loved Edmund. And the truth of that matter stung.

Never mind that she'd waited for him to return. He'd been foolish to even acknowledge his feelings returning for her.

Poppy's searching gaze brought him back to the present, but he couldn't bear it any longer. Standing abruptly, he stood from his seat and walked away without a word, though he felt her piercing gaze shooting into his back as he left.

He was finished. Finished with the party, finished with Cornwall, finished with Poppy. Finished with *feelings*.

He would wait out the remainder of his time at Golowduyn. He would help the Kendrickses. But he would no longer spend a single moment in that woman's presence.

He couldn't wait to leave this forsaken place. The sea was enough for him, and tonight was the perfect reminder as to why.

CHAPTER EIGHTEEN

*P*oppy watched Lieutenant Harris stomp away from the party, his head low as he stormed past the attendees until he ultimately disappeared around the house.

She knew she was imagining things. After all, she was prone to do so. But she couldn't help but think that he'd left because of her kiss with Cadan.

If she could even call what they did a 'kiss.' She'd barely made contact with his lips before they'd separated. Honestly, she'd kissed seashells longer than that when she was a child and found her first unbroken scallop shell.

And it wasn't as if she could have denied him that kiss, humiliating him in front of everyone and thereby owing another forfeit herself. No, accepting his small, hen-peck of a kiss had been the best thing she could've done.

"Poppy?"

She turned away from where the lieutenant had disappeared, facing Cadan as he approached her with a sheepish grin.

"There ye be, ye vellan," she said, swatting him playfully on the arm.

A few people glanced in their direction, and Cadan waited

until they left to respond. "I'm sorry about that, Popp," he said softly, still smiling with a half-grimace. "I figured you'd be the best girl to kiss since all the others…"

He finished with a shrug, but she knew exactly what he was trying to say. "Since all the other girls would think ye liked 'em."

"I knew you and I were good enough friends for there to be no misunderstanding."

He waited expectantly, and Poppy nodded at once. Cadan had made it very clear that he had no interest in falling for any girl in the coming years—at least not until he had established his own way of life.

At any rate, Poppy was fine with that, as she and Cadan were better as friends than anything else. She could never fall for a man who didn't have a competitive bone in his body.

"No misunderstandin' at all, Cadan," she reassured him.

Then she paused. Well, there'd been no misunderstanding at least on her part. Lieutenant Harris, on the other hand…

"I'll make it up to you, I swear," Cadan said. "I won't pinch any of your desserts for a week." She gave him a look of disbelief, and he smiled. "All right, a day."

She laughed, then he placed a kiss to the back of her hand once again before backing away. "I'm on duty at the light-house tonight, otherwise I'd love to stay and chat. You enjoy yourself tonight, flower."

Then he was gone, taking his boundless energy with him as he crossed over the fields. Would he meet Lieutenant Harris on the way back to Golowduyn?

She sighed, her mind returning to the lieutenant. She knew she'd seen anger on his face—just as clearly as she knew he'd been terribly discomfited as Cadan drew nearer to her. Did that prove that Lieutenant Harris was envious of Cadan kissing her? She didn't know what else it would be. Unless he was simply hurt that she'd never kissed him.

But then, surely he would not even remember such a fact.

It had been so long ago. She'd only pulled away because she didn't know if she could leave Cornwall for him and didn't wish to lead him on. But now, that non-existent kiss had become one of her greatest regrets.

Her worried musings continued throughout the rest of the gathering until the sun began to set and the party dispersed. Poppy walked home with Morvoren as the two discussed the party.

Finally, and expectedly, Morvoren's tone lowered, though they walked alone across the countryside. "'E was watchin' ye," she said.

Poppy didn't have to ask who Morvoren was referring to. "I know."

She'd seen from the corner of her eye how Lieutenant Harris had shifted away from her and Cadan, how his arms were flexed as he folded them, his lips in a rigid line.

"I just don't know why 'e be so upset," Poppy said.

"'Cause 'e didn't like seein' ye kiss another man, that be why."

Poppy hesitated. "Even be that true, it don't mean anythin'. I still want to stay 'ere, and 'e still wants to remain at sea."

Morvoren tipped her head back and forth, though she said nothing.

"What?" Poppy pressed.

"I don't want to encourage ye like I did the last time and cause ye to be injured again. But...no one can e'er know why a man behaves the way 'e does when 'e be in love."

Poppy's shoulders lowered. "But that be just the problem. 'E doesn't love I."

Morvoren softened. "No one knows the inner workin's of another's heart. I s'pose all we can know is our own."

The words settled over Poppy, seeping into her mind well into the evening and throughout the night when she should have been fast asleep.

She lay awake in bed, staring up at the shadows cast on the ceiling from the small fire in the hearth. There had been moments at the Hawkins's that evening, moments where her eyes had connected with Lieutenant Harris's and the past seemed to collide with the present. Moments where she thought, just maybe, they could put their heartaches behind them.

Then that kiss with Cadan had occurred.

Either way, Morvoren was right. No one could know the workings of another's heart. But Poppy did know her own. And only now could she acknowledge that she hadn't moved beyond her feelings for the lieutenant after all.

The following morning, with her knowledge of her own feelings coming to fruition, Poppy had every intention of determining for herself how Lieutenant Harris felt. But with the rain pouring down for hours on end, and with the lieutenant in the tower watching over the lamps, she never got the chance.

Knowing there was nothing else to be done about the matter that day, she left Golowduyn with Isolde. Fortunately, for their sake, the rain had finally let up in the later afternoon, though not early enough to prevent the both of them from having to traipse across sopping fields and muddy pathways.

"What song ought we to sing now, Issy?" Poppy asked, helping her niece sidestep yet another puddle.

"'Bout duh mermaids?"

Poppy smiled. "Excellent choice." She took a deep breath, eying the raindrops still clinging to the blue cornflowers sparkling like sapphires. "'There's a mermaid I know who's as fine as can be. She dwells at the far end of the deep, blue sea with her coral red hair, and her seaweed green eyes, and a tail that stretches straight up to her thighs.'"

Isolde caught a word now and then, but mostly she sang off-tune in mere gibberish that pulled a smile on Poppy's lips.

"'Beware the maid o' the sea,'" she continued, swinging Isolde's arm playfully back and forth. She glanced out to the sea, the water seeming to glisten all the brighter now that the clouds had mostly dispersed. "'She's as wicked as wicked can be. With her siren's voice, she gives men no choice to fall for a maid as treacherous as—'"

"Poppy?"

Poppy gasped, whirling around and bringing Isolde along with her. Lieutenant Harris walked toward her with a stern expression.

For how long had he been following her? Her singing and the sea below must have drowned out any possibility of hearing him.

"Lieutenant 'Arris," she greeted as chipperly as she could manage. Such a task was difficult, though, what with the scowl that marked his brow. "Ye be needin' somthin'?"

Isolde tugged on her hand. "We see Mama now?"

"Just one moment, love," Poppy responded before facing the lieutenant again.

He drew a step closer, extending a folded correspondence to her with his free hand. "A letter for your brother. From Mr. Kendricks."

She stared at the folded paper, accepting it as the lieutenant immediately backed away.

She frowned. That was it? He would say nothing further to her? "'Ave ye any idea what it be about?" she asked, raising the letter in the air. If he wouldn't speak with her, perhaps she'd make him.

Lieutenant Harris paused, though he still remained a few paces away from her. "I believe it is in reference to Tristwick." He gave a nod to signal his departure, then turned to leave once again.

"Auntie," Isolde said, tugging on Poppy's hand again.

"Just one moment," she repeated softly, then she called after the lieutenant again. "Where did ye leave last night in such a rush?"

He stopped, hesitated, then turned toward her once more. "I returned to Golowduyn to see if I could offer my services to Mr. Kendricks, as no one else was there to do so."

Poppy narrowed her eyes. Had he meant that as pointedly as it had sounded? "Ye be referrin' to Cadan?"

His silence was answer enough.

"I'm sure ye noticed that 'e left for the lighthouse soon after ye did."

He looked away, clearing his throat with impatience. "Yes, I am aware." He shifted his body away from her, signaling his desire to end the conversation once again.

But she wasn't quite finished with her snooping. "So ye didn't leave 'cause of I? Or anythin' I did?"

"No, of course not." He smoothed out the sling along his left arm, seeming to favor the limb more than he had before. "So you'll see that the letter is delivered to your brother? Mr. Kendricks wished for it to be handed to him directly."

She knew he was trying to distract her from their conversation. Little did he know, she wished to pursue this topic, as well. "Ought ye not give it to 'im yourself?"

He gave a haughty look of amusement. "I think it better for me to not appear before your brother again, for obvious reasons."

He was hinting at what had occurred between them. She was sure of it. And blast, if it didn't increase her curiosity all the more.

"Why be that, then? Do ye not wish to see me brother?"

He looked at her without flinching. "It is more that he does not wish to see me."

She thought back to the moments she'd seen them scuffling over the ball during the hurling. Had more happened beyond the pushing?

"Did the two of ye quarrel yesterday?"

"I suppose you could say that."

He was not being very forthright, was he? Well, it was no matter. It would not take much to assume what had occurred between her brother and the lieutenant.

"Auntie Poppy," Isolde said, tugging at her hand again. "See Mama?" She took a few steps away, attempting to pull Poppy along with her.

Poppy held fast to her hand. "Yes, Issy. I promise. One moment." Isolde frowned, her little blonde eyebrows pulling together. But Poppy looked back up to the lieutenant. "Trevik be under a great deal o' stress," she explained, choosing her words carefully. "When 'e feels like 'is family and 'is 'ome be under attack, 'e does whate'er it takes to protect 'em."

"Yes, I'm well aware of your brother's actions, thank you. But if he truly wishes to protect Tristwick, perhaps he ought to focus his energy on accepting help from others, as opposed to living in the past."

Poppy narrowed her eyes. What was he on about?

But the lieutenant clearly did not wish to continue. He motioned to Isolde. "Are you finished with your interrogation yet? I believe you have a niece who wishes to leave."

She frowned. As if he had the right to tell her how to watch over her own family. Instead of being distracted by his words once again, Poppy focused her attention on what he'd said before. "Trevik do be acceptin' 'elp from others. None o' we want Tristwick to change, so we all be doin' what it takes."

He had the audacity to scoff.

"What be that for, then?" she asked, her patience thinning.

His jaw twitched. "If you ask me, neither of you seem very concerned at all about Tristwick."

"Be that so?" she challenged.

"Yes," he said, his eyes honing in on hers. "Because if Trevik was concerned with helping Tristwick, perhaps he would take my suggestions instead of pushing me down an alley and commanding me to leave." He leaned toward her. "And if you were concerned with helping Tristwick, perhaps you ought to do more than stare out at the sea and kiss half the men in Cornwall."

Poppy flinched, his words digging into her heart. How could he say such cruel words? Had he not just complimented her the night before about staring out at the sea? Besides, she *was* doing more than that. The sea merely helped her feel at peace. And Trevik…

"Auntie Poppy?"

Poppy shook her head, only vaguely aware of Isolde's continuous tugging on her hand. Unfortunately, Poppy wouldn't be surprised if Trevik had pushed the lieutenant down an alleyway. Her brother had not been himself lately. It was no excuse, of course, but it was certainly a reason.

As for his accusations against her, she could hardly believe his boldness.

Lieutenant Harris ran his fingers through his hair and backed away. "This conversation is futile. Please, forget I even started it."

But Poppy could not. "Ye cannot leave after accusin' me family o' such things, sir. Ye at least ought to allow me the chance to defend meself."

"You do not need to," he stated. "I already understand you perfectly."

"No, ye don't," she said, anger steaming up inside of her. "First of all, I ain't kissin' 'alf the men in Cornwall."

His eyebrows rose in doubt.

"And what's it to ye if I do?"

He shrugged. "Nothing at all."

She could see the truth in his expression, the irritation in his green eyes. "Really? 'Cause it seems to I that it bothers ye a great deal. I just can't figure out why."

"It doesn't bother me at all."

"Auntie Poppy!" Isolde's voice hit a pitch higher as she

tugged harder and harder on Poppy's hands until finally, she slipped free. "I see Mama," she said with a stubborn frown.

"Yes, I just need to speak one minute more."

But Isolde stomped down the pathway. Poppy couldn't be frustrated with the girl who clearly could not give a care about her auntie's drama with this naval officer.

The cliffs they stood upon did not drop directly to the sea, but undulating hills scattered with rocks and drops eventually led to the churning waves and treacherous cliffs below. All the same, Poppy couldn't let the girl go alone, especially with the slippery pathway.

Her argument with Lieutenant Harris would simply have to be wrapped up more swiftly.

She turned back to face him, walking backward toward Isolde. "If ye ain't bothered 'bout whom I kiss, then why did ye really leave early last night? And why were ye so angry when Cadan kissed I?"

The pain that flickered across his features—though veiled quickly by a mere frown—stunned her into silence. She'd...hurt him?

"As I said." His voice was deep and slow and dangerous. "We shouldn't have even started this conversation. I—" He stopped abruptly, his eyes flickering over Poppy's shoulder before widening in panic. "Wait! Isolde, stop!"

Poppy whirled around, fear rippling down her insides the moment she caught sight of her niece, leaning close to the edge of the cliffside to smell a yellow flower, the mud beneath her shoes already beginning to slip.

"Isolde!" Poppy screamed, but it was too late. In the next moment, the girl slipped over the edge, and her screams pierced the silent air.

CHAPTER NINETEEN

*P*oppy was the first to race toward the little girl, but Edmund wasn't two steps behind her. Fear clawed at him like a wild animal, his heart ramming against his chest. If only he hadn't started that conversation with Poppy, if only they'd both been watching the girl instead of arguing, this never would have happened.

Before they reached the edge, Isolde's screams grew silent, and Poppy's legs pumped faster.

"Isolde!" she cried out again.

Edmund caught sight of the mud Isolde had slid down. If Poppy didn't stop soon, she'd slide right after the girl.

Swiftly, he reached out with his right hand, feeling the twinge in his left arm as he strained forward. Grasping his hand around her upper arm, he stopped her.

"Let go!" she cried out, wrenching her arm free.

"If you don't stop, you'll both be hurt," he said swiftly, trying to stop her again.

Finally, she listened, slowing her pace as she neared the edge.

How had Isolde gone so far in such a short amount of

time? And how—*how*—could they have allowed this to happen?

Carefully, they inched forward, peering over the cliff's edge to see the steep decline covered in large boulders and carpeted with grass.

At the second boulder farthest away from them lay Isolde, a spot of red already appearing in her blonde locks.

"No!" Poppy cried, tears streaming down her eyes. "Isolde!"

The girl remained still.

That was all it took for Poppy to begin moving again, taking a step toward the mud, clearly intent on retrieving her niece herself, but again, Edmund stopped her.

She whirled around to face him, anger pursing her brow.

Instantly, he released his hold of her. "You'll injure yourself," he stated, motioning to her long, blue skirts.

She raised them up without hesitation, but he shook his head again. "I will retrieve her myself."

She paused, surprise flickering across her features as she glanced down to Isolde, then back to his arm in a sling. "Ye'll be no good with that."

"I wear it only as a reminder to not use it so very often," he lied, motioning to the sling. "I can bring her back safely. I swear to you, I will."

She stared into his eyes, a battle clearly raging within her until she finally nodded.

"Please do," she relented, then she took a step back and allowed him passage to the cliff's edge.

As carefully and swiftly as he could manage, Edmund stepped toward the thick mud, Isolde's small footprints disappearing as his boots stepped atop them.

He slipped a time or two, Poppy's gasp from the clifftop reaching his ears before he righted himself each time. Fortunately, there was still a thick layer of grass attached to the cliffside, so he secured himself on the blades as he slipped and slid his way down.

Finally, after nearly falling another time and only just catching himself in the mud—a shock of pain shooting up his left arm—Edmund reached the girl still unconscious on the boulder.

"Be she breathin'?" Poppy called from above.

Edmund knelt down beside her, noting at once the slight movement of her chest and stomach. "Yes!"

He felt her pulse in her wrist—faint, but noticeable—then assessed her as best as he could. He knew from his days at sea that moving a person who'd suffered a fall like this could injure them further. So how could he move Isolde and risk that happening?

"Isolde?" he said softly, brushing her hair back from her face to see the wound to her brow. He couldn't tell with the amount of blood, but the gash looked deep. Deep enough to need sutures? He couldn't be sure.

Isolde moaned, and he pulled back, staring at her intently as she shifted.

"Hold still, darling," he instructed, but the girl moved her head back and forth without crying out in pain.

Relief filled him to know she was not further injured, but they were not out of deep waters yet.

"Be she well?" came Poppy's worried question from above.

He nodded. "As well as can be expected."

"Praise 'eavens. Isolde? We be gettin' ye back to Mama now!"

Isolde whimpered.

Removing his sling from around his neck, Edmund tied it round Isolde's head to keep it secure near the wound. "I'm going to pick you up now, all right? Nice and easy. Then we'll get you home to your mama."

She didn't respond, and Edmund wondered if she was cognizant of anything that had occurred.

Carefully, he assessed her arms and legs once more before lifting her up. Though she was light, Edmund's arm protested in pain, no doubt thanks to his scuffle with Trevik the day before.

That had been caused by his inability to stop himself from arguing, as well. This incident would simply push the final nail into his coffin.

With far less stability and speed than sliding down the cliff-side, Edmund clambered his way back up, praying fervently with each step he took that he maintained his stance. Using Poppy's watchful gaze as his anchor, he finally reached the top.

Poppy's eyes were red with tears. "I need to get 'er 'ome," she said, smoothing the girl's hair from her brow as she sniffed.

Edmund shook his head. "She needs to see a physician. Swiftly. You are the faster runner, Poppy. Find Dr. Kent, and I will bring her back to Tristwick."

Again, fear flashed deep within her eyes. There really was no reason for her to trust him, and his heart ached at the real-ization.

"What about your arm?" she asked.

He shook his head. "She's as light as a feather."

Again, she hesitated, her eyes boring into his. "Ye prom-ise?" she breathed.

Edmund swallowed hard. "Yes. I promise."

She nodded, then without a glance back, fled down the pathway. Mud flew out behind her, kicking up from her boots, and the letter he'd given her to deliver to Trevik was still clutched tightly in her hand.

His heart swelled uncomfortably in his chest at the weight of responsibility given to him. Poppy trusted him. After all this time, after all that had occurred, she trusted him.

This time, he would not fail her.

The journey to Tristwick was exhausting. Isolde's weight—though light as she was—grew heavier against his arms with each step he took, his left arm throbbing. The girl began to cry halfway across the cliffsides, though whether from fear or pain, Edmund couldn't be sure. He tried to whisper words of comfort to her, but he knew the girl needed medical attention —and her family.

With gritted teeth and focused eyes, Edmund continued forward, refusing to dwell on his protesting muscles and his fear over the girl's continued safety until finally, Tristwick's stone houses came into view.

Spurred on by the sight, he skittered past the cellars and empty houses until he reached the Honeysett's home.

"Trevik!" he called out, kicking the door with his boot. "Mrs. Honeysett!"

Isolde's cries had grown since he'd climbed the hill, and Edmund winced.

Please, please be at home.

In the next moment, footsteps sounded, and a bewildered Morvoren opened the door. She took one look at Edmund before her eyes fell on her daughter. Instantly, she dropped the rag from her hands and shot toward them.

"Oh my—Trevik!" she screamed over her shoulder, taking Isolde in her arms at once. "What 'appened?"

Isolde clung to her mother as Edmund swiftly explained how she'd slid down the cliffside, Morvoren lifting his sling to peer at Isolde's wounded head.

"I can't be certain of anywhere else she may be injured," he said helplessly.

Trevik came around the corridor, appearing in the doorway. He frowned at Edmund, then fear flashed across his features as he took in the sight of Isolde in her mother's arms.

"She fell down the cliffside," Morvoren said.

Trevik didn't look away from his daughter. "We must clean the wound," he said, leading her back into the house. "I'll run for Dr. Kent."

"Poppy is already on her way there," Edmund interjected.

Trevik's eyes fell on Edmund, but in the next moment, he disappeared into the back of the house with Morvoren and Isolde swiftly in tow.

Edmund stood there alone, his breathing heavy from exertion. Not a minute passed by before Poppy appeared around the ridge next, followed closely by Dr. Kent.

"She found me on my way back from the lighthouse," Dr. Kent explained, jogging forward. "Where is the little girl?"

"They've already taken her to bed," Edmund explained.

Dr. Kent delivered a brief nod, then entered the home. Poppy did the very same, though she took a moment to glance at Edmund with a quick, "Thank ye, sir," before she disappeared within the house, as well.

A stillness filled the air once Edmund was alone—a deafening silence not even the sea could drown out. Slowly, he reached forward, closing the door to the Honeysett home as he stood outside of it.

That was where he belonged—always on the outside looking in, whether it be a home or a family.

With slow steps, he made his way back to the lighthouse, yet another location he had no permanent attachment to. He wanted to stay in Tristwick to ensure Isolde was well. After all, he'd been the cause of her fall. But he knew his presence would merely be a sore reminder of what had happened.

How could he have been so foolish? Goading Poppy about kissing Cadan, pretending he didn't take issue with it. He was completely unhinged. An utter embarrassment. Just like he had been as a child.

His mother's words echoed in his mind, filling him with more shame.

"Why must you always embarrass the family, Edmund?"

"Why can you not be more like your brothers?"

"Why must you always force the firm hand of discipline as the only way in which you will not humiliate your mother?"

He never allowed his mother's words to take residence in

his mind, but tonight he deserved them. He'd put a child's life in grave danger simply because of his selfish desires.

And because of that, he deserved to be berated.

Edmund avoided the others at Golowduyn after telling them what had occurred. He knew the Kendricks's didn't blame him, but he couldn't bear anymore consoling words as he hunkered down in his room and pretended to retire early.

Since he'd watched the lamp all day throughout the storm, Edmund had the evening off, having every intention of catching up on his rest. But when sleep evaded him—the clock chiming a mere six o'clock—he snuck away from the house and headed to St. Just, seeking to numb his feelings at the inn.

However, after one sip of brandy, he put the glass down and didn't pick it back up. He didn't deserve any of this relief, as temporary as it would be. He deserved to remain fully aware of his actions. He deserved to feel the ache in his arm that now hung at his side instead of being held up by his sling.

After declining an invitation to play a game of cards—and being approached by a woman with red lips—he left the inn no better than when he'd arrived.

It was just as well. He knew only one thing would give him some semblance of peace, and though he still didn't believe he deserved it, he had to know for himself if the little girl was all right.

Now to pray Trevik didn't kill him for returning.

Edmund made his way slowly across the countryside, the rain having begun again as just a misting, though it covered the pathway in mud, providing even more of a reminder of how he'd failed the Honeysett family.

His guilt increased tenfold by the time he reached their home, so much so that he simply could not get himself to even knock.

What was he doing there? He was nothing special to this family. Surely he would receive news of Isolde's status alongside the rest of Honeysett's acquaintances when they saw fit.

"You were always daft, boy."

His mother's raspy tone slipped into his thoughts, and he backed away from the door.

Before he could take another step, however, the door opened, and Morvoren drew back with a short gasp. "Oh! Lieutenant." She paused. "Did ye knock?"

Her eyes were red and swollen, but a soft smile curved her lips. Did that mean…

"No, I did not," he replied.

She waited before opening the door wider. "Will ye come in from the rain?"

He raised a hand to decline her offer. "No, thank you. I do not wish to bother you. I only came to see if Isolde…"

His breath caught in his throat as Trevik joined his wife, a deep crevice down the center of his forehead.

"Lieutenant 'Arris came to see 'ow Issy be," Morvoren said with careful words.

Trevik merely eyed Edmund in silence.

Edmund knew he shouldn't have come. After all, hadn't Trevik threatened him over and over again not to hurt his family? Now that he had, would Trevik finish what he'd begun in the alleyway in St. Just?

Frankly, Edmund would be relieved if he did. He deserved it.

Trevik drew a deep breath. "Isolde be well. Dr. Kent did say she'll make a full recovery." He paused. "We 'ear that be thanks to ye."

Edmund cleared his throat. "I did nothing but carry your daughter here."

"Me sister said ye retrieved 'er from the cliffside yourself, to keep Popp and Isolde safe."

Edmund paused, using his right hand to subconsciously rub at his aching left arm. "That may be true, but I was also the one who pulled Poppy's attention away from your daughter to begin with. She might not have fallen had I not been there, and I...I cannot express my regret enough for playing a part in her injury."

Morvoren shook her head. "Poppy already tried takin' full responsibility. But we don't blame either of ye. We know 'ow easy it be to lose track of a child. Don't we, Trev?"

The woman was a veritable angel. He was nowhere near deserving of such kindness.

Fortunately, Trevik was there to bring him straight back down to earth. He merely grunted in response to his wife, then slunk back inside the house without another word.

Well, at least Edmund hadn't been beaten to death.

"'E be goin' through a lot," Morvoren explained with an apologetic wince, motioning to where her husband had left.

"I understand. I've injured far too many in his family for him to ever forgive me."

She looked very much as if she wished to protest his words, but she couldn't. Because they were the truth. He'd caused Isolde to fall, and he'd broken Poppy's heart.

At the thought of the woman, his eyes involuntarily looked past Morvoren into the home, but he pulled them away. Poppy no doubt wished to avoid him, as well.

"She ain't 'ere," Morvoren said with a knowing look.

Was he truly so transparent?

"She left 'ome 'bout an hour ago," Morvoren continued. "I don't know where she left to, but we know she be takin' a lot o' the blame on 'erself."

Edmund's shoulders fell. That wasn't right. She should be feeling nothing but anger toward Edmund.

"If ye 'appen to find 'er, would ye mind seein' that she comes 'ome safe?" Morvoren asked next.

Edmund hesitated. If Trevik knew his wife was asking

Edmund to seek out Poppy, surely he'd have something to say about it.

Still, Edmund had every intention of finding the woman as soon as possible, if only to alleviate her guilt. "I will," he agreed.

Morvoren gave him a grateful nod, then Edmund turned to depart. The door closed, but he only managed a few steps before it opened again.

Edmund faced whom he assumed would be Morvoren again, but his palms clammed up as Trevik emerged instead.

He approached Edmund with a stoic expression, extending a dark blue piece of cloth to him. "I believe this be yours."

Edmund's sling. He'd forgotten about it, despite the ever-present ache in his arm. "Thank you," he said, accepting the fabric.

"Me mother washed it clean of Isolde's blood. That be why it's wet."

Edmund's heart pinched. He looked up at Trevik, the man's eyes guarded, as usual. But Edmund couldn't bear it any longer. He needed to say something, to clear the air between them, or he was going to burst.

He faced Trevik with all the humility and sincerity he could muster before beginning. "Trevik, I am truly sorry for what occurred between Poppy and me, and for what happened to Isolde." He swallowed. "I know we haven't been friends for some time now, nor do I expect you to ever befriend me again, but I hope you know, I would never intentionally hurt any member of your family. I am only sorry that I have done so. I do not expect forgiveness, but I...I just wished you to know."

Trevik's lips remained in a straight line, his eyes stalwart and hard, just as Edmund expected.

But he had said his piece, and nothing more could be done about—

Trevik offered his hand to Edmund, succinctly ending his thoughts. Unsure of what was even occurring, Edmund accepted the fisherman's hand, firmly shaking it as emotion rose within his throat.

"Thank ye for savin' me daugh'er," Trevik said. "And for ensurin' Poppy didn't go down that cliffside 'erself.'"

Edmund could only muster a nod in response. The handshake was over just as swiftly as it had begun. Trevik pulled back and slipped inside his house without another glance, leaving Edmund in stunned silence.

He could only imagine what it must have taken for Trevik to do such a thing. After all, he'd been upset with Edmund for nearly six years now. But then, what were old quarrels when compared to the safety of his family?

Slowly, Edmund turned away from the Honeysett home, following the pathway as his eyes continually surveyed the beaches and cliffsides, searching for any sight of Poppy.

Soon enough, just as he'd expected, he found her sitting on Tregalwen Beach, the water just out of reach from her location on the sand. He couldn't see her face from his vantage point, nor could he be certain the brown coat she wore was hers, but he knew in his heart she was Poppy. No one else would find solace in the cold rain at the edge of the sea.

Edmund winced. There would be no more putting this off. It was time to fix what he'd been foolish enough to create.

CHAPTER TWENTY

Somehow, Poppy knew she was being watched before Lieutenant Harris even reached her.

"Did me family send ye out 'ere?" she asked the moment he appeared in the corner of her eye. She sat in the sand, her attention fixed on the storming seas.

He hesitated. "How did you know?"

She pulled her legs up, wrapping her arms around them and resting her chin on her knees as she shrugged in silence.

"They are worried about you."

And rightly so. Poppy hadn't felt this low since Father had died and Lieutenant Harris had left. If only Father were there now. He'd wrap her up in his comforting embrace and let her know that all would be well. He'd know just what to say to remove the darkness, even if it was simply to watch the sunset together or eat milk cake with tea.

But she had a duty now to remove the darkness herself. She simply could not allow it to stay, no matter how horrible she felt for nearly causing the death of her own niece. Trevik and Morvoren both said no one was to blame in the situation, but Poppy would never forgive herself.

"I'll return 'ome soon," she responded, mumbling into her arms. "Ye be free o' your duty to find me now."

For so long, she'd attempted to be around the man, to extend their time together, if only for a moment. But what good had that ever done? She wanted him to leave now, before something else occurred that they'd both regret. Another argument, another fight. Another moment where she began to question her choice to not be with him.

She shook her head. His presence in Cornwall was too confusing. Too painful. A mere constant reminder of how her life had once been so close to perfection, never to be realized.

"Do you mind if I stay a moment?" Lieutenant Harris asked.

She hesitated but ultimately shook her head without a word.

He sat down beside her, the water from the sea-soaked sand no doubt rushing straight through his breeches.

Together, they sat in silence, Poppy pulling her coat more tightly around her shoulders to ward off the chill that had taken to the air.

She did not know why he wished to remain, but she didn't have the energy to explore such a question. Instead, she focused on the crashing waves.

The sun was hidden behind swollen clouds and sea mist, cloaking the earth in a dim, grey light. Such a moody setting had been known to draw many a spirit lower, but the contrary occurred within Poppy. The lessened light was merely a thick blanket that spread calm and peace across her soul.

Fierce winds picked up the water in powerful, unending movements, sea spray lingering in impenetrable mists. The roaring waves overpowered her senses, drowning out all other thoughts as moisture ran down her cheeks, her tears mingling with rain like the old friends they were.

"You must be pleased Isolde is well," Lieutenant Harris said, his deep voice soft, though raised to be heard above the rushing water. He sat with his feet planted on the ground, his back slightly hunched forward as his arms rested over his bent knees to link in the middle. "I called to see how she fared."

Poppy focused harder on the rushing waves. "Did they give ye back your sling?"

He nodded, pulling it out from inside his jacket, the cloth limp from its dampness.

"It be nice of ye to use it on Isolde."

"It was the least I could do, seeing that I was the one at fault."

Poppy frowned, looking up at him. Only then did she realize how closely he'd chosen to sit beside her, their shoulders a mere few inches apart. "Twasn't your fault, Lieutenant. It be I, and I alone, who be tasked to watch o'er 'er today."

"But you surely cannot deny the fact that, had I not been there to upset you and distract you and provoke you, you would have never let her out of your sight."

Tears filled her eyes again, the realization of what had occurred—and what might have occurred—overcoming her once more.

"You see?" Lieutenant Harris said softly. "You are not to be blamed for what occurred, Poppy. I am." He blew out a sigh, running his fingers through his wet hair. "I am to be blamed for all of it."

Poppy hesitated, wishing to look away from him, afraid of what staring at him might do to her heart, but she couldn't help herself any longer.

She allowed her eyes to trail over his features, so close she could see the raindrops clinging to his eyelashes and the wrinkle lines at the edges of his eyes as he peered out to the sea. His jaw was shaded with whiskers unshaven from the night before, and his green eyes were darker, wearier than she'd ever seen them.

"I must apologize, Poppy," he said, his deep voice slow. "For provoking you. For my unkindness. For the ungenerosity

I've treated you with since my return. I was always told by my mother that I had a sharp tongue, but I..." He paused, seeming to think better of his words as he shook his head.

Poppy's ears perked. He'd only ever mentioned his two brothers and father in passing when she'd pressed him for information on his family years before, and something about his mother pushing him to the sea. Apparently, he'd lost all contact with them.

Clearly, he regretted speaking of his mother now, but what she still couldn't understand was why. What had happened between him and his family members to have created such a division?

Instead of receiving any answers, Poppy held her tongue, listening to Lieutenant Harris as he continued.

He hung his head and stared at his hands still clasped together, his fingers now covered with rain that slid down the strong lines of his knuckles.

"I never should have come back here without informing you of my intention to do so," he said. "It was unfair of me to disrupt your life and your family's, especially during this difficult time. And for that, I am truly sorry."

The warmth caused by Edmund's unexpected words tried to pull Poppy up from the depths she'd found herself in, but she dampened them with cool logic. She couldn't keep dragging herself back and forth from the past to the present. He might be apologizing, but that meant nothing for the state of their future.

Still, the sincerity within the depths of his eyes overcame her so greatly, she had to look away.

"Thank ye," she said. "I be sorry for me own words and actions. I do think neither o' we 'ave been on our best behavior."

"No, indeed."

They sat in silence, a wave slamming against the beach in front of them, spraying mist across the sand.

"Did you really wait for me to return all those years?" Edmund's question cut through the air, settling around her shoulders as a heavy weight.

Her instinct was to play naïve, to deny the very fact that she knew exactly of what he spoke. But the load she'd carried for over three years depleted her resolve.

"Yes," she replied in hushed tones. "I did."

Admitting the truth brought forth untapped feelings, as if she was watching him leave Cornwall all over again, and her grief pulled more tears from her eyes.

Lieutenant Harris's shoulders lowered. "I…I didn't know."

His words were simple, but they were shattered, broken. Somehow, she knew he felt remorse for putting her through such anguish. Yet she could not be angry, not when she'd wounded him in return.

"I know ye didn't," she said softly. "But ye don't 'ave to feel badly 'cause of it. It was me own fault, me own baseless 'ope. I knew from your letter that ye didn't know if ye'd return, so I 'ad no reason to believe that ye would. But still I…"

"Still, you waited," he finished, no question in his words.

She nodded. "Like a fool."

He frowned, shaking his head. "I should have been forthright with you so you could have moved on sooner."

She nearly laughed, mirthless and biting. Moved on sooner? The man had been deceived by her words. She had not moved on. Not even the slightest amount. She still considered often how her life might have been different if she had married Lieutenant Harris and moved to Derbyshire. She'd be with the man she loved, perhaps would have a child of her own, and she'd be running a household without a care in the world.

But as per usual, the same question always came into her mind—where would she be without the sea? Without Tristwick and her family?

And yet, another question slipped into her thoughts, one she had not dared to ask herself until now.

Where was she without Edmund Harris?

Silence settled between them again, the sulking seas and darkening skies lending itself further to Poppy's mood. She may have felt peace with such weather, but nothing could improve the sorrow now hanging above her like her own personal storm.

"I missed ye," she said, the words slipping past her lips before she could stop them. Her voice broke as she spoke, unleashing the flood she'd kept behind her closed-off heart for years. "I missed ye more than I could bear. The months apart were fine enough to 'andle when I knew ye were comin' back, but the second time ye left…" She broke off, shaking her head. "And now that ye be in Cornwall again, it be e'en more painful, 'cause ye *ain't* 'ere. Not really. I know we can't turn back time. I know we can't be what we were, but I wish…I only wish we could be friends again. 'Fore it all got too complicated to maneuver 'round."

She finished, refusing to allow herself to be embarrassed for sharing the truth. Even if Lieutenant Harris walked away right then without a word, she would not regret speaking of how she felt, as those words had been begging to be released since the moment she first saw him back at Golowduyn.

"Well, then," he finally said, looking at her over his shoulder, "perhaps that is exactly what we ought to be."

Their gazes met, and she drew a steadying breath at the softness that had appeared in his green eyes.

"Be that even possible, after everythin'?" she asked, not wishing to pursue false hope yet again.

His eyes took on a faraway look. "I would like for it to be so," he said softly, fiddling with the sling still in his hands. "Because truth be told, I missed you, as well. I miss you *still*."

Poppy's breath was snatched away from her. He missed her? Lieutenant Harris missed her? She knew a friendship with him wasn't what she wished for in the deepest parts of her heart, but surely it was better than what they were before —acquaintances, or even, at times, enemies.

"When I first left Cornwall," he continued, his voice as soothing as the sea's waves, "I thought of you night and day. The second time I left, I refused to think of you at all, though months passed before I could fall asleep without envisioning you in my mind." He glanced at her sidelong. "We attempted to move beyond friendship, but perhaps that was our mistake all along. Perhaps remaining friends—being what we were in the beginning—would be the best for us both."

Poppy should have been elated by his words. After all, she now discovered that he did not despise her.

But then, hearing how he'd regretted falling for her in the first place was nearly too much for her to bear. Especially when he was wrong. She never started off as his friend. She'd been in love with him from the moment she'd laid eyes on him. She was in love with him *still*.

So how would a friendship work between them if she wanted so much more than that?

"Would you like that, then, Poppy? To be friends again?"

The answer was simple. She did not. But if the choice was between having Lieutenant Harris as a friend or having no part of him at all, she knew what she would choose.

"I would," she said softly, giving him a smile.

"Then it is settled. We shall be friends again. That is, so long as Cadan does not oppose."

Her brow furrowed. "Why should 'is opinion matter on this?"

He shrugged. "The two of you seem to be...I merely assumed..."

He left his sentence open, clearly wanting her to either affirm or refute his words. Poppy had a mind to let him wonder a bit longer, but then, if they were friends, surely she should no longer do such a thing.

"Cadan and I be friends," she said simply. "And that kiss ye saw 'tween us was our first—and dare I say, last—that shall e'er occur."

He leaned back, watching her to see if she was in earnest.

"And to answer your previous question," she continued, "no, I 'aven't kissed 'alf the men in Cornwall."

He winced. "Yet more words I fear I must apologize for."

Poppy gave a flippant raise of her shoulder. "It matters not, now we be friends."

Lieutenant Harris nodded, and they both took to staring out at the sea once again. "So you have no desire to be with him, then?"

Why did he care so greatly if they were merely to be friends? "No, sir."

He visibly relaxed. "That is a relief."

"Why?"

He gave her a sidelong glance, the twinkle in his eye flickering like a flame weakened by the wind. "I simply found it difficult to believe that you could ever be happy with someone so utterly useless while playing games."

His words pulled out surprised laughter from her lips, his own grin warming her straight through. But in that same second of alleviated tension, a moment of weakness overcame her, and her eyes dropped to his lips—those perfectly chiseled, perfectly masculine lips.

What would a kiss feel like from Edmund Harris? Of course, she'd thought of that before. Countless times, in fact. She'd often envisioned his kiss to feel something akin to the way the sea caressed her skin as she walked across the beach, or the way the sun warmed her face right after a storm.

But infinitely more powerful, infinitely more beautiful.

Feeling his eyes on her, she looked up, a wariness pursing his brow. Yet he did not look away. Instead, his gaze, too, dropped to her lips, but only long enough for her heart to stutter.

Time stood still between them. They were friends, only friends. But an energy pulled them together, drew them closer in involuntary waves. She shifted in the sand, and their shoulders pressed together, sending chutes of warmth spiraling up her arm and swirling round her heart.

Lieutenant Harris looked away first, focusing hard on the sling in his hands as he cleared his throat. "So, we are friends, then."

Had the words been meant to remind her or himself?

Raging heat flushed throughout Poppy's body. Thank heavens for the frigid rain that now soaked through her coat. She needed something to cool her down after where her thoughts had strayed.

"Yes, Lieutenant. Friends."

"Then I suppose you ought to call me Edmund again. After all, I've been calling you by your given name all this time."

As well he should. She liked her name far too much to be called anything different. "Very well, Edmund," she said with a smile, if only to prove that she was unaffected by the moment they'd just shared.

"Well, as your friend," he began, "might I suggest we return to our respective homes so we avoid becoming sick from lingering far too long in this weather?"

Disappointment sank within her chest, but she nodded all the same.

He stood, extending his hand to hers, and Poppy hesitated but a moment before accepting his offered help. His fingers gripped her hand firmly, despite the slippery rain that encased both of their hands, and he pulled her up with ease, releasing her the moment she stood.

Breathless, she thanked him, noticing as he favored his left arm once again. He must have injured it more than he'd let on. But was he more affected by his tussle with Trevik or having to carry Isolde to Tristwick?

"Shall we?" he asked, motioning for her to precede him up the beach.

Poppy nodded, falling in step beside him. She folded her arms as they walked against the spitting rain. "I ne'er got the chance to thank ye properly for helpin' Isolde today. 'Tis a noble thing ye did, rescuin' a life that 'as no bearin' on your own."

He looked down at her. "She has a bearing on my life. She's connected to you." His face searched hers, then he looked away and swiftly added, "And we are friends, of course."

Of course. Friends. They needed to remember that. "Well, I do appreciate ye."

"I was glad to be of service. At any rate, I could hardly be considered a part of His Majesty's Navy if I didn't have a desire to help those in need. I..." He paused, a frown pursing his brow.

"What?" she asked, her boots pressed hard in the sand. If it hadn't been so blasted cold out, she could have removed them.

"I only...had a thought."

She waited for him to continue.

"Have you ever heard tell of a lifeboat, Poppy?"

She narrowed her eyes, thinking hard. "Do they not 'ave one in Penzance?"

"I believe so. They send volunteers during storms to rescue stranded men."

She waited, wondering at his purpose in telling her this.

"I was merely thinking that, perhaps if the men of St. Just knew they had a crew ready to rescue them at sea, they would not be so hesitant to join Trevik's crew."

His words percolated in Poppy's mind, simmering like a stew until the heat popped to the surface. "So instead o' convincin' fishermen to sail in dangerous seas, we convince 'em to fish in seas where a rescue boat be available."

"Precisely," he said, his eyes alight, his features growing more animated. "I've heard tale of men rowing out to rescue stranded sailors during shipwrecks and storms. Even *I* have experience firsthand with Mrs. Kendricks rescuing Captain Kendricks and myself. Having a boat filled with able-bodied men would most certainly encourage fishermen to stay with Tristwick, would it not?"

His excitement was contagious before another thought occurred, and her face fell. "But who would man the lifeboat?"

Edmund paused as they reached the cliffside, the ocean's roaring behind them and the wind less fierce. "We could always find ways to encourage volunteers. Have a tip for passing ships and their captains, like they do for lighthouses. Encourage the community to raise up funds." His words picked up speed as his excitement continued. "There could also be an incentive for new fishermen—new homes from Mr. Trevethan, enough room for larger families to grow into. If Tristwick grew enough, Trevik could even split the crew into shifts—half of them fishing, the other manning the lifeboat if needed."

Poppy stiffened. Edmund's idea was flawless, apart from one important factor…encouraging Tristwick's growth. And changing the face of Tristwick—the home her father built—would surely change her memories of her father, perhaps wipe them out completely.

Worry stormed in her belly like the storm behind them. "Would it not cost a great deal to purchase a lifeboat? 'Ow would we e'er get the funds?"

His face fell, and Poppy was overcome with simultaneous guilt and relief. She knew Edmund was merely trying to help, but perhaps there was another way to save Tristwick without changing it entirely so she could no longer recognize it.

Edmund rubbed a hand to his jaw. "Perhaps I could visit Penzance and see how they were able to fund their boat."

Heavens. Was he willing to do such a thing? Again, conflicting feelings arose within her. Appreciation and fear. Worry and hope.

She still held fast to the belief that Tristwick could be saved without changing it entirely from what it had been when her father was alive. But then, Edmund's offer was so generous. So thoughtful.

"Perhaps you could ask Trevik what he thinks," he suggested next. "I would be more than willing to seek out any information of which he may be in need."

Poppy nodded, forcing a smile as she attempted to remain balanced in her feelings. Too much was changing for her to remain steady.

Yes, she and Edmund had made amends, but to what end? He would still be leaving, sending her life into upheaval in a matter of weeks, if not days. Then she'd be left to once more pick up the threads of a life she wasn't sure she wanted in the quaint, peaceful Tristwick—the Tristwick her father created, the Tristwick where she was comfortable—no longer existed.

The darkness she'd felt before with the injury of Isolde had shifted to a dim grey with Edmund's help. But now, another dark seed had been planted in her heart. And no matter how desperately Poppy tried as Edmund walked her home in the fast-approaching darkness, she could not draw enough light to stamp it out.

CHAPTER TWENTY-ONE

*T*revik took to the lieutenant's idea in an instant, commissioning Poppy to deliver a letter to Edmund, asking if he really wouldn't mind traveling to Penzance in order to discover for himself how they were able to obtain a lifeboat.

"And ye be certain ye don't want to ask 'im yourself, Trev?" Poppy pressed the next morning, unsure if she wanted to be the messenger between her brother and the lieutenant.

She had taken the day off from the lighthouse to be with Isolde, so the thought of walking to Golowduyn for no other reason seemed futile—especially when delivering Trevik's message could very well change the face of Tristwick.

"I be sure, Popp," Trevik said. "Thank ye." Then he left to meet Mother at the cellars.

Morvoren approached Poppy shortly after, speaking in hushed tones, though only Poppy was near enough to hear her words.

"Trevik be nervous to see the lieutenant again, and for good reason," Morvoren explained. "I saw 'im shake 'ands with the Lieutenant after Isolde fell."

Poppy's mouth fell open in shock. "Ye did not."

But Morvoren nodded. "With me own eyes. 'Twasn't long, but 'twas an 'andshake if e'er I saw one." She motioned over her shoulder toward the door. "I'll stay with Isolde for a few hours, so ye can rescue your brother. Trev simply doesn't know 'ow to treat a man 'e once despised and now appreciates."

Poppy could hardly believe Morvoren's words. She simply couldn't fathom her brother humbling himself enough to do such a thing. But then, he loved his family, and he wasn't so prideful as to not recognize Edmund's benevolent service.

Knowing there was nothing else to be done, Poppy readied herself for the day, accomplishing her chores at home first, helping Morvoren change Isolde's bandage on her wound—which had fortunately not required sutures, after all—and baking an extra lot of fresh figgy 'obbin to take with her to Golowduyn.

She'd need something to offer Edmund when she requested him to ride nearly eight miles to discover more about a lifeboat she hoped he would learn nothing about.

After leaving Isolde with Morvoren and a few figgy 'obbins for her niece, Poppy left for the lighthouse alone, acutely aware of how silent the world was without her niece's constant gibberish chatting.

But of course, she would not allow such a thing to dampen her spirits for long, focusing instead on the rushing of the waves below and the herring gulls squawking above.

It was a beautiful morning. The rain the day before had deepened the green of the grass splayed out across the fields and had caused the colors of the sea pinks to pop with their delightful, circular heads. The birds seemed to call louder overhead as they found worms atop the soil, and the wind exhibited a gentle caress, instead of the violent pushing it had taken part in yesterday.

The moment Golowduyn's tan structure appeared in the distance, the cliff behind it still casting a shadow over half the lighthouse, all peace fled from her heart as it tapped enthusiastically against her chest. Her heart, it would seem, was far more anxious to see Edmund than her mind.

Of course she was looking forward to the notion that they were both friends again. But then, how would such a thing work? How was she supposed to even behave? And more importantly, how was she to remain happy once he left her to deal with a Tristwick so changed she no longer recognized it?

These thoughts and more continued to swirl through her mind until she finally reached the lighthouse and found Edmund brushing down Glastaish just outside of the stables.

She approached slowly, taking a moment to observe the way his shoulders rolled against his waistcoat as he stroked the brush down the horse's curves. His left arm was in his sling again, reminding her once more what this man had done for her family—and what he was offering to do, as well.

With a deep breath, she headed toward him, purposefully sliding her boots across the dirt so he might be alerted to her presence earlier. Sure enough, he lifted his gaze toward her.

She wasn't certain what she'd been expecting when he first saw her—hesitation, perhaps?—but when his expression brightened, his eyes shining with warmth, her heart fluttered.

"Good morning, Poppy," he greeted, resting the brush against the horse's back as he turned to face her.

She stopped a few paces away, holding the basket in front of her with both hands. "Mornin'," she greeted in return, a sudden shyness overcoming her. She looked around, wondering what to say when she settled on the grey horse in front of them. "Did ye ride already?"

Edmund nodded, sliding the brush down the side of the mare's stomach. "I did. And it was a brisk one, at that." He glanced back at her with a half-smile. "So what brings you to the lighthouse today? Kendricks told me you were taking time away."

"I was supposed to, but I be tasked by me coward of a

brother to ask for your 'elp." She raised the basket in her hands. "And I've brought a little somethin' to persuade ye."

He patted the horse's back, tossed the brush into a nearby pail, then approached Poppy. "You know you do not have to persuade me to help." Still, he accepted the basket she offered, then paused. "It isn't stargazy pie again, is it?"

His wink nearly did her in. "I s'pose ye'll 'ave to see for yourself."

He peeked beneath the cloth that covered the raisin-filled, rolled dessert, and his smile grew. "I can see I made the correct decision in becoming friends with you, Poppy Honeysett. These are, quite possibly, my favorite desserts in all of Cornwall."

Poppy beamed. "'Ave ye not said the very same 'bout blueberry and lemon posset? And elderflower syllabubs?"

He shrugged. "What can I say? I am a man of many passions."

They shared a smile, and the tension in Poppy's neck eased.

"So, I assume you have spoken with your brother about my traveling to Penzance, then?"

She nodded. "'E be quite excited 'bout it," she said, trying not to feel too jaded about the fact, as Trevik hardly seemed concerned about the change that might occur within Tristwick if they pursued such an idea. "I be certain 'e was envious that 'e didn't come up with the idea 'imself."

Edmund chuckled. "I'm sure he would have, eventually." He took another sniff of the figgy 'obbins. "He wishes me to visit Penzance, then? See what I can discover?"

She winced. "Would ye mind so terribly? "We'd 'ate to put ye out."

He already shook his head. "Not at all. I can leave as soon as this evening."

Poppy's lips parted. How did the thought of him leaving

St. Just cause her chest to tighten so suddenly, as if a rope was cinched around her, unable to be removed.

"Is something wrong?" he asked, having must have noticed her hesitation.

She smiled, albeit strained. "Nay. I be merely thinkin' 'bout your arm, wonderin' 'ow ye be after yesterday."

He raised a hand to his sling. "I was a little worse-for-wear, but I woke up feeling better than ever. How is little Isolde?"

"She be doin' fine. Morvoren's been strugglin' to keep 'er abed already. She just be wantin' to play."

He smiled. "That's very good to hear."

Their eyes met. A moment passed, and she recalled their closeness last night on the beach before the sound of an approaching carriage rattling toward them pulled their attention to the road leading to Golowduyn.

"Be the Kendrickses expectin' a guest?" she asked, noting the fine coach fast approaching.

Edmund narrowed his eyes. "I don't believe so."

They waited in silence until the carriage came to a stop near the house, the footman hopping down to open the door. A woman whom Poppy guessed was older than fifty years of age emerged first, squinting up to peer at the lighthouse, her tall-brimmed bonnet stuffed with lace.

Then she turned sharp, green eyes on Poppy and Edmund.

"Well," she said, her voice raspy, "if it isn't Lieutenant Harris." She pulled a smile on her lips, though it looked foreign to her face, as if she wasn't accustomed to showing the action. "How are you, my darling son?"

Poppy's lips parted, shock rushing through her body like a sudden rainfall. Edmund stiffened beside her, the color in his face drained, leaving behind a stark white complexion as he faced the woman Poppy hadn't been certain even still lived.

"Mother."

CHAPTER TWENTY-TWO

*E*dmund's heart pounded against his chest, his palms cold and his head spinning. He never thought he'd see this woman again—and certainly not in Cornwall. Eighteen years had passed since he'd observed that tight smile, and even now, it was too soon to be seeing it again.

How had she found him? *Why* had she found him?

"I can see you're surprised," Mother said, interrupting his thoughts with that familiar raspy tone. He'd always told her that her voice was caused by how often she shouted at him. To which she responded in the same way—with a strike across his face and a command to leave her presence. "Come, son. Do you not wish to greet your mother with a kiss?"

She took a step toward him with an outstretched hand, but Edmund retreated with a step back, cursing his decision the moment he did so. She was the last woman in the world he ought to be revealing any weakness to. He was a full two heads taller than her now. Surely he should no longer be intimidated by her presence.

"What are you doing here?" he asked plainly, acutely aware of Poppy's surprise as she flicked her eyes between him and his mother.

If only Poppy could hear his silent petition for her to take shelter inside. He did not want her poisoned by the darkness Mrs. Dorothy Beacham was capable of.

"I should think it obvious, Eddy," Mother said. She wore her dark hair still the same, pulled stiffly away from her face as to limit the wrinkles across her cheeks and brow, though her temples were now streaked with grey. "I'm merely here to see you, of course."

As if he could ever believe such a lie. The woman had avoided Edmund as much as he'd avoided her, not once reaching out by way of correspondence, not once inviting him back home. Not that he would have responded had she contacted him, of course.

"How did you know where to find me?" he asked next.

Poppy's eyes focused on him. She had to be wondering why he was speaking so void of emotion to his mother. Trevik would never dare to speak to their mother in such a way. But then, Mrs. Honeysett was not Mrs. Beacham.

"Why, your letters, of course," she responded.

Letters? He did not write any letters to her. Only…Algernon.

Of course. Of course his eldest brother would share Edmund's location with Mother. He and Cecil adored their mother, and she adored them.

But Edmund had always been too similar to Father to have earned her regard.

Curse his decision to tell his brother of his convalescence in Cornwall. Never in a million years did Edmund even consider that his mother would come to find him, though.

He made no response to her words, though he regretted his silence as Mother took the opportunity to cast her attention to Poppy.

"Will you not introduce me to your friend, Eddy?" she asked, her eyes slowly trailing up and down Poppy's person.

Edmund gritted his teeth. He wouldn't wish to offend

Poppy by not introducing her, but then, how could he willingly offer up any information about his friend to his mother?

"Eddy?" Mother prodded, sighing with impatience. "You always were swift to disregard Society's norms." She faced Poppy herself, then. "I am Mrs. Dorothy Beacham, Eddy's mother. And you are?"

Poppy cleared her throat, glancing to Edmund as if for permission, but Edmund didn't look away from his mother. "Poppy 'Oneysett, ma'am."

Mother blinked, doing nothing to mask how unimpressed she was.

Edmund clenched his hands into fists. She'd always been a master at hiding her emotions. He knew full well his mother's reasoning in showing her disapproval of Poppy.

"Well, Eddy," Mother said, turning to face him again, "I do wonder if we might find somewhere a little more"—she glanced sidelong at Poppy again—"private for us to speak."

Poppy clearly took the hint. With quick movements, she stepped toward the door. "I'll bring these inside for ye," she murmured.

She took the basket he'd forgotten he'd still held in his hands, then disappeared within the door of Golowduyn.

The moment he and Mother stood alone, what little hope and light he had felt before vanished due to Poppy's absence.

"That was unkind of you," he said, facing his mother. "Dismissing her in such a way."

Mother gave a flippant scoff. "Come now, no more wasting our time. I wish to speak with you." She motioned to his sling. "I see you've gone and injured yourself again."

Again? She knew of the other times he'd been injured at sea? Had she seen it in the papers, or had Algernon told her that, as well? He knew Cecil wouldn't have. He hadn't spoken with Edmund in as long as Mother had. She had poisoned Cecil against him since the very beginning.

Ignoring her words and pushing his other questions aside,

Edmund gathered what little confidence he could to the fore-front of his mind. With Poppy gone, he no longer had to force politeness, nor did he have to worry over what Mother would say to her.

He had always been Edmund, the greatest disappointment of his mother's life. But now, he was so much more than that. He was a lieutenant in the Royal Navy. A grown man of nearly thirty years. He had done much healing at sea. And he would die before allowing this woman to wreak anymore havoc upon his life than she already had.

"I will ask you again, Mother, and I expect the truth this time. Why have you come here?"

Her eyes narrowed a fraction. "I've already told you, son. We are here to see you." Her eyes traveled the length of him, sizing him up as she had Poppy. "You might rival Algernon's height now. Who would have ever thought, what with your frail frame as a child."

Yet another way Edmund had never been able to measure up to the high pedestal she'd placed his brothers on. He had always...

Pausing, he recalled her earlier words. "We?"

She gave him a look of confusion before looking over her shoulder at the empty space behind her. With a sigh, she walked back to the carriage. "Come along, Mr. Beacham."

Edmund had managed to remain in control of his reactions upon seeing his mother. But when her husband emerged from the carriage, poking his head out with a wary glance at Edmund, anger burned through his veins.

"Edmund," Mr. Beacham said, straightening his jacket and tipping his head in greeting, as if this was a cordial meeting. "My, but you've grown."

The audacity of the man to show his face to Edmund again. Mr. Beacham had always been a fine-looking gentleman, with handsome features and a tall figure—the perfect match for Mother. Both of them appeared to be delightsome, wholesome individuals.

But only Edmund knew the truth about them both. The truth that Mr. Beacham had broken his family apart more than Mother ever could.

Mr. Beacham stepped forward with an extended hand, as if he truly thought Edmund would wish to greet him in such a way.

Instead, Edmund spoke firmly, his right hand up to halt the man's progression. "That is far enough, Mr. Beacham." He looked to his mother, who'd lost her feigned smile.

Memories threatened to intrude on his mind, producing feelings of inadequacy and fear. But he would not allow such things to continue.

He drew a deep breath, reaffirming his stance and looking at them both without flinching. "Before the both of you imagine you can pretend your way into creating a farcical parent-child reunion, you ought to know that will not be occurring. You are not welcome here on this land, nor are you welcome in my life. I suggest the both of you leave immediately."

To his utter satisfaction, Mr. Beacham slowly slunk behind his wife. Edmund had lost count of the number of times that man had done Mother's bidding by striking Edmund or holding him secure for her to do the duty herself.

To tower above the man who was now clearly frightened of Edmund was a balm that finally smoothed over one of his many childhood wounds.

Mother, however, only hardened her eyes. "I had hoped that the navy would have beaten that lack of respect out of you, boy."

"No, Mother. Only you attempted to do such a thing."

Her eye twitched. "I did not come here to quarrel with you."

"Then why did you come? I will not speak more until I have heard the truth."

She glanced to Mr. Beacham, and he placed a hand at her back, as if to give her strength. "Mr. Beacham and I are here on holiday. We heard your name at the Golden Arms, I inquired as to where you would be and was then given the instructions to the lighthouse." She raised her eyebrows. "I thought it only right that I pay you a visit, after you have yet to pay your poor mother one after nearly twenty years."

Edmund scoffed. The woman did not wish for a visit from the only son she despised. He knew she'd just as soon wish him dead. As for the rest of her words, however, he was inclined to believe them.

"Will you not invite us in, then?" Mother asked, motioning to the house.

"It is not my home to do so." Nor did he believe Kendricks would welcome them in either. If the captain heard all that Mother had done, Edmund was certain Kendricks would just as soon throw the woman off his property as well.

Mother gave Mr. Beacham a knowing look. "Then perhaps we might instead dine together at the Golden Arms this evening."

Edmund couldn't hold in another caustic laugh. As if he would ever knowingly put himself him through such a miserable meal.

"I don't believe—"

His words ended abruptly when the door to Golowduyn creaked open and Poppy froze in the doorway with wide eyes and the empty basket in her hands.

She glanced between Mother and Mr. Beacham, finally landing on Edmund with an apologetic wince.

Edmund grimaced. He did not blame Poppy for coming outside. After all, she couldn't very well stay there forever. But he would be hanged if he allowed his mother to disrespect her again.

With rattled nerves, he faced Mother, speaking in hushed tones. "If you leave this minute, I will agree to meet with you in St. Just this evening. Five o'clock." That would give him a mere half hour before he'd have to catch the stagecoach for Penzance.

Mother smiled, no doubt pleased she'd gotten her way. "Very well. We shall greatly look forward to our visit then, son." Her eyes flitted toward Poppy, then back to Edmund. "Until tonight."

Mr. Beacham barely managed a single tip of his hat in Edmund's direction before swiftly urging his wife into the carriage and ducking inside himself without a glance back.

As the carriage pulled away, Poppy came to stand by his side. He'd expected the tense feeling in his shoulders to leave the moment he watched his mother ride away, but unfortunately, it remained.

"I be sorry I interrupted," Poppy said softly. "I be needed at 'ome."

"It is no trouble, of course," Edmund said softly. "Frankly, I was grateful for the excuse to send them off earlier."

Her curious gaze lingered on him. "So...that be your mother, then?"

He gave a single nod, unwilling to divulge any more information about the woman.

"And the man she be with..."

"Her husband."

She nodded. "I gather ye didn't know they be in Cornwall."

"No, I was not aware of their presence." He pressed a hand to his throbbing brow. "And now, for some asinine reason, I've agreed to dine with them both tonight."

Poppy's brown eyes were filled with more questions—questions Edmund did not wish to answer. So he did what he always did when thoughts of his mother returned. He buried them deep within the darkest parts of his soul and focused on the sunshine.

"I suppose dinner will be worth it, knowing I have those figgy 'obbins to eat on my trip to Penzance," he said with a wink in her direction.

Her cheeks deepened to a lovely pink, the same shade as the flowers dotting the cliffside.

"I placed 'em on your bed in the rag. Ye can just return it later."

The thought of her in his room was enough to distract his mind from his mother for half a second. "Thank you. And thank you again for bringing them."

"Thank *ye* for goin' to Penzance for we."

He nodded, looking back to the road where the carriage could no longer be seen.

"Edmund?" Poppy said softly. "Are ye well?"

His name on her lips warmed his heart from the coldness that had taken root there. He peered down at her, wishing to tell her the truth.

Instead, he settled with, "Of course," then he found his best, convincing grin.

But the truth of the matter was, he was not well. Not in any regard was he well. But this was not another burden he wished for Poppy to bear.

He'd handled it fine on his own up until this point, and he'd do so again. And the moment his mother left town, he would bury all the memories she'd brought back with her— her cruelty and animosity toward him—and he'd ignore the fact that they'd ever resurfaced.

Because that was the only way he'd ever learned to live.

CHAPTER TWENTY-THREE

*E*dmund sat rigidly in his seat, leaning away from the table at the Golden Arms, attempting to create as much distance as possible between himself, his mother, and Mr. Beacham.

He leaned his leg against the portmanteau he'd dropped beside himself, reminding himself once again that this evening could end the moment he wished for it to.

"Are you going somewhere, son?" Mother asked, motioning to the bag.

"I have business to attend to out of town," he responded simply.

Images of himself jumping away from the table in the dimly lit inn and darting past regulars drinking their brandy danced around his mind, but he set them aside. He would not flee, if only to prove he'd grown beyond his mother's treatment of him and would never again be forced into submission.

"You will not eat?" Mother asked as meals were placed before her and Mr. Beacham.

Edmund shook his head. "I am not hungry." That was, in part, true. In reality, however, ever since partaking of

Poppy's dishes, he didn't have the stomach for anything served at the inn. Furthermore, he didn't have much of an appetite for anything, now he was seated with these individuals.

He took a sip of the brandy in front of him, his mother watching him with a look of disapproval.

"I am concerned for you, son," she said. "I don't believe you are doing your best to care for yourself."

Mother, concerned for her youngest son? He could have laughed. When had she ever shown such a sentiment?

"I'm fine, Mother," he said stiffly. "No need to start worrying yourself over me now."

She gave him a pointed look but wiped it clear when a passerby shuffled past their table. "Do tell us about your time in the navy, Eddy. I feel as if we know very little about it."

Edmund took another drink, not bothering to remove the permanent scowl that had etched itself across his brow since his mother had first appeared at Golowduyn.

"You don't wish to hear about my time in the navy, Mother," he stated.

If she was still the same woman as before—which he knew she was—Mother would never wish to hear another word about the navy. She'd always hated the organization. Father had paid more attention to his career as a naval officer than to his wife.

Little wonder. Father had escaped to the sea just as Edmund had.

"Algernon tells me you are a first lieutenant," she said, finishing a bite of her food. "I do wonder why you have not yet become a captain of your own vessel, though."

There it was. That's why she'd asked about the navy, to criticize him. No matter how she attempted to hide her disdain and disappointment for her last child, there was no way she could.

"I felt no need to become a captain," he responded,

lounging back in his chair and pulling a devil-may-care look across his features.

Mother's nostrils flared—something they always did when he'd gotten under her skin. He still enjoyed this, saying words just to upset her. It was the only way he'd ever been able to stand up to her.

"You felt no need to better yourself?" she asked, her voice low and raspy. "To aspire to something greater than what you are now?"

He pulled in his lips and shook his head, remaining silent. It was the truth, funnily enough. Becoming captain of a ship brought on a slew of responsibilities and problems Edmund had no desire to aspire to.

"Typical," Mother muttered under her breath. "I suppose I should not be surprised. You were never one to apply yourself. Unlike Algernon and Cecil." She glanced to Mr. Beacham with a smile. "They are a credit to their name, are they not?"

Edmund looked to Mr. Beacham. The man skirted his eyes away from Edmund and took a bite of his food.

"Do you know, Cecil is a barrister now?" Mother continued, the proud smile on her face similar to what it had been when Edmund was a child. "The education he was required to receive was shocking, was it not, Mr. Beacham? We are just so proud of him. He is married to a lovely woman who's bestowed the family with two sons and a cherubic daughter."

Only Mother would boast about having a barrister for a son more than a lieutenant of the royal navy.

"And, of course, you've been in contact with Algernon," Mother continued. "So you will already know what a help he has been to us all. Running the family's estates, ensuring we are all cared for. He married a remarkable young woman—a daughter of a baronet—who has already blessed him with an heir."

Edmund took another drink. It hadn't taken long for

Mother's true colors to emerge. She would often do this, compare him to his brothers, boast about their strengths while tearing Edmund apart.

"Why can you not be more like them, Edmund? You behave as a leech, attaching yourself to each member of your family until we have been drained of all life."

He'd always resorted to making some offhanded joke, which then evoked her wrath even more. Of course she never struck him when Father was around. When he'd died, however, he'd felt the fullness of her brutality, for that was when he'd learned the truth about her relationship with Father.

How could Mother not have changed after eighteen years? Did she not wish to move on with her life? Did she still truly not understand how her issues had very little to do with Edmund—and *everything* to do with Father?

"Yes, we are quite proud of our sons," Mother said with another smile at Mr. Beacham.

What an interesting use of the word 'our.' Edmund bit back another scoff. Mother continued to drone on and on about his brothers' other accomplishments before delving into their desires—which matched up perfectly with Mr. Beacham's, fishing, reading, and horseback riding.

Such a thing was not impossible to believe. After all, Algernon and Cecil had now spent longer with Mr. Beacham than they ever had Father. The fact that they had many similarities with the man was not so very strange, since Edmund already knew the truth about the situation.

"Yes, my dear Mr. Beacham has become very fond of the sport," Mother continued as Edmund drifted in and out of the conversation. "That is one of the reasons he had the desire to come to Cornwall, to explore the fishing that runs so deeply through the area."

She turned admiring eyes on her husband, and Edmund grimaced, feeling the sudden urge to purge the contents of his stomach. Mother's admiration for her second husband had always surpassed her tolerance for her first, but that didn't make it any easier for Edmund to accept it.

"Tell Eddy where we've been thus far, Mr. Beacham," Mother said before taking another bite of her potatoes.

Mr. Beacham hesitated, then launched into a vapid retelling of the locations they'd visited. "The whole industry is fascinating," he continued, chatting to Edmund as if they were old friends, instead of being the man who had overseen his wife's cruelty. "I am but a humble, recreational fisherman, but these Cornishmen have perfected the entire trade."

Though he was loathe to admit it, Edmund had to agree. He'd seen that perfection and hard work exhibited by the Honeysetts. Mr. Beacham would no doubt highly enjoy meeting the fisherman's family.

Too bad for him.

"Our next stop after St. Just will be Sennen Cove," Mr. Beacham continued. "I've heard it comparable to Bude, which we highly enjoyed, as well. We experienced quite fine weather there, as opposed to what they are prone to experience. I fear they have suffered a great deal of shipwrecks. So frequent an occurrence it is, they have positioned a lifeboat nearby to rescue—"

"A lifeboat?" Edmund blurted out, lowering his emptied glass.

Mr. Beacham's brow rose, and Mother narrowed her eyes at his outburst.

Edmund inwardly grimaced. He hadn't meant to reveal such emotion to these people.

"Have you a particular interest in lifeboats?" Mr. Beacham asked hesitantly.

Edmund rolled the words around his tongue, debating whether or not to allow Mother and Mr. Beacham a glimpse into his life, though small as it was.

235

Surely, for the sake of Tristwick—for the sake of Poppy—he could.

"No," he finally responded. "That is to say, I know of someone who was asking after them." He paused, staring into his glass to feign indifference. "I was not aware Bude was in possession of a lifeboat."

Mr. Beacham glanced at his wife, then continued, albeit uncertainly. "Yes, it is a fascinating story, really. Apparently, they were gifted one by the navy."

Edmund narrowed his eyes. "However did they manage that?"

Mr. Beacham shrugged. "The fisherman I spoke with could not tell me anything other than the navy saw a need and thought it worth their time to give them one."

Edmund looked away, rubbing his jaw. He wasn't too familiar with Bude, but he knew the Admiralty would never agree to gift a boat to a town until it benefited themselves heartily.

Whatever had Bude done to receive such a reward? And could Tristwick do the same?

"Do you happen to know how large the boat was?" he asked next, ignoring Mother's pursed lips—a definite sign that she was losing more patience, no doubt because the conversation no longer centered around herself.

"Oh, large enough to fit twelve people, at the very least," Mr. Beacham said.

"And they had volunteers running it?"

"I believe so."

"How did they find people enough to man it?"

Mr. Beacham winced. "I am unsure. The man wasn't terribly forthcoming, I'm afraid."

Edmund sighed. He was on the brink of something. Hope? Relief? Either way, this could be the answer they'd been searching for to save Tristwick, to bring more people into the hamlet.

His thoughts settled on Poppy once again and her clear desire to keep Tristwick that same, closeknit community it had always been. He couldn't understand her reasoning. Would she not be willing to do anything for her home? Surely, she'd come round to this idea if the choice was between saving Tristwick or not.

He rubbed his fingers along his chin, only then realizing his mother's and Mr. Beacham's eyes settling on his. He'd revealed too much excitement, hadn't he? Unfortunately, he wasn't quite finished with his questions.

"Have you visited Penzance yet?"

"No, we shall make our way there in a few days."

Blast. That might've saved Edmund a trip, kept him near Poppy for longer. But it was no matter. He was only glad to be going to Penzance before his mother and Mr. Beacham would be.

"Well," Mother said, breaking into their conversation with a pointed look at Edmund, "I do believe we would find ourselves regretting the time we spent together if we did not maximize it to its fullest. That being said, the time has now come for us to address why I truly desired to speak with you."

Edmund hunkered down in his seat, his portmanteau pressing against his leg once again, reminding himself that he did not need to stay a moment longer than he wished to.

"Now," Mother said, setting her plate aside and squaring her shoulders, "I have come to inquire after your intentions for Sunningdale."

He paused. Sunningdale? That was why she'd come to speak with him? Algernon had Norest Park, the primary estate inherited from father, and Cecil had been handed Boarstrode Manor, a lovely home, as well. Mother married into wealth with Mr. Beacham, who had his own estate to run. So why did she care one ounce about Sunningdale? She'd despised the house because Father loved it.

"It is a drab, dusty little hole," she'd say bitterly about the dark paneling and old, red tapestries hanging from the walls.

"What of it?" Edmund questioned carefully.

In all honesty, Edmund had no attachment to Sunningdale apart from it being gifted to him by Father. It was far too close to his family for comfort. A day's carriage ride and they'd be there, able to visit even if he asked them not to. He'd only ever considered living there when he'd thought Poppy might have appreciated his offer of a large home to raise a family within.

Pain shot through his chest, but he held it at bay.

"We are merely concerned that it is not being utilized to the best of its abilities," Mother said. "Now we've heard that you have leased the property." She closed her eyes, shaking her head. "Whyever would you do such a thing when you've family who would take care of the house better than any stranger?"

Edmund scoffed. As if she even needed to ask that question. "The house was given to *me*, Mother," he said, releasing a heavy breath and scooting forward on his chair, careful not to bump his arm—once more in his sling—against the edge of the table. "So I am doing with it as I see fit."

Her eyes hardened. "That is really quite selfish, Edmund."

She would know selfish, wouldn't she? "How do you figure that?" His fingers gripped the handle of his portmanteau. The coach would be leaving in a quarter of an hour. He doubted he would last that long at this table.

"It is a large home," she said, her voice cold. "Fit for many children, as opposed to Boarstrode Manor."

Edmund paused. He had been there before. It was smaller than Sunningdale, but Boarstrode had at least six rooms and was large enough for a growing family.

"What are you saying, Mother?" he asked, though he already knew the answer.

She raised curved eyebrows. "I am merely suggesting that if you have no plans to ever maintain the house yourself, or fill it with children and a wife of your own, it is your duty to do right by your brother and allow him to run Sunningdale, as opposed to these strangers living in our family's home. After all, it is what your..." She paused, her nose slightly wrinkled with disgust. "What your *father* would have wanted."

The resentment in her tone chilled Edmund to his core. He released a breath and shook his head. There was no chance he'd allow his father's place of refuge to fall into his mother's hands by way of Cecil. Her middle son had always been his mother's favorite, while Algernon was her pride.

And Edmund? He'd been a thorn in her side from the moment he'd chosen to take after his father.

Edmund had given up any thought of ever living at Sunningdale, and he was more than happy with that fact. But he would far rather see strangers care for the home than Mother or his brothers.

"I hate to disappoint you," he said without a hint of sorrow, "but Sunningdale will be remaining under my control. I shall continue leasing it to those current renters for the fore-seeable future."

Mother's lips pinched tightly together, and Edmund's chest constricted. Still, he refused to back down.

"Do you see what becomes of young men in the navy, Mr. Beacham?" Mother said, her frigid eyes focused on Edmund. "Their families are fed lies to believe they will become respectable, honorable gentlemen, when in reality, they are taught to become insolent, prideful men who haven't a care for anyone but themselves." She shook her head with disgust. "What was the purpose in sending you to the navy at all?"

The words stung. Mother had never wanted him to join the navy, unwilling to have him lead the life of his father's— the life that ruined hers. Only when Edmund threatened to expose her and Mr. Beacham's secret had Mr. Beacham finally talked sense into her, signing the papers for Edmund himself.

With a set jaw, he leaned forward in his seat, his hand still around the handle of the portmanteau. "You did not send me to the navy, Mother. I *escaped* to the navy. Just like father did."

He stood from the table, squaring his shoulders. Mr. Beacham still ducked his head, having at least the decency to appear ashamed. Mother, however, kept her chin level with the ground, only her eyes rising to meet his.

"I found honor and respect there," he continued, "things I was never shown by either of you. Now, you must excuse me. I've somewhere I need to be."

He didn't bother extending a departing nod, simply clutching his portmanteau with his right hand and making to leave.

"That girl from the lighthouse."

Edmund froze at his mother's words. Everything within him screamed for him to leave. No good would come from having whatever conversation Mother had planned in her warped mind.

And yet, the mere mention of Poppy pulled out his defenses. Slowly, he turned to meet his mother's gaze.

"What of her?" he asked.

Satisfaction filled her eyes, no doubt at her ability to get him to remain. "Are you attached to her?"

He glanced around them, wondering who was overhearing their conversation, though he didn't say a word.

"As I suspected," Mother said with a slow shake of her head. "A lieutenant of His Majesty's Navy, falling for a serving girl."

Edmund's jaw twitched. Serving girl? Poppy was so much more than a serving girl. She was—

"You were destined for greatness, son. You could have amounted to something like your brothers. But instead, you chose to squander it away. You chose to tarnish the Harris family name."

His lips parted, and he shook his head, astounded—though he shouldn't have been—at her sheer audacity to deny the truth. "Oh, Mother," he began, "you have already done your part to bring ruin upon the Harris family name." Then he sent a pointed look to Mr. Beacham. "Has she not, sir?"

Mr. Beacham finally looked up from his plate, his cheeks a bright pink before his gaze darted away.

"I trust I shall not see either of you again," Edmund said. "Good day to you both."

He left the inn with measured steps, though all the while, he had to fight to keep his limbs from giving way beneath him.

The moment he stepped outside, he leaned against the side of the inn, drawing in a deep breath of the fresh air around him.

He'd done it. He'd stood up to the woman and her husband. And now, he'd never have to see them again.

Or so, at least, he hoped.

CHAPTER TWENTY-FOUR

*P*oppy could not stop her mind from dwelling on Edmund. A mere day and a half had passed since she'd seen him at Golowduyn, but it seemed as if a lifetime had come and gone already.

She knew her attachment to him would lead only to heartache—just as before—but she could not stop her desire to be near him, to hear his laughter, to feel his smile long before she even saw it.

After another full day had passed by without a sign of the lieutenant's arrival, Poppy returned to Tristwick to spend the evening with her family. They ate a quick dinner of tattie cake, then the Honeysetts walked the short distance to Tregalwen for a stroll across the beach before the sunset.

Poppy and Isolde scoured the sand for seashells with Mother as Trevik and Morvoren walked a short distance ahead of them. The two of them had been silent all evening, which was nothing out of the ordinary of late. But something within their expressions that evening, the worry in their eyes, caused concern to swirl in Poppy's heart.

"More shells, Auntie Poppy," Isolde said, bounding toward Poppy with fists of broken seashells. One would have never guessed the girl had been involved in a cliff fall only days before, what with her skipping steps and broad smiles, only a bruise on her head that was halfway covered by her locks of blonde hair.

Poppy peered down at the shattered shells Isolde held before her with open hands. "Oh, I only be needin'…" She paused, unable to lower the girl's spirits by telling her she only required whole shells.

Instead, she lowered herself to Isolde's eye-level and opened her old reticule. "That be a fine collection, Miss Issy. Thank ye."

Isolde beamed as she dumped the shattered seashells and gloppy sand into the reticule. Poppy would merely clean the reticule and sort out the shells later.

"Ye be such a fine 'elper, Issy," Mother said. "Are ye to find more?"

"Yes! More!" Then she hopped ahead of them with her eyes roving about the sand near her parents.

Poppy smiled before she caught sight of Morvoren watching her daughter, though instead of the signature smile that always accompanied watching Isolde, Morvoren merely regarded her with sorrow.

The concern within Poppy grew. "'As somethin' else 'appened?" Poppy asked Mother, motioning to Trevik and Morvoren.

Mother followed her gaze, and her eyes clouded over. "They be worryin' 'bout the same thing as usual."

Poppy was afraid of such. "Do they not think the lifeboat'll work out?"

Mother shrugged. "None o' we be sure 'bout anythin' now, love."

With sinking shoulders, Poppy could only agree. She'd wanted Edmund to return so she could speak with him. Yet, she dreaded the news he would bring back—whether that was

Tristwick and her memories changing forever, or Tristwick and her family unable to live throughout the winter.

"Poppy," Mother said, motioning toward the cliffside.

Poppy followed her mother's gaze, only then discovering the man walking across the pathway above the beach.

She recognized Edmund's confident stride at once. He'd finally returned, then.

"We ought to wave 'im o'er," Mother said, igniting a flame in Poppy's chest. "Trevik'd wish to know straightaway what 'e's found."

The both of them raised their arms, waving until Edmund's head focused in their direction. He paused, then raised a hand in a returning gesture. Finally, he made his way down the incline and headed for them across the sand.

Mother pointed out his approach to Morvoren and Trevik, who turned hopeful eyes on the lieutenant. Poppy's heart reached out to them. Clearly, they were hoping for good news, just like the rest of them. Unfortunately for her sake, whatever news Edmund held, she knew it wouldn't be good for her.

He finally reached them after a few moments, greeting Mother, Morvoren, and Isolde with smiles, Trevik with a hesitant nod, and Poppy with a lingering gaze. She tried to decipher what news he held within him, but he was the perfect picture of placidity.

"'E just be gettin' back from Penzance?" Trevik asked, getting straight to business. He shifted his feet uncomfortably in the sand, allowing Morvoren to take his arm when she slid it through his.

"Yes, the stagecoach arrived only a quarter of an hour ago." The portmanteau he gripped in his right hand was evidence enough of that fact.

Poppy watched the men closely, still shocked that they were speaking civilly with one another. She'd always taken the blame for their friendship ending. After all, had she not shown her marked interest in the lieutenant, Trevik would have never had any reason to hate him.

So now, to see the two of them trying their best to be amicable yet again, a weight lifted from her shoulders that she hadn't been aware of until that moment.

"I assume you would all like to know what I have learned," Edmund said. His impassive expression faltered, revealing dismay in his eyes. "However, I must warn you, it was nothing exceptionally useful."

Relief rushed through Poppy's limbs until Trevik's demoralized expression filled her with shame and worry. She needed to remember her family, to stop dwelling on herself.

"By all means, lieutenant," Trevik said softly. "We'd love to know what ye learned. Whate'er it may be."

Edmund nodded, skirting a glance toward Poppy before beginning. "I was unable to learn how Penzance managed to afford their own lifeboat. Perhaps more regrettably so, I learned that they have yet to even cast their boat into the sea to help wayward ships."

"Do ye know why?" Trevik asked.

"I'm afraid not. There may not have been a great need in these last few years for a lifeboat. Or more believably, the volunteers may have simply lost their courage to withstand the perils of a storming sea."

"Which could very well 'appen 'ere," Morvoren mused.

"Precisely," Edmund said. "It is a terrible shame. Rescuing those in need would be a fine way to live out one's life in a rewarding manner. However, not all hope is lost. I heard word of another lifeboat recently from my…" He paused, shaking his head. "Well, never mind from whom. I merely learned that Bude acquired one from the Admiralty as a gift."

Trevik pulled back. "'Ow'd they manage that, then?"

"I haven't the faintest notion. They've launched countless times, however, with enough men to help."

Trevik's shoulders squared once again, and he rubbed his

fingers to his chin in a thoughtful manner. Unfortunately, with Trevik rising from the depths, Poppy sank faster and faster.

This was a good thing, and she knew it. Yet, she simply could not shake the dread and the fear creeping up over her shoulder like a shadow at night.

"If Mr. Kendricks isn't in need of my help, I'd be happy to travel there next," Edmund offered.

"Oh, no. That be too far for ye to travel for we, sir," Mother jumped in at once.

Trevik looked slightly displeased but nodded following her words. "Ye've already done more 'an enough for we, Lieutenant." He paused. "Unless ye can some'ow 'elp we to receive a boat from the Admiralty."

"About that," Edmund began. He glanced to Poppy, then averted his gaze once again. Why could he not face her? Was it because he knew she was unhappy with how this would change Tristwick?

"I...I hope you do not mind," he continued, "but I've already written the Admiralty to discover what would need to occur for them to gift a boat to Tristwick and its surrounding areas. I delivered it to the civilian office in Penzance who have been hired to work for the Admiralty. They have promised a quick delivery to the naval port in Portsmouth."

Poppy's breathing halted. Edmund was simply trying to help. She knew that. But...

"Ye did?" Trevik asked, clear excitement in his eyes.

"Yes," Edmund said, still avoiding Poppy's gaze. "I explained how there have always been shipwrecks near Dulatha Cliffs, and elsewhere, despite Golowduyn's efforts, and how a lifeboat would help the navy, as well as the trade route and fishing industry. However, I do not expect an answer for a week or two, at the very least."

"Thank ye so much for doin' that, sir," Morvoren said.

"It do be a fine thing, Lieutenant," Trevik said next.

Mother nodded in perfect agreement. Everyone seemed

pleased, thrilled, even, with the prospect of being gifted a
lifeboat. Poppy was…She didn't know what she was. She was
happy that this was working out for her family. And if a
lifeboat was given them and it did help to save lives, then she
would fully support it.

But what would happen to Tristwick? What would happen
to what her father had created?

"Be there anythin' we can do for ye to repay the favor?"
Trevik asked.

Edmund glanced to Poppy. "No, thank you. I was happy to
be of service."

Poppy knew he wished for her own gratitude, and rightly
so. But she couldn't voice it. She couldn't even feel it. Of
course she was thankful for his efforts. But her mind was a
bleary darkness.

"I've been wonderin' 'ow we get volunteers," Trevik said
to Edmund, her brother's voice distant to Poppy's ears. "I
think I'll visit the Roskelleys in St. Ives, see if Hedrek'll change
'is mind 'bout not comin' back if 'e knows we be fixin' to get a
lifeboat."

Mother chimed in next, her words sounding even farther
away. "Per'aps ye ought to bring the lieutenant. If Hedrek
'ears a firsthand account o' bein' rescued, it might persuade
'im further."

"I'd be happy to assist in any manner I can," Edmund said
with a nod.

"Can Kendricks spare ye for an afternoon in, say, two
days?"

"I can always ask to be certain."

Poppy was hardly aware of what was occurring outside of
her own body. Her head spun, her lungs struggling to draw in
a breath.

Everything was changing.

She couldn't hold onto the past any longer.

She couldn't hold onto Father and Tristwick and the sea.

Nothing lasted forever.

"Poppy? Poppy?"

She looked up, Trevik's words poking through the clouds of worry that burgeoned before her.

"Yes?"

"I know what ye be thinkin'," he said with a glance to Mother.

Why did they all look between each other to share secret glances as if she couldn't see them or didn't know that they were all skirting issues around her?

"Tristwick be changin'," he said. "'Tain't ideal. But we 'ave to look into it or we might..." He broke off with a sigh.

"We might, what?" she asked, her words echoing in her ears.

He stuck his tongue in his cheek, his shoulders lowering before he responded. "Or we might not be able to remain in Cornwall at all."

All at once, Poppy was watching Trevik with perfect clarity, the haze lifting as she was shocked into attention. Not remain in Cornwall? Was her brother having a laugh?

"Ye can't be serious," she said.

But his expression—and the stoic faces of all the others—told her the truth. The breath rushed from her lungs, her heart squeezing tight. "Ye be considerin' leavin' Cornwall?"

Trevik nodded. "If it comes down to it, we just might 'ave to. Ye know 'ow much we be strugglin' now, Popp. 'Tain't wise to keep pretendin' all be well. There be more work in Devonshire, perhaps. Maybe e'en more up north."

North? Away from the sea? She shook her head, unwilling to even consider her brother's words. Leave Cornwall. She really would lose herself, then.

"And ye be fine with this, Mother?" she asked next, keenly aware of Edmund's eyes on her, though she was the one unable to meet his gaze now.

"No, I ain't." She responded with a look of compassion

that nearly broke Poppy. "But if the choice is between seein' me family starve or leavin' me 'ome, I think ye know what I'd choose, love."

Poppy shook her head. No, this was not possible. This could not even be an option. How could they even be considering this? Surely there were other possibilities. Other things that could be done. Surely they could find other people.

"'Ow can ye be willin' to leave what Father made," she said, taking a step back from her family. "Leave 'is legacy behind? 'Ow can ye all just be so willin' to give up? When Father died, it was just as 'ard, but 'e ne'er gave up."

Trevik shook his head. "That was different. We 'ad a crew, then. And less mouths to feed." His eyes settled on Isolde, who was sitting down in the sand, scooping the particles onto her skirts with a focused gaze. "I ain't givin' up. We—"

But Poppy was finished. She shook her head and walked away from her family, though they all stared after her.

"Poppy?" Mother called out for her, but she didn't stop.

"I need to clear me 'ead," she said over her shoulder. "I'll be back 'fore dark."

Silence followed. She strode across the sand, trailing the water's edge as she moved farther north. Her cheeks burned red from embarrassment of having reacted in such a way around Edmund, but she hadn't been able to help it. She simply couldn't fathom for one moment Trevik's thinking.

She drew deep breaths, willing the ocean air to calm her troubles, but nothing worked. The darkness was too strong. She knew what would come next if she didn't fight it—finding no joy, feeling no love, experiencing no hope for the future.

If she left Tristwick, she would lose her one connection to Father. Her one connection to stability. Then where would she be?

"Please, 'elp me, Father," she whispered into the air, folding her arms as the wind slid through her hair. "I can't feel it again. I can't go back to that darkness."

Tears spilled down her cheeks. She was drowning with no knowledge of how to swim. She would leave Cornwall. Leave Father. Leave her life and her home. But she couldn't.

She sent more prayers heavenward, seeking relief, seeking a semblance of peace, but nothing could penetrate the darkness.

"Poppy?"

CHAPTER TWENTY-FIVE

*P*oppy stopped her progress across the sand at the sound of Edmund's voice. She knew he would come. Just as she knew who had sent him.

"Ye don't 'ave to find me just 'cause me mother says so," she said, turning back to look at him.

A quick glance over his shoulder, and she discovered her family walking in the opposite direction, headed for home.

"You know your mother well," Edmund responded, his eyes focused on her. His portmanteau rested by his feet in the sand.

Poppy didn't meet his gaze. How could she after her embarrassing display a few moments ago?

Instead, she faced the sea, the sun settling lower and lower into the sky, sinking into the plush clouds on the horizon like a weary soul settling his head deep into a feather pillow.

How she wished to rest her own soul. How she longed for freedom from the thoughts she constantly battled. Fears. Worries. Darkness. It was a never-ending barrage against her spirit, and she was tired of it.

"Are you well, Poppy?"

She'd nearly forgotten Edmund was there. And yet, how

could she ever forget his presence? She felt it in her very soul whenever he was near. She always had.

"I 'ardly know," she answered truthfully. "I ne'er thought they'd leave Cornwall."

Edmund nodded, as if he understood. Then again, perhaps he did. He had to leave the sea, hadn't he?

"I am sorry that I could not return from Penzance with better news," Edmund said.

Poppy lifted a flippant shoulder. "Tain't your fault, sir. At any rate, I deserve no less than this fate."

He gave her a quizzical look.

"I prayed ye wouldn't return with good news," she said, finally admitting the truth aloud. "I wanted ye to discover nothin' 'bout the lifeboat so Tristwick mightn't be changed if we acquired one. I thought there be nothin' worse than Trist-wick changin'." She let out a quiet, caustic laugh. "'Ow wrong I be."

She focused on the pinks and oranges swirling in the sky like ribbons gliding in the wind, instead of the regret rushing over her in relentless waves.

"Had I known you did not approve of my going to Penzance, I would not have gone. And I certainly would not have sent the letter to the Admiralty. I can only beg your forgiveness now for doing so."

Poppy squeezed her eyes shut, the regret in his tone causing her further shame. "Please, don't apologize again, Edmund. 'Specially now, when your actions might be our last 'ope." She finally turned to face him, looking up into his eyes that were as green as the countryside. "I do be grateful for your 'elp. Truly."

He tipped his head in acceptance of her words. "I do not pretend to know the extent of your attachment to Cornwall. After all, I cannot understand something I have never had. But I know how much it would pain you to leave here. I can only pray for your sake that matters will not come to that."

The layered waves gently slid toward the sand, white and a cream-colored orange as they reflected the skies above. She always felt such a calmness with visions like this before her. But as Edmund spoke with her, his words so soft and understanding, she was startled to realize that his remarks had filled her with more peace than even the sea had.

"Thank ye," she said, unable to say anything further.

He waited a moment, then faced her more directly. "May I ask as to why you *are* opposed to a lifeboat being brought to Tristwick?"

Poppy chewed the inside of her lip, wondering how to go about answering his question. She needed to speak the truth, of course, but she didn't wish to sound like a mad woman. Then again, what did it matter? If her family found a new home in the north of England, she'd never see him again.

Ignoring the pressing feeling in her lungs, she responded. "I simply didn't want things to change. That be all, really."

He seemed to mull over her words. "And what is it about change that frightens you so?"

She could have easily taken offense at his words. Truthfully, had they not agreed to be friends three days past, there was a very high likelihood that she would have snapped back with an accusation that he was afraid of something himself.

"Are ye not frightened o' change, sir?" she responded instead.

He shrugged. "I am wary of it. But I would not say I am so very frightened of it."

Poppy certainly couldn't say the same.

"It is not so terrible to be frightened of change," he clarified. "I merely asked to understand your feelings a little better."

As any gentleman would. But could Poppy reveal her vulnerability? Share the real reason behind her fear of change?

Drawing a deep breath, she tested the waters. "I s'pose I

just ain't very stable," she said with a raise of her shoulder. "I can count on one hand the number o' times me life 'as changed. Some o' them be good—like Morvoren and Isolde joinin' the family. But more often than not, the change rattles me, and I…I find it difficult to be 'appy."

Edmund's eyes did not waver from hers, his brow creased in the center. "Forgive me, but I find it difficult to believe that you, of all people, struggle for happiness. You always seem so lively and joyful."

She looked away, even then, the darkness hovering over her. "Not always."

He watched her, waiting for her to expound. Perhaps out of her longing to feel at peace, to feel normalcy once more in her life, Poppy continued.

"Me father and I were close," she said softly, allowing the rhythmic waves of the ocean to calm her flapping heart. "Trevik took after me mother, wise and sensible. But I took after Father, cheerful, with a bright outlook on everythin'. I took great pride when others would point out the similarity, as 'e was me best friend."

The lump in her throat grew, and she swallowed hard to be rid of it. "When 'e died, I lost sight o' meself. I felt a sickness in me mind. One o' darkness. I felt joy in nothin'. Love with no one." She closed her eyes, shaking her head as if reliving the moment all over again. "I did me best to fight it off, but I couldn't. For a year I suffered with it, and me family too, as they couldn't do anythin' to 'elp either."

She recalled the days, weeks, and months Mother had spent coaxing Poppy from her bed, encouraging her to continue moving forward. Trevik had done his best to cheer her up, as well. But nothing worked. They were each grieving in their own ways when Father had died, but neither of them had known what to do with the heavy weariness Poppy struggled with.

She opened her eyes then, drawing in the light from the

sunset, reminding herself to pull up from that darkness. "Eventually, I returned to me right frame o' mind. Started enjoyin' food again and laughin' with others. It returned only once after Father's death, but since then, I've 'ad this never-endin' fear that the sickness will return. I'd do anythin' to ne'er experience it again."

She stopped, turning to face Edmund, who had kept his eyes on her as she spoke. "Father's death changed Tristwick to the point o' no recognition. Trevik became in charge and lost 'is childhood. Men left the crew, new men joined. New 'ouses were built to accommodate larger families." She swallowed again, shaking her head. "With everythin' so different, and without that stability from me father, I 'ad nothin' to grasp onto for safety, and I sank 'ard and fast. I s'pose I just be afeared o' that 'appenin' again."

She ended in a shrug, turning away from Edmund as her vulnerability nearly crushed her. She knew he wouldn't reject her. He was far too honorable about that. But would he simply brush off her fears as inconsequential? A simple, pain-free ailment?

"What brought you out of the darkness first?" he asked after a moment, his voice soft.

He wished her to continue, then? She motioned toward the sea. "Livin' 'ere," she responded. "These waves be the only thing that gave me joy durin' those long months o' sorrow. Which is why the thought o' leavin' 'ere be just…" She trailed off, unable to even finish her thought. "I'll lose me connection to me father in Tristwick, and I'll lose me connection to peace in the sea. And who am I if I lose 'em both?"

The question hung in the air between them, unanswerable. At least to Poppy it was. She didn't know who she'd be if she left Cornwall. Of course she would not simply cease to exist. But then, had she not felt that way after Father had died?

Edmund was silent for a long moment, eventually

responding with his eyes fixed on the sea. "I know how you feel, to a degree."

She waited. Did he? Or was he simply saying so to make her feel better? "Ye do?"

"Do you recall what I told you of my family?"

Poppy struggled to produce any information at all, as he'd never given her very much to go off of. "Ye said that ye lost touch with 'em after your mother sent ye to the navy," she offered.

"Yes. But I fear what I told you was only a partial truth."

She narrowed her eyes, listening as he explained. "You see, I drifted apart from my mother long before I went to sea. And she did not send me. I chose to go myself when I reached the age of eleven."

Poppy reeled. Edmund had *chosen* to leave his family? She could hardly fathom wishing for such a thing, and at so young an age.

"We did not part on good terms. I have not spoken with one of my brothers since I left, and my eldest brother only exchanges infrequent letters of business every year or so. And until two days ago, I had not seen my mother since I left for the navy."

Poppy tried to take in the information. Of course she'd wondered about Edmund's past. But he'd hardly seemed bothered with speaking of them at all. Now all she could wonder was why. What could have occurred between them all to have caused such a division between this son and his parents and brothers?

She paused. He had forgone mentioning one member of his family. "And what o' your father?"

His eyes took on a faraway look. "He died a few months before I left."

The air escaped Poppy's lungs, though she had expected Edmund's words. "I be sorry," she whispered. "I 'ad no notion 'bout any o' this."

He gave a half smile. "Which is how I prefer matters. I do not relish living in the past, so I do not speak of it. Not even Kendricks knows the half of it."

He was sharing with her things he hadn't even told Mr. Kendricks? Despite the heaviness of their conversation, a warmth bloomed in her heart.

"I merely wanted to tell you because I, too, have tasted the darkness of which you have spoken."

Their eyes met, and an understanding passed between them, the likes of which Poppy had never before felt. She had always been attracted to Edmund on a physical level. She'd also felt connected to him due to their similarities and propensity to find joy in the mundane. But this was the first time she'd felt an emotional connection with him—a spiritual connection—that helped her to understand that she was not alone.

And suddenly, the world did not seem so very dark..

"'Ow did ye…" she began, her voice cracking. "'Ow did ye overcome it?"

He faced the sunset, light hitting the tips of his high cheekbones and glancing off his dark hair. "With time and a great deal of distraction. I was similar to my father as well, in features and in manner. Instead of ignoring memories that can be, at times, painful, I welcome them in as old friends. This helps me to feel him close by."

She nodded, understanding his sentiment perfectly. She'd attempted to squelch memories of her father, but the moment she allowed them in, the ache of missing him still remained—though the reminder of how much he'd loved her had returned along with it.

"When he passed," Edmund continued, "I was given my father's small officer's box that had belonged to him when he served. It held his name—my own name written on the side of it."

"He was in the navy?" she asked.

"He was. The finest captain you'd ever met. Which was where my love for the sea was born."

"So ye must've got on well with 'im, then."

"I did. I always looked forward to when he returned from his months at sea. He was a dedicated man." His eyes focused on something in the distance as he continued. "When the *Valour* was shipwrecked near Golowduyn, most of my belongings, including his officer's box, were lost."

"No," Poppy said, her brow furrowed. "Did ye find it?"

"Funnily enough, Gwynna Trevethan delivered it to me many years ago, before she married Mr. Trevethan. Apparently, it had washed up on the shore."

Poppy shook her head. "Incredible."

He nodded. "But in those weeks where I did not have this officer's box, I realized that I did not need one of Father's possessions to remember him. All I needed were memories of him. His love for the sea. His propensity to eat pastries. His need to be free." He turned to Poppy, his face softening. "All of this is to say that if you leave Tristwick behind, you are not leaving your father behind. He is with you, so long as you keep his memory alive."

His words sank in, his anecdote working perfectly to calm her troubles.

She looked back to the sea, the sun no longer visible, though the warmth of its light remained. "Sunsets," she said softly. "Father and I used to watch the sunset every night together when 'e didn't 'ave to fish. 'E always said 'is favorites were the red ones 'cause they reminded 'im of the poppies and meself." She glanced to Edmund, tears flooding her eyes. "If I 'ave to leave Tristwick and the sea...at least I know I'll 'ave a sunset where'er I go."

Edmund nodded his head, a soft but proud look in his expression as he regarded her.

Poppy still had no desire to leave Tristwick, nor Cornwall —nor Edmund. And she still held trepidation for the future of her home if change was going to occur. But somehow, in that moment, standing with Edmund at the edge of the sea, the future did not seem so very frightening after all.

"Poppy," Edmund said after a moment, his eyes still delving into hers, "you said earlier that you only ever felt darkness like that twice. Once when your father died. May I ask what occurred to cause the second occurrence?"

Poppy held her breath. She couldn't share such an intimate detail about her past feelings for Edmund. Surely that would create a wedge between their friendship again.

And yet, as his eyebrows raised, pain flickering deep within his eyes, she knew she didn't have to say a word.

He already knew that his departure from her had been the cause of her deep, unbearable sorrow.

CHAPTER TWENTY-SIX

*E*dmund had felt the sting of regret before. Countless times, in fact. But this pain was different. It was far more poignant. Far more personal. After all, as he'd told Poppy before, he'd felt that darkness, that sorrow before. Now, to know that he had been the cause of it for Poppy, filled him with inconsolable pain.

"I'm sorry," he said softly, unable to look her in the eyes as his gaze dropped to the sand.

She nodded, though neither of them said another word.

Honestly, what more *could* Edmund say? That he wished he hadn't injured her so deeply? That he should have remained in Cornwall with her? How could he say such a thing when he did not know if that was true?

Now, more than ever, he understood her desire to remain in Cornwall—her fear of leaving Tristwick tied intrinsically to her father's death. Edmund never should have asked her to leave Cornwall, to create such trauma in her life, nor would he ask her to do the same now.

Perhaps Captain Jones had been right all along. Maybe Edmund *had* needed time away from the sea to right his mind once again.

He still held fast to his decision to break apart from Poppy, though. She belonged to Cornwall just as he belonged to the sea. Besides, while he now understood her decision and why she refused, that still did not change the fact that he was not enough of a man to make her happy. He was not enough of a *person* to make her happy.

After seeing his father not be enough for his own wife—and Edmund not be enough for his own mother—how could he accept any less?

"Thank ye for speakin' with I, Edmund," Poppy whispered, her voice steady. "And thank ye for all the work ye did for Tristwick."

Edmund finally stared down at her, her words echoing in his mind.

For Tristwick? Poppy thought he'd done it all for Tristwick?

For a moment, he considered allowing her to believe such nonsense. Never mind how deeply he'd missed her over the last two days. Never mind how he now dreaded returning to sea because he feared the loneliness that would inevitably strike him the moment Poppy was no longer by his side.

Allowing her to know the truth behind his actions would only prove to draw them closer together, which was something neither of them could afford.

And yet, as the last few days flashed through his mind—eating the dessert she'd baked for him, traveling to Penzance to save her home, enduring a conversation with Mr. Beacham solely for her sake—he could no longer hold his tongue.

His eyes roved about her features as he stared down her. "I did not do it for Tristwick, Poppy. I did it for you."

The moment the words left his lips, he knew he shouldn't have allowed them to. What had he been thinking, that admitting his actions would only solidify their friendship more? Surely the opposite would happen. Surely such words would encourage her to feel more for him, and him more for her.

And yet, as Poppy's gaze locked with his, the tears welling in her eyes like crystal pools made it difficult, indeed, for him to feel much regret at all.

She blinked, and a single tear escaped her eye, curving down her cheek until it disappeared under her smooth jaw. A trail of moisture was left behind, blazing a mark around his heart forever.

He'd been the cause of many tears of hers over the years, and yet, he'd not been there to ease her burden, to wipe them away and give her the comfort she needed.

Until now.

He knew he should not reach out to her. He knew a single touch to her face would be enough to seal his feelings for the woman forever. But the pull he had to Poppy Honeysett was impossible to resist.

Slowly, he reached his hand forward, hesitating just out of reach of her skin before finally giving in to his desires. He brushed the tear from her cheek, stroking his thumb over the moisture in slow movements until her skin dried.

And yet, he did not remove his hand from cupping her face. Her wide eyes watched him with vigilance as she no doubt wondered at his actions, but still, he caressed her, his fingers sliding partway between her jawline and her neck.

Then perhaps even more foolishly, his eyes dropped to her lips. They had parted at some point in his caress, those smooth curves that beckoned him closer.

How he longed to answer their call. He so badly wished to partake in all the affection they had to offer, those lips that had smiled at him like no one else ever had. Those lips that had once spoken of her love for him.

Would he ever hear her say those words again? Or could she perhaps share her feelings *without* the words? Slowly, he drew closer to her, his fingers sliding to the back of her neck as she raised her chin to maintain his gaze—the same motion she'd made...when Cadan had kissed her.

Edmund tried to shake the thought from his mind. She'd said she and Cadan were only friends, after all. But then, was Edmund not her friend?

His heart dropped low in his chest. He never should have touched her. He never should have entertained any thought of how she might still feel for him. She had kissed Cadan, but she'd only ever rejected Edmund. Who was to say she would not do so again?

He had never been able to do enough for his mother to make her choose him. He didn't want his marriage to be the same. Especially because he could not give Poppy what she wanted.

With pained movements, Edmund tore his eyes away from her and took a step back, his hand dropping to his side, empty and cold.

"I must go," he said, his voice raw. He retrieved his portmanteau still at his feet and took a step away. "Kendricks will be awaiting my return. Please, tell your brother I will wait for his word concerning St. Ives."

Poppy nodded, but Edmund couldn't meet her gaze as he struggled with his resolve to keep away from her.

"Goodnight, Poppy."

"'Night, Lieutenant 'Arris."

He forced himself to walk away without another glance back. She had used his title, and he knew it had been on purpose, for it was just another piece of evidence that the two of them could never be together.

CHAPTER TWENTY-SEVEN

*E*dmund slowly wandered back to the lighthouse, arriving after dark and in desperate need of sleep. He hadn't received a wink of it the night before at the inn in Penzance due to the noise from the men drinking below.

Unfortunately, with his thoughts racing, it didn't appear as if he would be receiving a great deal of sleep that evening either.

He entered Golowduyn with a soft turn of the knob, praying he did not awaken Mrs. Kendricks. The poor woman deserved all the sleep she could receive. She'd remarkably kept the delivery of her baby at bay for nearly two extra weeks, and Edmund knew Kendricks's prayers had done much for that cause. If she could make it but another week, Edmund was sure all would be well.

Or so at least *he* prayed.

With as much silence as he could muster, Edmund closed the door behind him before heading down the corridor to his quarters. Before he could take two steps, however, a voice stopped him.

"Harris?"

Edmund started, looking up to find Kendricks standing in

the doorway to the circular room, where the spiral stairs led up to Golowduyn's tower. He held a pail of oil in each hand.

"Did I wake you?" Edmund asked with an apologetic grimace.

Kendricks shook his head. "Not at all. I was just about to take these up to Cadan to save him a trip down tonight."

Edmund nodded. At the mention of the lighthouse assistant, that familiar jealousy burned in his chest, but he pushed it aside. It wouldn't do to have such feelings any longer. He wanted Poppy to be happy, with or without him. Even if the thought wounded him to his core.

"Did you just return from Penzance?" Kendricks asked.

"Yes. Though, I stopped by the Honeysetts first."

Kendricks raised the pails in his hands. "Perhaps you could carry one of these up with me so I can hear of your travels."

Edmund hesitated. The last person he wanted to see right then was Cadan, but he could hardly deny Kendricks's request for help.

After adjusting his sling, Edmund retrieved one of the pails, then he and Kendricks began their ascent of the one hundred and seventeen steps up to the tower. As they did so, Edmund recounted all that he had to the Honeysetts, his voice just loud enough to be heard over their boots clanging against the iron staircase.

"So will you travel to Bude, then?" Kendricks asked when he finished. "See what you can discover there?"

"No, the Honeysetts did not wish me to. At any rate, I received all the information I could from Mr. Beacham. I'm certain I'd be unable to find anything further."

Kendricks was silent for a moment, walking just ahead of Edmund. "How was your meal with your mother?"

Edmund hesitated. He'd told Kendricks about his require-ment to meet with Mother and Mr. Beacham, but nothing beyond how he'd dreaded spending time with them.

"As horribly as you could imagine," he responded.

He'd explained to Kendricks long ago how he was estranged from his family—if he could, in fact, call them his family—but had never explained why.

"Did she ever tell you why she was in town?" Kendricks asked next.

Yes, to steal what was rightfully Edmund's and deliver a home she never wanted to the sons she actually loved. "She was merely visiting Cornwall with her husband."

"Will you see them again, do you think?"

Edmund's arm began to protest from the strain the heavy pail had placed on his muscles, but he couldn't shift to his left arm, no matter how badly he wished to. The ache had only just begun to subside after the incident at the hurling competition and then carrying Isolde across the cliffside.

"No," he answered Kendricks's question assuredly. "There is no reason for me to do so. At any rate, they are sure to be off to the next town by now."

Kendricks paused on the landing marking the midway point up the steps and turned to face Edmund. "I hate to tell you, Harris, but they are still here."

Edmund's stomach tightened. He lowered the pail to the floor, stretching out his arm. "What? Are they?"

"Yes. I saw them late this afternoon in St. Just."

Of course. Edmund should have known his mother would not have given up so easily on something she wanted. Her remaining in St. Just could mean only one thing—that she still had every intention of obtaining Sunningdale for Cecil.

Edmund would simply have to avoid St. Just, then. And pray she didn't attempt to infiltrate Golowduyn again. At least he'd be away in St. Ives soon enough.

At the thought, he faced Kendricks. "I forgot to mention before, Trevik asked if I was available to accompany him to St. Ives on Monday to see if I can help bring back men for

Tristwick. I told him I would, but only if you will not be in need of me."

"No, not at all," Kendricks responded, then he raised a brow. "Has the man forgiven you, then?"

"Forgiven? I hardly think so. Barely tolerates is more accurate."

Kendricks chuckled, motioning toward the steps. "Shall we continue?"

Edmund nodded, following after him once again as he picked up his pail.

"So are you ever going to tell me what is occurring between you and Poppy?" came Kendricks's next question.

The tower was dark apart from the few lanterns that hung every thirty steps or so. Edmund had to focus hard not to miss a step. "Nothing is occurring between us that I'm aware of," he replied, feigning ignorance.

Kendricks chuckled in front of him. "Forgive me, but I have a difficult time believing such a thing. I've seen the looks the two of you have shared."

Looks? As if that was indicative of anything. "I hate to disappoint you, Kendricks, but Poppy and I have simply agreed to be friends, that is all."

"And you are fine with that?"

"Absolutely." He forced a lightened tone as he recalled the evening he'd just spent with Poppy. He could still feel the smoothness of her skin on his fingertips. "You know me, Kendricks. I prefer not to be tied down anywhere unless it be by a rope made of food."

Kendricks didn't laugh, clearly seeing through Edmund's jokes.

As their breathing grew labored, Kendricks stopped at the next platform, his eyes once more on Edmund. "So you have no plans to retire ever?"

"Of course I do. When I'm eighty-nine."

Kendricks gave a humorous smile. "All right, then what will you do after that?"

"Hire a fine cook and live out the remainder of my days eating in peace."

"That sounds horrifyingly lonely."

"Not to me."

Kendricks shook his head. "You truly have lost all desire to wed Poppy, to live at your own estate?"

Edmund stared at his pail on the landing, beginning to regret his decision to help Kendricks with it. He should've known this conversation would occur. He could only hope Cadan couldn't hear from his place in the watch room above. "I will never live at Sunningdale," he replied softly. "My mother's visit here has successfully sealed that chapter of my life closed."

"And...marrying Poppy? Do you not have feelings for her still?"

Edmund had not responded to that part of Kendricks's question on purpose. But of course his old captain would notice.

"My feelings matter not," he said flippantly.

"And why is that?"

"Because in my experience, feelings of the heart are as useless as a ship without sails. They will lead you nowhere but to heartache."

Kendricks raised a brow. "Spoken by a true, single gentleman." He picked up his pail of oil again. "If you ask me, my old friend, I think you are simply ignoring the truth of how you really feel."

"Well, I *didn't* ask you."

Kendricks watched him with a careful eye, and Edmund cringed. How had he allowed such unkind words to leave his mouth? Especially directed at Kendricks?

He blew out a breath and ran his fingers through his hair. "Forgive me, Captain. I..."

Kendricks shook his head, hardly looking offended. "I shouldn't have pressed the issue. I only wish for you to find the happiness that I have found. That is all."

Shame overcame Edmund even more. "I know, sir. And I am grateful for your efforts in that regard. Truly. But there is nothing else to be done. Even if we still shared feelings, even if we...if we wished to pursue marriage again, her attachment to Cornwall, to her family and to Tristwick, are far too strong."

"Is that so terrible a thing, to have an attachment to one's family and home?" Kendricks asked sensibly.

"No, of course not." He shook his head with a heavy sigh. "I offered her the world, but she did not want it. If we ever did marry, I would always fear that I was not enough for her, that she would regret her decision."

He had promised himself that he would retire from the navy when he found the woman he wished to marry, and he had been willing to do so with Poppy. But when she'd revealed that he wasn't enough for her before they were even engaged, warning flags had posted in his mind, and he'd fled.

He winced as his mother's words flooded through his ears.

"I never wished to marry your father in the first place," she would say when he was away at sea.

Eventually, she sought attention elsewhere from Society, friends...and Mr. Beacham. What if that very same thing occurred to Edmund?

"Call me mad," he explained, "but I wish for a wife who needs me, who wants me, more than anything. When marriage becomes difficult, as I know it does, I would not wish for any reason for my wife to regret her decision to become attached to me."

Kendricks nodded thoughtfully, though he remained silent.

After a moment, Edmund gestured for him to continue. "I know you have something to say. You always do."

Kendricks sniffed out a laugh through his nose. "I merely think you are mad."

His blunt words caused Edmund to chuckle. "Why am I not surprised?"

Kendricks lowered his pail to the floor again, leaning toward Edmund. "Marriage should not require one to give up *everything* about oneself. Yes, both must be willing to sacrifice to a degree, and be willing to listen and to change. But one should never be allowed to lose his or herself entirely in the process. After all, we choose to marry that person for a reason." He tipped his head to the side. "Would you want Poppy to change who she is as a person?"

"No, of course not. And I'd never ask her to do such a thing."

"Are you quite certain?"

Edmund pulled back. He would never require Poppy to change anything about herself to satisfy his own desires. He loved—he had loved her just the way she was.

"All I asked of her was to come to Derbyshire with me," he said defensively. "I do not believe that is so heinous a crime."

"No, not at all," Kendricks said at once. "But perhaps that is not all you were asking of her."

Edmund waited, wondering what his friend was about.

"I know Poppy quite well," Kendricks continued. "In the years she's worked here, I've come to see how very similar she is to my wife in one specific regard. Being asked to leave Cornwall behind would be like being asked to leave her very soul behind."

Edmund's shoulders fell. "I know," he said, defeated. "I discovered as much tonight from Poppy herself. And I regret ever asking her to even consider doing such a thing. But that still does not change the fact that I..." He broke off with a sigh. "I am not good enough for her, Kendricks. She made that clear three years ago when she wrote to me of how there was nothing in this world which would persuade her to leave Cornwall."

Kendricks grimaced. "Just observe her, Harris. That's all I'm saying. Observe her here, in Cornwall. See the way she behaves, how she feels. And perhaps you will see that it is not about how you are not good enough for her—and everything about what *Cornwall* is to her."

Edmund stifled his frustration. Kendricks was trying to help, but Edmund simply didn't see what good it would do for him to watch Poppy's admiration of Cornwall when he already knew she felt more for the county than anything she could ever feel for him.

"Trust me," Kendricks continued. "If Poppy makes you feel half of what I feel for Abigail, you should stop at nothing to be with her. I would sacrifice it *all* to be with Abigail." He gave a smile. "In fact, I did. And I have not once regretted my decision."

"I'm afraid I am not as altruistic as you, Captain," Edmund returned.

Kendricks retrieved his pail once again, a mischievous look in his eye. "That is where most people assume wrong. I was not behaving entirely selflessly when marrying Abigail. In fact, my offer of marriage was fairly greedy, as I was but a hopeless fool desperately in love with a woman I had only just met and could not fathom a life without her."

Their eyes met, and Edmund couldn't help but return his smile.

Still not wishing to see where he paled in comparison to the incomparable Cornwall, he finally nodded. "Very well. I shall take your advice and observe Poppy. But I don't—"

His words were cut off by the sharp trilling of the bell below at the foot of the iron stairs.

One ring. Two. Three. Four.

There was only one person left in the lighthouse who could ring the bell at the bottom.

Edmund's eyes connected with Kendrick's. "Is that…"

"Abigail."

Kendricks lowered his pail with a thud, the oil splashing out over the side of it, then he tore down the stairs as Edmund followed directly behind him.

CHAPTER TWENTY-EIGHT

*P*oppy awoke to a loud rapping against the front door. The night was still dark, the waves rushing outside her window as she threw back her covers with a pounding heart. There was only one reason for someone to come knocking at such an hour. Had there been an accident? Had Trevik been injured on the *Pilferer* that evening? Or was he...

She refused to allow the thought to enter her heart. Donning her nightdress, she fled from her room, meeting Mother and Morvoren in the corridor as the three of them raced to the sitting room.

Mother opened the door first, and Poppy pulled back as Edmund stood before them.

"Lieutenant?" Mother questioned, clearly feeling the same confusion as Poppy. "Whate'er be the matter?"

Edmund's eyes glanced to Poppy. "Mrs. Kendricks has gone into labor. I rode for Dr. Kent, who bade me to fetch you for assistance."

Mother was already backing away from the door. "I'll be but a moment. Poppy, ye must fetch Elowen. Bring 'er here to stay so she don't hear 'er mother's frettin'." Then she whirled around and disappeared down the dark corridor.

"Be she well?" Morvoren asked, remaining by the door as Poppy began her retreat, as well.

Poppy only heard the beginning of his response.

"I do not believe so, ma'am..."

In a matter of minutes, Poppy and Mother were traipsing across the dark countryside toward Golowduyn, guided by the light of the moon and a single lantern Poppy held outstretched before them.

"I would have brought the wagon had I known I'd be retrieving the both of you," Edmund said apologetically, leading Mrs. Kendricks's horse beside him.

Mother shook her head. "We be no strangers to walkin' these cliffs, Lieutenant."

He nodded, glancing to Poppy with a searching gaze before focusing straight ahead.

She wasn't sure what his look had meant, but she did her best to set it aside, concentrating instead on keeping one foot in front of the other, despite her churning stomach.

Mrs. Kendricks and her baby would be well. They had to be. Mr. Kendricks couldn't survive without them.

Silence punctuated the air between them from that point forward as they rushed to the lighthouse, arriving just after midnight. Mr. Kendricks met them at the door as they filed into the entryway, Elowen clinging to his neck, her dazed eyes wide open.

"Thank you so much for coming," Mr. Kendricks said, strained lines stretching across his brow and beneath his eyes. "Dr. Kent has done his best to prevent the baby from coming, but it will occur this evening." He hesitated, motioning to Elowen as he spoke in a hushed tone. "She has not released her hold of me since she awoke to Abigail's moaning."

Poppy understood her task at once. "Elowen," she said

softly. "Would ye like to come play with Isolde and me in Tristwick?"

Elowen reached out for Poppy at once, who embraced her with all the love and comfort she was in need of in that moment.

Mr. Kendricks released a sigh of relief. "Thank you," he whispered.

"'Ow be Mrs. Kendricks?" Mother asked.

He grimaced, his eyes red. "She is not in a good state. Dr. Kent is worried if she does not strengthen her resolve, both she and the baby might not…" The words choked in his mouth.

Mother nodded compassionately, though her brow was set. "We'll not allow that to 'appen, Mr. Kendricks. May I?" She motioned to the back room, and he nodded for her to continue.

He turned back to Edmund, Poppy, and his daughter. "Are you certain…"

Poppy was already nodding her head. "I'll watch o'er 'er at Tristwick. The minute ye send word, I'll 'ave 'er right back."

Mr. Kendricks nodded his gratitude, the fear in his eyes rattling her confidence.

A moan from Abigail broke the silence, and Mr. Kendricks was gone without another word, leaving Edmund and Poppy alone in the corridor with Elowen.

Edmund kept his gaze averted, rubbing the back of his neck before facing the door. "Allow me to ready the wagon, then I can take the both of you back to Tristwick."

He left before she could even decline his offer or express her gratitude. She knew something was bothering him, but she could not decipher if it was concern for the Kendrickses…or the time they'd spent on the beach, when he'd caressed her with such softness, she'd nearly melted into a puddle at his feet.

After gathering a change of clothing for Elowen, a warm throw, and the girl's doll, Poppy made her way outside just as Edmund finished securing Glastaish to the wagon.

He held a silent Elowen as Poppy climbed into the wagon, then delivered the girl back into her arms. The wagon seat shifted and creaked as he climbed up next to them, wincing as he had to use his other arm.

"Do it 'urt?" she asked.

He shook his head. "Not more than I can handle." Then he clicked Glastaish forward.

Elowen fell asleep as the wagon jolted and jostled across the road. Every now and again, Poppy's shoulder would bump into Edmund's, causing a warmth to settle about her like a comforting blanket, but the two of them remained silent to avoid waking Elowen.

Soon enough, they reached the upper edge of Tristwick. With the pathway in front of the house too small for a wagon, they situated themselves on the ridge behind the house.

After securing the horse, Edmund came around to help Poppy down from the wagon, once more taking Elowen with another wince as his arm pinched.

Poppy climbed down the wagon, then reached for the girl, but Edmund paused. "Will you allow me to carry her inside for you?"

"Are ye certain it won't 'urt ye?"

"Not at all," he whispered. Then he followed Poppy as she led the way to her home.

Morvoren met them at the door, circles beneath her eyes. "I 'eard the wagon approachin'," she whispered, leading the way to her room where Isolde still slept.

She motioned for Edmund to place Elowen on the spare bed she'd fashioned out of a few blankets and pillows, and together, she helped him lower the girl, who miraculously remained asleep.

Edmund made to leave the room at once, though he hesitated a moment near the doorway.

"I'll watch o'er 'em for a moment," Morvoren said, giving Poppy a knowing look.

Grateful for her sister-in-law's care, Poppy led Edmund to the front door once again.

"Thank ye for bringin' us back," she whispered, taking a step outside, the cool night air instantly nipping at her cheeks.

He paused on the pathway, turning to face her. "Of course. I'm grateful to be of any service I can." He looked away, the light of the moon barely revealing the edges of his features. "I've never seen the captain like this before, not even at sea."

Her throat ached with emotion for the captain and his lieutenant, who felt his friend's pain as his own. "It be understandable," she whispered. "That be the love of 'is life fightin' for 'er own."

Their eyes met, and the intensity with which he watched her, apparent even in the dim light of the glowing moon, forced the breath from her lungs.

She wished she could say the intensity was for her sake, that he felt something for her that was akin to the Kendricks's feelings for each other—something that would keep him in Cornwall with Poppy.

But she knew he was merely feeling compassion for his friends.

"Mrs. Kendricks'll be well," she tried to reassure him.

"You are so certain?"

"Ain't nothin' to do with 'ow certain I be, and everythin' to do with 'ow strong Mrs. Kendricks be."

"Yes. Yes, you are right."

Once again, their eyes connected, but instead of that same intensity, a softness crossed his features. "Poppy," he whispered, taking a step toward her.

She held her breath. But in the next moment, he shook his

head and stepped away. "I shall send word tomorrow how the Kendrickses fair."

Disappointment rushed over her, but she nodded all the same. "Thank ye."

He withdrew further, giving a simple nod before disappearing into the darkness. Poppy closed the door as she retreated within her house, leaning back against the wood with a sigh.

Worry consumed her. Worry for Mrs. Kendricks. Worry for her baby. Worry for Elowen and Mr. Kendricks.

And worry for her own sake as she attempted to contemplate how she would once again bear a life that did not include Edmund Harris.

CHAPTER TWENTY-NINE

*E*dmund feared he would get in the way at Golowduyn, having nothing to offer the suffering Kendrickses, but the moment he returned, Mrs. Honeysett and Dr. Kent put him straight to work, delivering clean rags, linens, and soap, opening windows, and boiling water.

Edmund was no stranger to the dangers of childbirth, having heard all his life how often women and children did not survive the harrowing ordeal. But Dr. Kent seemed capable enough, though his practices seemed a far cry different then what most physicians performed.

Knowing how private a person Mrs. Kendricks tended to be, Edmund avoided entering the room at all, always delivering any items he'd been tasked to find to Mrs. Honeysett outside of the door. But that did not stop the sounds of Mrs. Kendricks's agony from spreading throughout the home.

How a woman could withstand such pain was beyond him. He was only relieved Kendricks had chosen to remain by his wife's side, as she would clearly need his support, as opposed to most women being without their husbands during labor.

After Mrs. Honeysett tasked Edmund to boil more water

for Dr. Kent to wash his hands—yet another practice the physician had adopted—Edmund set the kettle on the stove-top, then returned to the room to see what else was needed.

Waiting outside the room, he held his hand above the door, ready to knock. But when other voices sounded—only Kendricks's and his wife's—Edmund paused.

"Gavin, I cannot do this."

Edmund had never heard Mrs. Kendricks's voice filled with such despair, such fragility.

He peeked beyond the crack of the open door, finding Dr. Kent sitting in the corner of the room, his eyes closed to reveal a moment of weakness as he slept. Mrs. Honeysett must have gone outdoors for a moment to give her a boost to see through the night, as well.

"You can, Abigail," Kendricks whispered, capturing Edmund's attention once more. "You must. You must find the strength to go on."

Edmund winced. He should not be there, listening in to this private conversation. But when he attempted to move, his feet remained rooted to their spot.

"I don't have the strength," Mrs. Kendricks whispered. "What if…what if something happens to the baby?"

"You mustn't think such things." Kendricks spoke with tenderness, but the underlying fear within his tone nearly broke Edmund. "All will be well. We—"

His words were interrupted by another of Mrs. Kendricks's moans as she struggled to breathe. After a moment, Kendricks began again.

"You must fight, my darling," he said in a fierce whisper, as if to fortify himself, as well. "Fight for us, just like before. You have the courage. You have the strength. Do not give up now. Not after you've overcome so much. We need you." He paused, his voice shaking as he continued. "*I* need you."

Shuffling occurred, and Mrs. Kendrick's sobs were muffled, no doubt as Kendricks embraced her.

With tears burning in his eyes, Edmund finally pulled away. He had no place to listen to such intimacy, such love. And yet, he could not regret overhearing their vulnerable words.

Mother and Father had never verbally expressed their love for one another, not to Edmund's surprise, for he did not believe they ever did truly love each other.

Not like the love the Kendrickses shared. Not the type of love to break a man at the mere thought of his wife giving up the fight and leaving her life behind.

Desperate to calm his emotions, Edmund left the house, quietly closing the door behind him and drawing the cold air into his lungs.

Kendricks's words from before echoed in his mind. *"I would sacrifice it all to be with her. In fact, I did. And I have not once regretted my decision."*

Edmund had seen that time and time again. Kendricks would truly be lost without Mrs. Kendricks at his side.

Then another thought occurred, one he could not keep at bay as it forced itself to the forefront of his mind.

How would *he* be without Poppy? Would he not also be a broken man? Had he not been a broken man without her these three years past?

"Ye need a bit o' fresh air, too?"

Edmund started, swiveling his head to the side to where Mrs. Honeysett stood. The dim light from the lantern in the kitchen window cast across the grass and lit half of her features.

He'd forgotten that she'd come out there first.

"Yes," he responded. "Just for a moment."

She nodded with understanding. "Ye've been a great 'elp to 'em this evenin', sir."

"If only more could be done. Captain Kendricks is…I wish I could do more for him."

Mrs. Honeysett looked away. "Ye be doin' more 'an

enough just by bein' 'ere." A soft smile spread across her lips, the twinkle in her eye resembling Poppy's. "I know Trev would've appreciated a man's support when Morvoren 'ad Isolde. Poor man fainted dead away."

Edmund gave a soft chuckle. He had no doubt he would do the same when his wife had children.

The humor slipped away from him. When? *When* he would have children? To his greater annoyance and further disturbance, Poppy's image appeared in his mind's eyes.

Slowly, he reined his thoughts in. That ship had sailed long ago. There was no returning to the past. Or was there?

He shook his head. Somewhere in that dark evening, in his delirious, sleep-deprived state, his senses had taken leave of him.

"No one blames ye for what 'appened 'tween ye and Poppy, ye know," Mrs. Honeysett said.

Heavens above. Did the woman possess some secret device with which she could decipher his very thoughts?

He shifted uncomfortably on the grass they stood upon.

"That bein' said," she continued, "all o' we, Trevik included, were upset when things didn't work out 'tween ye and Poppy. 'Course, we just want ye to be 'appy, and if that be possible only separate, we support ye both."

He nodded his gratitude, not knowing what else to say. He'd always loved Poppy's mother. She had welcomed him with open arms from the beginning and made him feel at home—something he'd never even felt at his own home.

"*Are* ye 'appy, Lieutenant?"

He hesitated. There really was no point in telling a falsehood. Not when the woman would perceive it.

"I am trying to be," he answered truthfully.

"I be glad to 'ear that. I do 'ope it comes to ye one day."

"Thank you." He swallowed, shifting his gaze anxiously to prevent more words from exiting his lips.

"I'd better return to Mrs. Kendricks now." Mrs. Honeysett

walked past him with a loving pat on his arm, then moved to the door.

Edmund hesitated. He was terrible at sharing any sort of emotion, but that was no excuse when this woman had done more than enough to always be kind to him.

With a deep breath, he turned toward her. "Mrs. Honeysett?"

She stopped with her hand on the door handle. "Yes?"

"I…I just wanted to thank you for your kindness. Now and always. I know you did not have to do so after I left, but I…" He trailed off, not knowing what else to say.

Mrs. Honeysett's warm smile spread across him like the sunshine, just like Poppy's always did. "Whether ye marry me daugh'er or not, sir, ye'll always be part o' me family. I 'ope ye know that."

Then with a silent nod, she retreated indoors.

Edmund stared after her, his heart overflowing with warmth, though his chest tightened with discomfort. Did Mrs. Honeysett still wish for him to marry Poppy? Or were her words spoken out of just simple kindness?

He squeezed his eyes closed, trying to bring back all of the reasons he was going to return to the sea by the end of the coming week, but as he stood in the darkness, Golowduyn's light flashing over his head, the sea's waves steadily rushing in his ears, he could think of nothing else but when he would be able to have the fortune of seeing Poppy once again.

Two hours passed before Mrs. Kendricks was ready to deliver her child. Mrs. Honeysett had requested Edmund to remain close.

"Ye must be 'ere for Mr. Kendricks if she doesn't…"

Edmund had understood his duty at once. Though sick with the fear of such grief, he paced the sitting room back and forth, wincing with each and every shriek Mrs. Kendricks released until finally—finally—the heartachingly sweet cry of the baby pierced the air.

The breath rushed from Edmund's lungs, and tears flooded his eyes at the sound he'd never heard before—the sound of a babe fresh from heaven's doors.

She'd done it. Mrs. Kendricks had done it.

CHAPTER THIRTY

*P*oppy had been unable to sleep the night before, anxiously awaiting any word from the Kendrickses about the state of Mrs. Kendricks and the baby. When news finally did come early the next morning that both she and her new baby boy were miraculously well, Poppy had never been more relieved.

She was tasked to bring Elowen to meet her new baby brother, so in the afternoon, the two of them—Isolde remaining with her mother—made their way to the lighthouse.

Poppy would have never guessed that baby Benesek, with his thick, dark hair and chubby cheeks, had been delivered a week early.

"I'm only relieved I didn't have to wait another seven days to have him grow any larger," Mrs. Kendricks joked as she rested in her bed, Gwitha at the foot of it.

Poppy was relieved to see Mrs. Kendricks's color already having returned to her cheeks, the burden of the last few weeks finally removed as she held her child in her arms.

Elowen had been uncharacteristically quiet when she'd first entered the room, but once she'd been allowed to sit beside her mother in the bed, her chattering became endless once again.

"Are ye feelin' well, Mrs. Kendricks?" Poppy asked when there was a break in Elowen's comments about how small Benesek's fingers were and how soft his hair was.

"I'm more than well, thank you, Poppy. Ready to climb to the top of that tower just as soon as Dr. Kent gives me permission."

Mr. Kendricks shook his head from the side of the room, an amused smile on his lips, though dark half-circles still hung below his eyes. "Then I shall pay Dr. Kent to force you to wait at least a month."

They shared a smile, then Poppy took her leave, allowing the family of four to spend time together alone as she went about her regular chores at the lighthouse.

Poppy felt much joy for them, much relief. And yet, she could not help but wonder if such joyous moments would ever be for her own life—with her own children and husband.

Naturally, Edmund popped into her mind next, but she had to push the thought aside. He did not wish to remain on land any longer. Nor did he wish to marry her.

He was content with his life, so she would be, as well.

Or so, at least, she'd try.

The next morning, Poppy rose early with her mother and Trevik, dressing and eating a simple breakfast of porridge before walking to St. Just together. Only Trevik and Edmund were supposed to go to St. Ives that day, but after much deliberation, Mother thought it would be better to have as much of their family visit the Roskelleys as possible.

She'd sent a letter a few days before, informing them of their visit, but they did not have time to await a response.

"I do 'ope they don't think it be an ambush," Trevik said

as the three of them walked down the road to town. "There be so many o' we goin' now."

"I'm sure they'll be right 'appy to see us," Mother reassured him. "I imagine they be in need o' some familiar faces after so long."

Poppy couldn't help but agree. She'd been excited at the prospect of seeing her old friend Demelza Roskelley again, the sister of Hedrek being only a year younger than Poppy.

With a dismal catch the night before, Morvoren had volunteered to do what little fish processing was required, then promised she would see to the Kendricks's needs, as well, so Poppy was free to travel with her mother and brother.

And, of course, Edmund.

Attempting to distract herself, she focused on the sheep bleating in the distance as they crossed over the fields, but it was no use. Edmund had become a permanent fixture in the chambers of her mind, unable to be moved, unable to be ignored.

She hadn't seen him at the lighthouse the day before. Apparently, he'd stayed awake all night and all morning to help with the Kendrickses and had finally slept in the afternoon.

His actions didn't surprise Poppy. The man had always been noble, as was evident by the fact that he'd be joining them in St. Ives that morning.

Now all that Poppy had to do was find the patience to wait to see him again.

With the coach set to leave for St. Ives at ten o'clock, and the Honeysetts arriving a half hour early, Trevik went to the inn for a heartier bite to eat while the women headed to Mrs. Follett's Modiste.

That morning, Morvoren had mentioned in passing that she needed to remember to restitch her stockings that had already been mended nearly six times over. Mother, wishing to surprise her daughter-in-law, spoke with Mrs. Follett about obtaining a discounted pair.

As Mother did her best to negotiate a lower price, Poppy wandered about the shop, eying all the fine fabrics, parasols, and bonnets on display until her patience thinned.

After signaling to Mother that she would be waiting outside—Mother responding with a distracted nod—Poppy slipped from the modiste and out into the fresh air once again.

How she despised lingering in those stuffy shops. She'd much rather remain outdoors where the smell of rye bread and English walnut cake swirled about the air in delicious waves.

She sniffed again, glancing toward the bake shop at the end of the street. She had no extra money to spend on anything there and looking at the pastries was sure to be torture. But that smell could not be refused.

After a short walk, she reached the shop, eying the goods from the glass window outside, fresh strawberries on small tarts, buns with raisins adorning the top, orange custard puddings. The baker had certainly been busy that morning. Busy and detailed. They all looked of perfection.

"Pardon me," a woman said beside Poppy in a raspy voice.

Poppy stepped to the side. "Apologies, ma'am," she mumbled, having obviously been preventing the view of the sweets to the woman.

Something about that voice sounded oddly familiar.

"Pardon me," the woman said again, and Poppy's stomach tensed.

Of course. She knew where she'd heard it before. Slowly, she turned to look at the woman standing beside her. Sure enough, Edmund's mother—Mrs. Beacham, was it?—stood by her side.

"You are the serving girl from the lighthouse, are you not?" the woman asked.

Poppy couldn't hide her surprise at the woman recognizing her. "Yes," she responded simply.

She didn't think she needed to clarify that she wasn't *just* a serving girl, but something within her told her that the woman hardly cared.

Mrs. Beacham pulled on a tight smile. "I thought it was you. There was no mistaking your darling face. I do not know if you recall, but I am Mrs. Beacham."

Beacham. So she'd remarried after Edmund's father died. "Yes, ye be Edmund's mother."

The woman's brow raised high, and Poppy cringed. "Lieutenant 'Arris's mother," she corrected swiftly.

Her cheeks warmed under Mrs. Beacham's continued appraisal. "Forgive me, but I cannot recall your name."

"Oh. I-I be Poppy 'Oneysett." What was the matter with her? Why was she stuttering and acting so foolishly? She never cracked under pressure.

But then, this was Edmund's mother, for heaven's sake. His *mother*. Surely Poppy should be doing her best to impress her. Then again, he'd recoiled when the woman had attempted to approach him and hardly seemed to care about his mother's opinion at all.

"And do you reside permanently at the lighthouse, Poppy Honeysett?" Mrs. Beacham asked next, reciting her name slowly.

"No, I live...just west of 'ere, in a small fishin' hamlet."

For some reason, she instantly regretted her delivery of such knowledge. If Edmund didn't seem to trust this woman, Poppy shouldn't either. Or had there been some simple misunderstanding between them that resulted in mislaid suspicion? Mrs. Beacham seemed kind enough, if not a little too serious.

"A fishing hamlet," she said with the barest lift of her voice. "How charming. My husband dabbles in the sport."

Dabbles? Sport? In Tristwick, they wouldn't even recognize the words.

Poppy glanced over her shoulder to Mrs. Follett's modiste. Curse her desire to ogle these pastries. She never should have left her mother's side.

"I'm certain Mr. Beacham would love to see how the fishing works in your part of the world," Mrs. Beacham continued, as if expecting an invitation.

But Poppy could not deliver one, not without first discussing the matter with Edmund. The last thing she wished to do was betray what trust had flickered between them by speaking with someone he did not wish her to.

"Our fishin' do be quite efficient, ma'am," she said, taking a step away. "Forgive I, but I must get back to me mother. She be waitin' for I, see."

Mrs. Beacham stepped forward, resting a hand on Poppy's arm. "Oh, but could I have just one more moment of your time?"

The look of pleading in her eyes made Poppy stop, though she glanced around anxiously. What if Edmund happened upon them?

"Please," Mrs. Beacham continued, her fingers tightening around Poppy's arm.

Finally, Poppy nodded. "Very well, ma'am."

Mrs. Beacham released her. "Thank you. I simply must speak with you about…about my son."

How Poppy regretted her decision to stay. The woman's only wrinkle lines appeared in the middle of her brow and at the edges of her mouth, as if she'd never spent a day in her life with a smile.

"I couldn't help but notice," Mrs. Beacham continued in her oddly gravelly voice, "the two of you seem quite close to one another."

Again, Poppy's cheeks warmed. Close to her son? Blast it all, Poppy had nearly *married* him. She hardly doubted Edmund had told his mother anything about their past, though.

"We be friends," she responded carefully.

Mrs. Beacham's lip twitched. "Well, I'm terribly glad to hear that. Our Eddy always had a difficult time making friends, as I'm sure you know."

Poppy didn't respond, finding that to be her safest route when she could not decipher the woman's words as truth or fiction.

"He was such a troubled little boy," she continued. "Always misbehaving, always finding himself in a bother. He could never make friends when he was away at school because he was…well, he was quite disturbed, you see. More so after the death of his father."

Worry stirred in Poppy's belly. None of this sounded like Edmund. Except, of course, being upset by his father's death. Was that because Mrs. Beacham was lying? Or because Edmund had done his best to hide his past?

Mrs. Beacham carried on, hardly aware of Poppy's discomfort. "He found himself in so many scuffles at school that we eventually had to pull him from Eton and hire a private tutor so he could continue his education from home."

Poppy looked over her shoulder. Maybe Edmund would arrive, or Trevik or Mother. Someone had to eventually come to help her escape this conversation.

"I truly thought I could help him heal while he was at home, but I'm afraid matters only worsened until he received his wish to be sent to the sea." Mrs. Beacham shook her head with a weary sigh. "I have only ever wanted the best for my son—to know he is living happily. I wrote him frequently, but I never received a letter in return." She hung her head. "Not once."

Poppy wasn't certain what she was supposed to be feeling at the moment. Sorrow for Mrs. Beacham's plight? Confusion over Edmund's seeming disregard for his mother? Misbelief or trust?

"Even now, I have come all this way to visit with him, and

he…" She paused, clearing her throat. "He will not speak with his poor mother. All that I wish to do is share my love for him. All I wish is to speak with him, just for a moment. Surely you understand my desire, Poppy?"

Concern grew broader and broader in Poppy's mind, like a ship fast approaching harbor. She knew people could change. She knew she did not know every little thing about Edmund.

But then, something was missing in Mrs. Beacham's words —some feeling Poppy could not place. But without being able to do so, she nodded in silence.

Mrs. Beacham looked pleased—if her face had been capable of such an expression. "I knew you would. You have a good heart. Now I hope I can trust in your good heart to please, tell my son that I love him. That my greatest desire is simply to speak with him and share that love." She reached toward Poppy, wrapping her fingers around her arm once again. "Would you ever be willing to do such a thing for a poor woman who has lost her son?"

Poppy willed herself not to wriggle free from the woman's too-familiar grasp. She hardly thought speaking with Edmund about his mother was her place—and she highly doubted that it would do any good.

But in that moment, all she wanted was to be free from this woman's presence. Something seemed odd about her, strangely off, and Poppy simply wanted to escape.

"I can try," she said with a nod. "But I do 'ave to find me mother now. Good day, Mrs. Beacham."

She took a step back, and Mrs. Beacham finally released her hold of her arm. "Oh, bless you, Poppy. You do a poor mother's heart much good. It is no wonder my son admires you so."

She gave a gracious nod of her head. Poppy barely managed a stiff curtsy in return before turning on her heel and scurrying up the street. Finally away from the woman's presence, Poppy drew a deep breath, refusing to be affected by the last thing she said, about Edmund admiring her.

Truthfully, she did not know what she could believe and what she could not. And that was what bothered her most of all.

After finding Mother just leaving Mrs. Follett's, she told her a quickened version of what had just occurred.

"I don't like it, Poppy," Mother said with a frown. "It seems unfair of a woman to put ye up to somethin' like that."

Poppy couldn't have agreed more. They continued their conversation until they reached the inn, finding Trevik and Edmund standing around the corner, stiffly speaking with one another once again. Relief flashed across Trevik's features once he saw Mother and Poppy approaching.

Edmund, however, took one look at Poppy, and his face brightened.

"It is no wonder my son admires you."

Poppy did her best to smile at Edmund in return, but his mother's words cast a shadow over her delight in seeing him once again.

"Your brother was only now telling me that the both of you will be joining us," he said with a polite smile. "I am pleased to hear it."

"We couldn't let the both of ye 'ave all the fun," Mother teased.

How could Mother speak so easily with the man after Mrs. Beacham's words with Poppy?

"The coach ought to arrive in a quarter of an hour," Trevik said, peering down the road. "I suggest we wait 'ere to ensure a place inside."

The others nodded in agreement, but Poppy had hardly heard her brother's words. Edmund was watching her now, his eyes slightly narrowed, as if he noticed something different with her behavior.

Of course he would notice. She was not so adept at hiding

her emotions as Mother was. So how was Poppy to bear an entire day with Edmund, all while she knew this secret that he deserved to know?

She glanced to Trevik and Mother, who were deep in conversation about what to expect at the Roskelleys. Edmund still watched her.

She needed to tell him. She did not wish to make him angry, but then, wouldn't she be betraying his trust if she did not tell him what his mother had said?

With that, her decision was made.

Taking a step forward, she spoke to Edmund directly. "May I speak with ye for a moment?" She glanced to Trevik's and Mother's inquiring eyes. "In private?"

Edmund hesitated, looking to the others before nodding. "Of course."

Poppy ignored the look Trevik gave her as she led Edmund away from him and Mother. Her brother would be fine. Mother could explain matters. Either way, he could handle a few moments of not being fully aware of everything going on with everyone.

Once she'd reached the far end of the side of the inn where fewer ears could overhear their words, she turned to face Edmund.

"Are you well, Poppy?" he asked, concern creasing his brow.

"Yes. I only...I do 'ave somethin' to say to ye that might make ye upset."

Worry swirled in his eyes. "What is it?"

She drew a deep breath. "Your mother was speakin' to I just now, and I thought ye'd like to know."

Instantly, the worry vanished from his eyes, replaced with a look as hard as steel. "What did she say?"

Poppy rushed forward, anxious to speak the words before he could assume the worst. "She spoke a bit about your past. The letters she wrote to you. 'Ow...'Ow ye ne'er responded."

His jaw twitched, fury burning across his features as his lips disappeared in a frown. "Whatever that woman said to you, you must know that she cannot be trusted. She was never known to be a great defender of truth."

For some reason, his words quelled Poppy's concerns, and she nodded in silence.

"Is that all she said to you?" His lips still tightened in a straight line.

Poppy recounted a few more of the items she could remember, and Edmund's frown deepened further and further until she ended.

"She asked if I'd get ye to speak with 'er," she finished with a wince. "Then I left 'fore she could say anythin' more."

He closed his eyes, shaking his head with a mirthless huff, not saying another word.

Poppy glanced back to her family, who looked away when they caught her gaze. "I didn't know if I should tell ye or not, but tain't fair for me to be 'tween ye both. I only thought ye'd like to know since she be quite adamant. Forceful, e'en."

His eyes snapped to hers. "Forceful? Did she touch you?"

The question was so sudden, she nearly took a step back in surprise. "No. Well, she 'eld me arm, but—"

"Did she injure you?"

Poppy frowned, taken aback once more by his ferocity. "No, Edmund, she didn't."

His jaw flexed, and he looked away. Why had such a question come to his mind at all? Clearly he did not trust his mother. Poppy, too, had felt a degree of discomfort around her, but she hardly thought Mrs. Beacham would have injured her. Who would do such a thing?

Slightly regretting her decision to tell Edmund after all, she crossed an arm over her body. "I be that sorry, Edmund, if ye be upset with I. I thought ye ought to be aware, that be all. I wouldn't wish to betray your trust for nothin'."

To her relief, Edmund released a slow breath, clearly

attempting to soften his heart. "Thank you, indeed, for informing me. I am not upset with you. I only…I fear I need but a moment." He looked up the street. "I shall return before the stagecoach arrives."

Without hesitating, he stormed away and disappeared around the corner of the inn.

Mother and Trevik came up to her with worried expressions.

"What 'appened, Poppy?" Mother asked, concern laced in her tone.

Poppy shook her head in dismay. "'E just said 'e needed a moment."

Trevik glanced over his shoulder to the street. "The coach ain't waitin' for 'im."

"'E said 'e'd return," Poppy said.

And she had to believe the man would keep his promise.

CHAPTER THIRTY-ONE

*A*fter a well-placed bribe of a few coins and a kind smile to a maid sweeping down the lower corridor of the inn, Edmund learned which room his mother was staying in.

Thanking the maid, he stormed up the stairs, his smile disappearing as he pounded his fist against her door.

He knew she would be there. Her words to Poppy were a clear message—a threat.

"Speak with me, Edmund, or you shall live to regret it."

Seething, he waited until it opened, and Mr. Beacham's ashen face appeared in the doorway.

The man backed up with wide eyes. "Dear…" he began.

Edmund moved into the room, slamming the door behind him. All sense had fled from his mind the moment he'd heard Poppy's words, rage blinding him when he'd learned Mother had touched her.

Of course she would still be using her controlling tactics. Anything to get Edmund to do as she wished.

Mother stood from the chair near the window, putting her book down and staring at Edmund with a look of innocence he recognized all too well.

It was the same one she held up to her face like a mask in public. Always the portrait of perfect serenity.

"How dare you?" he said, facing her with clenched fists and a tight jaw.

Mother tipped her head to the side. "Whatever do you mean?"

"You know exactly what I am referring to."

A knowing smile spread across her lips. "Oh, you mean speaking with the little serving girl?"

Tension slid up Edmund's spine.

"I knew you'd be upset with me, Eddy, seeing how protective you are of the little creature, but honestly, you left me no choice."

"No choice but to what, harass an innocent woman, twist the truth of the past to your own advantage?"

It was true he'd had a difficult time in school, but that was nothing compared to how mother had treated him afterward.

"She *is* innocent, isn't she?" Mother gave a soft laugh. "So impressionable. So naïve." She turned to Mr. Beacham. "Do you know, her family works in the fishing industry? I've a notion to see them."

Mr. Beacham didn't even attempt to respond, his eyes remaining out of the window.

Edmund knew she was only saying such words to crawl under his skin. Unfortunately, it worked. Now it was time to do the same thing to her. "Whatever you said to her did not work."

Mother pulled in her lips. "On the contrary. I wished to convince her to get you to speak with me."

Poppy had clearly been intimidated by Mother. Who wouldn't be? But he couldn't deny the relief that had come over him to know Mother's words hadn't stopped Poppy from telling him the truth.

Still, if Mother planted any seed of doubt in Poppy's mind...

He shook his head. "I did not come here to speak with you. I came for one purpose, and one purpose alone."

"And what is that purpose, pray tell?"

"To warn you. If you ever speak with Poppy again, or anyone in her family, I will see that—"

"What?" Mother snapped, interrupting his words and taking a step toward him.

As a child, he'd always flinched back, but not now.

"You remember who you are speaking with, Edmund Harris. I am your mother." Her voice dropped, her eyes carrying a dangerous light. "You know what your idle threats brought you before."

Oh, he recalled all too well what had occurred after he'd attempted to stand up to her. A bloodied lip. A bruised cheek. A swollen eye.

Did she truly believe she could intimidate him with such tactics now?

"Now," she said, drawing her chin up to appear taller, "after befriending a lovely physician's wife, I have come to understand that you were once quite close to becoming engaged to this little fisherman's daughter."

Edmund's stomach tightened. Mrs. Rennalls. Of course she would be the one to speak with Mother.

Now that she knew of his attachment to Poppy, Mother would do everything in her power to use that to her advantage.

"I cannot tell you how heartily disappointed I was to learn of this." Mother clicked her tongue as if he was eleven years old still. "Have you no shame?"

Edmund's chin dropped in disbelief. "I suppose I learned from the best."

Her eyes pinched. "You still have that sharp tongue about you. Just like your father."

His heart twisted at the mention of him.

"How I despise you, Edmund. You and your father," she'd say over and over again.

As her spiteful words echoed again in his mind, Edmund shook his head. He did not need to be there any longer.

Rising to his full stature, he pointed a finger at his mother. "You stay away from the Honeysetts. Or I shall tell everyone."

Her nostrils flared. "Tell them what?"

He didn't need to say a word. He knew she was fully aware of what he was referring to.

Her jaw clenched. "You hateful boy. We had an agreement."

They did. Edmund was fully aware of it. She had signed for him to enter the navy, and he would keep their secret.

But for the first time in his life since that moment when he was a child, he felt the power return to his side. "That agreement will be void if you speak with Poppy again. I swear, I will tell everyone. Including Algernon and Cecil. I will tell them what I know about you…" He pointed a finger at Mr. Beacham. "And him."

She raised her chin, though fear flashed across her features. "They would not believe you."

"Perhaps. Or perhaps everything will make sense to them then. The coincidental timing of your first meeting with Mr. Beacham. The bruises they saw across my face and back when we swam in the lake at Sunningdale the summer before Father died. The reason I was kept away from them and the rest of society for weeks to allow the bruises to heal."

Recalling these moments seemed to injure him all over again. He was certain his brothers already suspected Mother's cruelty, but why would they say a word when she loved *them*?

Still, he knew they were unaware of the truth of her and Mr. Beacham's relationship, and revealing such would set the truth in motion.

He raised a brow. "The seed will be planted in their

minds, and doubt will be continually sewn for the rest of their lives."

"You'd be willing to destroy the lives your brothers have created by spreading baseless rumors?" she said ceremoniously.

He shook his head. He had no desire to upend anything. Even if they had both received the love Edmund never had, his quarrel was not with them.

"No, Mother. Not baseless. For you know it is the truth. And I will not be at fault for destroying their lives. You will be."

Her lips twisted, pulled in with utter hate. "I never should have allowed you to enter the navy. I should have kept you home, forced you to comply with my wishes. You were always the greatest reminder as to why I never should have married your father."

The words pierced Edmund's heart. He'd heard them before—how she'd regretted her marriage to Father, how she regretted having Edmund—but such words could never *not* hurt.

In an effort to secure his spirit, he pulled up his defenses and forced an apathetic tone. "And being near you, Mother, has always been the greatest reminder of why I chose to follow Father."

Her face screwed up with rage. She pulled back her hand to deliver a blow to his face, but he caught her wrist with his fingers, holding her securely away from him.

She struggled to break free, though he held fast. Mr. Beacham stood back, eyes wide, face white.

"Unhand me, you ungrateful wretch," Mother said, pulling her arm again.

Finally, he released her, having no desire to injure her in return.

She took a step back, holding her hand to her chest as he spoke.

"I will never allow you to strike me again," he said. "You destroyed my life, but I'll not allow you to do so again. Nor will I allow you to destroy the lives of anyone in St. Just. Mark my words. If you do, I will tell the world what I know."

She looked up at him as if daring him to say more, but he didn't need to. She knew he was telling the truth.

With a quick glance to Mr. Beacham, whose eyes were still filled with fear, Edmund walked out of the room, leaving the door ajar as his hands shook with pent-up fear and frustration.

He would never see his mother again.

CHAPTER THIRTY-TWO

*P*oppy sat across from Edmund in the coach, glancing at him for what seemed the hundredth time as the carriage rumbled its way to St. Ives.

She still didn't know where Edmund had gone after she'd told him about his mother, but wherever it was, it hadn't done him any good. He came back silent, brooding, and pensive, despite forcing a smile and conversation at the beginning of their journey.

Now, however, nearly halfway there, Edmund did not even attempt to speak as he merely stared out of the window, his chin propped between his thumb and bent forefinger.

She had an inkling he'd gone to speak with his mother, but of course Poppy couldn't be sure. How she wished to ask him —about his mother, about his childhood, about it all. But the man seemed bound and determined to keep that part of his past under lock and key.

Her concerns continued as the coach arrived in St. Ives, and she drew her attention to the busy streets of the town, the houses stacked one after another up the hill, as if in a hectic scramble to reach the top.

After tipping the coachman, Poppy and the others made

their way through the busy streets, weaving in and out of buildings, shops, and houses until they reached the smaller homes situated down a tight road.

As soon as they found the Roskelleys' house—a white-washed, two-story home squished between seven other dwellings—they knocked on the door and awaited a response.

Poppy looked over her shoulder, peering down the street as she hoped to catch a glimpse of the sparkling sea the harbor town was situated beside, but there was no sight of it.

Was this in Poppy's future, a sea-less view from her home that was packed between the others as tightly as a hogshead of pilchards?

Her conversation with Edmund echoed in her mind from two nights past on the beach, and she reminded herself that her memories of her father could be brought with her wher-ever she traveled.

But her fear of being thrust into the darkness with no escape had not changed. She supposed it was simply part of her life now, a permanent appendage to her mind that she would simply have to learn to live with.

The door opened, and Mrs. Roskelley appeared with an expectant look. The moment she settled her eyes on the Honeysetts, her chin quivered.

"Oh, my goodness," she breathed, and Mother reached forward to embrace the woman. "I was so 'appy to receive your letter, sayin' ye'd be comin' to visit."

"'Ow we've missed ye and your family, Rose," Mother said.

Poppy, Trevik, and Edmund looked away, allowing them a moment of privacy before Mrs. Roskelley ushered them inside her small home—nearly half the size of what they'd possessed in Tristwick.

She situated the women on the small wooden bench near the miniscule hearth, the men standing beside them before Demelza rushed into the room. She squeezed her way onto the bench with Poppy and her mother, clinging to Poppy's hand with her own as Mrs. Roskelley sat on a chair she'd brought in from the kitchen.

"It be so wonderful to see ye again," Mother said, beaming at them both, though there was a hint of sorrow behind her smile—behind everyone's smiles. "Are ye adjustin' well?"

Demelza hung her head, her stringy black hair falling out of her bun as Mrs. Roskelley nodded with a tight smile. "The fish processin' be different 'ere," she responded. "Tain't no singin' involved and very little talkin'. Most women just wish to get done swift-like. But we 'ave work, so we mustn't complain."

She looked to her daughter. Demelza didn't say a word, though Poppy felt the young woman's hand tighten in her own.

Poppy squeezed it in response, not knowing what else to do to support her friend.

"And 'ow be Hedrek?" Mother asked next, her tone light. "Be 'e likin' the seinin' business?"

Mrs. Roskelley's smile faltered. "I do think 'e misses Tristwick."

Poppy didn't blame him. While Trevik fished with long drift nets aboard the *Pilferer* at night, seiners fished during the day with multiple boats and grand nets. Seiners—especially in Tristwick—were known for their greed and workhorse behavior, as opposed to drifters, who loved their work deep in their bones.

Poppy glanced to Trevik, whose brow was creased, then to Edmund, who stood watching her with a stoic expression. Her heart skipped a beat, but she looked away. Was he still upset with the news she'd given him of his mother? Or did something else now bother him?

"Tell us what news ye 'ave o' Tristwick," Demelza said

next, turning her dark eyes on Poppy. "We be desperate to 'ear what 'as 'appened at 'ome."

Poppy forced a smile, then launched into a monologue of all that had occurred, carefully toeing the line between making the Roskelleys not miss home too greatly, and not wishing to depress them with the stark reality that awaited Tristwick without the *Pilferer's* crew.

After a few moments, however, the door opened to the outside, and Hedrek appeared. He looked around the room, sliding off his cap and closing the door behind him.

"My apologies for not being 'ere earlier," he said simply.

Trevik brushed off his tardiness with a shake of his head, reaching forward to shake hands with his old crew member. "It be good to see ye again."

Hedrek nodded, his tall figure even broader than Trevik's and Edmund's. No hint of a smile touched his lips, but that was nothing new. Hedrek had always been a serious individual —made even more so with the death of his father when he was a young boy, now even more so with the death of Kenver.

"So," he said as those about the room watched him, "I s'pose ye all be 'ere to try to convince us to move back to Tristwick."

An awkward silence settled in the room.

Mrs. Roskelley gave a quick shake of her head to her son, but he seemed not to notice. Demelza's hand held Poppy's even tighter.

Poppy's heart ached at the discomfort, the injured hearts that filled the room. So much pain had been suffered by each person there. She could almost feel it all herself, so much so that tears flooded her eyes.

She looked down, blinking away the moisture. Tears would not help convince the Roskelleys to return to Tristwick.

But Trevik might.

He focused his gaze on the family they visited, a look of compassion on his brow. "To be honest, yes, that be why we came. To tell ye all what be changin' so ye might 'ave the desire to return."

Hedrek was already shaking his head. "Trev, I told ye 'fore…"

His words trailed off as Trevik took a step forward. "We need ye, Hedrek. We need your family. Ye remember Lieutenant 'Arris?" He motioned to Edmund, who nodded as Hedrek did the same. "'E do think we'd benefit from a lifeboat. If we can obtain one and find men enough to run it, we can do that as well as fish. We can…we can save men who we might've saved 'fore. With ye and other men returnin', we might bring even more men in, and we—"

Hedrek stopped him with a shake of his head, raising a gentle hand between him. "Please, ye must stop Trevik. I appreciate ye comin' all this way to see us. And I do 'ope this lifeboat works out for ye all. But as I said 'fore, livin' in Tristwick be too painful now for the lot o' we. It bears too many reminders of all that we've lost." His jaw was tight, no doubt to keep his sorrow at bay. "Ye know what it be like to live in a place with a near-constant reminder of a family member's death. I be grateful for ye comin' all this way. But me family be stayin' put right 'ere."

Demelza's hand shivered in Poppy's, her chin quivering.

This had been a mistake, coming here. They'd hoped to convince them to return, but instead, she feared they'd only made matters worse.

"Why don't we 'ave a cup o' tea," Mrs. Roskelley offered softly, attempting to ease the tension around the room. She motioned for Demelza to join her, and the girl hung her head as she followed her mother to the kitchen.

As his sister and mother left, Hedrek winced. "I know they think we be better off at Tristwick, but we ain't," he said to the others. "In time, they'll see."

No response was made as Hedrek's shoulders fell. "Look, I'd 'ate to waste your journey 'ere, so I'll tell ye, I did 'ear of a few men who be weary o' workin' for seiners. I be meetin' 'em at the Red Boar for drinks 'fore dinner. I ain't interested in returnin', but if ye come to the inn, I'll introduce ye 'em. Per'aps *they* might be interested in what ye 'ave to offer."

New men, new families. Poppy's stomach swirled. She closed her eyes, reminding herself that this was a good thing. This meant that she would not have to leave Cornwall. At least not for now.

"Thank ye, Hedrek," Trevik said, his lips pulled down. He lowered his voice. "My apologies for comin' 'ere. I only wished to…"

"I know. Ye just be doin' your best for your family. Same as I. I only be sorry I can't 'elp more."

A sudden rush of humility came over Poppy. That was precisely what Trevik was doing—attempting to help his family. And that was what Edmund had been doing, too, for her family.

And what had she been doing? Worrying, faithless and fearful. She knew her fears were warranted. She knew they were valid. But that did not mean she couldn't try just a little bit harder to have hope.

After all, was life not worth the effort?

CHAPTER THIRTY-THREE

*T*he rest of the visit with the Roskelleys passed by fairly quickly, as did the next few hours that the Honeysetts and Edmund milled about St. Ives until four o'clock in the afternoon came around and it was time to make their way to the Red Boar and meet with Hedrek's friends.

Edmund sat back in silence—as he had all day—as Trevik explained to the three seiners about the lifeboat. To their relief, these men seemed far more interested than the Roskelleys. Still, they were not entirely convinced.

"Me son and I ain't particularly attached to seinin'," one of the men said who had experience as a skipper. "But what incentive would we 'ave for movin' 'ouse and disruptin' our families' lives?"

Trevik launched into a description of newer housing, more land than St. Ives, and the ability to perhaps have time away if they volunteered for the lifeboat—though they were still uncertain if they'd receive it.

Still, the men seemed hesitant. Clearly, Trevik was just missing the mark on what they were looking for, and Edmund had just the idea as to what it was.

With reticence, he leaned forward in his seat, facing the men who sat across from them at the elongated table.

"If I may, Trevik," he said.

Trevik's jaw twitched, but he leaned back with folded arms. "By all means."

All eyes fell on Edmund, and he drew a deep breath. He was still feeling the effects of his mother's work on Poppy and himself, but he'd been asked to come to St. Ives for a reason. He didn't have the chance to convince Hedrek to return to Tristwick, but he'd do his best to convince these men to do so.

"I know it may seem mad to uproot one's family," he said, "and to begin a new working schedule. But I'm sure I may safely assume that it matters not where you live nor what you do, so long as you have food enough to feed your families?"

The men rumbled with affirmation.

"Do your wives feel the same?"

The response was far less enthusiastic, and Edmund smiled. "You may be paid a small amount less at Tristwick, but there, you will find a sense of belonging that will make up for what you lack in funds."

The men listened, a few of them leaning forward as their interests were piqued. Trevik, Mrs. Honeysett, and Poppy, as well, focused their attention on him as he continued.

"Trevik here has laid out all the benefits of working in Tristwick, but none of what would benefit you by *living* in Tristwick. The sense of community there is unmatched. The views, unparalleled. And the people…" He paused. "They are the very best you shall ever find."

His eyes shifted to Poppy's, a warmth in their cinnamon depths as she watched him.

"The women sing in the cellars," he continued, "finding lasting friendships with those they work alongside."

A man with blonde hair raised his brow in surprise while another rubbed his rough hands across his weathered jaw in a thoughtful gesture, their responses encouraging Edmund to carry on.

"They gather together often to spend time on the beach. They share all they have so no one goes without. You truly have not experienced a community—have not witnessed true beauty—until you've stepped foot in Tristwick with its hidden houses and breathtaking views."

He leaned forward, his words coming out even more forcefully as he felt them deep within his soul. "If you come to Tristwick, you will see that it is not just a place to exist. It is a place to thrive. You will be surrounded by the best people you will ever have the privilege of knowing, in one of the best places you could ever have the privilege of living."

He ended his speech, the fair-haired seiner nodding his head as the other men mulled over Edmund's words. The Honeysetts also remained in silence.

Had he said too much? Been a bit too dramatic with his words?

He glanced to Poppy, intending to take a quick reading of her face, but when he saw the starry-eyed look she gave him, his heart pattered against his chest.

Swiftly, she blinked the look away, though the dimples in her cheeks still revealed her smile.

No doubt she had been stunned with his words about Tristwick. In truth, he was, as well. He never knew he had such strong opinions about the hamlet, but he *had* been speaking the truth.

Granted, his envy of the county still stood, knowing Poppy chose Cornwall over him. But little by little, he was beginning to understand how warranted the others were in their devotion to Cornwall—especially the little pockets of heaven like Tristwick.

The seiners eventually responded with encouraging comments, leaving their names with Trevik and promising to visit Tristwick at their earliest convenience before taking their leave.

Once the men had left, Trevik blew out a sigh of relief. "Blast it all, 'Arris, if we don't owe that all to ye." He let out a strained chuckle. "They didn't even need the promise of a lifeboat. I knew we'd done right by bringin' ye along."

He clasped Edmund's shoulder with a look of gratitude, which Edmund struggled to respond naturally to. A week before, Trevik had been pushing Edmund down an alleyway to threaten him. Now he was speaking to him like the friends they'd once been.

Meanwhile, Poppy and Mrs. Honeysett watched them with warm smiles.

Edmund could hardly comprehend what was occurring. What was this, this sense of inclusion he felt? Is this what it felt like to be part of a community—part of a family? He'd felt something similar to when he was aboard a ship, having friendships with those whom he served alongside.

But those friendships—apart from with Kendricks—had all but faded away. In truth, Edmund was quite sure that he, just like all the other men in the navy, were replaceable, and made to be so.

If what Edmund had said about Tristwick was true, then being a part of the community like Tristwick, being a part of a family like the Honeysetts, was not fleeting. It was lasting.

What would it feel like to be a part of something so permanent?

Trevik continued expressing his hope for the future as the four of them made their way to the front of the inn to await the coach. When it arrived, they piled inside with other strangers, unfortunately preventing any hope of their private conversations continuing.

Of course, that meant that Edmund's mind had the opportunity to stray to more unpleasant things, namely his mother still being in town.

He knew he needed to speak with Poppy about her, if only to ensure Poppy truly had come away unscathed by the viper. He also needed to thank Poppy for believing in him, instead of allowing Mother's words to get under her skin.

Or so at least he hoped they had not.

He squeezed his eyes closed, forcing the thoughts to clear from the muddled mess that was his mind. He had no business dwelling on the permanence of families and communities. Not when he'd made a promise to Captain Jones to return to sea. Not when he *wanted* to return to sea. Or did he not any longer?

To his relief, and the relief of his ever-worrisome thoughts, the journey back to St. Just was swift and uneventful. After an hour and a half, he and the Honeysetts set off on foot across the countryside at seven o'clock, following the curve of the road until they reached the pathway that split into two—one toward Tristwick, the other to Golowduyn.

Edmund hesitated by the family, his eyes lingering on Poppy, though he had no notion how to ask her to remain behind for a moment. He couldn't risk Trevik's wrath again, not when things had only now become amiable between them.

"Thank ye again, 'Arris," Trevik said.

"Indeed," Mrs. Honeysett said. "We be indebted to ye, sir."

Edmund gave a humble nod, then once again, he glanced to Poppy. She opened her mouth to speak, then hesitated, looking to her mother.

"Well," Mrs. Honeysett said, "don't stay out too late, Popp." Then she turned to her son. "Trev, will ye 'elp your poor mother 'ome? I be as stiff as a door."

She looped her arm through his and pulled him away, though Trevik glanced between Edmund and Poppy with a wary brow before eventually facing forward.

Praise that blessed woman.

"You are welcome to return with them," he said to Poppy. "I know it has been a very long day."

But she shook her head. "I'd not be sleepin' anyway if I returned now. I still need me walk on the beach." She paused. "We could take a walk together if ye'd like."

Their eyes caught, then he motioned to Tregalwen.

Together, they made their way toward the beach, the sun's early evening light casting bright rays across the cliffside. The sea pinks glowed nearly white in the golden sunshine, tall green grass blowing back and forth like the gentle waves of the sea.

Silence marked the air between them, but the rushing water and herring gulls' calls painted the silence into a peaceful serenity.

And yet, with their impending conversation, Edmund found it difficult to feel any peace at all. If he brought his Mother into their discussion, Poppy was sure to have questions about her, which was only fair. But was he capable of answering her questions without becoming defensive?

Just as he found the courage to speak up, they reached the sand, and Poppy plopped down to remove her boots and stockings.

Edmund watched her for a moment, not fully aware of what he was viewing until he saw the smooth curve of her lower leg.

"Are ye not takin' your own boots off?" she asked.

Starting, Edmund swiftly pulled his attention to her eyes, realizing all too late that he'd been caught staring.

Attempting to hide his blushing cheeks, he sat down away from her, then worked to remove his footwear with only his right arm.

"I be glad to see ye be takin' me advice," she said, slipping one of her stockings into the boot she'd already removed.

He regarded her questioningly, grunting as he forced his left arm to remain still in its sling.

"From the forfeits I 'ad to pay," she explained. "Givin' ye three pieces of advice?"

"Ah, yes. Of course."

Why was he so addle-brained that evening? His answer was given the moment the image of her leg flashed in his mind's eye once again.

Once the two had removed their boots and stockings, they secured their belongings near a large boulder protruding from the edge off the cliffside, then finally headed toward the sand.

As the gilded light rolled across the beach, the undulating sand cast shadows from its ridges, creating a lined pattern across the shore that was disrupted with each footprint they created.

With his focus once more shifting to his mother, Edmund struggled against the stability of the sand, unable to move as swiftly as he wished to until he heard Poppy speaking behind him.

"Are ye in a footrace, sir?"

He looked behind him, noting he was several paces ahead of her teasing smile.

"My apologies." He stopped, allowing her to catch up.

"'Ave ye forgotten 'ow to walk in the sand, too?"

"Whatever do you mean?"

"Well, ye oughtn't tramp about at a horse's pace," she continued. "It ought to be leisurely. Like a fawn grazin' in a meadow, see." She walked gently across the sand, and he slowed his pace to match her own. "There ye be. Far better, yes?"

He nodded, his feet still sinking deep into the sand, but he no longer felt as if he was fighting against the beach with each new step.

"Sand ain't meant to be walked swiftly in," she said next. "It be only for leisurely strolls. And foot races, 'course."

A pleasant smile stretched across her lips as she stared into the distance, puffy clouds outlined in a brilliant white near the horizon.

He observed her for a moment, though she hardly seemed aware of his attentions. Instead, her eyes were captured by the sea, the cliffside behind them, the clouds in the skies above, and the sands they walked upon.

With each new direction her eyes focused, her smile grew wider, and the peace she exuded touched his spirit.

He'd recalled seeing this side of Poppy often when she was younger, when everything had seemed right in the world. But then, nothing was right in her world now, was it? Everything she'd feared was occurring, so how could she exude such peace?

Kendricks's words echoed in his memory. *"Being asked to leave Cornwall behind would be like being asked to leave her very soul behind."*

Finally, Edmund understood. Yes, change was coming, and Poppy had to be aware of that fact. But there was one thing different about her that evening that he hadn't noticed until now.

Her hope had returned. It overflowed from her spirit, filling every inch of his own. Cornwall was in her soul, and now, it was—

"Did ye mean what ye said today?" Poppy asked interrupting his thoughts at just the right moment. "All your kind words 'bout Tristwick?"

They stopped, the retreating waves hardening the sand beneath their feet.

"I did," he replied.

He averted his gaze, unable to meet hers, for he knew what she was thinking.

If he loved Cornwall, if he loved Tristwick, what was stopping him from making a home there?

CHAPTER THIRTY-FOUR

*I*n truth, Edmund did not know how to answer such a question.

Why, indeed, would he not make a home in Tristwick for himself?

Yes, he still held a deep love and respect for the navy, but he was beginning to realize that Kendricks was right. Officers' duties were taxing, the food unappetizing, and the men, well, men. Being aboard a ship for months, even years at a time, *was* unbearably lonely.

But in Cornwall, he was never lonely, especially not with Poppy. Despite all of his attempts, he was falling for her all over again. Perhaps he had never stopped falling for her. He was in a constant state of plummeting past logic and sense in the rash and foolish hope of being caught in her love.

He could envision a life with her here, and it shone brighter than any future he could have imagined for them in Derbyshire. Living in Cornwall, he would say goodbye to the navy, but never to the sea. They would have a modest home that Poppy could be mistress of in between processing fish, visiting with her family, and doing whatever else she wished to do. Edmund could join the crew of the *Pilferer*, or perhaps find work in town, something fulfilling and rewarding. Something that would allow his arm the rest it needed—and his mind, as well.

He could not afford a lifeboat for them, but he could certainly manage to keep his wife and her family happy. He would be her rescuer, the reason Poppy could remain in Cornwall.

Then just like that, the vision popped in his head like seafoam on the sand, disappearing into the briny air.

That was just the issue, wasn't it? Poppy may love him. But a marriage with him was not enough for her to move to Derbyshire. He would *never* be enough for her unless he was in Cornwall.

"You will never be good enough for anyone."

Mother's voice rattled in his mind, settling deep within his heart to nudge out any remaining hope he had for the future he'd concocted. That was the reason he could not stay in Cornwall with Poppy. Because she wanted to be in Cornwall more than she wanted to be with Edmund. He understood her reasoning now, but that didn't change what she desired. It was better this way anyway. At least without him being closer to Poppy, Mother would remain away from her, too.

"Edmund? Are ye well?"

Only then did he realize how silent he'd been over the last few moments. "Yes, I am quite well."

"Are ye certain? Ye seem a bit…distracted."

Distracted? Yes, he was distracted. He'd come out there for one purpose, and now he needed to see to that purpose before returning to Golowduyn and wedging some much-needed distance between himself and Poppy.

"I was merely thinking of your conversation with my mother this morning," he began. "I wished to see if you are well after her mistreatment of you."

He waited as he watched the lilting waves.

"Ye needn't worry. She didn't treat me unwell."

Edmund stiffened. Was Poppy…defending her? No, that couldn't be right. Surely she could see past Mother's ruse.

"Did she not?" he asked, unsure if he wished to pursue this conversation.

"Not truly. I didn't expect 'er to speak with I at all, due to me station. But she was bein'…pleasant."

She wouldn't meet his gaze, though Edmund couldn't begin to understand why. Was it because she'd fallen for Mother's ruse and now could not face Edmund due to his supposed cruelty for abandoning his mother?

He tried to remember that morning, the fact that Poppy had told him straightaway of his mother's actions, but he could no longer think straight with the ache in his stomach and the twisting of his heart.

"She *can* be pleasant," he said stiffly, "especially when she is receiving what she wishes."

Poppy turned to face him. "That be just the thing though. She doesn't 'ave what she wishes, does she?"

If only he could have warned Poppy earlier, told her the truth of Mother so she might not have allowed the woman to trick her. But then, what could be done now that Poppy was already on Mother's side?

"What do you mean?" he asked.

"She said this mornin' all she wants is to speak with ye." She shrugged, hesitant. "As I said, I don't know your relationship with 'er, but she did seem upset 'bout not speakin' with ye for so long."

Mother *was* upset, but not for the reasons Poppy assumed. It was because Mother could no longer control him.

"Would…" Poppy hesitated when he remained silent. "Would it benefit the both of ye if ye just spoke with one another?"

His jaw twitched. It was his own fault that Poppy was not aware of his history with Mother. How could he have thought for one moment that Poppy would blindly take his side without knowing any of the facts? No one ever had. And no one ever would.

"I did speak with her," he said flatly. "Right after she spoke with you, in fact. But I'm sorry to say no good came from it." Except, of course, that Mother would now stay away from him due to his threats.

But he could hardly admit such a thing to Poppy.

How foolish he felt for entertaining fanciful thoughts of staying in Cornwall with her, all while she was dwelling on how horrible of a son he must be.

"I be that sorry," she said.

He couldn't respond, his attention on the sea. The gentle waves seemed to mock the turmoil raging within him, taunting him for his stupidity.

"You thought you'd be happier on land than on sea?" the waves whispered up at him.

He'd learned his lesson before, that the decking of a ship was the only place he'd ever truly find peace. But this time, he would not forget it. He took a step away from Poppy. It was time he headed home.

No, not home. He did not have a home.

"Thank you for the lovely walk, Poppy," he said. "I had better return to Golowduyn before the sun sets."

She glanced in confusion to the glowing sunshine that had at least a solid hour of light left. But Edmund hardly cared. He couldn't remain by her side any longer. He couldn't remain in *Cornwall* any longer. He was due to leave Golowduyn in five days' time, but now that Mrs. Kendricks had her baby, what need did he have to remain?

"Edmund, I…"

But he shook his head, ending whatever protest she surely had for him. "Farewell, Poppy."

For it *was* 'farewell,' as he would not be seeing her again.

Turning away before she had the chance to speak a word,

Edmund strode back up the beach, regretting his decision to remove his boots and stockings after all.

Never mind. He'd wait to put them on at Golowduyn if he needed to. Anything to create more distance between himself and Poppy swiftly.

"Edmund?"

His heart dropped at the sound of her voice drawing closer. Why had she followed him?

"I apologize, Poppy, but I must be off," he said over his shoulder like the cad he was.

"No, Edmund, ye must wait!" Her voice jerked as she ran across the sand behind him, finally catching up to him. She stood right in front of him, giving him no choice but to stop. "What..." She paused, breathing hard. "What are ye doin'?"

He focused his gaze over her shoulder, the shadow from his stature engulfing her. "I have already said I am returning to Golowduyn."

"'Ave I upset ye?"

"No."

"Then why can't ye look at I?"

He stared down at her, if only to prove her wrong, but seeing the confusion in her eyes made him regret his harshness at once.

"If this be 'bout what I said concernin' your mother, I be that sorry. I just don't know what ye want me to say."

"You can say whatever you wish to," he said simply.

"But I can't. I don't wish to upset ye for speakin' badly 'bout your own mother."

He paused. She was *stopping* herself from speaking badly about her? Did that mean...

He blew out a slow breath. He moved to run his hands through his hair, forgetting the sling still cradling his left arm that suddenly twinged at his movement—which only proved to anger him further.

This was Mother's fault. All of this miscommunication,

this confusion. How he despised the fact that she came to Cornwall, that she spoke with him at all. Why did she wish to destroy every aspect of his life, time and time again?

"Edmund, please," Poppy said more forcefully than he'd ever heard her speak. "I want to understand."

She reached toward him with an outstretched hand, but in that same moment, with so many of his thoughts focused on his mother, Edmund envisioned the wicked woman in his mind reaching out in the same manner with that same forceful tone, and instinctively, he pulled back, ready to dodge another strike across his face.

When he realized what he'd actually done—avoided Poppy's touch instead of Mother's strike—he peered down at Poppy, surprise parting her lips.

Humiliation coursed through him. There he was again, just a boy, unable to protect himself, unable to earn his mother's love. And he'd revealed as much to the woman he…to the woman he loved more than life itself.

He looked away, taking a step back as he raked his hand through his hair. What a foolish error. What a stupid, embarrassing, humiliating…

"Edmund?" Poppy's soft voice above the waves was his undoing. "I wasn't goin' to 'urt ye."

He shook his head—in response to her words or his own actions, he couldn't be sure. He should have played off his pulling away, laughed about it as he typically did. But the damage had been done.

How could he still be affected by his mother like this? How could he have allowed himself to behave so stupidly?

He turned away, ready to make another escape. He would gather his belongings that very night, leave for St. Ives come morning. Anything to leave behind this shameful chapter of his life.

"I must go," he said, then he stepped around her and stormed across the beach.

But Poppy followed right after him, his footsteps in the sand no match for her quick footing. "Wait, please."

He held out a hand behind him. "No. You must allow me to leave."

Even saying the words broke his heart. He didn't want her to. He wanted her to follow him, to coax the demons out of his past. But he wouldn't allow her to. She was far too pure a woman for him to burden with his past. A past he should be man enough to leave behind.

"No, Edmund," she said, still following him. "I can't let ye leave. Not like that."

"Poppy, I cannot do this. I cannot speak of…"

"Yes, ye can. If I can speak o' me father, ye can speak o' your mother."

He whirled around, and she skittered to a stop just before she would have slammed against him. "Your father loved you," he barked. "And my mother…" His words clung to the tip of his tongue, digging in their claws of fear and disgrace.

"She what?" Poppy asked, staring up at him, her hands at her side. Was she worried she would again frighten the weakened boy inside of him?

He shook his head, looking away.

"Ye can tell me, Edmund," Poppy said. "Ye can tell me anythin'."

Still, he remained silent.

Still, she waited.

He stared out at the sea, the sunshine's brightness reflecting in the water in a strong line, pure and golden white.

Finally, Poppy took a hesitant step toward him. "Did she injure ye, Edmund? When ye were a child?"

Hearing the words aloud from someone other than himself for the first time in his life rattled the iron gates round his heart. He bit hard the inside of his cheek, attempting to ward off the tears suddenly billowing in his eyes, tears that had no business being there at all.

He wanted to run away, to flee from having to face the truth of the matter, but there was no point now. He knew Poppy would follow him wherever he went—just as she'd always done.

But he was behaving ridiculously, childishly. How could he still be weeping over his mother's cruelty? How could he still be affected by her lack of love?

"Edmund?"

As Poppy pressed, so continued his defenses to crumble. Would Poppy think he was lying? Would she laugh at the ridiculousness of it all? Or would she…Dare he hope that she believed him?

"No one will believe you," Mother had said.

But what if Poppy *did*?

Swiftly, he blinked away the moisture from his eyes and stared into the sunshine, the light exuding so similar to his Poppy's.

"Yes," he finally replied. "Yes, she did."

Poppy nodded. "Often?"

"Yes," he responded, nearly breathless from admitting the truth about his childhood aloud.

Poppy didn't respond with words, then. Instead, she took a tentative step toward him, as if approaching a feral animal, afraid of what he might do.

Honestly, Edmund did not know what he would do, either. The emotions from his childhood had resurfaced, emotions he'd thought he'd buried so far down, they would never see the light of day again. How could he overcome them again?

"Edmund." Poppy's voice was soft, soothing like wind through the grass growing along the cliffside.

She waited, silent, patient, until finally, he dared to meet her gaze.

Her eyebrows were drawn high, eyes reflecting tears that mimicked his own. And with a broken voice, she spoke. "I be so sorry."

That was the final straw. Edmund had sworn to never voice what had happened to him as a child, humiliated and afraid that no one would believe him. When he'd dared to hint at what had occurred, he'd been teased mercilessly by school-mates and then ship's boys.

So to have this precious woman before him believe his words, have compassion for his experience, even if she did not know the half of it, he could hardly bear it.

He was defeated. Broken. No longer strong enough to withhold the words inside of him, to keep the iron gate around his heart. Instead, it fell to the ground, clanging loudly and reverberating within his ears.

And ever silent, ever patient, Poppy waited for him.

"I suppose you wish to know why and how such a thing was able to occur," he said with a mirthless huff, attempting to dispel the darkness of his past.

"Only if ye wish to share it."

With a deep breath, Edmund nodded, lowering to the sand with his infuriating sling still pulling at his neck. Poppy followed suit, tucking her legs beneath her as they faced the sea, though her eyes were directed at him as he began.

CHAPTER THIRTY-FIVE

"*My* mother was pushed to marry my father by her parents," Edmund recounted. "They saw it as an advantageous match for their fourth daughter to wed a then-lieutenant of the Royal Navy. She was left often when Father went to sea, as she had no desire to live aboard a ship for months at a time. The more he left her, the more she began to despise him and her life, so she..." He paused, lowering his gaze to the sand they sat upon. "She took comfort in another man's arms while Father was away."

Poppy remained still, listening as if this was not the sordid tale that it was.

"She was so angry with Father for leaving her, so angry with the life she had been forced to lead, that she began to take out her fury on me as a child. As I mentioned earlier, I took after my father in many ways, looks, desires, even our names. So the similarities spurred her hatred to grow."

Poppy shook her head, dismay etched on her brow. "Did she do the same to your brothers?"

He hesitated. "No. My brothers were never injured because they were not my father's sons."

Her eyes widened as understanding dawned.

"Desperate for control over her own life, Mother planned a way to bear children with the man she loved, instead of the man she married. She bore my elder brother, Algernon, first. Father knew the truth, for though he'd been at home long enough for Society to believe the child was his, he and Mother had not been…together for many months."

He averted his gaze from Poppy, desperate not to see the disapproval that was sure to be on her brow. "Father did his best to make amends with Mother, remaining at home for a few months after Algernon's birth, but she was verbally vicious to him whenever he was present. So soon after, she conceived her second child, Cecil, once again with the other man.

"Father knew the truth, but to save his own pride, his wife's reputation, and his two pretended sons' lives, he took them in as his own, providing for them and loving them as best he could. But, once again, he returned to sea."

"And that be when ye were born?" Poppy guessed.

"Not exactly. You see, my father experienced an awakening of sorts on one of his many assignments. He returned months later, fully prepared to make amends with his estranged wife. He wooed her, courted her, spent time with her for the first time since they were married. But soon enough, the sea beckoned him, and he answered its call. This time, my mother was pregnant with her third child. She begged him not to leave, but the sea's call was too strong for him to ignore. Mother never forgave him for leaving, nor did she forgive the child with which she was pregnant."

"Ye," Poppy finished.

"Precisely."

She shook her head in amazement. "So ye be your father and mother's only legitimate child?"

"To my detriment, yes. At every turn, I am a reminder of how Father ruined her life, now how I have ruined her life." His voice hardened as he recalled the many times she'd said such to his face. "If I had not been born, she could have lived out her life happily with her two sons and Mr. Beacham."

Poppy paused. "Mr. Beacham, 'er 'usband now. 'E be the one…"

"Yes. He was the one she wanted to marry before my father. He is my brothers' real father."

"Do they know?"

"I'm certain it has crossed their minds before, but I understand why they do not pursue such thoughts. Mother taught them how to despise my father, as well."

"'Ow did ye come to know 'bout all this?"

He shifted against the sand, bending one leg and resting it beneath the other, which arched above the sand. "Before my father died, he sealed a letter with all the information inside, requesting it to be given to me on my eighteenth birthday by the executor of the will."

"Was it a shock to ye?"

"Not necessarily. Some of the information I received, yes. But most of it I had already assumed and learned of my own accord. You see, I discovered the tryst between my mother and Mr. Beacham myself, finding them alone in the gardens one night."

Poppy's brow contorted. "That must 'ave been 'orrifyin'."

"It was. But I used it to my advantage." The words slipped from his tongue before he had the chance to pull them back.

Poppy eyed him. "'Ow so?"

He grimaced. "I'm afraid you will think less of me if I tell you."

"It can't be any worse than allowin' your own niece to fall off a cliffside 'cause ye be too busy arguin' with a friend."

He released a small laugh before sobering. "After Father died, Mother refused to allow me to join the navy when I expressed my interest in doing so. 'I'll never allow any son of mine to follow after your father's footsteps,' she'd said.

"I could have run away, but I wished to one day rise up in

the ranks honorably with signed papers. Only when I...I threatened her to reveal the truth about her and Mr. Beacham's affair did she finally sign for me."

Poppy tipped her head to the side. "I always thought she forced ye into the navy."

He shook his head in shame. "No. I was required to change my story after I was laughed at mercilessly as a child, for I was the only one who did not have a mother's love awaiting me back home."

She didn't respond for a moment, and he could only imagine how ashamed she must be of sitting next to such a man as he.

"I've only ever threatened her with my knowledge twice," he said. "I know it is not admirable by any stretch of the imagination, but I did what I had to do to be free of her."

"What be the second time?"

"When she spoke with you," he said softly. "I could not bear even the notion of her causing you or your family harm. I thought perhaps she'd threatened you to get to me. So I warned her to stay away from you."

She nodded, mulling the information over in her mind. Again, he grimaced. This was why he'd worked so hard to hide his past from everyone—especially Poppy. She was far too pure, far too generous and good a person to even comprehend his terrible actions.

"I know I shouldn't have," he said, assuming her thoughts. "I was simply afraid. Afraid of you believing her over me. I was taking the coward's way out, I suppose. Just like I've done all my life."

To his surprise, she scoffed. "Coward?" The look of disbelief in her eye captured him. "Edmund 'Arris, ye be the last man in the world who I would e'er call a coward."

Still, concern gripped his chest. "You do not think poorly of me, then?"

"'Ow could I possibly think poorly of ye?"

He gave her a sorrowful, knowing look. "Because I am not capable of inspiring a mother's love."

"Ye be blamin' yourself for what she did? Nay, sir. Tain't no one's fault but 'er own. She only be tryin' to make 'erself feel better after the mistakes she's made. It be nothin' else but that."

A calmness rushed over him at her words. How could he have ever thought this woman would have doubted him?

"Why ye be smilin'?" she asked.

He hadn't realized until then that he was. "My father wrote to me those very words in his letter."

Her eyes twinkled. "'E be a wise man, then."

They shared a smile, and their eyes caught. A moment ticked by in silence before her features sobered. "One thing I can't understand is 'ow ye managed to cope through it all. 'Ow be ye still standin' as strong as ye are?"

Edmund had always brushed aside his feelings from his childhood, refusing to allow the ache to enter his heart. But in that moment, with Poppy's goodness, he no longer felt the need to brush them aside.

"I assure you," he replied, "I have not coped as well as I should like. I have learned, however, that if we spend our lives fearing the darkness, we lose the chance to live. We must acknowledge the past. Be mindful of the future. And live for the present."

She hummed in acknowledgement, leaning back on her hands and stretching her legs out before her. "That be the difficulty though."

He couldn't help but smile. "Just so."

Their eyes locked again, and their smiles faded as they stared at each other. The air changed around them. The peace from before vanishing as an invisible power filled the space between them like flashes of lightning deep within the clouds—the light nearly visible and the energy potent.

He knew he should look away, perhaps even stand up to

break the spell forged between them, but he couldn't. Instead, his eyes dropped to her lips, their pink curves calling to him. How he longed to answer their call, to finally taste of their sweetness that was sure to satisfy all of his desires—yet surely create more.

But that was just the problem. He could not satisfy all of his desires where Poppy was concerned. If there was one thing he'd remembered that evening, it was that love was fragile, easily broken, easily forgotten. His mother's had been for his father, and Poppy's had certainly been for Edmund's.

Hadn't it? Did he dare to find out? Or was he truly the coward Poppy was so convinced that he was not?

"Do ye e'er wonder," Poppy began, her eyes flicking to his lips, "what life would be like 'ad I gone with ye, 'stead o' stayin' 'ere?"

Edmund's breathing shallowed. Had he thought of such a thing? Yes. He had. More often than not, he'd imagined her walking the corridors of Sunningdale, replacing all of his painful memories with new ones of her smiles and the laughter of their children.

"Yes," he responded, unable to prevent himself.

Her eyes took on a light he had not seen before. Should he not squelch it, dim it before it could brighten? Stamp it out before he had to remind himself just how deeply he'd loved her all those years ago and life at sea became unbearable all over again?

"But I do not anymore," he finished.

She nodded slowly. "I s'pose ye be wise for not drudgin' up the past."

Her eye shone still, as if she did not believe a word he'd just spoken. She kept her gaze on him, his breathing ragged, his heart thumping painfully against his chest, but he couldn't move. "We want different things now," he said, if only to remind himself of the fact.

"Do we still?"

"Yes," he said, still forcing himself to believe it. "You need Cornwall. And I need the navy."

She leaned forward, pushing up from her hands so she sat level with him once more, bringing their faces closer together. He told himself to lean back, but he couldn't bring himself to create more space between them.

"Be ye sure, Edmund?" Her voice was soft, almost raspy as it unraveled the threads of his heart.

What in heaven's name was she doing? Did she not know how dangerous this was? How this would only make his departure all the more difficult?

"'Cause I can't 'elp but 'ope," she continued, her eyes dropping to his lips once more, "that per'aps things be different now."

She rested her hand in the sand between them, a mere hair's width from where his own fingers were positioned.

He swallowed. He would maintain his ground. He would stand firm. No matter the desire racing through his pulse, no matter the stirring in his heart.

"We cannot do this, Poppy," he said, his voice catching in his throat. "Even if things are different now. It is too hard. It was too difficult to…"

The ache in his heart increased, though his whole body was aflame with desire as her lips parted.

"What be too difficult?" she whispered, leaning closer toward him. The pressure from her fingertips pressed into the sand until it shifted, and their hands touched.

He closed his eyes, the energy from their contact overcoming him. His chest rose and fell with measured breaths. "Leaving you," he said, breaking through his hesitation.

She needed to know. She needed to know how he'd felt when she'd denied him, when he'd left her.

He opened his eyes to meet hers. "Overcoming you was

the most difficult thing I've ever had to do. And I cannot do it again."

Tears brimmed in her eyes as they moved about every inch of his face. "Then why must ye? I can't be parted from ye either, Edmund. I can't bear it again. My heart be whole only when ye be near."

CHAPTER THIRTY-SIX

*E*dmund winced, the truth in Poppy's words echoing the same sentiment in his heart.

She said nothing further, keeping her eyes on him, unmoving.

He knew what she wanted. It was the same as his own desires. But as she stared up at him, unmoving, he knew she was allowing him the chance to make the decision for himself.

He could either attempt to kiss the woman he loved and be rejected again, or he could *leave* the woman he loved and be alone again.

She didn't want you, Edmund, he reminded himself. *She chose Cornwall instead.*

Would she choose the same again if given the chance?

The sunshine brightened her eyes, created a glow about her hair, and drew attention to her lips—those perfect lips that had always spoken such lovely things to him. Those lips that now awaited just out of his reach.

He leaned closer, still fighting with his conscience. He couldn't keep away from her much longer. But then, was she aware of what would occur? Was this truly what she wanted?

"If we kiss," he breathed, staring at her lips, "there will be no turning back. Things will be harder for us, more difficult than ever."

Her eyelids fluttered. "I care not. I love ye, Edmund."

The breath rushed from his lungs. She'd said the words once before when she was sixteen, but this was different. This time, there was more feeling, more depth to how she spoke, and he could hardly bear it.

He had always wondered if he hadn't suggested leaving for Derbyshire, if they both would have expressed their love for one another by the end of that fateful evening.

But now, hearing what he'd always wondered, what he'd always wanted, that Poppy truly loved him, he could no longer keep himself from her.

He drew a breath, trying to brace himself for whatever would come as their lips touched. And yet, when they did, nothing could have prepared him for the rush of emotions that overwhelmed him. His heart pounded into his chest, the perfect contrast to the softness with which Poppy's lips met his, and for the first time he could remember, he breathed life.

They held still for a long moment, their fingers still touching in the sand where they sat beside each other. Edmund relished in the feel of his lips pressed against hers. He'd wanted this moment for so long, had spent countless frustrating nights dreaming of how it might feel. And yet, all of those experiences, all of this time, simply made the moment all the more beautiful, all the more memorable and poignant.

He'd thought all this time that he'd been happy at sea. That he'd felt fulfilled sailing with the waves. But nothing, none of that held a candle to how he felt in that moment kissing Poppy.

The desire to be closer to her, to finally caress the smoothness of her skin, tugged his left arm forward, only to have the sling stop him once again.

He hesitated to break contact, to pull away from Poppy for

fear of the moment ending, but his desire to draw closer to her could not be stinted.

Gently, he pulled back, his lips cold without Poppy to warm them as he tore the sling from around his neck and dropped it in the sand to the side of them.

He shifted his seating as he faced her again, covering his right hand with hers and using his left hand—finally—to caress her face. Hang his still-recovering arm. Any pain was worth being able to properly kiss the woman he loved.

He stroked his thumb across her jaw first, her skin as soft as he'd imagined it to be, just as warm as her heart was. Then he tipped her chin as he looked into her eyes. She watched him with such innocence, such longing and love, his chest constricted, and her lips were his once more.

He never knew joy until this moment with Poppy. He never knew love until their lips touched. Edmund had nothing in his life. No parents who loved him. No home. No secure standing with the navy.

So why did being with Poppy, kissing Poppy, make him feel as if he had everything?

He already knew the answer. It was because Poppy *was* everything to him. Even now, after she'd chosen another life. Even now after three years had passed with him attempting to numb his feelings until he thought they no longer existed.

How wrong he was.

As the depth of his love overcame him, his limbs weakened, the strength of his arm failing as he leaned closer to Poppy, drawing more power from her lips.

He drew closer, and she slowly slipped back, as if she could not remain upright on her own, either.

Desperate to maintain their affection, to not lose the connection between them, Edmund followed her until she lay in the sand, their mouths working in unison as they shared the love they'd repressed for too many years.

He hovered above her, propped on his right arm that

rested to the side of her head, his left hand on the other side of her as he leaned to the side and deepened their kiss.

He knew their actions would change the course of their future, whether for good or for bad.

And yet, in that moment, he could not begin to regret his decision to finally kiss the only woman he'd ever loved.

Poppy could no longer breathe, captive as she was to Edmund's affections. She'd dreamt of this moment for so long, and now that it was finally here, she wasn't sure she quite believed it.

The soft pressure he placed upon her lips with his mouth, the gentle way he held himself above her, keeping his body chastely away from hers—all of it captured her, all of it caused her to fall deeper, to fall more madly in love with her childhood dream.

She loved him. She loved him for how he treated her. She loved him for how he playfully competed against her. She loved him for how he shared and entrusted his past with her.

How she wished to protect him, to keep him safe so no one might ever injure him again—herself included.

Tears sprang to her eyes, her spirit overcome with emotion. They ran down her cheeks, cool compared to the sun warming them as they laid upon the beach. He raised his hand to her face, gently pressing his fingers at the back of her neck to hold her more securely against him.

She responded in turn, bringing her hand to explore the hair at the nape of his neck. A soft moan sounded at the back of his throat, and he pressed his lips more firmly against her own.

This. This was a kiss made of dreams. Haunting, and beautiful, and perfect dreams. She knew she would have to wake up. She knew when this kiss ended, Edmund would depart. She would awaken from this lovely dream and question if he would return from the sea all over again.

But right now, she would relish being caressed. Being *loved* by him. For that was how this felt—that he did love her still, perhaps even more than he had before.

She did not know if it meant anything would change. He seemed bound and determined not to allow that to occur. But by heaven, she would enjoy this kiss, and she would cherish it for the rest of her life.

She opened her eyes for a moment, if only to be sure that she was, in actuality, kissing Edmund Harris. Her heart skittered at the sight of his brow drawn together, as if their affection was nearly too much for him to bear, as if he struggled to keep his desires at bay.

She understood the sentiment perfectly, forcing herself to breathe steadily, to calm her racing heart, but it was of no use.

Edmund had captured her, and there was no turning back. This would not last forever, though she'd do nothing to stop it herself.

Time stood still as they kissed, though how much time had passed by since they'd begun, Poppy was entirely unaware. All she knew was that it had not lasted long enough when their kisses slowed, and Edmund finally pulled back.

She opened her eyes in a daze, seeing him caress her features with his gaze. "I did not want that to end," he whispered, brushing a strand of hair across her brow as he stared down at her.

"Nor did I," she responded.

"But...I must return you to your family before Trevik discovers us and gets rid of me once and for all."

She smiled at his teasing, though his statement was actually very true.

He stood up from the sand first, gripping his limp sling in one hand and helping her to stand with the other. She raised, being pulled up with ease toward him. Her feet sank low into the sand, however, and she stumbled just a foot forward, resting a hand against his chest.

Breathless at their proximity once again, she looked to his lips, but Edmund pulled back.

Not allowing disappointment to enter her heart, she followed him up the sand and did her best to not allow her spirits to sink. They replaced their stockings and boots—Edmund shifting away from her as she did so—then he helped her up from the sand once again.

She'd expected him to release her as she stood, just like before, but his fingers laced between hers as he led her from the beach and walked along the pathway to home.

She wanted to speak, to ask him what all this meant, though she held her tongue, merely wrapping her other arm around his as they walked.

Finally, Tristwick appeared around the ridge, the stone cottages glowing brightly in the golden light.

"I can walk you the rest of the way," Edmund offered as they stopped at the cliff's edge.

But Poppy shook her head. "I'll be fine on me own. 'Sides, I'd not wish for me brother to kill 'e, as I'd quite like to see ye again."

He gave a gentle laugh, but the humor from her words faded. "Will I? See ye again, I mean?" she asked.

Again, their eyes met, unspoken questions drifting between them. Had the kiss meant more than a simple exchange of their love? Had it held a promise of a future together? Or was the affection merely a tragic goodbye?

He stared down at her, then placed a kiss to the back of her hand. "Yes. You will."

She nodded, attempting to take what hope she could from his words. Slowly, she pulled away from him, turning to leave, but he caught her hand in his and pulled her swiftly back against him, pressing his hands into the small of her back to remove any distance between them.

She smiled up at him, breathless, then he reached down and bestowed another kiss on her eager, willing lips.

When he pulled back, he stared deep into her eyes. "That is so you do not forget me until tomorrow."

She smiled. "'Ow could I e'er forget ye, sir?"

"I suppose you are right about that." He winked, then finally released her.

She walked down the pathway, glancing over her shoulder now and again to see if he still watched her. Each time, he smiled in return.

She still could not believe what had just occurred.

She, Poppy Honeysett, fishermen's daughter, serving maid at Golowduyn, processor of pilchards, and caretaker of toddlers, had kissed Lieutenant Harris. And that was something she would treasure forever.

CHAPTER THIRTY-SEVEN

*E*dmund left Poppy that night afraid that he would awaken from the euphoric dream she'd cast about him. He tried to tell himself to be logical, that morning would come and his fears would return.

But to his surprise, he awoke the following morning feeling even more renewed. Poppy's kiss had rejuvenated him. Set his heart aflame with light and joy. Speaking with her about his past had done wonders for his soul, bringing to him a hope for the future he'd never before had. He did not know what that future would look like, but he did know having Poppy a part of it was something he wanted, more than anything he ever had before.

What that would look like, he was not certain. His promise to return for another assignment with Captain Jones still stood, but would Poppy be willing to wait for him again—and more importantly, did she still wish for him to join her in Cornwall? He knew she loved him, but he had asked her to wait so often, what if she couldn't any longer?

Intent on speaking with her as soon as possible to end his worries, Edmund made ready that morning before the sun had even risen, pulling on his sling, though his arm felt better that morning than it had in weeks.

To his dismay, however, he learned from Kendricks that Poppy would be taking the day away from Golowduyn to work with her family in the cellars.

"Do you need her for something?" Kendricks had asked heavy-handedly.

Edmund had merely smiled. "Perhaps I do."

"Well, then," Kendricks had replied, playing along, "perhaps you ought to head to St. Just to see if Golowduyn has any correspondence awaiting us. If it takes longer than usual, I'll just give your excuses to my wife."

His captain's knowing smile had buoyed Edmund's spirits, so he'd taken his leave and now awaited the post to open to retrieve the mail.

When it finally did, Edmund swiftly retrieved the letters, ready to leave when he was handed a correspondence for himself.

Thanking the postmaster, Edmund was momentarily distracted as he peered down at the letter. Who could have written to him? Surely not Algernon again. But when he flipped the letter over, he saw the seal of the Admiralty pressed into the maroon-colored wax.

A moment of confusion settled around him, then his heart picked up. Could they be responding so soon to his inquiry about a lifeboat?

With a racing heart, he broke the seal, unable to wait a moment longer. But when he glanced up to ensure he would not walk into anyone, his eyes caught sight of his mother and Mr. Beacham standing just outside the inn, sober expressions on both of their faces.

Edmund's stomach tightened, though he was sure they had not noticed him. If he turned around right then, crossed the road to the other side, they would not see him at all.

And yet, for reasons he could not begin to understand, he

hesitated. Speaking with Poppy, having her belief in him remain, had given him more validation in those few moments than he'd ever received in his life. Surely those positive feelings would flee if he spoke with the Beachams again.

But then, what if he did speak with them and gently closed that chapter of his life instead of slamming the book shut as he'd attempted to do before with threats and pointed fingers?

Such a thing would be far more admirable.

With cautious steps, he made his way toward the two people who he'd thought had destroyed his life irreparably, though Poppy and her love had seemed to finally repair it.

"Acknowledge the past. Be mindful of the future. Live for the present." Just as he'd told Poppy.

It was time he moved on. This time for good.

With a deep breath and Poppy's smile in his heart, he headed for the Beachams, who stood with a few other individuals waiting for the coach.

Mr. Beacham startled at his approach, taking a step back. If Mother was surprised, she only revealed so with a quirk of her brow.

"Mother," Edmund said, "might I have a word with you both?"

He motioned to the side of the inn where they could speak with more privacy, making his way there without awaiting a response.

Mother raised her chin, hesitating a moment before she and Mr. Beacham joined him. "Speaking with us again, are you?" she said bitterly.

How he longed to walk away right then and never speak with the spiteful woman again. But he had a task to see to, and he would not shirk.

"Are you leaving St. Just?" he asked.

"Do you not know already, after the threats you have assailed against us?" she asked, as if Edmund ought to feel ashamed for his actions.

Heaven help him, but he did not. "I did not come here to argue," he said quietly. "Nor to threaten you again. I merely came to…" The words tasted bitter in his mouth, like burnt chocolate in the morning, but he pushed them out anyway. "I came here to tell you that I forgive you."

Not even her years of practice could hide Mother's surprise, though she quickly masked it with another sneer.

"I did not deserve the treatment you gave me," he said, gaining confidence as he spoke, "simply for being the only legitimate child you bore with a man you despised. You were in the wrong wholeheartedly, despising me through no fault of my own. But I do not wish to follow in your footsteps. I do not wish to become embittered. I know the pathway to forgiveness is long and ever-changing, but I will learn to forgive you, to move on with my life, as you could never do with my father."

Her tight lips turned white. "And what of…" she glanced around them. "And what of your threats?"

His head swirled as he made his decision. "I will keep the knowledge to myself."

She raised a dubious brow. "And why should we believe you?"

"Because I am a man of honor. A man of my word. And I will not destroy my brothers' lives, nor the lives of their children, as you tried to destroy mine."

Mr. Beacham lowered his head, his ears beaming red. Mother remained unchanged. "And Sunningdale House?"

"I will hold firm in my decision to lease the property out to other families," he said decidedly.

Mother narrowed her eyes. "You selfish boy. You will not give Cecil what ought to be rightfully his just out of bitterness?"

Edmund held fast to the peace he felt the night before, remembering Poppy's smile, remembering how he felt sharing his past with her, how he would feel being with her again.

"I do not believe I need to remind you that both properties

Algernon and Cecil were given are not rightfully theirs. As my father's only heir, I have every right to take possession of Norest Park and Boarstrode myself."

Fear flickered in her eyes, though she masked it with another frown.

"But worry not," he continued. "My brothers shall always possess the homes *my* father gave them." He looked to Mr. Beacham next. Edmund had planned for years to deliver a well-thought-out speech to the man who'd spurred Mother on to leave Father, but he realized now, it would not do any good.

Instead, he settled on his final words. "Goodbye, Mother. I sincerely hope, if we ever meet again, that I will find you a changed woman. One whom your children and grandchildren can respect and love."

Her nostrils flared, but she remained silent.

Edmund took his leave, then, nodding his head to them both and walking away, his chest swelling with emotion.

He'd done it. He'd begun his journey, and what a relief it was.

Now all he wished to do was tell Poppy about it.

A paper crinkled in his hand, and he looked down, having entirely forgotten about the letter from the Admiralty.

He shifted it around in his right hand, bringing it up to his left arm still in the sling. Unfolding the edges, he scoured the contents. His mood slowly lowered as he read the words over.

With a sinking stomach, his worries solidified. How was he ever going to tell Poppy?

Poppy hadn't expected to see Edmund so soon after the previous night, especially standing in the processing cellars of Tristwick.

Mother had pointed him out first, the lieutenant standing

resolutely within the doorway, his eyes roving over the courtyard.

She waved, catching his attention, but the tight smile with which he bestowed her secured the knot in her stomach.

Before, she'd imagined seeing him with hidden smiles and stolen glances. But now, she knew whatever words he held within him were not of a pleasant nature.

She wasn't a stranger to men and their loyalty to the navy. She knew he could love her and the sea in the same regard. But then, if he did fulfill another assignment, would he return? Was their love strong enough to begin a new life in Cornwall, or was he there to ask her to go to Derbyshire again?

Slowly, she approached him, wiping her salt and fish covered hands on her apron before meeting him. "Edmund," she greeted, attempting to keep her happy spirits. "What brings ye 'ere so early?"

She eyed the tall cellar walls, the sun having yet to peer over them.

He hesitated. "I received a letter from the Admiralty. I came as soon as I could to speak with your family."

Worry settled in the pit of her stomach. Whatever news he'd received, it was clearly not what they'd hoped for.

Regret for her desires before stabbed at her chest. How could she have ever hoped that Tristwick wouldn't receive a lifeboat? What did that mean for their future? For their home in Cornwall?

"I'll gather me family," she said softly.

Edmund nodded, and within a matter of moments, Poppy, Mother, Morvoren, and Trevik—with Isolde being watched by Mrs. Bosanko—joined Edmund outside of the cellars' large, wooden doors.

"I received word from the Admiralty," he said, facing the family with a stoic expression. "And I'd like for you all to read the letter yourselves."

He extended the correspondence forward, Trevik accepting it at once and bringing it closer to his person.

"Read it aloud, son," Mother said softly.

Trevik nodded, and Poppy kept her eyes on Edmund, though his gaze focused on the dirt path beneath their feet.

Lieutenant Harris,

We were pleased to receive your letter and quite intrigued to hear of Tristwick's desire to obtain a lifeboat for their waters. Of course, we are aware of the need in many locations for such a service and have been aware of the dangers of Dulatha Cliffs and the surrounding areas for quite some time, including when the Valour—*the very ship you were on—collided with the cliffs and nearly took your life.*

Due to your letter, we are interested in providing a boat to Trist-wick, as we did for the town of Bude.

Trevik paused, his eyes alight as he looked to his family. "This be the best news," he said with a shocked laugh.

But Poppy kept her eyes on Edmund. She knew this would bring all manner of change to her home, but she was finally willing to accept such change. So long as *one* didn't occur—Edmund's departure.

"Please, continue," Edmund said to Trevik, his eyes still averted.

That being said, we are, understandably, unable to extend a lifeboat to just any area, as they are quite cost prohibitive. As luck would have it, we have come to the knowledge of an eight-man boat that might do well for the hamlet. However, we would require the people of Tristwick to provide proof that such a small area could provide enough men to care for the lifeboat.

Furthermore, as we have had a few experiences in the past that have proven not as lucrative for us, we shall also be requiring you, Lieutenant, to be in charge of the lifeboat. As a naval officer, we know you shall have vested interest in ensuring the lifeboat is used to rescue both fishermen and naval ships alike.

Should you not wish to accept this task, might we suggest that you find another officer willing to do the same? Otherwise, we have complete faith in your abilities, being the well-respected individual that you are. Of course, we shall miss your services aboard the Defense, *but what can be more noble than manning a lifeboat and rescuing your lost brothers at sea?*

Do inform us of your decision. We look forward to the possibility of collaborating our efforts to create a safer, more sustainable sea.

Signed,
Mr. Patrick Williams
Clerk

Trevik lowered the letter, turning to his family with an excited smile. "I cannot believe they will heed our request."

Mother and Morvoren nodded in silence, though their attention remained on Poppy. Poppy, however, looked at no one else but Edmund, who still had yet to meet her gaze.

"So," Trevik continued, entirely unaware of what was occurring around him, "all we must do now is find an officer to help man the lifeboat."

Poppy couldn't blame him for his enthusiasm. He'd just been handed a lifeline, a way to save Tristwick and his family. He had every right to celebrate.

But Poppy could not join in.

"Trev," Morvoren said softly, giving a subtle shake of her head.

Trevik narrowed his eyes, paused as he seemed to catch

her meaning, then turned to Edmund. "'Course ye be the obvious solution, Lieutenant, but seein' 'as 'ow ye be expected back in St. Ives in just a few days, we can 'ardly ask ye to do the task."

All eyes shifted to Edmund, and finally, he met Poppy's gaze. In his own, she saw only hesitancy.

"I…I *am* expected in St. Ives."

He said nothing further. Did he wish for a direct request? A specific invitation for him to remain? She opened her mouth to deliver such, then paused.

This was exactly what had occurred last time. She'd written to him, asked him to stay in Cornwall with her, then everything had fallen apart. If she asked him to do the same again, would he flee as he did before?

Acutely aware of the expectant eyes of her family weighing down on her, she began. "Ye'd do a fine job 'ere, Lieutenant. We'd love to 'ave ye remain if ye wish it…for Tristwick's sake." She added the last words in a rush, if only to let him know he was not beholden to stay for her, if he did not wish to.

But his expression sobered, his eyes clouding over as he dropped his gaze. "Thank you for the offer. But I…I have promised Captain Jones that I would be returning to his service. I have a few officers in mind who would all make fine leaders, though. I will leave you with the names."

Poppy scrambled to keep her heart from tumbling to the ground. This was expected. Edmund was a man of honor. He would *have* to return to sea when he'd *promised* to return to sea. But then…one question remained.

"And…" she began, "will ye return?"

Edmund wouldn't meet her gaze. "I…" His eyes flitted toward her family, who looked away with discomfort. He lowered his voice before continuing. "I must clear my mind before I offer any such answer."

Poppy's head swirled. She told herself this was not as

before. His response allowed her some hope. But then, would she again await his return for another three years? Despair at his departure then fall in love all over again when he returned.

"Excuse me," Edmund said, lowering his head and backing away.

Poppy watched him turn around and make his way back up the cliffside, her nightmare continuing.

"Poppy," Mother said behind her, and Poppy turned to see her family facing her with looks of concern.

"Be this happenin' again?" she asked, releasing a disbelieving breath.

Mother came forward, resting a comforting arm around Poppy's shoulders. She didn't say a word, but Mother didn't have to. No one did. They were all thinking the exact same thing that she was.

Poppy, what a fool. How childish she was to allow this to occur again.

She closed her eyes, willing the thoughts to stop. Her life had been so close to perfection the night before. She'd had so much hope. So much to live for. She knew Edmund loved her. As deep as her blood ran Cornish, she knew he loved her.

So what thoughts did he need to clear before he answered her request?

Her breathing increased, her heart rapping against her chest. She would not allow this love to slip through her fingers again. She would not remain silent as she did before. She would face him. She would beg him for his thoughts until she received his reasoning.

"I must go," she said, pulling away from Mother's embrace and heading for the cliffside.

"Poppy, don't," Trevik said, attempting to stop her, concern etched across his features. "Don't go after 'im. 'E'll just 'urt ye more."

"I have to know," she said, her determination growing. "I have to know why 'e be leavin' again."

"'E's married to the sea, Popp," Trevik said gently. "Men like that don't change. Please, don't go after 'im. I can't see ye 'urt anymore than ye already be."

Pausing, she turned to face him more directly, hearing the emotion in his words, seeing the pain in his expression, and she softened. "Trev, ye've taken care of I since Father died. Ye can't know 'ow I appreciate it. But I ain't sixteen no more. I can take care o' meself. If I get 'urt, I get 'urt. But it be an ache I be willin' to risk."

"And if 'e asks ye to leave Cornwall again?"

The fear with which he spoke caused an ache in her heart she could barely manage. "I love ye, Trev," she said, unable to answer his question. "And there ain't nothin' that'd stop the love, no matter where I be."

With a nod of departure to her family, she removed her apron, Mother taking it with an encouraging nod before Poppy fled from the cellars and up the hill in search of Edmund.

She knew he loved her, just as she knew why he fled when he was upset. And yet, as she reached the top of the cliffside, with no sight of Edmund in any direction, her determination waned, her spirits falling once again. Had he gone to Golowduyn or St. Just? Or had he taken a different route not on the pathway to avoid being discovered?

Deciding on the pathway to the lighthouse, she forged ahead, willing her courage to continue. But as she drew closer and closer to Golowduyn, leaving Tristwick and Tregalwen behind, still out of reach of Wheal Penharrow and Lowena Cottage, she stopped, her spirits crushing within her to the point where she could no longer move.

There was no sight of Edmund from the undulating fields and cliffsides she stood upon. No sight of him at all.

Praying for relief from the pain in her heart, she turned to the sea, only then realizing where she stood. The poppy fields of Porthlenn had finally bloomed, and she had not even noticed.

The sight was stunning in the early morning light. The sun shone through the full, red petals, causing them to glow as they opened toward the sunshine. They swayed in the gentle morning breeze, covering the field in a blanket of silk rubies that took her breath away.

She'd been waiting so long for these poppies to bloom, to see the sight once again, praying this time, that those fields would hold more hope for her.

But once again, darkness loomed. Would she sit there just like before, awaiting Edmund's return?

A tall ship sailed by in the distant sea, just visible above the extended green stems of the poppies. Would that be Edmund soon, sailing away from her as she, the ever-foolish girl, sat in those fields and prayed for his return?

She had lost hope that he ever would. And now, she had lost that hope again. Would she never find relief from this ever-constant ache? This ever-constant longing to be with the man she loved? The man who kept running away?

Tears streamed down her cheeks, but she did not bother to hide them. She needed to let go. She needed to move on. Permanently this time. Because Edmund would not return. Not this time. Not—

"Poppy?"

CHAPTER THIRTY-EIGHT

*P*oppy gasped, whirling around as Edmund's voice broke through her thoughts.

"Edmund?" she breathed, not trusting her eyes as he stood behind her.

His cravat and jacket had been removed, his hand grasping them at his side as the wind rushed past him, rippling his collar against his neck and opening his shirtsleeves to reveal the base of his throat. His chest rose and fell as he stared at her, feet braced apart, shoulders squared. The look of focus in his eyes made her heart tremor.

"Ye came back," she breathed, still unable to believe her eyes.

He walked toward her with deliberate steps. "I did. For you."

What was he saying? Was he...was he saying he would stay? "Edmund, I don't understand."

He nodded, his brow pulling together with emotion. "I know. And I cannot beg your forgiveness enough for that. I merely..." He stopped, shaking his head as he began again. "I have spent my entire life running, Poppy. Running from my family, running from friendships, running from you because I feared I would never be good enough. Indeed, the moment you told me you did not wish to leave Cornwall, I took that as evidence that you did not love me as I loved you." He shook his head, taking another step toward her. "Then I realized how absurdly I was behaving. How I was expecting far too much. And just now," he trailed off, scoffing at himself. "I left because you asked me to stay for Tristwick, and not you."

Understanding rushed over her. Of course, of course he would take her words in that way. She remained where she was, the poppies tapping against her blowing skirts as the wind swirled around them. "I only said as much so ye wouldn't feel obligated," she explained.

A soft smile stretched across his lips. "I know. But it helped me to finally see what it is I truly wish for. It helped me to realize how foolish I've been. You love me. But even if you did not, even if you only wish to be with me for the sake of Tristwick, I am finished running away. I am finished being parted from you. I love you, Poppy, with a love that will never fade."

There was no stopping her tears now, though she smiled with trembling lips. This could not be real. This could be nothing but a perfect dream.

And yet, as Edmund closed the distance between them, his hands cradling her face, his thumbs brushing aside her tears, she knew, somehow, this was reality after all.

"Marry me, Poppy," he whispered. "Marry me so we may remain in Cornwall together. So we may raise our children by the sea, carefree and happy forever."

Her breath caught in her throat. "I will, Edmund. I will marry ye. But we don't 'ave to live 'ere if you don't wish to. I will go where'er ye wish to live. Sunningdale, aboard a ship, in the middle o' the sea. I care not. I cannot be parted from ye any longer, for I need ye to be whole. No one else, *nowhere* else."

He closed his eyes, a deep sigh escaping his lips as his shoulders fell, as if a great weight had been taken from him. When he opened his eyes again, their green depths sparkled with moisture like the Cornish seas. "No, Poppy. I do not wish to live anywhere but here with you. Cornwall is now just as much a part of me as you are. I could no sooner ask you to sprout wings and fly than for you to leave your home."

She laughed, sniffing away her moisture. "Are ye sure?"

He sobered. "I have never been more sure of anything in my entire life. It only makes sense for me to settle down here, the place where it all began. I was saved by Mrs. Kendricks from the storming seas. Now, if your brother allows me to, I will be able to manage a lifeboat to, in turn, help those whose lives are also at risk."

"Be that what ye want to do, then?" she asked, his words sounding better than she could have dreamt.

He brushed his thumb against her lower lip. "More than anything. Besides, what better place is there for me to retire than by the sea? And what better person to be with than the woman whom I love? You have given me something to live for, Poppy. And I will never take you or your love for granted again."

Tears filled her eyes, her mind swirling with the knowledge of his love for her. Then another thought occurred. "But ye 'ave to return to sea."

He nodded, the solemnity to his expression matching the ache in her heart. "I do, to fulfill my promise to Captain Jones, I do. But the assignment will only be for a time." He stared deep into her eyes. "And I promise you, Poppy. I will return."

Enveloped in his words, Poppy wrapped her arms around his neck, staring deep into his eyes and feeling the truth in his promise. For Edmund was a man of his word, and now she had his.

"Then I will wait for ye," she said.

And she would.

Together, they stood near the fields, poppies bouncing against their legs and the wind ruffling her skirts. Edmund's lips met hers again with a love that promised of a bright, unending future—for how could it not be for the little girl who had dreamt of love, and the man who'd made it a reality?

EPILOGUE

*P*oppy stood on the tips of her toes, straining to see past the men lumbering off the ship one by one and spreading into the teeming crowds around St. Ives.

"Can ye see 'im yet?" she asked.

Mother shook her head. "Not yet, love."

Poppy sighed with impatience. She'd waited long enough to see Edmund. Three months to be exact. But she was fairly certain she would die in the next three *minutes* if she did not at least catch a glimpse of him.

"There 'e be," Mother said sharply, and Poppy stood to attention.

"Where? I can't..." But in the next moment, she gasped, spotting the handsome lieutenant, her betrothed, the love of her life, finally appearing as he stepped off the ship.

Tears sprang to her eyes, and she pressed her fingers over her lips to keep from crying out his name.

Mother pressed a hand to her back. "Well go on up there, ye silly girl!" she encouraged.

Poppy beamed, giving in to her mother's urging and fighting through the crowds, keeping her eye trained on Edmund.

How she had missed him these few months past. Of course, she'd kept herself busy with a wedding to plan and a hamlet to save, but nothing had helped the dragging days and never-ending nights she'd had to spend away from her love.

"Edmund!" she cried out, unable to help herself any longer from calling his name above the others who embraced their own returned sailors.

Edmund perked up, his eyes surveying the crowds with an anxiousness that warmed her heart to the point of bursting.

"Edmund!" she called again.

She raised her hand in the air, waving it wildly back and forth until finally—finally—he spotted her. The smile she was rewarded with was worth every moment they'd spent away from each other, worth every letter shared, and every tear shed.

"Poppy," he said, though she could not hear him above the noise bursting around them.

They worked to run toward each other, weaving in and out of the crowds until Poppy barreled toward him.

He welcomed her with open arms, and she squealed, jumping into them. She wrapped her own arms around his neck, and he spun her around and around.

"Ah, my love," he breathed into her ear, burying his face in the crook beneath her ear. "How good it is to hold you once more in my arms."

Tears streamed down her cheeks as she pressed her face ever closer to his. They had exchanged letters often over their time apart, which had eased their separation to a degree, but nothing had made her heart warm like his presence once more in Cornwall.

"I missed ye," she said when he finally lowered her to the ground.

"I missed *you*," he returned. He took a step back from her, though he held tight to her hands as he looked the length of her. "Poppy, how can it be that you've only grown more beautiful since we were together?"

She pulled her hand away and gave him a playful swat to his chest, her cheeks burning. "Ye flatter me, sir."

He narrowed an eye with a playful look. "Tell me you did not miss it."

She laughed, reaching up to embrace him once again. "More than ye could e'er know," she whispered, and he tightened his hold around her all the greater.

This was the reunion she'd longed for all those years ago. A joyous one. A perfect one. And finally, she received it.

She pulled back, staring up into his eyes. Then right there, in front of all of St. Ives, he kissed her, with a kiss that curled her toes with delight and made her head spin.

Once their kiss ended—though certainly not when Poppy was finished with it—they found Mother, who embraced Edmund with warmth and love, as she always did. Then the three of them stepped away from the teeming crowds.

"Trevik borrowed the Kendricks's wagon to take us 'ome," Poppy said. "'E be waitin' for us at the edge o' town."

"How good of him," Edmund said, offering his arm to Poppy, who readily accepted it.

She knew it was awful, but she couldn't deny the pride she felt hanging onto the arm of his naval jacket, his cocked hat tall and stately, his uniform accentuating his broad shoulders as ladies left and right admired the handsome lieutenant.

How Poppy had ever captured this man's attention—captured his love—was beyond her. But one thing was for certain, she would never let go of him again.

Over the next few weeks, Edmund and Poppy did their best to be patient as they waited for the banns to be read at church, though there was still plenty to do to make ready for their coming nuptials.

Poppy still had to work between the Kendricks's and the cellars, all the while watching a growing Isolde, Elowen, and Benesek as Edmund worked hard to settle into his new routine as master of the lifeboat.

The last three months at sea had been just enough to satisfy his desire to return—and just enough to remind him once again how ready he was to retire.

Life at sea was wonderful, though nothing could compare to being with Poppy and his new family.

Still, it would be an adjustment, but one he was ready to make.

Everyone in Tristwick—including the new seining men who had recently relocated from St. Ives—welcomed Edmund with kindness. Even Trevik had seemed to have taken the last three months to do his best to forgive Edmund.

Matters became even more relaxed between them as they had to work together for the good of Tristwick. Over the weeks, Edmund worked hard to find men to agree to man the lifeboat, and though they still had yet to receive it, he'd been in contact with the Admiralty, who had plans to deliver the boat the moment he had the list of men competent enough to row it.

Meanwhile, the fishing had resumed in Tristwick, and Edmund had been invited to join the boat, which he agreed to do for a time.

More than anything, Edmund wished to forge his own path. He enjoyed the camaraderie aboard the *Pilferer*, how similar it was at sea, but only heaven knew if there was something else out there for him. Whether it was opening up a bake shop with Poppy, finding ways to sell her shellwork, manning a lifeboat, or fishing for life, he wasn't certain. But with Poppy's help, he knew he would discover what he wished to do.

The two of them had stolen away every moment they could together as Poppy and Morvoren prepped the house across the hamlet, where Poppy and Edmund would live together.

"Ye be certain ye wish to live in Tristwick?" Poppy had asked him over and over again.

To which he always responded the very same. "I do not care where we live, so long as I have you."

And it was the truth. Now that he knew he had Poppy's love, and he had his love for her, he felt the words deep within his soul.

Just so long as he didn't have to live in Derbyshire.

His Mother had not reached out to him since their inter-action in St. Just, nor had Mr. Beacham or Cecil. However, Algernon had wished Edmund a happy life when Edmund had written to announce his upcoming marriage to Poppy.

His work to forgive Mother continued day by day, some nights were worse than others, but always an uphill climb.

He genuinely wished them happiness, though that did not mean he wished to live right by them.

No, he was happy to continue to rent Sunningdale to those who wished to live there, and he was happy to remain in Cornwall with his love.

He knew life would be far different now, but he was ready to face it, for he had Poppy by his side. With her, he could face anything, and he would end up all the better for it, because that was what Poppy did—she made everything simply, purely better.

When the wedding day finally arrived, the banns had been completed, and the people gathered in the church, Poppy stood at the front of the chapel with Edmund, listening to the words of Mr. Biddle as he read from the Book of Common Prayer.

She could hardly hear what he said, however, as she stared into Edmund's eyes, seeing the love he had for her in perfect harmony with her own. How she had ever been so blessed as to marry the man of her dreams, she would never know.

As Mr. Biddle asked if there was any objection to their union, Poppy and Edmund cast their eyes to those in attendance, and only then did she truly see how full the chapel was with her friends and family.

Tears flooded her eyes as she met each of their gazes, everyone there to support the lieutenant and the fisherman's daughter whom they'd seen fall in love with each other from the beginning.

The Causeys and Summerfields smiled up with warm grins. The Hawkinses with their perfect blue eyes and flawless features sat behind them with happy looks, while next to them, the Trevethans and their children filed out to the side of them, Mr. Trevethan's arm around his wife as they grinned.

The Kendrickses sat at the front of the chapel, baby Benesek happily sucking away on his father's fingers as Elowen swung her legs back and forth with impatience. Mrs. Kendricks had tears in her eyes as she peered up at Poppy, a proud smile on her lips.

Morvoren and Trevik were seated on the front row at the opposite side, Morvoren looking like an angel with her blonde hair. Trevik chewed on his lower lip to keep his emotion at bay as Isolde watched those around her with curious eyes.

Mother did not attempt to hide her tears, though, dabbing at them with a handkerchief. And though she could not see him, Poppy knew in her heart her father was there, too.

Finally, she returned her gaze to Edmund as Mr. Biddle continued with his words.

"I love you," Edmund mouthed out to her, which she responded to with an, "I love ye too," of her own.

The words continued, the union created, and when the two were bound together, they shared a kiss at the front of the room.

It was a modest kiss, a chaste kiss, but it promised of so much more to come. A life filled with joy and laughter and love. With children running about, with hard winters and hot summers.

Life would not be easy—but then, life never was. Poppy and Edmund both knew that better than anyone. But what six years apart had taught them, was that life was better when they were together.

Yes, their love had been tested, as all love is at some time or another. But they had made the solemn promise to remain together, and with that fire burning inside them, they would make it. As all those in Cornwall did, for when it was a Cornish romance, it was a romance—a *love*—that lasted through the ages.

THE END

AUTHOR'S NOTE

The idea to write a Cornish Romance series came to me in 2015 after I watched Poldark for the first time. The show had been suggested to me often, but I simply didn't find the time to watch it until my second child was born.

The night I returned home from the hospital, I was wide awake with a sleeping babe on my chest, so I found myself at liberty to start a new series. *Poldark* appeared on my screen, I pressed play, and then I was swept into the majesty of Cornwall. From that moment, I never looked back. And honestly, I believe it was heaven sent. Finding Cornwall through *Poldark* helped pull me from one of the most difficult times of my life.

The recovery for my second child was very difficult. My husband was working at a horrible job that constantly took advantage of him. He worked thanklessly for hours and hours on end while I was at home with my two kids. As the months dragged on in a similar manner, Christmas came—and so did the darkness in my mind.

It only lasted a few months, and I wasn't really aware of how bad it had gotten until I was finally pulled from the depression. Looking back, it was like a dark cloud hung around me, impossible to penetrate, invisible to everyone, including myself, until I was brought into the light again.

Watching *Poldark* and seeing the beauty of Cornwall truly kept me from verging into dangerous territory. It gave me something else to focus on, something else to bring me joy. And I'll be forever grateful for it for that reason.

POPPY'S STORY

From the moment I wrote Behind the Light of Golowduyn, I knew Poppy and Edmund's relationship was going to be a favorite of mine. I couldn't wait to tell the story of a little girl growing up and marrying the man she'd fallen in love with so many years before.

When the time finally came to write her book, however, the story wouldn't flow. I brainstormed for months and months about where her life would be and how she'd end up with Edmund, but every new idea that I came up with fizzled out until I was once again left with nothing.

It wasn't until I traveled to Yellowstone with my husband and talked his ear off for hours and hours on end that I finally ended up with the main idea for the story—Poppy would be asked to leave Cornwall.

As authors, we're asked to push our characters to breaking point, so the happily ever after will be the sweetest it can be for them. It's quite healing as a person to write about a fictional person's suffering. But as I wrote the outline for this story, I came to realize that Poppy would suffer from depression. This wasn't supposed to happen. After all, I was happy to write about someone else's suffering. The last thing I wanted to do was write about my own!

I was so frustrated with this at first. Poppy was the happy-go-lucky character, the one who always found the sunshine. But that's when I realized that this storyline was perfect for her. I knew she wouldn't be depressed in the storyline, but having suffered with depression, she would be anxious about feeling it again—and she would do everything within her power to keep others from feeling the darkness themselves.

Still, I fought with this book. I wrestled with it daily. It took far too long to get myself to start at all, and when I finally did, each day, it was like dragging a cow through the mud. I felt like Anne Shirley falling face first into cow poop every single day.

Until finally, I finished. Only then did I see why I struggled so much with this book. I was fighting with it because I didn't want to relive it, just like Poppy. I didn't want to feel the fear anymore, the worry, the darkness. But that made finishing this book all the more satisfying.

DEPRESSION

I don't claim to know much about this awful, damaging sickness. Only what I've experienced and how I've attempted to stop myself from feeling it again. I hope you will give me grace if I didn't represent your own personal depression, as it is so different from person to person. I did my best to represent it in a way that still shows the light that can be found if we keep holding on.

I mourn for those who have chronic conditions, who suffer with this on a daily level—or even once in their lifetime. I pray for your relief and your courage to continue fighting the darkness.

I hope Poppy and Edmund's stories will inspire you, or at the very least, give you a bit of relief and joy. As always, that is why I write—to spread light in this ever-darkening world.

Now, in my author's note, I always like to share a bit about my behind-the-scenes process, including my name choices, as well as the storylines based on actual history. So let's dive in, shall we?

NAMES

I love adding interesting tidbits to nearly every name I choose in my stories, even if the characters and places are in the background and only mentioned once. It's a way to add a personal touch to each book, and From the Fields of Porthlenn was no different.

Character Names

First off, you may have recognized the names Demelza and Mr. Carne for side characters in the book. They, of course, are inspired from Winston Graham's *Poldark*. It was fun to finally choose the names as an homage to the great man and his writing. As well as to the great character of Demelza Carne Poldark!

Next, as for the daughters of Abigail and Gavin Kendricks and Trevik and Morvoren Honeysett. I chose Elowen Kendricks because her name is Cornish for "powerful like an elm tree." With parents like Abigail and Gavin, how could she not exhibit such strength? As for Isolde's name, it means "one who is beautiful and fair." And being the daughter of Morvoren, she couldn't be more beautiful. Furthermore, Gwitha, the Kendricks's dog, means "to protect," which I thought was rather fitting, and Benesek—the Kendricks's new bundle of joy—means "blessed." I'm sure you can surmise why I chose that name for the Kendricks's second child.

Finally, the name Cadan *is* historical and pronounced like "Madden." His name means "battle" and "companion." This just matched up with his personality perfectly. Quite obviously, he is Poppy's companion, and Edmund's battle!

Location & Misc. Names

First off, Edmund's ship. The *Defense* was named after an actual ship called the *Defence*. I couldn't find a better name for the ship that Edmund uses as a defense mechanism.

Likewise, another fitting descriptor was found from the name of Porthlenn. I combined the Cornish words *porth* and *lenn* to create the fields where Poppy awaits Edmund's return. *Porth* means *port*, and *lenn* refers to a *cloth*. I chose porth because the word is everywhere in Cornwall, and I just love the sound of it. Lenn, however, was chosen because I feel like Poppy uses the poppy fields as a cloth—or a cover—to protect herself, just like she uses hope to protect herself.

Also, as a sidenote, there are poppy fields in Cornwall, the most famous of which is the West Pentire Poppies. I have a life goal to be in Cornwall when they bloom because the images are simply spectacular.

HURLING

When I first traveled to Cornwall, my husband and I found the gorgeous crossroads in Bodmin Moor at the tail end of our trip. On our way across the moors, we saw mysterious stones propped up a distance away and couldn't figure out what they were. After a quick google search, we discovered that they were called the Hurlers Stone Circles. That led to another question. What are hurlers and why were they in a circle?

Finally, I found the history behind the site, and the legend that goes along with it. Many years ago, men played the Cornish sport of hurling on the Sabbath and were punished by being turned to stone to ward off others from doing the same. The minute I learned of this, I knew I had to put hurling into my story.

Side note, Cornish hurling—the one described in this book—ought not be confused with the Irish and Gaelic hurling, which is a stick-and-ball sort of game that actually has rules.

Cornish hurling isn't very popular nowadays. In fact, only a few places still play the sport, including St. Columb and St. Ives. Some of the cities only have children partake in the fun, but some places still hold fast to the tradition. I hope it continues for many years to come because what a tradition it is!

There has been one recorded death from hurling that occurred in 1705, but not much was said about it. It doesn't seem very unlikely to believe, however, what with how crazy the sport really is.

What Mr. Causey shouts to begin the game, "Town and country do your best, for in this parish, I must rest!" are the actual words recited at the beginning of each game, and the three cheers called out afterward is also historically accurate!

During my research, I learned that in one of the present-day hurling competitions, someone took the ball in a car and gained much ground that way. I figured if a car could do it, a man on a horse could, too!

Finally, one of my favorite discoveries while researching was to find out that the winner dips the ball into a pint at the local pub and passes the drink around for all to take a sip and partake of the luck the ball extends to others. I don't know about you, but I don't think I'd take a sip of that pint!

CORNISH WORDS

I used a few Cornish phrases and words that you might not have heard of until reading the book, so here's a list to help!

Vellan – villain
Pisky – pixie
Mimsey – minnow
Cakey – feeble-minded
Fitty – suitable

FOODS

I've been dying to add proper, historical Cornish food into my stories since the beginning, but time and time again, it just didn't fit my characters until I wrote Poppy's story.

I used my Poldark Cookbook for a lot of inspiration, as well as other websites and books to find the best food for Poppy to create at the Kendricks's. I do have to say, using stargazy pie had to be my favorite. I haven't tried the pie—nor do I think I ever will—but it sure was fun to see Edmund squirm at the sight of it!

HISTORY OF THE LIFEBOAT

In each of my Cornish Romance books, I've loved adding historical details about the county that I find simply fascinating. Behind the Light of Golowduyn included information about lighthouses. For the Lady of Lowena was all about the Cornish cottages dotting the cliffsides. Near the Ruins of Penharrow was obviously focused around the bal maidens— female mine workers—and In the Waves of Tristwick, about the fishing industry.

Each of these ideas came fairly easily to me. But From the Fields of Porthlenn was nearly impossible to discover what the story should center around. I did some digging to see what would help save a small hamlet, however, and I just so happened to stumble upon lifeboats in the 19th century. As soon as I read about it, I knew this would be just the thing for Poppy's story.

I had no notion that lifeboats were a "thing" until much later on, so when I learned about the Royal National Lifeboat Institution (RNLI) being established in 1824, I was pleasantly surprised. Since my story takes place in 1820, however, I had a bit more research to do.

In my reading, I discovered that Lionel Lukin built the first unsinkable boat around 1785. In the years following, more lifeboats were built, each improving more after the others until around 1789 that a lifeboat design competition was launched, asking for the best designs for a lifeboat. The reward was, get this, a whopping two guineas (around two pounds nowadays).

Instead of choosing a winner, however, the ideas of William Wouldhave and Henry Francis Greathead were combined. Both were offered half the prize money. Wouldhave was offended and walked away. Greathead, however, remained. He was asked to build the lifeboat from their merged designs and then came to be known as the inventor of the lifeboat. He named the boat the *Original.* Quite clever, if you ask me. They launched this boat in 1790 when rescuing a shipwrecked crew.

The best thing about Henry Greathead? He never patented any of his inventions so others could benefit from his ideas. He built thirty-one different lifeboats over twenty years, always trying to improve his design to save the lives of others.

After learning about this, I launched into the wide and vast world of lifeboats in Cornwall—the first one being stationed in Penzance in 1803.

It is true that the lifeboat in Penzance never launched, but a new one was stationed there in 1826 by the National Institution for the Preservation of Life from Shipwrecks (later the RNLI).

Now, not to disappoint you, but there were actually no lifeboats built in Cornwall between 1803 and 1824. (Shh. Don't tell anyone that I fudged the lines between fact and history.) However, in 1817, just like in *From the Fields of Porthlenn,* Bude *was* gifted a boat by the Admiralty.

After a great deal of research, I could find nothing about the details of this other than the fact that the boat was little used and "allowed to fall into disrepair." Edmund, however, heard from Mr. Beacham that it was a fine boat and used often. Perhaps this occurred to give him just the push he needed to discover his need to contact the Admiralty for a lifeboat for Tristwick!

Years later, after all of this, the Monarchy actually demanded that a set sum of money would be given to Bude so they could establish a working lifeboat to save the lives of the many ship-wrecks that occurred around their waters. I'm happy to tell you that this lifeboat did launch many times and saved count-less lives!

Sailing a lifeboat during any time would be harrowing, but even more so in the past with no radios or any of our modern technology. These boats were also known to capsize during certain rescues, but worry not. I have it on good authority that Edmund lived to a good old age.

EDMUND'S SLING

Most of the paintings back then revealed white slings, but there was one I was able to find with a man wearing a blue one, and I thought it would be just the thing to set Edmund apart from other injured sailors.

As always, I loved learning more about all that Cornwall has to offer. The research I've completed for each of these books has probably been my favorite part of the process—and of course hearing from readers about how they love Cornwall, too.

I'm so grateful each of you have come along this journey with me to Cornwall with this series. And I'm so grateful that I watched that first episode of Poldark all those years ago so I could discover the beauty, the incredible history, and the rich culture of Cornwall. I hope those who read this series can see my respect for all things Cornish. And I have just one last thing to ask of the Cornish people—will you adopt me into your culture? I have a great-great-great-great-great-great-great-great grandmother who was Cornish. Does that count?

Thank you again to all of my readers! If you haven't already, join me on Instagram and Facebook. I have many photos from my recent trip to the UK—and Cornwall!—as well as give-aways and the latest news about my books. I'd love to have you join me!

Also, if you enjoyed this book, please consider leaving a review here. Reviews help authors out so much because that is how people hear about our books.

Until next time!

Deborah

ACKNOWLEDGMENTS

Just like every book, there was no way From the Fields of Porthlenn would have seen the light of day were it not for my many friends and family members who helped me along the way.

I need to thank my mom and my sister Joanna first. Thank you for reading every single book I've written. Thank you for the hundreds of offers to watch the kids and to help around my house. Thank you for always being supportive and helpful and loving!

Thank you to my beta readers, Joanna Barker, Martha Keyes, Jess Heileman, Arlem Hawks, Jamie Ann Bartlett, Kimberly, and Jacque. I'm so grateful to each of you ladies for helping this book to shine brighter!

Next, I have to give a huge shoutout to all the bookstagrammers who have messaged me over and over and over again about their excitement for this book. Seriously, your messages and your anticipation for Poppy's story was LEGITIMATELY the only way I could push through this story. There were so many times I wanted to quit. So many times I told myself to give up, that no one would want to read this story anyway. And time and time again, your messages would come in, spurring me on. Thank you!

A special shoutout must go to @herliterarytravels. You share my love of Cornwall, and I'm so grateful for it. Thanks for being such a huge supporter!

Next, I need to thank Joanna Barker for her encouragement after this book was finally written. Again, I was *this* close to not publishing the blasted thing. Your words of encouragement, your boost of confidence, was just the thing I needed to go that final mile and publish the book. Thank you, thank you, thank you!

Lastly, my sweet, patient, wonderful husband. The last six months have been insanity, and I couldn't have made it out alive without your help. I'm so grateful for your companionship, for your love, and for your encouragement. I'm so grateful we share so many of the same loves and passions. With you, darkness is kept at bay, and my hope is stronger. Thank you for being the Thomas to my Hannah. The Gavin to my Abigail. The Frederick to my Sophia. The Jack to my Gwynna. The Trevik to my Morvoren. And the Edmund to my Poppy. How I love you.

ABOUT THE AUTHOR

 Deborah M. Hathaway graduated from Utah State University with a BA in Creative Writing. As a young girl, she devoured Jane Austen's novels while watching and re-watching every adaptation of Pride & Prejudice she could, entirely captured by all things Regency and romance.

Throughout her early life, she wrote many short stories, poems, and essays, but it was not until after her marriage that she was finally able to complete her first romance novel, attributing the completion to her courtship with, and love of, her charming, English husband. Deborah finds her inspiration for her novels in her everyday experiences with her husband and children and during her travels to the United Kingdom, where she draws on the beauty of the country in such places as England, Scotland, and her beloved Cornwall.

Made in the USA
Middletown, DE
13 October 2023